Annette Motley was a̶ ̶[...]
permanently in a book. [...]
years teaching English [...]
art before becoming a f[...]
lished short stories, magazine serials and a string of
historical novels. *The Oldest Obsession* was her first
contemporary novel; *Balancing Acts* is its sequel.

Annette Motley lives in a village in Surrey with her
husband, the inevitable cats and a lot of wildlife.

Also by Annette Motley

THE OLDEST OBSESSION

BALANCING ACTS

Annette Motley

WARNER BOOKS

A *Warner* Book

Published in Great Britain in 1998
by Warner Books

Copyright © Annette Motley 1998

The moral right of the author has been asserted.

A CIP catalogue record for this book
is available from the British Library.

ISBN 0 7515 2282 1

Typeset by Palimpsest Book Production Limited
Polmont, Stirlingshire
Printed and bound in Great Britain by
Clays Ltd, St Ives plc

Warner Books
A Division of
Little, Brown and Company (UK)
Brettenham House
Lancaster Place
London WC2E 7EN

for Suzanne Harman

Chapter One

'YOU ARE MY SUNSHINE, MY ONLY SUNSHINE,' Miranda sang to the plump mound of her stomach. 'You make me happy when skies are grey.' They were grey today. She could see them through the window from her bed, a turbulent impasto of pollution and bad-tempered weather, flying across a plate-glass sheet the size of the screen in a small cinema. Lying sullenly under them, the roofs, the towers, the cranes and craters and still, thank God, the beleaguered trees of south-east London waited for a change of mood. Close up below, sectioned between the red and grey buildings, the river stood in slabs like slate. Despite the commotion in the clouds it was a cool, flat panorama with a seventeenth-century feel to it, like the one dreary Christmas card you leave in the box, discovering it later to be a masterpiece.

'Dutch, probably,' Miranda said aloud. 'Come on, Moriarty, it's time we got up. I know you don't want to. Neither do I, very much, but there is a lot to do today.'

Moriarty grumbled and turned inside her. At minus two months she already had a mind of her own and her vote was that they should stay where they were, snug in the nest of warm red bedding cocooned around the warm red fleshpot in which she lived.

This small clash of wills had taken place on every

awakening for the last week. Amused by it, thrilled by the evidence that Moriarty so soon possessed a will to clash, Miranda idled and sang to her a little longer. Towards the end of 'I'm Into Something Good', the undisputed foetal favourite, she noticed a cup of cold coffee on the bookcase near the bed. Adam had made it. She smiled as the shaft of memory struck like sunlight. They had made love before he left. He had slipped into her from behind before she awoke, so that her first awareness was of deep, strong oceanic motion inside her. Startled, she had thought that perhaps she was about to give birth early, but Adam's hands had clenched in ecstasy upon her breasts and she had realised what was happening.

'It's rape,' she had mumbled, her mouth full of her hair.

'Mmm. But it isn't always a crime.'

He had moved a hand to her vulva, introducing himself and finding a welcome. Miranda moaned and arched. 'It's too nice,' she cried. 'I can't bear it.' He had pulled her backwards on top of him until she fell across his body like a ravished Sabine; the wicked one who had Roman fantasies, the one who lay back and enjoyed it. There must have been one. She entertained a short fantasy of her own featuring Adam in a centurion's kilt, the kind made of gilded leather strips. They were the sexiest things men had ever worn, and you didn't even have to take them off. She might try to bring them back into fashion one day. Vivienne Westwood would approve. There now, she had quite gone off the idea of getting up.

It didn't matter if she was late for college. At her present stage, near the end of the Easter term and with another year to go, there were few demands from a set timetable; but there was an impossible amount of work to get through, and unattainable standards to be reached. She would just have to take Hercules for her role-model and get on with it. Although none of that hero's labours had produced anything so rewarding as a baby, she found his image more appealing than the boldly going women in suits so widely esteemed by the media. The real problem was that there were too many art students, few of whom would make a living in the manner they would have chosen. Miranda was fortunate in that she did not aim to become a painter. She was not ungrateful for her talent for painting and drawing, she was even slightly in awe of it; it seemed so little to do with her, so much the gift of her genes. Grandfather Carrington was an architect and Grandma Joanna an interior designer, while her own mother, Chloe, was a successful painter and a visionary colourist who had tutored her, skilfully and without pressure, since she was a child. When art school had beckoned, her lessons had become more rigorous. Miranda was grateful for this, especially for her encouragement in the use of pastels, an elusive medium which even Degas, its finest exponent, had found difficult. Now, her pastel commentaries upon the working lives she saw around her in the city would probably gain her a distinction in the fine-art section of her degree.

Chloe herself painted with every receptor of her sensibilities, using her work as a continual channel of revelation and self-discovery. Miranda's relationships to her world were looser, less cerebral, more sociable. It had been clear to everyone who knew her, many years before she had considered going to college, that she had an uncommon talent for inventing clothes. She was not a little girl who sewed for her dolls; she had wasted no time on that. Her first effort, at four, had been to turn two tea-towels into a dress by knotting the top corners and safety-pinning the sides. She had worn it with pride until Chloe had taught her to sew an unsteady seam. In the next few years she had turned out a succession of basic, wearable garments in attractive materials she had chosen herself. Her seams were straight, her small fingertips calloused and her pleasure in her work increased with her discovery of its possibilities.

On her tenth birthday she was given a sewing machine.

Her father, Alain, a Frenchman and himself the epitome of understated style, added two great big, beautiful books, one a history of fashion from cave to catwalk and the other a guide to the work and methods of the great modern designers.

'Mme Chanel,' she decided, 'did things a bit like some of mine.'

'You can't put it that way round,' her brother Rufus had protested, an eight-year-old stickler for exactitude.

'She can if she likes,' contradicted his twin, Tilda, explaining with a truer logic, 'because neither of them knew about the other one.'

The first year of the sewing machine was brilliantly represented in the Olivier family photograph album for 1988. There is Chloe on her birthday, floating on a cloud of bias-cut cheesecloth, tie-dyed by Miranda to tone with her red and gold hair. Alain stands next to her in a soft blue collarless shirt (collars were difficult) made from an old sheet. Tilda wears the rather long khaki drawstring shorts that she still digs out every summer, cut down from an elephantine pair wheedled out of the Oxfam ladies for fifteen p, while Rufus, with an air of obvious relief, salutes the brim of a very creditable baseball cap fashioned to the maker's pattern. All you needed was a good eye and common sense.

Now, at eighteen, with a whole generation of hopeful designers to outshine and a new generation of Oliviers kicking beneath her ribs, she would also need outstanding flair and technical ability, unflagging dedication, and, what was more important on the nauseating roller-coaster of nineties' economy, an unfair proportion of good luck.

On bad days she doubted that she had any of these; on good ones she thought she had the full set. Her talent was confirmed both by her college marks and by the reactions her clothes provoked; she was proving her dedication by her efforts to organise her maternal future in terms of her work. As for luck, true, there had been a few occasions when it had broken down with as much drama and inconvenience as her venerable 2CV, but by today's standards she had more than her fair share of it, and especially now. She had a leading place in her college year, she had Moriarty to look forward to, she had a loving family – none of whom objected to her unwed state, who would welcome the baby with trumpets, cymbals and a savings-book – and most wonderfully and undeservedly, she had Adam, who lived with her and was her love.

Technically, Adam Cavendish lived next door in a studio similar to her own. Here too, luck had played a part. Their apartments were among a dozen self-contained units on the top floor of a Victorian bonded warehouse, converted in the seventies by a group of young artists and architects who had done most of the work themselves. Chloe had been one of them. She and Alain had begun their married life there and had rented it to friends when they bought their first house. When they had left London a year ago for the Surrey village of Sheringham, they had made Miranda their peppercorn tenant. In January her next-door neighbour had moved out, so Adam had tossed his laptop and his brief wardrobe into his car and driven straight round.

He had spent the first morning making exuberant love to Miranda and the afternoon staring out of the vast expanse of window, composing a Wordsworthian eulogy to the view. He did not often write poetry, but he had published half a dozen amusing and truthful short stories and made several attempts to begin a novel. More practically, for anyone whose heart is set on a modern literary career, he was completing the final year of a degree in journalism and had persuaded the *Surrey Clarion* to give him a job as a freelance columnist.

Thinking about him, Miranda smiled and stretched, her arms describing the infinite expanse of the pleasure of life. She plunged her nose into his pillow to recapture the scent of him. Adam smelled like tanned skin, like the Mediterranean, like herbs under the sun. It was all there, beneath her burrowing nose. She would have liked to stay there, in olfactory heaven, until he came back to her, but that was a luxury she could not afford. She searched for, found, and kissed a single dark hair left on the pillow; then, to Moriarty's disgust, she wriggled out of bed. Staggering as she piled on warm woolly layers in humming-bird colours, she decided this must be the last time she tried to climb into her leggings standing up.

'OK, OK, this isn't a disco,' she admonished the turbulence within. 'If I were you, I'd keep still and make the best of it. When you get out you're going to miss all this trouble-free transport. I just hope it won't be too much of a wrench for you, swapping your walking shock-absorber for a Moses basket in a 2CV. You'll have to think of it as character-building.' She made some fresh coffee and carried it with the phone to the broad window seat, settling with her feet up and her back against the deep embrasure. She dialled Adam's mobile.

'It's me,' she announced huskily. 'I just got up. Thanks for the coffee.'

'I'm glad you enjoyed looking at it. How are you? How's Moriarty?'

'We're fine,' she purred. 'Where are you?'

'In college. Will Hutton is giving a lecture this morning. I couldn't miss that.'

'Great. What about the afternoon? I'm going in to do some cutting, but I could leave by about five-thirty.'

'I'm not sure yet. Let you know later. Listen, Miranda.' His voice darkened. 'There's some news. My father called. About Joel.'

'Oh.' Her stomach tried to contract, Moriarty heaved and the physical world was suddenly less secure. 'What sort of news?'

'The police have decided not to bring charges.'

'Oh. I see.'

'Are you all right?'

'Yes. It's just – I'm fine.'

'I don't know about you, but I'm bloody furious. I can't bear to think of him getting away with all of it like this.'

'I suppose not.'

'What do you mean?'

'Well no, of course not.' She was cold and she felt sick.

'You don't sound too sure about it.'

'I am. Of course I am.'

'Are you?'

'Oh, Adam—'

'Well – you know.'

'You don't need to do this. We've done it all, long ago. And I am every bit as angry as you are.'

'I just wish—'

'Well, don't. Look,' she sighed, 'don't waste time over it. Go to your lecture and then come home. I'll stay here and work. I can do the cutting tomorrow. I want to be with you.'

His tone lifted. 'Me too. OK, I'll do that. See you soon. Love you.'

'And you. Bucketsfull. Bye.'

Joel. Her mind raced while her heart drummed up uncomfortable thunder. Moriarty's too, by the sound of it. Funny to think she had two hearts inside her now, like Doctor Who. What a pity she did not own a Tardis as well. Would she use it to take her back to the time before she had known Joel? And then take a magic leap forward to being with Adam, banishing those crucial months between, with their changes, their excess of pleasure and her first introduction to loss and pain? She began to walk up and down the long room, moving her hands over her body in soothing ellipses. If she were to excise Joel from her life, then she must also exclude Moriarty, and that was not only impossible but unwishable. It was no use telling herself that this could equally well have been Adam's child she was carrying. Moriarty was Joel's and that was that.

There came the sweet, soft, serpent voice that she had not heard for a long time, saying she did not want not to have known Joel, not to have loved him, not to have travelled with him into the realms of bliss with a price, and unbelievable hurt and disillusion.

Joel was notorious. He was also absurdly glamorous. At college, someone had sprayed the indelible letters on his locker: 'Joel Ranger – MB and D to K.' No one who knew him took this for irony. As though to collude with this publicist, Joel wore constant black, rode a gleaming Harley Davidson and resembled a modern fallen angel; Alain Delon, or maybe Nicholas Cage in *Wild at Heart*. He got away with this exquisite kitsch because he was the most exciting and sought-after sculptor, painter and general maker to knock his tutors' eyes out in years, and because every woman he met wanted to sleep with him or murder him or both. Joel took this, and the women, for granted. Their opinions of him did not much interest him. He liked sex and needed a great deal of it, but like his pristine bike, he needed to keep himself free of luggage – which was how he saw other people's emotions when unnecessarily attached to himself. This was how he had presented himself to Miranda. Herself the happy product of the warm and intelligent relationship between her parents, she had taken his two-dimensional self-image to be a convenient mask. She supposed it assisted him to work with the demonic intensity and commitment which left him so little time for what she thought of as life, as opposed to work; but when she came to know Joel better she realised that for him there was no such dichotomy. He lived to work and sex helped to provide him with fuel. Having made this discovery she had fallen into the predictable female error of trying to turn sex into love as she understood it.

It was an easy mistake to make. Joel as a lover was pure physical poetry. He had taken her virginity with careless, teasing conversation and a tender sensual attention, a religious concentration that astonished her and made her his avid acolyte. He knew every nerve of his body and learned every one of hers. He taught her a hundred ways to give him pleasure and gave her a hundred back. He demonstrated the sweet, sharp conspiracy between pleasure and pain and stretched her on a scudding wheel of sensual extremes. She had felt ecstatic and endangered, living on the brink. They became each other's harmonic instruments, perfectly attuned, each note a throb from the throat of Orpheus. It had seemed to Miranda that her own lessons were also beginning to succeed and that perhaps he *was* falling in love with her. He spent more time with her than he had with any of his previous girlfriends. He ate meals with her, was seen about with her. He let her stay in his flat; they were almost domestic together. He liked talking to her and listened to what she had to say about his work. He would make love to her at all hours of the day or night, anywhere and everywhere, ramming into her in back alleys, serenaded by late-night drunks, or gently and discreetly sodomising her beneath a blanket in the noonday, sun-worshipping park. She loved it, all of it; she could not get enough of it. He was an addiction, he was deep in her blood.

Many were jealous, particularly Cally Baker, who had once been Miranda's friend, and who claimed to share Joel's dedication to sex for its own sake. When Joel agreed to spend brief weekends at her parents' house in Sheringham, Miranda really thought she was winning. He had been charming to her family, who, all but Tilda, had drunk and failed to see the spider. She was sure she detected signs of increasing affection. Wary, she avoided emotional statements as much as she could; but even when she could not, when she just had to tell him how much she loved him or die of repression, he did not appear to object.

It was enough. She was not making any plans. They

were beautifully right as they were. So right, you might suppose, if you subscribed to an idealistic order of things, that Moriarty was conceived.

Joel subscribed to no order other than his own, which decreed that he was a person without social commitment whose only definition of himself was to be found in his work. There were good reasons for this in his history; perhaps they were even excuses, but they were of no service to Miranda. When she told him she was expecting his baby he was quiet, controlled and not unkind. He explained that he did not wish to be a father. Furthermore, he did not wish her to become a mother.

His ultimatum was clear and cruel. 'Either you lose this baby or you lose me.'

Knowing how badly he had hurt her, he did what little he could to modify the damage. She cried a lot and he was forbearing. They made love even more frequently and, for Miranda at least, with a new depth of passion born of longing for the impossible.

And now it was impossible to know what might have happened; whether or not he would have left her, or if she might even have committed an act she knew instinctively to be murder. She did not believe she could have done that, but she would never know for certain because events had overtaken them in a manner which neither of them could have foreseen in a million years.

Even today, when she looked back at that afternoon, at the scene that had stunned the nerves of her retina more like a shocking piece of art than a living reality, she had to shake off disbelief again and renew her acceptance that, in that moment, all their lives had undergone a change that was not good and could not be undone.

On a winter Sunday at Sheringham, she and Joel had wandered hours deep into the country. At the turn of a woodland path, a valley had opened out below them, and with a vivid abruptness she found herself gazing into a landscape both familiar and unknown: the unseen private country of her mother's pictures, only half inviting them to explore.

At its centre lay Arden House, the towered and ivied edifice of dark red stone whose frost-fired windows recalled the great, flaming canvases Chloe had done at the height of summer; paint translated into the live energy of heat and light, flagrant, somehow exulting, as if the empty house itself were alive.

Now, it seemed a place forgotten, its beauty asleep and waiting, a host to briars and solitary birdsong. The fairytale image persisted when they found a small, warped door ajar at the back. They entered on quiet feet, whispering like children as they roamed the elegant, deserted rooms. Upstairs there were dusty corridors, more empty rooms. Another open door.

Joel glanced through it. An expression of question and pleasure came into his face, as if, after tedious years, he had found something new. He had pushed her forward. So that she had to look.

Had to see the lovers lying on the bed, their naked bodies wrapped about each other in the innocence of sleep, pale limbs tangling with darker ones in folds of faded brocade the colour of dead petals.

So beautiful together, the light so soft. She had thought of Correggio. She could still see them now. Chloe and Luke Cavendish, Adam's father.

To see her mother – her mother! – in another man's arms had been to comprehend with outrageous suddenness that nothing in the world was as she had trusted it to be. There was only betrayal. Chloe's betrayal. Joel's betrayal. They were all one.

The pain that had dazed and enraged her every night since she had told Joel about the baby, that was all one with this.

Her anger swelled, a boiling in her veins, forcing upon her a clarity of vision she had previously contrived to avoid.

She saw how her relationship to Joel was governed not by her love for him but by her fear of losing him. And this for the man who was so calamitously lacking in the ability to love that he wanted her to kill his child in her womb. She had been abject, she had humiliated herself. Each further moment she spent with him would be nothing but a shoddy, shameful compromise.

Miranda shivered, her eyes refocusing on the city spread before her window, wearing the beauty of this particular morning like a very old cardigan. Damn Joel. She had not wanted to think about all that.

She had known when she had started reworking her life without him that the only direction in which to look and move was forward. Not that there was any real danger in her memories. She had Adam now; he had made her proof against them. She felt a sherbet burst of love and gratitude. She had lost herself, for quite a long time, before Christmas. She had been like a building whose foundations had been gutted by fire or by an earthquake. Lovingly, with humour, taking infinite pains, Adam had replaced every brick. Now she stood rock solid, facing the world even more confidently than before. She could not have done any of it alone. She would have toppled into rubble.

Every time he came home to Miranda, as well as the sensual melting in his lower abdomen, Adam had the enjoyable feeling of playing house. He knew they were not engaged in a mere game, especially in view of Moriarty, and that real men do not play house, but that was the feeling. He supposed it must be something to do with his parents' divorce. Since the age of eighteen months, his experience of houses had consisted of racketing from palazzo to piste with his actress mother, Helen, as she made her triumphal ascent to the theatrical heavens; or wolfing nourishing chunks of family life in Sheringham with Luke, his second wife Dinah and their children Oliver and Belle. Since he had lived with Miranda he took a simple pleasure in just opening the door and finding her there, knowing that neither he nor she would later get up and go home, that they *were* at home – it gratified the rootless child in him. Miranda's welcoming smile was as wide and luscious as a slice of melon. It was like that today.

'I *am* glad you're back,' she beamed.

'So am I.' He kissed her. She tasted not of melon but of lemon curd.

'I can't help it,' she said as he licked his lips. 'It's my latest pregnant craze.'

'Brother of the more well-known pregnant pause? Fine. I like it, too.'

'Good, because I'm going to plaster it on toast, roll it up in pancakes and lather it all over tarts.' Consciously she maintained her tone of airy nothingness. 'Bit of a pig about Joel, isn't it?'

Adam laughed. 'More of a whole hog.' He observed her bright face. Too bright?

'I hope it didn't bother you – hearing about him.'

'Only for a minute. Did Luke say why the police have given up?'

'Lack of evidence. They couldn't find a thing to connect him with drugs. His flat stayed clean through several searches. He has met with no known dealers or suppliers, exchanged no suspicious packages, nothing. They can't afford to spend any more time on him.'

Miranda sighed. 'It doesn't surprise me, really. He has always known how to cover his tracks. He would have stopped dealing at the first warning you gave him. Soon he won't even need the money. His exhibition is coming up in July. He'll probably sell everything he does after that.'

'So that's it, then?' Adam looked grim. 'After all the damage he has done. And tried to do.'

'I guess so. Unless – oh God,' she said nervously, 'you don't think they'll try to get Rufus to give evidence, do you? And Dwayne.'

'I don't think so, not after they've already let them off with a caution.'

'But you're not sure?'

'I'll find out. Don't *worry*.'

'Mum would be so upset. After all that effort, keeping him out of court. What if the whole thing starts up again?'

She could not help worrying.

She said, 'No matter what the law wants, it just wouldn't be right to put pressure on Rufus. He made Joel his hero and his loyalty is a matter of self-respect. I admire him for it. I know Dad thinks I'm muddling morality with sentiment, but I don't see how one can avoid it.'

'I think it's all right until you have to choose between them.'

'Well, I choose sentiment. Rufus is my brother. I love him and I don't want him to have to think less of himself than he already does. You know he blames himself for Joel's surveillance.'

Rufus had been an idiot to get involved; he already held the track-record among the hashisheen of his south London playground.

When she had first brought Joel home and the boy had been dazzled by him and seduced by the Harley, Miranda had no intimation of introducing a nemesis to the house. She knew that Joel smoked dope, but had no suspicion of his history as a dealer No one discovered that until he had been supplying Rufus for some months with selected merchandise for sale at Sheringham School; cannabis at first, then amphetamines, Ecstasy and other fashionable designer items without a maker's label. When a bad E-mix affected his closest friend, Dwayne Cubitt, Rufus had wanted to stop trading. Joel had persuaded him to continue, and when he resisted again had resorted to blackmail, threatening to draw the attention of

Sheringham's headmaster, Philip Dacre, to the lively trade surrounding the school.

Rufus had panicked and Tilda, bless her, with a twin's intuition, had caught the whiff of it and extracted his confession. Tilda held the drug trade and its denizens in the deepest despite. She had been furious but also undeniably gratified to discover that Joel, whom she cordially disliked, was living down to her expectations. She discussed the problem with her best friend, Belle Cavendish, and they decided to seek Adam's advice. This was on the grounds that he was an adult, a journalist, in love with Miranda and would be madder than Mad Max with Joel. Belle was extravagently fond of her half-brother and liked to involve him in anything with which she could catch his interest.

Her judgement was sound. Adam had immediately called Joel and demanded that he let Rufus off the hook, threatening police action if he refused. This proved less sound; Joel's retaliation was neat, vengeful and aimed ultimately at Miranda, whom he did not forgive for leaving him.

Should the police be involved, he promised to contact a tabloid columnist he knew and offer him the saleable tale of the Senior Master of a well-known school who was committing adultery with the mother of one of his pupils, a well-worn scenario which never failed to titillate the *hypocrite lecteur*.

It was too much for Adam and Miranda to handle alone. Neither the threat nor its possible consequences directly belonged to them.

It had been left to Adam to acquaint his father with the dual prongs of Joel's fork; Miranda had not spoken two civil words to her mother since that inextinguishable moment on the threshold of a room in a deserted house.

After despatching Joel from her life she had sat for half an hour at the kitchen table, playing with the broken bits of her heart, until Chloe had come home, trailing clouds of adult glory and wearing an insufferable smile of bliss and ignorance. Miranda had wiped off both of these, called her several demeaning names and roundly renounced her as a mother. Chloe, despite the shock of finding herself and Luke discovered, had exhibited genuine distress on Miranda's behalf and an extreme reasonableness in the face of her attack. Miranda had taken a breath and gone on to renounce her, with redoubled fervour, as the grandmother of her forthcoming child.

This was the first that Chloe had heard of the existence of Moriarty.

Neither mother nor daughter had done well on these terms. They loved each other dearly and had rarely been at odds. They had gone through a horrible time together.

For Miranda it had been at its worst before Chloe had told Alain about her affair; she had hated knowing while her father was still in ignorance. And later, after Chloe had made her confession, Alain had seemed to forgive her so easily. Miranda could not bear that either. She had always felt especially close to her father and he had responded; he could not help showing it, always hugging her, touching her hair, asking about her life, wanting to keep her from harm. She was outraged for him. Soon he had sternly insisted that, if he could forgive, then it was not her business to indulge herself in judgement. It had been hard for her. She could not summon the generosity he must somehow have found. But gradually, as she watched how they were together, tender and considerate, still so very much married, both apparently determined to let the past lie in the past, the terrible tension in her had begun to relax. She became able to confront the fear that had been at the root of her anger. It was going to be all right. There was to be no cataclysm. No separations, no divorce. No further betrayals.

She and Chloe had begun to mend what was torn between them.

By now the mend was almost invisible.

                    *   *   *

'I think I'll call Mum and get her reaction,' she told
Adam. 'She'll want to know. She may even have some
idea what the police will do.' Adam pressed the button
for the Oliviers and handed her the phone.

'I'm getting the machine,' she said fretfully.

'She's probably in the studio.'

She tried again. 'Come on, Chloe. I really need to talk to
you. Oh, shut up!' she chivvied the prattling answerphone.
'You don't think things will start to go wrong now, do you,
Adam? Just when we've all settled back into our lives.'

'No, I don't.'

'But suppose Joel tried to get the papers interested
again?'

'He wouldn't get any further than he did before.'

'God, I hope not. I can still hardly *believe* he actually
went ahead and did it in the first place. If *only* I hadn't
made everything worse by making you take me to him
that night. If we hadn't said those things to each other.'

Adam grinned. 'Or if I hadn't hit him, and vice versa.
Or you hadn't dragged Cally Baker out of his bed by her
hair. There's no point in this, Miranda. It's over now. And
so far, it's all working out.'

They had found themselves part of an unusual conspiracy
between their parents in which they all acted together
to help maintain the friendships between the younger
members of both families and to deflect the harm that
Joel had tried to do.

Its successful outcome, as far as the public side of things
was concerned, had been largely due to Philip Dacre. The
Headmaster of Sheringham had no intention of losing
either the good name of his school or the services of
his friend and expected successor, Luke Cavendish. He
had alerted the mafia of his august and ancient family
and had flourished the ties of Eton and Balliol in a
couple of appropriate clubs. The upshot was that no

dangerous column been printed and no drugs charges had been brought at Sheringham. Rufus Olivier and his friends had been officially cautioned and spoken to with scorching severity by a high-ranking police officer, and the Drug Squad had been informed of Joel Ranger's secondary career.

Adam was right. So far, it all appeared to have worked like a charm. The Oliviers and Cavendishes treated each other with more kindness and civility than either Luke or Chloe had the right to expect, and they managed their occasional public appearances together, at school functions or family parties, with efficient grace, everyone employing their higher emotions to fine effect.

But Miranda pondered on the churnings of the lower emotions. She knew her mother and Luke Cavendish could not just have stopped loving each other. How did they deal with their feelings? How did her father deal with his? And poor Dinah Cavendish, who had been so close to Chloe before, and probably during the affair? Certainly everything could not be as neat and tidy as it had been made to look.

For herself, for a long time, despite her love for Adam, she had remained under Joel's spell, an old, decaying spell perhaps, but one that still had surprising rushes of strength in it.

Adam said she should try not to think about it any more. Adultery happened. People fell in love. They could not help that. They stayed together or they decided to part. Luke and Chloe had made a sacrifice. She should accept it and move on.

Now he told her firmly 'Nothing bad is going to happen. And even if it did, we would be able to handle it. The important thing is not to let Joel get inside your head again.'

'I won't.' She grabbed a dark red corkscrew of hair and

twisted it furiously round her finger. 'I don't even see him these days. He's never in college, not even in the coffee shop.'

Adam frowned.

'Not that I'm looking for him, of course. It's more like I'm noticing – what was that old detective novel called? – *An Absence of Malice*.'

Chapter 2

CHLOE OLIVIER HAD NOT ANSWERED THE PHONE because she had been deeply asleep. She had taken two strong painkillers and a sleeping pill sometime after two. It was now nearly six.

She began the struggle towards consciousness but her dream still lapped about her, holding her back. She floated, weightless, boneless, fingers and toes feathering gently, in a shallow summer sea, down at the bottom among fronded weed and rose-coloured rock. Tiny, iridescent fishes nibbled and tickled her skin. Her body sang.

'Luke,' she murmured, or perhaps only thought.

She reached for him. Had they made love? She was not sure now. The submerged world receded and her limbs grew heavy. She was aware of pain, still sleeping somewhere inside her. And something else; something black and suffocating that sat waiting on her chest. She tried to cry out but could make no sound. She was fighting for breath as she broke through and surfaced.

She opened her eyes.

'I didn't mean to wake you. I'm sorry, *chérie*.'

Alain stood beside the bed. He bent to touch her cheek and still she could say nothing because the blackness was inside her now. It was part of her. She had created it herself.

She turned her head away. She must not weep.

'Tilda was worried about you,' he said gently. 'She thought you looked very pale. And you do. What is it? Are you ill?'

The pain awoke, dragging at her abdomen.

'It's nothing. Just a heavy period. I didn't intend to sleep so long.' She began to pull herself up. She felt groggy and her sight was blurred. She smelled of blood.

'No, no. Stay there,' he insisted. 'I'll bring you some tea. Or a glass of wine?'

'No, honestly, I'm fine. I'll get up. Go and talk to Tilda. You have hardly seen her this week.'

There must be nothing out of the ordinary, nothing they were not accustomed to have her do. She was not a woman who slept in the afternoons.

'*D'accord*. If you are sure.' Alain was relieved, as he was lately when he knew she was not about to abdicate her life for more than five minutes.

'I'll cook dinner,' he said cheerfully. 'You can just sit and enjoy the smell of it.'

'Lovely.' She smiled at him and he left her, his mind already on a menu. Chloe lay back, unable to move. Her pretence for Alain had helped to keep the reckoning at bay. Without him, she was left with the enormity of what she had done.

She did not want to get up. She could not be with him again, not until she had found some sort of equilibrium that would enable her to behave as though nothing had changed. She hated the idea of it because to pretend further was going to make her very lonely.

She had thought she was done with deception.

But today she had altered everything. She had altered herself, though Alain did not perceive it. She had done him an injury and he must not know of it. She had done Luke a far greater one and he must never learn of it. The pain was severe now. She was grateful. It was not one millionth part of what she deserved.

She wept and curled on her side, holding her swollen, empty womb in her hands. She had destroyed her child, Luke's child.

Before she had done it, there had been nothing else to be done.

No one had known she was pregnant. She and Luke had parted at last, and she had stayed with her children and with Alain, whom she had never ceased to love in the way she had always loved him; which was not the same, but no less than the way she loved Luke. She had heard it said that a woman cannot love two men equally.

'Equally' made no sense to Chloe. She could and did love them both; differently.

She had made her choice. She had refused Luke's absurd romance of running away to live on paint, love and English as a Foreign Language among the sympathetic ghosts of Verona. Although he was as necessary and miraculous to her as the light by which she lived and worked, she would not take her personal happiness in exchange for that of the other people she loved. It had been the right choice, she did not question that.

And then she had found she was carrying Luke's child.

She had know at once that she could not give birth. There was a simple and horrible logic to it. If she were to tell Luke she was pregnant he would triumphantly reclaim her; everything they had suffered and striven to prevent would take place. She could not tell Alain because she would not ask him to bring up her lover's child. Nor was she capable of attempting to deceive him about its paternity.

She had told no one. She had twisted and torn in the trap her mind had become, searching for a way to keep her child. She had not found one. There had been only the single course left to her and she had taken it this morning. As soon as she had done so, that same mind-trap had closed again, suggesting that there had in fact been another possibility; she could have given her baby its life and her love and they could have lived together, somewhere apart.

She could not look into the logic of that; she was in no condition for reason. If she were still a Catholic she would be in need of a priest. As it was, she did not know what she needed, how she was going to be able to be. Absolution was not available.

She lay and thought the thoughts of an automaton, spare and precise. Anything else and she would start screaming and keening and would not be able to stop.

She had conceived a child and she had killed it, taken its life before it could be born. He or she had lived inside her for three months and one week, a tiny creature who already had fingers and toes and the vestigial mystery of a human soul.

It had been hers and she had killed it. She wished now that she, too, had died.

But that was not how it was going to be. What would happen was that she would get up out of this bed, now. She would take a bath and put on her clothes. Then she would go downstairs and smile at Rufus and Tilda and ask them about their day. She would kiss Alain on the back of the neck as she often did while he was cooking. Then she would call Miranda, to whom she spoke every day, and they would discuss the infinitesimal changes of pregnancy.

Alain loved to cook. He did it easily, with a lot of imagination and no fuss. It was one of his gallic pluses, like his pleasure in fashion, his elastic knowledge of art and music, and his logician's love of a good argument. He approached such things with the same dedicated enthusiasm that he brought to his work in the restoration of ailing power plants, an arcane profession which no other member of his family was remotely qualified to understand. What they did know was that it concerned the ability to predict, within certain useful parameters, the eventual fracture of large and vital metal components under stress – when a crack developed in a power station turbo-generator, Alain's expertise would establish whether it was dormant, slowly growing, or likely to provoke an event spectacular enough for a disaster movie.

In the early days of their marriage, missing him while he worked for days or weeks in Hong Kong or Manila or Frankfurt, Chloe would plunder the desk in his study. Glowing among the files and papers and computer print there was a hidden treasure of futuristically beautiful charts and graphs in jewel colours, their meaning their own secret, their sweetness of line and form rivalling Matisse. Some were close photographs of metallic shards with delicate fibroid structures like the underflesh of exotic mushrooms. Chloe had asked for some of these on the understanding that he was not to explain what they were about. They had been the source of her first non-representative work, an excuse for pure colour and instinctive, adventurous shapes that gave her a new freedom.

She and Alain had always enjoyed the oppositeness of what they did; it pleased them to be at once so close and so far apart.

It was the closeness that Chloe needed now. It was there; she could take it for granted. But she felt that to do so today would be a form of dishonesty. If she did not do so, however, Alain would be sure to notice and question. It was up to her to find a balance.

'Has anyone fed Baskerville?' she enquired when they were all sitting round the big kitchen table. Alain had made a sturdy fish soup with *rouille* and greedy croutons sliced whole from a baguette.

'He seems to be genuinely starving, poor thing.'

A convincing whimper supported this as she disengaged a plate-sized paw from her knee. They had found Baskerville, a good-natured giant, half Bernese Mountain

Dog and half Gothic imagination, lost and howling dismally on Dartmoor.

'He's probably got worms,' suggested Rufus helpfully.

'He can't have. Not after the grisly time we had getting those pills into him,' replied Tilda indignantly. 'I did feed him, Mum. But it's Hildegarde. She keeps stealing his food. She's too young to know she ought not to have dogfood.'

'Spotty,' Rufus said very clearly.

'Oh for goodness sake give up, will you? Or at least call her something feminine and half suitable. Spotty. Yuk!'

The object of dissent, a small, undeniably spotted tortoiseshell kitten, was sitting on the top shelf of the large oak dresser between a blue Italian jug and a reproduction of one of Nicholas Hilliard's languid courtiers. She looked uncertain.

'Here, Spotty,' Rufus called urgently.

'Hil-de-garde,' cooed Tilda.

The cat leaped happily towards the table accompanied by several fluttering postcards and the double-headed cock and hen egg-cup which the twins had fought over since Miranda had broken its companion at the age of ten.

'Oh no!' Rufus dived for the pieces. There were a lot of them. 'I really liked that,' he said regretfully.

'It seems we 'ave disposed of one argument,' Alain remarked neutrally, 'even if it was not the one in 'and.'

Chloe gazed at them blankly. It was as if she were watching a film she had given up trying to follow. The twins' ongoing dispute over the relative merits of Spotty Muldoon and Hildegarde of Bingen suddenly seemed bizarre to the point of surrealism.

She rose abruptly, pushing Baskerville away. 'I'm tired,' she said. 'I'm going back to bed.'

She left the room and their concerned voices followed her, twittering inside the hollow of her skull like swallows in a cathedral.

* * *

She had wanted to phone Miranda but had not been able to make herself pick up the instrument. It was too soon to be reconnected with so much joyous expectation. Her daughter, like herself, was a woman who wanted children. She had refused with contempt to do what Chloe had just done. Her child was longed for, named, already extravagantly loved. It was not that there could be any question of a rift between them; Chloe would make sure there was not. Nevertheless, she needed some kind of lacuna, a hollow where she could lick her self-inflicted wounds and try, in secrecy and with an unkind, necessary despatch, to bury her dead.

For an hour or more she lay drifting in and out of thought and sorrow, thought and sleep. At nine o'clock the bedside phone jolted her fully awake. She let it ring until someone answered it downstairs.

Five minutes later Tilda's neat head appeared round the bedroom door. 'How are you feeling?' she asked cautiously. 'Only, Miranda wants to talk to you.'

'I'm sorry.' She smiled at the gentle, worried face. 'I couldn't wake up quickly enough to take it.'

Tilda's emotional antennae were ultra sensitive; they would have to be intercepted with white noise.

'I feel better now, thank you, sweetheart.'

'Good.' Tilda examined her doubtfully. 'Sorry about the stuff with Rufus. It was idiotic of us.'

'Don't worry about it. I was just overtired. Have you practised yet?'

'No, I was just going to.'

'Would you play that Debussy prelude and leave the doors open so I can hear?'

Tilda beamed. 'Of course. And listen hard after that. I'm going to play something Paul just wrote. It's really good. We're going to orchestrate it and then maybe they'll play it at the Summer Concert.'

She clumped off downstairs on her seven-league heels. Chloe smiled. She had thought they had heard the last of those when Miranda left home. Last year's Tilda, aggressively shy and living almost entirely in her music, had despised the lightness of fashion, but since Belle Cavendish had claimed her friendship she had left open the doors of her ivory tower and all sorts of ordinary pleasures had trooped in. In their wake had come Paul Hughes, her first boyfriend, also a musician, who had lately begun to compose.

How would they eat, in the jobless future that was promised them, all these young lovers and providers of beauty in all its forms? Would Miranda have to wait on tables and decorate plates in order to subsidise her designs? Must Tilda be satisfied to teach a diminishing number of musical pupils instead of becoming the solo performer she so surely ought to be?

They kept her close to them with their needs, their dreams, her living, demanding children. They pinned her to the moment.

Wanting to be dead was not among her options.

She picked up the phone. Miranda was talking to her father.

'The guillotine it is, then.' The slightly husky young voice curled on a giggle. 'I could take the technicolour dreamcoat I'm knitting for Moriarty and watch his head roll.' A yelp followed. 'What am I *saying*? What a terrible introduction to life, being there when your father loses his head!'

''Ee would probably grow another one, that one; *tant pis*,' Alain growled. ''Ee 'as lost it before, *n'est-ce pas, ma fille*?'

'*Oui, mon père*,' Miranda said drily, 'but he wasn't the only one. Let's not start counting mistakes, shall we, or we'll be here all night.'

'Miranda?' Chloe thought it was time to interrupt.

'Oh, sorry Mum. Didn't know you were there. Good-night, Dad.'

'Good-night, Miranda. *Dors bien, chérie*.'

'Mum?'

'What on earth was all that about? It sounded a bit extreme.'

Miranda explained, adding her concern for Rufus.

'I'll check, but I'm pretty sure they'll leave him alone. The chief constable has already dealt with him in the context of the school. Joel is a different case in another bailiwick.'

'You don't sound too bothered about Joel.'

'Miranda, do you *want* this thing to go any further?'

'No. I want it to be over.'

'Exactly. So let's not get too bothered.'

It was not only Rufus who would be distressed if Joel were to go to jail. Whatever Miranda might say or think she believed, Chloe knew that her daughter would be the one to suffer most.

'Fine. Leave him to heaven. Anyway, there's something else I want to ask you about. You know Sam Shaw, that spaced out little guy in the one-room flat down from mine? Well, he's leaving next week to bum around the far-out Far East with his girlfriend for six months. He's asked me to look after the flat, to let it if I find the right person. What d'you think?'

'About what?'

'I thought you might like to stay there, instead of at my place, when you come over before the baby is born. It's small, but it would be all your own, and it's cheap. Sam wouldn't mind, and that way we could all have our own space – especially our own beds. I love to sleep with Adam, but I think I might like a bed to myself around the birthday, just till I get used to Moriarty being on the outside. So – shall I go ahead and fix it up?'

Chloe hesitated. A decision would bring the birth so near.

'I'm not sure,' she said. 'Will you give me a couple of days to think about it? It certainly makes sense.'

That was what she had said, not long since, when

Miranda had asked if the baby could live at Sheringham on weekdays during term time, so that she could give every possible ounce of energy to getting a good degree. By then Chloe had already known what must happen to her own pregnancy. After an initial drawing back, she had come to view the idea as a merciful one; a child given for a child taken away. Far more than she could have expected to hope for.

How simple and stupid that seemed now. Empty and aching, experiencing a grief and self-loathing she had previously been incapable of imagining, she could see nothing to come to her beyond further pain.

Two days later, every man, woman and child in the country was plunged into mourning for sixteen small children and one of their teachers murdered by a lunatic in the gymnasium of their primary school. The madman was a solitary deviant whose chief relationships were with the young boys who attended the sports clubs he organised and with the licensed guns he would use to kill them and their sisters, and afterward himself. It would later be explained that he had borne a grudge against the elders of his small community because they had put an end to his work with boys when they became suspicious of the nature of his feelings for them.

It was impossible for anyone to understand his deed or to imagine the inner life that found its expression in such horror.

'To kill little children, Mum,' Miranda wept, flying to the phone as soon as she heard the news. 'It isn't human. It's just not in our nature.'

'Are you alone?' Chloe controlled the tremor in her own throat. 'Where's Adam? Shall I come over?'

'No. It's all right. He'll be here soon. I just needed to hear your voice. Bless you, though.'

'Lie down, sweetheart, and try to be calmer. You must try not to disturb Moriarty.'

'I know. Oh God – just think if it's going to be her one day. I can't bear it, Mum. Why does the world have to be so bloody evil?'

'Because we are, I suppose; some of us. But very few. We can't give up believing that because of one man's madness.'

'It *isn't* just one man. There are more every day. It's the way the world is going, turning against its children.' Miranda sounded afraid. 'I saw a film about street kids in Rio the other night. They have no homes, no one to look after them. There are death squads – the government doesn't stop them – they shoot them as if they were rats. There was one little girl, she was only eighteen months old, living out of dustbins.'

'I know, I know,' Chloe said softly. 'I saw it too. And there *are* people working to stop it, all over the world. Don't cry, my lovely. That can't help anyone.'

'It just makes me feel so goddamn guilty. And all I ever do about it is write useless letters for Amnesty.'

'They aren't useless. You know that, really. And you must not confuse guilt with grief. You have nothing to feel guilty about.'

For the rest of the morning, Chloe struggled to assimilate the shock of the sixteen innocent deaths. In a few hours Rufus and Tilda would come home from school with their own burdens of sadness and incomprehension. She would have to try to find the right things to say to them; she did not think she had done very well with Miranda.

It seemed important to keep busy. The occupation of the hands was said to calm the spirit. But although she disposed of a large number of small tasks, none of them could hold the enormity at bay.

Beneath the surface of her sorrow for what had happened at Dunblane, something else was taking place in her mind, some new picture evolving over which she, the artist, had no control. It was not yet clear, but its mood was unquiet.

There was something in it that frightened her. She began to feel enclosed, as though there were not enough air in the room. She put down the jar of brushes she had been cleaning meticulously, one by one, fetched her coat from the hook in the lobby and left the house. She was going to visit the only person to whom she could attempt to describe what was happening to her.

In the garden she whistled for Baskerville who appeared, grinning, from nowhere and dashed eagerly ahead of her up the shallow hillside behind the house. On the crest of it they followed the mile-long track to the village, fenced on one side to protect the sheep who lay piled in drifts against the hedges, sharing their heat. The big dog ignored them virtuously and pounded on towards the fork in the path, where he sat down to wait for Chloe. Would she carry straight on into the heart of Sheringham, and incidentally past the butcher's, or turn off down the narrow lane that came out at the back of the church?

St Mark's it was. Ah well, another day, another bone. Baskerville nosed open the gate on the south side of the churchyard and made for the warmth of the porch where there was a bench he liked to lie on. Chloe followed, saluted by the appealingly dissolute ranks of gravestones, raggedly uniformed in lichen. In the porch she hesitated, listening for any activity inside the building. As she had hoped, she heard nothing. Out of affectionate habit she scanned the parish lists on the noticeboard above Baskerville's bench. She was looking for Dinah's name.

There it was, on the flower rota. Nine a.m. Friday. Dinah Cavendish. Dinah did not believe in a deity but she had a strong sense of community. Her flowers were for her fellows, not for God.

Chloe touched the familiar signature as if it were a talisman, wishing sadly and with profound unreason that she could unburden herself to Dinah now. They had been edging towards friendship again, in a careful, unemphatic way, ever since the family *rapprochement* which the children had innocently forced upon them at Christmas.

As far as Belle and the twins were aware, nothing had ever changed between them. Dinah, once she had made up her mind to it, had enabled this to look like the truth with an ease that baffled Chloe, who knew better than to consider herself in the slightest measure forgiven. No, the changes between them were ineradicable; she accepted them as part of her punishment. But how much she missed Dinah, whom she loved; almost as much as she missed and longed for Luke.

You can't have it both ways, she told herself with tired contempt, and turned to push open the broad west door.

Although the church was empty she had no sense of being alone. A thousand years of intense life resided in the whitewashed walls and pillars of Purbeck stone, in the praying arches and the net of tracery ramping above her head, as busy as the roots of buttercups. Pale daylight slunk in, water-coloured, through the tall stained windows, but in each dark corner the primrose aureolae of candles redeemed the absent sun. The place breathed gently to a slow, ancient rhythm and Chloe felt the calming of her own erratic pulse.

Stepping carefully over the bronze knight set into the pavement above his tomb, she carried a rush-seated chair from the chancel and placed it against the north wall next to a small opening shaped like a four-leaf clover. Near this a channel was carved square and slantwise through the two-foot thickness of the stone. These were the quatrefoil and squint. In the fourteenth century they had been the conduits of food, conversation and holy communion to the narrow cell behind the wall where the Anchoress of Sheringham had lived. Her name was Catherine Chandler, and it was she whom Chloe had come to visit.

Chloe had made Catherine her confidante last summer when she had needed so badly to talk to someone about Luke. It seemed to her that they had something in common. Within three years of taking her vows as an anchoress, Catherine had first recanted and returned to the world and later pleaded successfully to be re-enclosed. Chloe had taken this as a metaphor for her own behaviour in the context of her marriage. She had talked to Catherine as if addressing a diary, part stranger and part her own reflection. Whether by power of her own imagination or intuition, or of something other than these, she had not felt that their conversations had been one-sided.

Inconsiderate of death and time, Catherine's was a vivid presence. Her spirit invested the space behind the wall, listening, communing, awarding sympathy and, on rare occasions, judgement.

'It's done,' Chloe told her, leaning her head against the grille of the quatrefoil. 'It is so much worse than I feared. I don't know what you would think of me. Do I qualify for forgiveness? Because I don't believe I am going to be able to forgive myself. You see, what happened this morning – all those children – and the others, those Miranda talked about? Well, she is right. Everywhere, all over the world, we are destroying our children. And now I have become a part of it – can you understand that, Catherine?'

Tears fell on her hands. She wiped them abstractedly on her coat.

'I have made myself a place in a hierarchy of destruction to which Thomas Hamilton also belongs. Today he killed sixteen children. Two days ago I ended the life of my own unborn child. You can see how we are linked together. Is there so much difference between us? Was Thomas Hamilton demented and Chloe Olivier sane? And if she is, and he was not, which of them was more guilty?'

She had thought she was calm and sensible now, was surprised to find herself very near to hysteria. Her head ached; there was a dull throb in her temples. She pressed her face against the stone to cool it. She listened intently, as though she held a shell to her ear, half expectant of voices from out of the sea.

Think, Chloe, think what you are saying. Do you really believe yourself the moral equal of a mass murderer, a creature whose distorted and unrecognisable psyche will perhaps never be deciphered? Isn't there an inverted arrogance in thinking yourself so great a sinner?

'Killing is killing,' she said aloud.

You used not to think so. When you were younger you argued for a woman's right to value her own needs above those of a thirteen-week embryo.

'I had not had an abortion then.'

So you no longer believe in that right?

'I think I still do, intellectually. But it doesn't stop me feeling like a murderer.'

You are living in the last decade of the twentieth century. What you have done is no longer regarded as murder in England. It is not even illegal.

'No, but that doesn't affect either my conscience or my emotions.'

Why did you do this, Chloe?

'Because it seemed the only way to avoid hurting so many people.'

And did you expect to feel so much remorse?

'I knew I must regret it, but not how much.'

So you chose to suffer the pain of remorse yourself rather than cause pain to others whom you love?

Yes. 'No!' she cried out. 'I chose to destroy my child rather than cause them pain.'

Did that child suffer?

'I don't know. I don't think anyone does, yet. It makes no difference to how I feel.'

And who is suffering now?

'I am. I have no alternative.'

Then suffer. But do not allow your life to be nothing other than suffering. That will be of no use to those whom you wish to protect, and of even less use to yourself. You have a good mind and a strong spirit. You should not willingly place them in jeopardy.

'I don't feel strong. I feel weak and despicable.'

The weakness will pass. The self-despite is more difficult. What you need is time and a place in which to reflect. Your mind is not clear. You should paint. You have always gained clarity from your work.

'I can't paint. Not now.'

Have you tried?

'No. I know I can't.'

Nonsense. You are punishing yourself. You think that because you have destroyed the thing you created, you have no further right to create.

'Perhaps. It seems logical.'

It is dangerous. You already know you have no leave to destroy yourself. You must try to work. There is healing in good work. You must make a committed effort. Without desperation. Even without very much concentration. Let it come as it will. Eventually you will find the release you are looking for.

'How can I?' Chloe moved restlessly. Her cheek was cold and stiff now. She rubbed it and found the imprint of the quatrefoil where she had leaned against the stone.

'Whether I work or whether I can't, it won't change what happened. And it's no use telling me I can learn to accept it.'

Is it not?

Abruptly, she stood up. 'I cannot go on with this – I have to go now. The children will soon be home.'

She turned away and walked quickly up the aisle. She felt ungracious but she could not help that. If something was unfinished here, it would have to remain that way.

In the porch she snapped her fingers at Baskerville, who had expected a caress and some acknowledgement of his patience. He gave her a puzzled look but followed her without complaint. They went back the way they had come, up the lane to the path across the fields, Chloe taking long, tense strides with the dog close at heel.

Just beyond the fork, at the top of the ridge, they came to

a vast, uprooted trunk set back in the grass. A wind-scoured dinosaur among trees, this was the Lightning Oak. It had lain there since the gales of 1987, supporting successive colonies of insect life and generations of villagers who liked to clamber up its tangle of roots and line up along the massive length to be photographed. When Chloe had first seen it she had thought of Ozymandias, so singular was its effect upon the landscape. She had made several sketches of it in charcoal and had scaled its six-foot radius to get a deeper perspective on the valley below, with the village scattering off to the left and the hillside sweeping up behind it to the medieval forest guarding the Pilgrim's Way.

Breathless after her headlong walk, she leaned gratefully into the bark, smoothed and polished by the wind that was almost constant up here on the ridge. She tipped back her head and closed her eyes, resting her hand on Baskerville's warm skull.

'I'm sorry, boy,' she told him. 'We'll go to the butcher's another time. I just couldn't face talking to anyone today.'

Baskerville pricked up his ears at the word 'butcher', then subsided into his lion pose, looking more puzzled than ever.

They stood silently, each thinking as nearly as possible of nothing. There was a slight freshening of the wind. Chloe slid down the trunk to sit in its lee, folding her legs under her coat and putting her arm around the dog, appreciating the warmth of his enormous body. He lolled his head against hers, fond and content. After a while his ears went up again. He stiffened, uttered a bass huff of joy and was suddenly off across the field. A rabbit, Chloe thought resignedly, but soon she heard the sound of further frenzied barking, Baskerville's deep belling surmounted by lighter excited yelps and snaps whose tones she instantly recognised as those of Holmes and Watson: Luke's dogs. She moaned aloud. She could not face an encounter with Luke. Not now, not today.

She stood up, shivering with nerves. She could turn back to the village and hope to avoid him that way. But she knew better than that. Luke would not permit her to escape. She stayed where she was, leaning, out of real necessity now, against the supportive oak, shutting her eyes again like a child who hopes by such pathetic means to dispose of what may be lurking in the dark.

It seemed a long time before she heard his voice, its notes fitting precisely into some waiting shape in her mind, or perhaps her soul.

'Chloe, this is wonderful. I couldn't believe it when I saw Baskerville.' Deep, furred and vibrating with happiness, the sound of him made a nonsense of her closed eyes and shut-down senses.

'Hello, Luke,' she said weakly. She put out a hand to stop him coming any nearer but he knocked it gently aside and pulled her against him inside his coat. His black hair, always a little too long and wild, blew into her eyes and her mouth, blackmailing her memory.

'Chloe. Oh my God, I've missed you.'

Her lips, open, framing the word no, were meet for his kissing. They were both shaking. He tasted salt on his tongue.

'Don't cry, my darling. Let's be happy together, even if it's only for a few minutes.'

'Happy?' She repeated the word clumsily as if it were in an unfamiliar language.

'Why not? Ah Chloe, I've been starving for you.' He drew back to look at her carefully, his eyes glittering with cold and the old piratical need for possession. 'This is a gift from the gods. From Tyche, to be exact – she's the one who likes to give people things they want. You do still love me, don't you?'

'You told me about her before.' Her voice was still strange to her. 'She's also the sister of Nemesis – the one who likes to take things away. We have already been visited by both of them.'

'Well, then it's Tyche's turn again.' He sounded like a schoolboy who has won a game, or like Alain when he had floored the family with an especially meaty chop of logic. He seemed to have no sense of her despair.

'You are so beautiful,' he said. 'It's not that I forget; but the eye of the imagination can lack intensity. You are really here.' He reached for her again. 'I want you, so much. It's like a great block closing up my life. I can't breathe without you.'

His physical presence was overwhelming her. 'Please, Luke,' she said, as synapses snapped to attention, corpuscles became more corporeal, juices flowed.

'Please, Chloe,' he mocked gently. There was the sharp tug in her uterus that had been her first warning of him, shocking in its strength. Its pull, though entirely sexual, was also similar to the sensation she was still experiencing as her endometrial lining came away after the termination. It shamed her. She appeared to herself utterly demoralised.

'I can't bear this,' she said.

'Do you think I can?' Luke asked angrily. He pulled at her shoulders, shaking her. 'It's no good; I have to be inside you. I've been in the desert; you know that. Come on – we can go up there into the trees.' His face lightened, looking at her, his smile unnerving. One of life's born enhancers, he smiled as if he had invented it. 'It *is* a gift, this meeting,' he insisted. 'For godsake, let's make use of it.'

How could she walk away from him now, when everything in her that wanted to live was tugged towards him?

'No.' Her voice tore her throat. She pushed at him violently. 'Didn't you *ever* listen to me? Hear what I meant? I can't be with you, not ever again, especially not now.'

'Why?' he demanded furiously. 'Now is all we have. And yes – I heard you. But I didn't believe you. And I don't believe you now.'

'That doesn't alter anything,' she shouted. 'What is the

point in your being this monster of selfishness? Just leave me alone. You make everything impossible for me.'

'Is that really how you feel?' he asked very quietly. 'You see, I can't believe that either. That isn't how it is between us.' He made no more attempt to hold her but stood still, watching her face. She was silent. This time it was he who had shamed her.

'What is it?' he asked, with the kindness that she loved in him. 'There is something new. Tell me.'

'There's nothing. Just let me go.'

His tone tightened. 'Tell me, Chloe.'

'Nothing – it's only – oh, then, those poor children this morning.' She was appalled that she could so abuse their deaths. She had not meant to do it; but she perfectly understood why she had snatched them from the air to serve as her shield against the truth.

Luke bowed his head. 'I know. It is a terrible thing; an offence against our nature.'

Chloe tried to be calmer. 'Yes. Miranda said something like that.'

'Did she? You would see how she must feel, at this time in her life. I saw her last week, did you know? Adam brought her home one evening. I have never seen a woman so happy to be pregnant.'

'Yes. She is. I'm sorry, Luke—' She felt as if her chest must burst. 'I just can't—' She could not finish her sentence. There was nothing she could say. She shook her head and made for the path, breaking into a run when she reached it.

'Chloe!' He called her once, then let her go. There would be another time. He wondered at the strength of her distress, uncertain if he ought to accept the explanation she had given. On the whole, he thought not. He wished she could have told him so that he might have tried to comfort her in some measure. Although it sometimes irritated him, her apparent need to carry both pain and blame had always aroused his compassion. He hoped Alain was not giving her a difficult time. It seemed unlikely; he had been more than generous. But things might well have changed between them. And what an interesting state of affairs *that* would be.

In the next but one field Chloe found the dogs. They were joyous, dancing with acute concentration in the intricate steps of one of their mock battles. Baskerville stopped for a moment to greet her, then returned to the delicate fray. She let him stay there. He missed Holmes and Watson. He could not know that they were no longer part of the same story.

It had been Baskerville who had introduced her to Luke, stealing his copy of *Sonnets From the Portguese* and bringing it to her as a trophy, delivering all that passion and intellect so lightly at her feet. Their first shared laughter had been over the names of the dogs. Their first debate had followed, upon the nature of coincidence. She must remind Tilda to take Baskerville with her more often when she visited Belle at the Cavendish house.

Luke called her next morning. She had known he would.

'You worried me yesterday,' he began.

'I won't talk to you.' She put down the receiver, leaving it off the hook.

'I'm not going to lose you,' Luke told her, unheard.

Chapter 3

THREE DAYS AFTER THAT, CHLOE SPOKE TO Miranda.

'I've decided to take the studio. What did you say the rent was?'

'That's terrific, Mum. It's only fifty a week to friends. There's basically only one room and a bathroom; but the light's great and, well, you've already seen the view.'

'"Earth hath not anything to show more fair." That's fine. I'll take it for the full six months; that will give me some leeway.'

'*How* long?'

'I've been thinking. I know this is not what we planned, but it suddenly seemed silly for you to have to lug the baby and all her possessions over here every week, when it would be much simpler if I were over there to take care of her. Or him. That's if you would like that?'

'Her, her! Well, yes, it would be really marvellous. It's just such a surprise. What does Dad think? How will they all manage?'

'They are all quite capable, you know; even Rufus, up to a point. But all right; it isn't just you and the baby. I really need a change of some kind in my life just now, Miranda. I haven't been able to work since Christmas. The brush has gone dead in my hand. So you see, this

— 41 —

seems a heaven-sent opportunity to get away and find a fresh perspective.'

'You're not – it isn't Luke, is it?' Miranda was troubled.

'It's – oh, a mixture of things. Look, don't ask me questions, lovely. Just accept that it will be good for Moriarty.'

'Sorry. I didn't mean to pry. Of course, I'm thrilled. I can't wait to tell Adam. Hey, by the way – Radio 4 has bought another of his stories, and they want to see some more. That means he'll be working flat out. So it will be extra fantastic to have you here.'

'That's very good news. Tell him congratulations from all of us.'

'I will. And thanks so much, Mum. This will mean a lot to me. For one thing, I can stop being so scared of the actual birth. You can keep telling me how easy it is.'

'I'll tell you the truth, which is not so bad.'

Chloe relayed Adam's news to the family at the dinner table, to general acclaim, saving her own for Alain in the bedroom. She told him quickly, stumbling over words, addressing his reflection behind hers as she took off her earrings in front of the mirror. Their positions made them seem to her like actors on a small screen, in a TV soap, perhaps; so that her intention appeared less real and therefore less painful. Alain heard her out gravely, his eyes upon hers, ignoring the nervous movement of her hands.

He said neutrally, 'It would have been kind if you had told me this before it became a *fait accompli*.' He pronounced the h's carefully, as he did when he was tired or disturbed.

'I know – but I didn't dare.' She could not look at him; the glass did not, after all, allow her a sufficient remove. 'I don't think I could have decided to do it at all if I hadn't done it this way. I am sorry. It was selfish of me. I see that now.'

He touched her shoulder very briefly. 'Perhaps, a little.

— 42 —

It doesn't matter. What is important is that you should feel like your old self again. Or perhaps a new self, I don't know. I'm worried about you. I know you are unhappy. But you don't talk to me.'

'I would. But there's nothing,' she reiterated tiredly. 'It's my inability to work that's depressing me. Truly.'

'I understand that. But it isn't – you are not regretting your decision to stay with us – with me – are you, *chérie*?'

'Oh no. No!' She turned to him, vehement. He had never suggested this before. 'You must not think that. Please. I've never regretted it.'

Alain nodded. 'I have not liked to ask.'

'I wish you had. I don't ever want us to stop talking about things. I didn't intend to do that. And I won't go to London if you don't want me to.'

He smiled. 'Of course you must go, if that's what you need.'

'I'll come home for weekends. And you'll come up to see Miranda and the baby.'

'*Bien sûr*. It will be good to change the pattern of things.'

'Yes, it will.'

He sat down beside her on the bench and put his arm around her.

'Everything will be fine, as long as you don't want to stay away for ever.'

Wretchedly, Chloe began to cry. 'I'm sorry.' She hated herself more at this moment than she had when she had told him about Luke.

'It's all right,' he told her. 'It will be all right.'

He felt that he held a distillation of loneliness in his arms. He wanted to make love to her, to bring her back to some sense of herself and of the union between them which, for each of them, had become part of their definition of self. But this was not the time. She was too far away. They went to bed and he held her until she slept or pretended to sleep. Alain lay awake, tormenting himself with thoughts of Luke Cavendish. He did not know what to do to help Chloe, except to let her go as she wished, without constraint.

'But how long will you actually be away?' Tilda tried not to look anxious. It did not seem the sort of thing her mother did.

'I'm not sure. But I'll be here quite often, and you'll have so much to do, there won't be time to miss me.'

'But why now? The baby's still ages away.'

'Well, there's a lot of preparation. Mental, as well as physical. Miranda is very young to have a baby.'

'Lots of girls have them young.' None the less she had been astounded to discover that her sister would be one of them; she had always been so level-headed, her sights set steadily on her future career. There had been boyfriends, of course, lots of them; Miranda was so stunning. But nothing serious; not until Joel had come along, all white teeth and black leather, and driven his fiend-gotten Harley straight through her cerebral cortex. Tilda despised Joel more than any other human being she had met, and, by daylight at least, judged him more harshly than even Adam ever could. At night, when her judgement fell, dreaming, to the wolves of her secret self, he spun his vampire wheels above her supine, compliant body and took her with him on a greedy, dirty, demonically exhilarating ride towards a sabbath of satisfaction that was never reached. She would wake, sobbing, drenched in her own bodily fluids and the civet scent of his, rich as blood and strong as imagination.

'I still can't believe Joel is the father,' she told Chloe righteously, her nose thin with disdain. 'Oh, I *wish* it could be Adam!'

'It will be, in every way that matters, as long as they are together.'

'I suppose so. But you don't think they would ever separate, do you? I mean, they seem to be wild about each other. Unless the baby got to be too much for Adam later, with his writing and everything?'

'Well, that's one good reason for me to be there; so that the load doesn't get too heavy for anyone. You can help too, later on.'

'Of course. And Rufus. Oh, Mum—' She screwed up her features tightly. 'We'll look after her properly, won't we? We will be able to keep her safe?'

'Yes, we will, darling. Don't worry.'

'I was supposed to tell you,' Tilda recalled with sombre relevance, 'Mr Cavendish is having a Remembrance Service for the children of Dunblane. It's on Tuesday. You will be coming, won't you?'

Luke and Dunblane in one suffocating room. It was not possible.

'I can't, I'm sorry. I'm leaving on Sunday.' She had meant to wait a week.

'But surely you could stay?'

'No.'

'But you must. Everyone is going.'

'Please dont make an argument of this.'

'I don't understand you just now, Mum, really I don't.'

'You are not required to,' Chloe snapped.

Her daughter turned on her heel and left the room.

'There isn't anything wrong between you and Mum, is there?'

Tilda put her question hesitantly. A few months ago she would not have dreamed of asking it, but recently her father had begun, she thought, to recognise who she was. He was even beginning to treat her, just a little, the way he had always treated Miranda. It had come late, but she welcomed it because she loved him unreservedly. Miranda's absence had slowly relieved her of a sibling jealousy which she had found uncomfortable and degrading, so that now she moved about her inner world with a new lightness, and the outer one with increasing confidence.

'Now, why should you think like that?' Alain asked. She caught the note of amusement, intended to reassure her.

'I don't, exactly. I just wondered. It's so odd, her leaving us like this.'

'I see.' Alain took on his considering look. He reminded Tilda of a severe but benevolent saint from a niche in a medieval cathedral.

'*Eh bien, ma mie*, per 'aps you should look at it differently. Chloe is not leaving us so much as she is going to be with Miranda. *Tu comprends*?'

'*Oui, mon père. Je comprends*.' She smiled at him cheerfully, not because he had convinced her, but because she had recognised his need to do so.

Later, when Paul Hughes came round to work with Tilda on the orchestration of his piano music, he was surprised and delighted by the warmth of her welcome.

'Hey, if you're going to kiss me like that, I think we ought to sit on the sofa, not the piano stool.'

'I'm not.' Tilda grinned. 'It was just the one.'

'I live in hope.'

'Do you? What do you hope for, Paul?' She was not teasing, as she so often did.

He shrugged. 'I don't know. I want to get closer to you, I suppose.'

'Physically, you mean?'

'Not only physically. But that would be nice, yes.'

They kissed again. Tilda liked the way it made her feel, as if something were beginning, very slowly, to unfold and grow inside her. It was slightly scary but somehow right. It had something to do with the music they shared together, something to do with the care he showed her, and quite a lot to do with the effect upon her of a lazy, contemplative quality he had, and the way his blond hair fell across his forehead when he bent over his manuscript. It was the same effect, almost, as had certain themes in Mozart or Prokofiev, which lifted her heart and also brought her to tears.

The kiss went on a long time. Eventually she pulled away.

'What's the matter?' asked Paul.

'Nothing. Only I had the weirdest sensation. My lips were numb and so were yours. It was as if you were turning into me.'

He laughed. 'Didn't you like it?'

'Yes, I think so. But I couldn't breathe.'

'Ah. There's a knack to that. You'll soon learn. It's like swimming or riding a bike. Or even making love.'

'Have you?'

'Made love?'

'Yes.'

'Yes, I have.'

'How many times?'

'I'm not sure. A few.'

'With more than one girl?'

'What is this, the Spanish Inquisition?'

'I'm sorry. I suppose it *is* your own private business.'

'I've slept with two girls.'

'Was one of them Fiona Thompson?'

'Yes.'

'Oh.'

'Now, what's wrong?'

'You went out with her for ages. Why did you break up with her?'

Paul sighed. 'I guess it was because, in the end, we didn't really have all that much in common. She hates classical music; she's a natural born clubber. It kind of became obvious that there was nothing but the sex going for us. And realising that somehow spoiled the sex as well. Does that sound stupid?'

'I don't know. I have no experience of sex. Do you wish I had?'

'No, why should I?'

'Because then I would have no excuse not to sleep with you.'

'Do you want an excuse?'

'That's not really what I mean.' She frowned. 'It's more

as if – I don't like the feeling that you are used to being slept with. I mean, what happens if I don't want to? If I don't feel ready to, not yet?'

'We go on as we are. We're OK, aren't we?'

'You say that, but don't you miss it?'

'Tilda, I think we should stop talking about it and get started on the music. This is getting us nowhere.'

'I suppose not,' she agreed sadly.

'Brighten up, will you? Look, I'd rather be with you than anyone else I know. Let's leave it like that, for now.'

Tilda would have liked to ask Chloe, describing an hypothetical case, of course, how long it might be safe to leave it before Paul might be expected to lose interest; but she did not think Chloe would like to be asked that sort of question at the moment.

It was no use asking Belle; *she* treated the entire opposite sex as if they had been especially created to worship and serve her.

Except for Adam, of course.

On Sunday Chloe found a small pile of gifts beside her breakfast plate.

'What are these for?' she asked.

'Surely you haven't forgotten?' Rufus gaped. 'It's Mother's Day.'

She froze and recovered on the edge of an instant. 'I *had* forgotten.' She distributed a fractured smile. 'What a surprise.'

'Open them, then.' Rufus loved presents, even when they were not for him. 'Mine first. The knobbly one.'

'All right.'

Family tradition dictated that Mother's Day gifts must be made by the donor. Rufus had made her a necklace of brown and gold glass beads, fashionably threaded on a bootlace. When she held it to the light they glowed like sweets sucked smooth.

'Nice, isn't it?' he said proudly.

'It's beautiful, darling.' Chloe kissed the top of his head where the hair still stood up like Just William's.

'Now Miranda's,' suggested Tilda. 'She posted it to me at school, so it would be a secret.' She indicated a plain black shoe-box with a hole in the top through which protruded a mouse-ear of dull gold satin. Chloe pulled gently, coaxing it into the daylight as if it were a magician's handkerchief, releasing a cloud of flame and amber, scrolled and gilded like a Klimt. It was a kaftan, a thing she loved to wear for its ease and sensuality. Like everything Miranda made for others, it was intended, she knew, to express the spirit of the wearer. She looked at the singing colours that had been chosen for her and thought, despairing, that she should have been given sackcloth.

'Don't cry,' said Alain, smiling. He put Tilda's small parcel into her hand. It was obviously a tape.

'It's to remind you of all of us when you get homesick,' Tilda said shyly. 'Everyone is on it. There's Chopin and Debussy from me and one of Paul's studies. Dad's reading your favourite French poems, and Rufus is doing some early monastic plainchant with Dwayne in their not-Angles-but-Angels manifestation.'

'Thank you,' Chloe whispered. 'All of you.'

I don't deserve this, she wanted to say. I am not the good mother you think I am. I have destroyed your brother, your sister, who might have sung, have played, have strung glass beads.

But such a speech could serve no decent purpose. 'I'm homesick already,' she said.

Tilda seized what she saw to be an opportunity. 'Don't go today,' she begged. 'You wouldn't have, not if you had remembered what day it was. Stay till Wednesday. Come to the service.'

Chloe looked at Alain, who said nothing.

'No. I think I had better go,' she said awkwardly. 'Miranda and Adam are expecting me. It's best to leave things as they are.'

Tilda had one last shot. 'What about Baskerville? He's your dog, really. He'll pine.'

'He is everyone's dog,' Chloe said firmly. 'You must not allow him to pine.'

'Is it OK if I go over to Dwayne's?' Rufus asked Alain when they had waved goodbye to Chloe.

Tilda gave him a dark look.

'It *is* the only real time we get together,' Rufus insisted. 'And it's more than half over today, because of Mum.'

'Then you had better waste no more of it,' Alain told him briskly.

'I suppose I couldn't stay a bit longer? Just an hour or so. To make up?'

'No. You will home by five-thirty as usual. The three of us will have a good dinner together and discuss household management.'

'Aargh!'

'Don't worry; it won't be so painful. Mrs Cubitt will give us extra time.'

'Things certainly can't get much worse,' Rufus said despondently. Since their uncomfortable interview with the assistant chief constable, Rufus and Dwayne Cubitt had conducted their friendship under stringent conditions. They were permitted to exchange phone calls only twice a week and to visit each other on Sunday afternoons. Their social mobility was restricted within the boundaries of the village and the grounds of Sheringham School. They might as well, they felt, be in an open prison. So far there had been no remission for good behaviour.

On the road into Sheringham Rufus was struck, with Pauline force, by a possible conversion of the inhuman virtue that had been thrust upon them. Dwayne looked doubtful at first. 'You'd never have thought of it if your Mum hadn't gone away.'

'Don't talk twat. Just keep your big floppy ears on the

business plan.' As a matter of fact, the daft old turnip had probably got something there. The world would certainly be about forty per cent more free for him to bustle in without Chloe always on his case. Dad was away half the time and spent half of the rest of it working in his study. Even Tilda was less of an interfering old bossy boots now that she had Paul Hughes panting after her.

'I've worked it all out, the figures and stuff. Even got a name for us – Walk the Plank Enterprises. What d'you reckon?'

'Could be prophetic.' Dwayne chuckled.

'You got to have faith, my son.' Rufus was proud of his Bob Hoskins imitation. 'Not to mention endless dedication and true commitment.'

'You also have to be a genius to make any money. Everyone knows video-pirating is a mug's game unless it's really big time.'

'OK, so it'll be a bit of a challenge. That's half the fun, isn't it? I'm working on a programme for the pricing. But so far it looks as if it makes sense to ask the punters to provide their own tapes for the vids and charge them, say, two to two-fifty for the copying. That will cut down our initial costs. When we've made a bit of money, we can buy tapes in bulk and provide the whole service. Cassette tapes need only cost a quid, so we could charge from three to four for music tapes.'

'How much will we make in a week?'

'I use our Double-Decker at home, and you get brother Elvis to lend you one, right? If we set up a tape-deck in school as well, we should be able to record two vids and two tapes each, every day. No sweat.'

'Elvis is running a business; he might want some rent. But maybe.'

'Come on, arsehole, you only have to push the buttons.'

'I suppose.'

'Don't be such a miz. Look, we should be able to make two pounds on each video and fifty p to a quid on the tapes. That's six pounds each on a good day. Six days a week. Almost forty quid a week.'

'Jaysus!'

'I haven't quite worked out a scale for the costs yet – it might be less for a while. Stock will be expensive.'

'Aye, there's the rub; there's the consideration that makes for probable calamity.' Dwayne had taken to Shakespeare like a swan to the Avon.

'Well, we only want to do stuff that's just out, at first, to grab the punters. Later we can do special orders and really good old movies.'

'*Battleship Potemkin*?'

'I was thinking more *Diehard*. Anything you like, is the point. Then, when we've built up a library, we can lend as well.'

'Wouldn't that defeat the object?'

Rufus sighed. 'To tell the truth, I just don't know. There's more to this racket than there was in flogging drugs. I'll mug up on it all.'

'Do that. Preferably *before* we begin. And one small thing – isn't all this just a micron on the wrong side of the assistant chief constable?'

'Yeah, but *only* a micron. They'd never bother with it, even if they found out. And there's no reason why they should if we're careful.'

'Famous last words! I could lose my scholarship if we're caught.'

'Listen, all they ever think about is drugs.'

'Just so long as we don't end up giving all our proceeds to bloody charity again. I hate to think of all those pampered little acid-heads drying out at our expense.'

'You're right. I reckon, after losing all that dosh, the world owes us a bit of a living.'

'I don't know.' Dwayne was thoughtful. 'It's like, do

we really want to make a living as petty criminals, or do we want to get down to it and get ourselves into Cambridge?'

'Why not both? God, Cambridge isn't so squeaky clean. Think how many politicians went there.'

'You do have a point. I guess most of society has one foot on either side of the law these days. And it *is* getting a bit boring round here.'

'So, you're up for it? Great.'

'Don't I have to be, if only to stop you landing us in the shit with your well-known overenthusiam?'

'I hope you're not going to grow up to be dull and worthy, Dwayne.'

'I think I hope I *am*.'

'Chloe called me this morning,' Dinah Cavendish told her husband in a deceptively chatty tone.

'Indeed?' Luke continued to read the Governors' Report on Available Finance. 'Did she have a particular reason?' he murmured.

'Just a friendly call. We are still friends, after all.'

He waited. Dinah reached towards the *cafetière* on the table near her sofa and, dreaming of dynamite, depressed the plunger.

'She wanted to say goodbye.'

'Oh?'

'Yes, she has quite settled into the studio or loft or whatever. Apparently the view is sensational.'

Luke laid down his report. 'Dinah, what are you talking about?'

'You know. Her new apartment, near Miranda and Adam.'

'No, I *don't* know. You may have the unquantifiable pleasure of telling me.'

Dinah widened her large brown eyes. 'You mean she didn't say she was leaving?'

'Less heavy on the incredulity, if you want to be convincing.'

'No, truly. I am surprised. I thought she would have told you.'

'When would she have done that?'

'How do I know?' Dinah waved a vague hand. 'At school, on the phone, a chance meeting in the village café. I don't know. It shows strength, though, keeping it to herself. Unless, of course,' she smiled shakily, 'in the light of these colder days the *amour* is not quite so *fou* as it used to be.'

'Don't be bitchy,' Luke said gently. 'Why on earth should she go to London? Surely she hasn't left Alain?'

'No, she hasn't. Sorry to dash your hopes. At least, I don't think she has,' she added more seriously. 'She was a bit strange on the phone, I thought. Kind of keyed up and nervy. Hard, bright, not like Chloe at all. She said she was going to live in this flat, she didn't know for how long, and then she apologised again. I don't know why. I mean, we've worked through all that already. I'm worried about her, Luke. There's something not right, there.'

She watched him struggle with dismay. 'You really didn't know, did you?' she said kindly.

He shook his head. 'No. I suppose – perhaps you could ask Miranda what it's all about?'

'You can ask Chloe herself,' she said neutrally. 'Next time you visit Adam and Miranda.'

Illumination came to Luke. 'God, Dinah, so that's what this is about. You thought Chloe had gone off to London so she and I could start meeting again – the clandestine tryst, the slouch hat and muffler, the rubber-soled shoes?'

'I guess I did,' she admitted. 'You must allow it's a convenient address.'

'Convenient! Next to Miranda? You know how *she* feels. She would have Chloe torn apart by four horses rather than let me come near her.'

'Yes, I had thought of that.'

'Well, then.'

'Well, what?'

'Just—' He lifted his hands in a pacific gesture, 'Don't worry, that's all.'

'I am trying not to.' Why did men hate women to worry, especially when they patently ought to? She hesitated. 'It would help if you would tell me one thing.'

'What?'

'Are you still seeing her?'

He sighed. 'We have never met by arrangement, not since the moral rearmament at Christmas. We have occasionally done so by chance, when our behaviour has been – immaculate. Dinah, isn't all this a little regressive?'

We. Our. The syllables were a gauge of remnant pain.

'You are absolutely right,' she agreed cheerfully, surprising him. She came over and stood behind the armchair where he sat, bending to lean her cheek against his. She breathed in and held the breath.

'Mmm. Nice,' She placed an experimental kiss on the most sensitive part of his ear, the object of the experiment being herself rather than Luke. He reached for her hand and held it.

'So then – how are things? Generally?' she enquired tenderly.

'Oh, they're – things.'

'But you are OK?'

'I'm fine, I think. You?'

'Yes, it's – I'm good; thanks. Really.'

They both laughed.

'It's ridiculous,' he said. 'We're talking like strangers.'

'That's what we've been, for a while. We don't have to be, though.' Her voice had descended to the note he recognised as sexual invitation.

'No, we don't,' he said. 'Perhaps we ought to celebrate that idea?' His reaction was a double one, both parts equal in sincerity: the desire to make Dinah happy and the knowledge of infidelity to Chloe. The emotional dualism was nothing new; it had existed ever since he had

— 55 —

first met Chloe. It was uncomfortable, but it was not unbearable.

What Dinah's experiment had taught her, however, was that she did indeed wish to celebrate in the usual connubial fashion, but that she could wait. He still wanted her; that was something. She tried to be dispassionate about her relief. They had slept together only twice since the break with Chloe, once when she had aroused him with her rage and again, a few days after, to make up for that lapse.

'Oh Luke, I'm sorry. I have to go out in a few minutes.'

'Do you, now?' He raised a sardonic brow. 'You seem to lead a remarkably busy life lately. What is it today?'

'It's my flying lesson. I wrote it on the calendar.'

'Oh? I didn't notice. How many lessons does it take?'

'I'm not sure. I think about fifty hours if I want a pilot's licence. Or maybe a hundred.'

'Do you want one?'

'Might be fun.'

'Only if Philip will let you borrow his plane for the rest of your days – or its own, which may well be numbered.'

'Don't be rude. I'm doing splendidly.'

'I'm amazed that he lets you get your hands on it.'

She longed to say, with explicit vulgarity – you would be astounded if you knew what he lets me get my hands on, and how keenly I return the compliment. But although her sense of humour extended all the way from the merely zany to the madly barking, Dinah was not a vulgar woman.

In the sky, skimming the cloud layer off the top of the oldest forest in England, she lifted her long green skirt and settled herself accommodatingly over Philip's penis. It was one of the first manoeuvres he had taught her, and neither of them had made any tired jokes about joysticks. Their particular closeness, clutching each other fast like adventurous children, together with the porn-shop crudity of naked breasts and hard-working genitals, gave her the fiercest amount of raw sexual pleasure she had ever had. Philip modestly put this down to the great age of the plane which juddered and shook, he surmised, at precisely the same frequency as her orgasmic spasms.

He helped her off with her little jacket and her bra and carefully, without pulling, removed the clip from her twisted bundle of hair. He watched her shake it down around her shoulders, curled and striped gold and brown like soft shavings of polished wood. He sighed, an intensely happy man.

'I would like to own a never-ending video of you doing that.'

'Just that?'

'That's all. It's a movement that seems to encapsulate everything there is about you, sensually. It's romantic and enticing and childlike, all at once.'

'How gratifying. And there I was, thinking I was prosaic and obvious, with the mental age of a disillusioned crone. Philip – I know I ask you this every time, but is this really safe? It isn't that I have any personal objection to a sudden death, and this would be a wonderful way to go – but I do worry about my potentially motherless children.'

'It's perfectly safe,' Philip assured her, 'as long as you do everything I tell you. For instance, just move your head a little to the left, so that I can see what I'm up to.'

He was an experienced pilot and, being a large man, managed to manipulate the controls of the aircraft as well as her own without obvious difficulty. None the less the arrival of his climax, a series of turbulent sensations reminiscent of *The Ride of the Valkyries*, stopped her heart more than once. When they had come back down to earth, Philip drove Dinah back to his house for afternoon tea, a daily ritual that had remained with him since childhood.

Sheringham Hall was an extensive Jacobean manor

— 57 —

house endowed by the merchant adventurer Sir Sidney Sheringham as a school for intelligent orphans like himself. His investments had prospered until the Civil War, after which the estate had gradually been reduced to the thousand remaining acres of farmland and forest which helped to maintain the school, the grounds and the lovely half wild gardens planned and planted by the younger Tradescant. The headmaster traditionally occupied the Dower House, a small, elegant echo of the Hall, set a mile away from it in its own walled garden. It was here that Philip had brought his wife, Catherine, twelve years ago when he had taken over the school. Catherine had been a gentle, tranquil woman, with the quiet good looks that are more restful than beauty. Like Philip she came from a 'good' family, or at any rate a very old one, and had shared his passionate conviction that teaching was the highest and most rewarding of all vocations. There could have been no couple better suited to the stewardship of Sheringham.

Catherine's death from cancer had been a great shock and a greater sorrow to Philip. For three years he had remained not so much inconsolable as without any desire for consolation. Luke and Dinah Cavendish had respected this and had encouraged him to talk about his life with Catherine, as he wished to do, rather than to behave as though she had never existed, which was what most people seemed to expect of him. Thus permitted to keep her with him, he found himself, by one of life's kinder paradoxes, slowly more able to let her go. His friendship with the Cavendishes deepened during this period, though they shook off the gratitude he tried to show them with the grace of those who do not know how much they give.

Although he considered himself conservative by nature, if not always by political persuasion, Philip harboured a rich vein of liberalism when it came to educational theory. He had turned Sheringham from the élitist, all male, public school it had become – complete with fagging, caning, homosexual exploitation and spotted dick for dinner – into a modern, independent establishment open to any intelligent student of either sex, with a few commonsense rules and no statutory punishments, an innovative curriculum and an excellent chef. He had put horses back in the stables, fast-forwarded the gym and other sports facilities and had recently added a state-of-the-art theatre and concert hall, built with funds bludgeoned and cajoled from the friends, relatives and heads of various high places who had shared his own outrageously privileged education. It was mortgaged well into the next century but Philip was confident that the payments would be met.

Sheringham was a success at a time when few such successes could be claimed, and Philip and his staff and board of governors worked diligently to maintain that status. If, occasionally, he was pricked by doubts about the changing culture of the young people in his care, their language, their looks and the incomprehensible sounds that pleased them, then Luke, the democratic heir of twenty thousand Cornishmen, would always reassure the conservative in him that the liberal had got it right.

'I'm going to need a bath before I go home,' Dinah said, counterweighting a transparently lustrous cup of lapsang souchong with a parodic little finger. She was always rather bemused by her own presence in Philip's beautiful house, surrounded by the exquisite acquisitions of generations of Dacres. Dinah's family had not been 'good'. Her father was a conservation officer, her grandfather had been a professional gardener and drunkard, and a great-great-grandfather had been the last man in his county to be hanged for arson. She supposed, in view of the horror of the penalty, that he must have had an excellent reason for his crime.

The Cavendish house, though also part of the Sheringham estate, did not possess exquisite acquisitions. It was an anarchist's jubilee of colour and clutter, bulging with amusing and attractive objects, though few of any value. The house lived hard and it showed. It was also immensely welcoming and extremely comfortable. Dinah's own appearance was similarly eclectic. Restricted to reassuring suits for her work as school counsellor, at any other time she revelled in a gypsy mix of shade and texture that was saved from mere bohemianism by a solid sense of style. In the Dower House, her movements hushed by deep velvet and followed by the eyes of portraits, alive and inquisitive in the candle-light Philip loved, she liked to imagine herself in older, darker times, a bidden guest in Bluebeard's castle. It pleased her to cast Philip as the murderous duke with his voluptuary appetites and his oppressive charm, the doors locked upon his secret, necessary deeds. Certainly she did not suppose he could ever have murdered Catherine or had any intention of disposing of herself; no, she was simply indulging herself in a gloriously decadent sexual fantasy, probably the first since her marriage. To do her justice, it was not the brooding weight of the house and its historic contents that inspired her; rather it was the manner in which Philip made love to her. The strength and depth of his sexuality had shocked and then taken her in thrall. With Luke, sex was an obvious key to his nature. It was in the energy that drove his athletic body and lit up his eyes and face, in the mischief with which he conducted his conversation, with men as well as women, in the lightness of spirit which came to him, undeserved, as his greatest gift. He was approachable, compassionate, and had the aesthete's touching belief in the eternal possibility of romantic love. Dinah had been the second great love of his life, Chloe the third. The first, his divorced wife, the actress Helen Cavendish, was one of the country's most famous proponents of the culture of romance, possessing all of Luke's attraction and a similar moral blind spot. It was a wonder they had managed to stay married long enough to produce Adam. An even greater mystery, to Dinah, was that after Helen, with her ageless beauty and her warm place in the hearts of the nation, Luke should have chosen herself. The affair with Chloe, which had caused her the greatest pain she had ever known, had justified her rooted insecurity; its termination, if in fact it had been terminated, had done nothing to alter this. In Philip, she had found both a distraction and a counterbalance against her love for Luke.

Now he left his chair and took away her cup. 'A bath is an inviting idea,' he murmured, his voice thick as molasses. 'But let's get dirty first.' He took her to his bed, a satisfyingly Gothic four-poster with claret-coloured hangings. There they enjoyed several light, relatively pain-less perversions of which he was fond. Stretched naked and face-down on the soft fabrics, with part of Philip, it seemed, filling just about every orifice, Dinah felt herself to be the epitome of the Mistress in a character that was wildly dramatic and in some way fictional. This was only a game they were playing, but a game in which the pleasures were both extreme and addictive.

When they had finished, he wrapped her bundle of hair in a towel, stood her under the shower and soaped her all over. This took longer than she expected and some parts had to be soaped again.

'Dinah, I am in love with you, you know,' Philip said to her when she sat, wrapped in his dressing-gown, in front of a lesser baronial fire. 'What we do together is wonderful, but it is your *self* I love. Remember that, when things become a little too heightened, won't you?'

'You don't have to say that,' she told him. 'Heightened is fine with me. The higher the better.'

Philip smiled. 'You mean you don't want to deal with it.'

'Do I?' She looked puzzled. 'I don't think so. You surprised me. I didn't expect a declaration.'

'Or want one?'

'I don't know. Need it make any difference?'

He laughed. 'Not if you don't want it to.'

'I think I probably don't. Not yet, anyway.'

'Then consider it unsaid.'

'No. It will be something nice and warm to carry about with me, like a little flask of spirits in my pocket.'

Chapter 4

SOON AFTER DINAH HAD LEFT THE HOUSE, LUKE Cavendish knocked tentatively on the door of his younger son's room.

'Oliver?'

The door opened. 'Yes?' said Oliver politely, his faun's face expressionless.

'Sorry to disturb you. I just wondered if you would be staying in this afternoon?'

'I hope so, yes. I've some reading up to do.'

'What about?'

'Liver disease in cats. It's tricky to diagnose. They usually have to have two or three expensive blood tests.'

'Not going to the surgery then?'

'I doubt it. Alastair's doing one of his "maximizations of available space" – so there won't be room for me. I'm on call, of course, in case there's an emergency. There isn't, usually, on a Saturday afternoon.'

'In that case, would you do me a favour?'

Luke made the request with less than his normal abundant confidence, uncertain how deeply the boy still disapproved of him. Oliver knew what had happened with Chloe and was very much Dinah's partisan. There was an impenetrable shrug. 'What is it?'

'Lisa Latham will be delivering some essays from the

Oxbridge Group. I wanted to see her myself but she's half an hour late already and I want to take the dogs out while there's still some light.'

'That's OK. I'll be here.'

'Thanks.' Luke hesitated. 'Give her a cup of coffee, will you, and talk to her for a while? She's had a rough time.'

'I know. I'll do that.'

'Thanks. I'll be off, then.'

'When will you be back?' The question came quickly.

'In a couple of hours, I should think.'

'Right.'

Oliver nodded and closed the door. Luke felt that he had both made and lost progress. He could not blame Olly if he were suspicious; he knew his mother would be out until five or six and he did not yet know that Chloe had left the village. However, there was nothing Luke could say without embarrassing them both.

He went outside and whistled up Holmes and Watson from the wilderness that was their favourite part of the garden. There would be no Chloe, but at least they could walk in the paths they had taken together.

Oliver had been unable to decide whether or not he was suspicious of Luke's motives. What he did know was that he himself would not have found it possible to get over Chloe in the course of a few convenient weeks. Judging by appearances, it looked as if his parents were in the process of achieving a genuine reconciliation. The atmosphere between them was not quite the same as it had been before Chloe; they were less spontaneous, more courteous in an edgy kind of way. But they were getting there. His mother was beginning to tease Luke again, a sure sign that she was happier. Oliver desperately wanted everything to be all right again; Adam was sure it would be, though Miranda had reservations. Belle, of course, had never even noticed that anything was wrong. She had missed all the *Sturm und Drang*, as Luke had irreverently called it, whereas Oliver had unfortunately come in for some of the worst of it. He had seen Dinah launch herself at his father like a tormented animal, tearing at him in a rage of pain, screaming obscenities about Chloe. But that was all over now. He did not like to think about it.

When Lisa Latham arrived, he showed her into the kitchen and made real coffee instead of instant, to make her feel special. She had looked apprehensive when he had let her in, but she seemed to relax when she realised there were only the two of them in the house.

'I'm sorry I'm so late. Tell your father, will you? I did a lunch-time shift in the restaurant and it got really hectic. Michelle didn't turn up, so I had to help clear up. You will tell him?'

'It's OK, really,' Oliver said gently. 'He said I should look after you.' She was a pretty girl, he thought, but these days she always looked anxious and unhappy. She had nice hair, dark, cut short in a way that showed you how delicate her bones were. She had a neat skull like a little cat. Nice eyes too, wide and sad, and a mouth that ought to be what Belle called 'bee-stung', but she folded it inwards as though it might say more than she wanted if she let it go. She reminded him of Winona Ryder, whom he used to admire before he met Chloe.

'I never see you in school since you gave up biology,' he said. It was hardly original but you had to start somewhere. 'Are you managing to keep up OK? It must be tough trying for Oxbridge after missing so much.' Oh hell, that was definitely *not* the thing to mention. Lisa saw him realise his gaffe. She also saw his kindness. Her mouth relaxed a little.

'The work isn't a problem,' she said. 'It's having everyone know *why* I dropped out that's difficult to live with.'

'I can imagine.' Oliver nodded, pleased by her reaction. 'But I'm sure there's no one who doesn't feel – well, sad that you had to try it – and glad you didn't succeed.'

She smiled nervously. 'That's a nice thing to say. But I'll bet they also think I'm a complete idiot. It was a such a stupid, loser thing to do.'

'They don't, honestly. They know it takes guts to do what you did. For every person who actually goes ahead and tries, there are a dozen who have thought about it seriously at one time or another. We all have bad times.'

'You really believe that?'

'Yes, I do.'

'Have *you* ever thought about it, Olly?'

'I've never considered actual suicide. I guess I'm not the type. I tend to get angry instead of sad. But I do have some idea of what you've been through.' He paused shyly. 'That is, if what my sister says is true.'

'What does she say?'

'That you did it because – you loved someone.'

'Who didn't love me?'

'Yes.'

'And you know what that is like?'

'Yes. It's been the worst thing that ever happened to me.'

'You, Oliver?'

She was looking at him as though he were suddenly someone else.

'Why not?'

'I'm sorry. I didn't mean – but you've always seemed so self-sufficient. You didn't even notice when Mandy Kane tried to chat you up. She was so discouraged she thought you must be gay. No one has ever seen you with a girl, not from school anyway.'

Oliver looked amused. 'She isn't – wasn't someone from school.'

'I see.' Lisa waited. Further questions might be unwelcome.

He grinned, his green eyes warming. His smile, like Dinah's, was slightly crooked and cheered others as much as himself.

'It's all right,' he said. 'We don't have to tell each other who they are. We don't need to know any more than we do now. But it is kind of nice, don't you think, to have someone around who knows how you feel? A relief.'

'I haven't been able to tell anyone. No one. But yes, it is.' She smiled.

'Ah! Bee-stung!'

'What?'

'Your mouth. It's what Belle is aiming at. She spends ages biting her lips to make them swollen. She tried to get me to inject them with saline solution, like Goldie Hawn did for some film; but I told her all I was prepared to do was to punch her in the mouth. Carefully, of course, to avoid breaking any teeth. She made me do it, too. The effect was pretty good, for a week.'

'Believable is not a word you'd apply to Belle. She'll always get what she wants. She's going to be famous one day.'

'Don't tell her. She has too much confidence already. How about you, Lisa? Do you have a burning ambition?'

'I'd like to teach English. I'm not sure at what level.'

'Is that Dad's idea? He's fanatical about the next generation of teachers.'

Lisa flushed. 'Not really. Well, I suppose he must have been the main inspiration. How are you getting on at the vet's?'

'It's great, I love it. I can't decide whether to take the gap year and carry on with Alistair, or go to vet college in October.'

'I'm the same about university. Though I can't be nearly as sure of Oxford as you can be about your A levels. But if I do get in I might take a gap year. College seems too much to handle this year. I think I need to get a better perspective on life after trying so hard to chuck it away. Mum and Dad like the idea. They want to lure me into Chez Claudie permanently, so they can keep me in their sights.'

'But that won't happen?'

'No. I hate cooking and I wouldn't want to be a waitress.

And if I'm really going to get over the bad times, I need to do it on my own. I don't mind staying at home – in fact I'd prefer it – but Chez Claudie, no.'

'Why do you prefer it?'

She examined her nails. 'Because I'm used to it, I suppose.'

'Not because you want to stay near to someone?' Her face burned. 'Shit, Olly! Did you have to say that?'

'As long as you're not fooling yourself.'

'No, I'm not. How could I? OK, I want to see him sometimes. Is that so bad?'

'Yes. Speaking for myself, it's usually pretty bad. Terrible. But wonderful too. I get high every time I meet her.' Lisa shook her head. 'What a pair.'

'We certainly are. And what a waste.'

Belle had arranged to go with Tilda, Paul and Cosmo Leigh to a concert at St Martin-in-the-Fields. On the train she became uncharacteristically quiet, and when they reached Waterloo she announced that she thought she would give the concert a miss.

'I've got a bit of a headache.' She looked wan and small. 'I think I'll go round to Adam and Miranda's instead.'

'Headache?' repeated Paul, amazed. Belle was the cause, not the victim, of headaches.

'I see,' said Tilda, who did see.

'It'd be a shame to miss the concert,' growled Cosmo, who was Belle's current escort and the receiver of her infrequent, very small favours.

'You don't go to a concert when you have a headache,' she told him with edgy patience. Cosmo was sometimes short on brains, though undeniably gorgeous in a rugged-but-haunted style and useful for carrying things and fleshing out excuses. He was considered very sexy.

Tilda pursed her lips. 'Very well. Meet you here for the 11.35?'

'I'll probably stay over.'

'I thought you might. Does Adam know that?'

'Not yet.' Belle grinned, then flinched and put a hand to her head. 'God, I hope this isn't meningitis – or a brain tumour.' Tilda rolled her eyes. 'And listen, you lot – work on Act Two on the way home.'

All four were taking part in the Middle School production of *Dracula*, which Belle was directing with occasional interference from Luke's assistant master, Mr Kaye, which she generally ignored. Paul was the musical director, and Tilda provided a melting Lucy Weston. The production eschewed the usual orthodontic absurdities, thus allowing the audience to experience the full pity and terror of Cosmo's monster of eroticism. The chief difficulty had been getting Cosmo to understand the concept of an erotic monster. Then Belle had taken him to see Klaus Kinski in *Nosferatu*, and the darkness had blessedly descended. Cosmo was bleaching his hair and letting it grow and affected a black velvet frock-coat out of school hours. He had begun to growl and mutter and present himself, as Belle savagely remarked, not so much like Kinski's ultimate Outsider as Matt Dillon's sad stab at Marlon Brando. She was not worried. She would whip him into shape in good time.

She refused his gallant offer to accompany her to Adam and Miranda's, applied a quick kiss to each of his dramatically hollow cheeks, and set off for the south bank of the river.

'Adam!'

'Belle.'

She flung herself on him. 'Oh, I have missed you so.'

He returned her hug for a second, then pulled her gently away and held her by the shoulders. 'OK, OK, then try not to destroy me.'

'Do you have to be like that?'

'Like what?'

'All wary and virginal.'

'Virginal!'

'You know what I mean. As if I were about to pounce on you and rape you.'

'Belle, do we have to have this?'

He took her coat and hung it in the small lobby. She twirled once to give him the benefit of her new stretch-velvet dress. 'No, there are lots of things we could have; brilliant conversation, a bracing argument, and please, a bottle of wine and something to eat. I am absolutely starving. Where's Miranda?' The living-room was pleasingly empty.

'Next door, asleep. She works too hard on her exam pieces and she gets tired more easily now.'

'Next door in your bedroom, or next door in her own place?'

'Her place.'

Belle beamed. 'I'm sorry she's tired, but it is nice to have you to myself for a while. I can't get used to you not living at home.'

'You'll have to. This is home now.'

'There you go again.'

She wandered into the kitchen and investigated the cupboard where Adam kept wine when he had any. 'Can I open this?'

'I shouldn't encourage you. Does everyone drink at your age now?' He heard the report of the cork.

'Yes. It's better than drugs. I don't do it much, actually. This is more for you; to lower your defences.'

Adam groaned.

'At least I'm honest about it. Let's have these cheesy things, OK?' She brought in the bottle and filled two glasses. As Adam had unwarily claimed the half of the sofa he usually occupied with Miranda, she was able to sit down close beside him. He shifted a little, leaving a gap.

'And frightened Miss Muffet away,' Belle said disdainfully. 'What do you think I am, a black widow?'

'Yes, if they are the ones who—'

'They are.'

'I'm not sure I like being cast as Miss Muffet.'

'It's part of the revolution of the sexes, the cunning plot to put all the girls on top. We turn the terminology of myth against you. It's like stealing your weapons while you're asleep.'

'Ah, but two can play,' said Adam, amused. 'Let's see – I think Little Jack Horner is the role for you.'

'Why?'

'He's a lad, or in your case a ladette, I suppose, who knows how to get what he wants and feel good about it.'

'I take that as a compliment.' Belle put down her glass and settled comfortable against Adam's side. 'So, now the opening hostilities are over, tell me things. What's the new short story about?'

'It's a fairy tale for modern times. Like the nursery rhymes, but in a softer mode. It's about Miranda and me, really. This guy, Jack, wonders how he will deal with the fact that he isn't the biological father of the baby his girlfriend is going to have. It discusses his doubts and the kind of – innocence – of the relationship between him and the girl.' Adam looked quickly at Belle, expecting mockery. She said nothing, waiting for him to continue.

'Well, in the end, when the baby is born, it looks just like him; like Jack. At least it does to him. Though not necessarily to everyone.'

'That's great. It uses how we all have to persuade ourselves, sometimes. That what we get is what we want. I like that.'

'You've got it. But also that there can be magic in it.'

'But since you know how the magic works, how can you hope that it will happen for you?'

'I don't. I'm just interested in the *way* it might work.'

'I wonder. We'll see.'

'Yes, we will,' Adam said soberly.

'It will be all right,' Belle assured him. 'The baby will be a little *wunderkind* and you'll love it to bits.'

'It's not that I'm worried about; it's the kind of father

I'm going to make. I just hope the right instincts are there. An awful lot depends on it. It's not something I was expecting to happen just yet. Belle, I don't know why I'm telling you this.'

She pressed her head into his shoulder. 'Because you know I care about you.'

'Is that it?' He smiled.

'More than anyone,' she said ambiguously. 'May I have some more wine?'

'Help yourself.'

'No, I like it better when you do it.'

'Very well.' Adam obliged and she watched his intent face as he poured. She could hardly bear not to touch it. She loved him so much that she lost all desire to control herself. She knew how dangerous this was; if she went too far she ran the risk of losing him for ever, and this was not the plan. They were each the half of the other. One day he would understand that. She moved restlessly, plucked at the cushions and sighed, releasing a drawn-out, two-note breath that she had perfected for the character of Minna, to suggest her conflicting fear and desire for Dracula. Receiving no reaction she repeated the sigh, noting that her control was better the second time.

'All right, Belle. What's the matter?'

'I'm not sure whether I should tell you or not. It may not be the right moment.'

'Only you can judge.'

'Yes, but it's difficult. Look – this is going to sound weird – but I'd have a better idea if you kissed me again.'

Adam sat up. 'You know that wasn't supposed to happen. I wish you'd just forget it.'

'Do you? Are you sure? Absolutely, completely sure?'

'Don't be idiotic.'

'Well, will you prove I am? Would you kiss me, just once? It can't hurt. It's only me.'

'Only the Black Widow.' He frowned. 'I wish you wouldn't play this game, Belle.'

'Why not? If it's only a game.'

'Because there isn't any point in it.'

'There is for me. Do you want me to grow up all bitter and twisted?'

'No, you exasperating child; I just want you to grow up.'

'Can't you see?' she shouted. 'That's what I'm trying to do. And I need some help.'

'I can't help you, not when you're like this.'

'You're the only one who can. I'm not a child any more, Adam, whatever you'd like to tell yourself. And that does have something to do with you.'

'You can't make me responsible for your feelings.'

'Not responsible. Neither of us is responsible. What there is between us, well – it just *is*. You're a part of me. I'm part of you.'

'No.' Adam grabbed both her wrists and shook her. 'You have got to stop this, Belle. Stop it right here.'

Very quickly she leaned over and kissed him. His hands tightened their hold and his lips parted involuntarily under hers. He made an instinctive bid for mastery, grinding his mouth unkindly against hers to turn her brave assault into subjugation before he pushed her violently away.

'There. You see?' she said shakily.

'No, Belle. I won't let you.'

Belle burst into tears. 'It wasn't all me. I can't bear it if you lie.'

'Oh God,' he said helplessly.

Belle sobbed quietly, looking bruised and somehow smaller.

'Don't. Don't.' He put his arms around her and stroked her wet hair out of her eyes. 'Sweetheart, it can't go on like this, you know that, really.'

'I can't help it,' she wept. 'It wouldn't be so bad if I didn't *know* you could feel the same way if you'd let it happen. You can't say you didn't want to go further that night we went to La Grenouille. Or now.'

'Belle, if things were different, I don't know,' he said miserably. 'As they are, nothing could make it right. You're my sister and that's an end of it.'

'I'm *not* your sister. Half-sister is completely different. There are enough different genes to make it perfectly OK – even to have children. What about the pharaohs, for godsake? They *only* married their sisters. And anyway, I'm not asking you to *marry* me, am I? I just want you to make love to me. That can't be such a horrible prospect, surely?'

Adam had to smile. 'Far from it,' he said gently. 'But I am trying, very hard, not to dwell upon it. Oh Belle, what am I going to do with you?'

She reached to stroke his cheek. His skin felt exactly like her own.

'Sooner or later, whatever you say, however you think you feel, you are going to take me to your bed; that's what you're going to do with me.' She turned and laid her fingers on his lips. 'I want you to be the first, Adam; that's what I wanted to say to you. I want us to stay close for ever. We can make a place between us where we can go for love and sanctuary for the rest of our lives.'

He could only stare at her. Her words were beautiful. His head turned with the tumbling world, without coherent thought. She picked up his hand, turned it over and pressed her open mouth against the palm. He could have sworn that the flesh burned.

'What am I doing?' he gasped. He leaped away from her and backed towards the door. 'I've had enough of this,' he said angrily. 'I'm going to wake Miranda. If you're staying you can make yourself useful. There's a pizza in the freezer. Shove it in the oven at 200, make a salad and open another bottle.'

'All right. There's no reason to be so cold and pissy about it.'

Adam uttered an unclassifiable sound and slammed the door behind him.

'I think you just sent her an alarm call,' Belle observed quietly. She scrubbed at her eyes, then found her bag and rummaged for her lipgloss and mascara. It would not do to look sad and bleary in front of Miranda. Not too much lip colour, though; Adam did not like it on her.

She briefly considered leaving herself pale and waif-like, with matching demeanour, so that Miranda would be bound to ask what was the matter, but decided it would be unwise to be so manipulative at this stage. Teasing Adam was justifiable; it would serve him right for being such a moral coward; but she was not certain where that exercise might lead. She must remember to take things slowly. She had a whole lifetime to win him over.

When Adam returned with a sleepy-eyed Miranda, he was pleasantly surprised to find Belle in the kitchen, mixing the salad and humming to herself. Her mood became warm and solicitous; within fifteen minutes she had secured herself a bed for the night and convinced Miranda of her fascinated interest in every detail of pregnancy, parturition and progeny.

'What does it *feel* like to be seven months?' she enquired as they were eating. 'I imagine it's like being invaded by an alien.'

'More like three sumo wrestlers,' Miranda replied wearily. 'And you see how it looks. I suppose I'm still in there, somewhere, too.'

'You sound as if you've stopped enjoying it.'

'Too right. I ache somewhere all the time. I've got piles—'

'Ugh!'

'I'm terminally tired. I'm usually depressed or furious, and occasionally downright hysterical. In fact, I'm sick to death of the whole damn thing. Apart from that,' she finished cheerfully, 'there's the small matter of college and my entire future as anything other than a great white whale. Sorry, Moriarty my darling – but this has been a bad day.'

'Sounds horrible,' said Belle in awe. 'I wish I could help in some way.'

'I help,' Adam stated. 'Chloe helps.'

'Yes, you do, and you're marvellous,' Miranda told him. 'But there is something, Belle, as it happens. I need a model. Size ten?'

'Yes.'

'Then follow me.'

Miranda levered herself up and led the way to her studio, which had given up any pretence at doubling as a living-room and had more in common with Caesar's tent on the eve of battle. She waved a hand at the east wall.

'That's what it's like, as near as I can get,' she told Belle. Twenty-eight pastels hung in sequence, one for each week of the pregnancy. They were tenderly observed but without sentimentality, the drawing very strong, colours pale and subservient to line, the concentration on the plastic qualities of flesh; how strong it was, how it could be stretched, what it might take to make it tear. In the early months they were very much portraits of Miranda, the young woman watching the changes in her body, wary, curious, apprehensive. This was Miranda's face, her way of sitting or standing, a complacent sexuality.

This individuality diminished week by week, until you were aware of the woman more importantly as a housing for the child. In one drawing, the sense of shared vulnerability was overwhelming, almost accusing; in another there was the triumphant unity of a perfect fugue. Looking, Belle paid them the compliment of failing to weep.

'I don't know how to say things about what artists do,' she said, feeling her way, 'but if these, all together, were a stage performance, I would think I had seen a very great actor at work.'

'Thank you,' Miranda said simply. 'Let's hope my tutors agree.' She moved to the long table where her pieces for the fashion show were laid out. They had been dyed, cut and tacked, but not yet machined.

'What wonderful colours,' Belle said at once. 'I love the burnt orange and the slatey blue; and this gold and tan and cream. And the shapes look like a human being, as well as pared down and sexy.'

The collection made up a capsule summer wardrobe in lightweight jersey, mixing the plain colours with narrow stripes. The basic garments were simple and easy to wear, and Miranda had added a covetable range of accessories; a scarf, a pareo, a belt, a bag and some painted beads and brooches.

'It's like Aladdin's Cave,' Belle said greedily. 'You really are a genius. I never realised before.'

'Let's see, shall we? Try the pants and the long-sleeved top first.'

Adam gazed out of the darkened window while she changed. As the lights on the north bank exploded into new constellations, he realised that his eyes were full of unshed, barely comprehended tears. He blinked them back and prepared to leave the two of them together; they did not need him and he certainly did not need any more of whatever was going on inside him now.

'How do I look, Adam?'

Belle sashayed expertly in front of the cheval mirror, making him a hapless voyeur of every wicked movement, each God-given curve. He wanted very much to hit her.

'They look very well,' he said.

'Yes, I think they do,' Miranda said, satisfied. 'Now the body – it can also be a swimsuit – with the wrap skirt and the jacket.'

Belle stripped in seconds and stood waiting, smiling at them both, her small magenta bra and pants blooming like Thai orchids against her creamy, slightly dusky skin.

Miranda gave her the pile of clothes, one hand pressed into the small of her back. 'You are just what I needed,' she said.

'I must go. I've got work to do,' Adam told them ungracefully, and fled. He would have liked to go down and talk to Chloe for a while; he had always liked her and he found her present air of gentle detachment calming in the face of the emotional gales in his own ménage, but Chloe was out that evening, having dinner with the owner of the gallery where she sold most of her work.

On May 1st Miranda went into college for one of the small brainstorming seminars that were her professor's speciality. He would examine the work done so far on the fine-art projects, then he and the class would hold an orgy of ego-bending self-criticism.

Wondering whether or not to trash Cally Baker's self-indulgent, belligerently toned portraits of pimps and hookers, which told you nothing about the subjects and everything about Cally, she straightened to realign her spine on top of her stool and, without the lightest intimation of necessity, released the contents of her bladder into the cushion beneath her. Clenching, she attempted to stop the flow, but it was too late. The last trickle ran insolently down her leg and into her boot. Oh wow! Pregnancy was full of surprises. Thank God she was wearing the plum and rust streaked kaftan; with any luck a few extra streaks might go unnoticed.

She slid gingerly off the stool, clutching the cushion to her backside, bringing it round to her side as she sank titanically to the floor and reaching under the seat for the carpet bag which – thank God again – she had stowed there earlier. She manhandled the waterlogged cushion into the bag and heaved herself back to her feet.

'I'm sorry. I think I'll go off home. I don't feel very well,' she informed the ten curious faces which, she now saw, were turned towards her. In fact, she felt perfectly well, but she could see no quick way out of her daft predicament. 'I'll leave the pastels and collect them later, if that's all right?'

'Surely,' the professor agreed. 'Come and talk to me on Monday at ten, instead. Take care, Miranda.'

Had any of them noticed anything? She really did not care.

When she had gone, Cally asked casually, 'Has anyone seen Joel recently? He isn't in his studio and he hasn't been around here for ages.'

'I heard he'd gone to Paris,' someone said.

'Really?' said another. 'I heard Amsterdam.'

'Yeah? Well, wherever he is, he's not there for pure pleasure. You can bet he'll be working his arse off for that exhibition.'

In the women's room, Miranda stripped off her sopping underwear and deposited it, with the cushion, in the bin. Then she turned her kaftan back to front and assessed the damage in the mirror. The stain was round and fairly compact and did not seem to smell of anything much. She switched on the hand-dryer. Sod it! It was out of order. She thought again. Removing the large clasp that held her hair in its exuberant knot, she used it to fasten the front of the kaftan into a single deep pleat, which more or less concealed the dark patch. It was not until she was struggling into new knickers and tights in a local boutique that she had the first recognisable contraction.

'Moriarty! It wasn't my bladder. You decided it was time to break the waters.'

She had been having twinges for a couple of weeks now, the mild Braxton Hicks contractions similar to the spasms of period pains; but the baby was not due for another two weeks.

'You careless child,' she admonished, shaking with laughter and terror. 'Why did I waste all that time teaching you to count?'

So it was that Moriarty May Day Olivier was born in an ambulance in a series of impassable traffic jams between Covent Garden and St Thomas's Hospital. The laughter and terror were tandem companions throughout the birth. The ambulanceman and -woman were heroic, kind and competent, while Miranda was vociferous and often profane. The pain, she discovered, and even more, the superhuman effort required of her, were far more outrageous than Chloe had said they might be. You pushed and you panted and you shouted in the rhythm imposed on you by the iron force that was trying to tear you inside out; at the same time you knew it was all right, it was what ought to happen, though there bloody well ought to be a better way and fuck you Joel, fuck you to hell and back, I'm going to get you for this one day!

She grappled grimly on to anything strong enough to sustain her, the sides of the bunk, some hanging straps, the uncrushable hands that came her way; she grasped and let go, grasped and let go, faster, faster, faster. She arched her back and roared and bellowed and laughed. Later she fell quiet. Everything became dream-like and concentrated inward; there was a great gathering of resources.

She heard herself panting, panting, her lungs a magnificently capable machine, keeping her panting and pushing and working with the furious instinct of Baskerville unburying something. Panting and shoving and shouting in joy and delirium, hearing someone say the head was coming; dying to see it, pushing again, harder, hard – no, it wasn't necessary because there it was – the head, the body, the whole perfect world in a few pounds of wrinkled pink and purple flesh.

'It's a girl, love.'

'I know. Hello, Moriarty. How do you feel? You've been through a lot.'

The nurse laid her on Miranda's stomach. She had black hair, sticking up in wet, punk spikes, stunning blue eyes and a better body than any Baby Jesus by any artist, ever. She was perfect. Life was perfect. Miranda had done the best thing she had ever done.

Moriarty screwed up her face and looked thoughtful; it made her look like Joel.

'You can stop that, right now,' her mother whispered, kissing the soft, spiky top of her head.

They were allowed to leave the hospital when the baby was a week old. Moriarty displayed none of the characteristics of a premature child, and their doctor decided that Miranda must have got her original dates wrong. Miranda was somewhat startled by this, as by her recollection it meant she had been a pregnant virgin. However, as Moriarty weighed an acceptable seven pounds, was modelled like an exquisite netsuke, and her fine, soft skin was packed with healthy organs, she was only too happy to agree. She couldn't wait to get home to Adam and begin to be a family.

Chapter 5

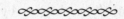

F OR THE NEXT WEEK, PROUD GRANDPARENTS,
aunts, uncles and assorted admirers flowed through
the lofts in a congratulatory stream, the current
controlled so that the older Cavendishes and Oliviers
might practise adroit avoidance.

On Friday evening Belle called Adam, her manner
mysterious and importunate. 'Listen and don't interrupt.
On Sunday, at twelve noon, I want you to take the Holy
Family and Chloe and flee to the nearest pub for a couple
of hours. Tilda and I are planning something special and
we need the flat to be empty.'

'What are you up to now, Belle?'

'Don't worry. You'll love it. It's a sort of present for
M&M. We may have to move a few things.'

'If you lay a finger on my laptop—'

The line fizzed with rude mirth. 'Chance would be
a fine thing,' Belle crowed. 'So – move it yourself.
OK?'

Adam sighed. 'I suppose so. I'd feel a whole lot safer if
you'd tell me what's going on.'

'You are safe. Tilda is in it too. Think how sensible *her*
shoes are.'

'Yes, but is that enough, I ask myself.'

'Trust me. And bring them back at two-fifteen on the dot, or you're dead.'

Parentally maintained ignorance of the emotional under-currents between their two families had allowed Belle and Tilda to plan a Grand Welcome to the World Surprise Party, which every member was commanded to attend. They thought it would be more fun if each household were also to be surprised by the presence of the other.

The organisation was swift and assured, involving two telephones and Belle's credit card. The only slight hitch in the actual proceedings was the time it took to persuade Chloe to go to the pub, rather than stay in and babysit.

A speeded up film of the next two hours would have shown Belle and Tilda, aided and outpaced by Paul and Cosmo, racing back and forth like overwound clockwork mice to the Turkish restaurant, the Bangladeshi minimarket, the French baker and the back of Cosmo's deeply sinister black van.

At two o'clock precisely, the van was joined by Luke Cavendish's venerable and elegant Citroën and the futuristic silver bullet belonging to Alain Olivier.

'O lord,' said Dinah, 'are we ready for this?'

Luke gave a low chuckle. 'I don't believe we have a choice.'

'What's the problem?' asked Oliver from the back seat.

'None at all,' Dinah assured him. 'Bring the presents, will you, Olly?'

'Hey, terrific,' approved Rufus, in the muzzle of the bullet. 'Looks like we've got company.'

'So we have,' said Alain, who had planned a long private talk with Chloe. As he regretfully opened his door there was a soft but purposeful shunt from behind.

'Look, Dad. It's Helen Cavendish. And she's got a Porsche! She's getting out. She looks terrific. This is going to be fun.'

'It will certainly be interesting,' Alain allowed.

He got out of the car and prepared to be engulfed by Helen.

Inside, there followed fifteen minutes of something very much like country dancing, as Olivier and Cavendish moved about the room clasping hands and brushing cheeks, while Helen kissed every man, including Cosmo, on the lips. Cosmo, imagining an opportunity to provoke Belle to jealousy, kissed her thoroughly in return, and in his sultriest Kinski, muttered the name of her perfume, which happened to be the one his mother used.

'So that's your Dracula,' Helen said smokily to Belle. 'I suspect this production is going to be a little different. Tell me about it.'

'The basic story is similar, but our version takes it into the modern tradition – more Anne Rice than Bram Stoker. You see, the sympathy is all with the vampires – with the loyalty and sort of kinship between them, the way they are bound together in blood. It shows how they can't help what they are, but that they can learn to make something noble out of it by loving each other.'

'And this is all your own idea?'

'Yes. There's an obvious parallel with the way people with AIDS look out for each other. Non-vampire society is seen as hopelessly out of date, spiritually impotent and emotionally paralysed by all the old, authoritarian concepts – religion, marriage, a justice system that has become irrelevant. Oh – and I make them indestructable.'

'Good God, Belle, you're living dangerously, aren't you? I hope the burghers of Sheringham are tough enough to take it.'

'It frightens Adam out of his skull, if that's any criterion.'

'Poor Adam. I'm afraid I have not been a proper, morally conservative mother. His sense of rebellion is all inside out.'

'I expect that's why he likes playing happy families,' Belle said wistfully. 'Come to rehearsal, Aunt Helen. Not yet. Soon.'

'If I can. I'm doing a three-parter for ITV; then I'm back in Paris for another run of Shakespeare.' She wrinkled her nose. 'Juliet's mother. I do my best to make her seem like a woman with a love life of her own. My reward is the lead in the Scottish Play.'

'Wonderful. You'll be extraordinary. If I pester Dad, maybe I can get to see you. Helen – do you think we shall ever act together again? Being with you in *Earnest* has spoiled me for anything less.'

'Ah. Funny you should say that, my darling, because there is an audition I think you should do. A children's serial for the BBC; one of those big house mysteries with lots of twists and a strong, sparky heroine. You'd be just right for her, and this is exactly the thing to kickstart your brilliant career. I play the evil housekeeper who is trying to deflect your rightful heritage to her own child; a rather handsome boy, as a matter of fact.'

'Wow. Do you think I'd really have a chance?'

'I think you have a very good one. And most of the filming will be in August, in the holidays. You ought to try for it. It would impress the drama schools tremendously.'

'Time is a bit of a problem. I want to make a real success of the play.'

'I know, and I think you will. This is a good opportunity, Belle. Think it over and let me know in the next few days. But now is the time. Next year you'll be doing your A levels.'

The contents of a souk had transformed Adam's sofa into a Renaissance dais where Miranda and Child were holding court. The Infant Moriarty, swathed in lacy wool, lay sweetly asleep while her mother, her long hair falling on the shoulders of her madonna-blue gown, accepted compliments and solicited advice. Gifts were strewn about them, their gilded wrappings pillaged by Rufus on behalf of his niece.

'Not too sure about this,' he admitted, opening his own offering. 'Only, I can't seem to get the hang of her being a *girl*.' He produced a lovingly cut and pasted mobile, hung with a dozen of the world's most covetable motor-cycles. At the top of the hierarchy was the superb Harley Davidson Electra Glide, the model in the current possession of Moriarty's natural father.

'Wicked, isn't it?' he observed proudly, unembarrassed by any more subtle emotion. 'I hope she likes it, anyway.'

'She'll love it,' smiled Miranda. 'It will help her to learn about colour and movement.' She knew there was no guile behind the gift.

'You look tired, Chloe,' Alain said anxiously. He drew her away from the sofa where they had worshipped together in a besotted admiration last experienced at the birth of Rufus and Tilda.

'I'm not sleeping well,' she confessed.

'Why not, do you think?'

'Probably because I still can't paint. I try and try and nothing works. It wrings me out. Maybe it will get better now the baby is here.'

'But surely you will be even more exhausted?'

'It's a different kind of tiredness. And after all, it's what I am here for.'

Alain sighed. He knew that this was not the truth, or not all of it. He wished that he could know, with any certainty, just what all of it might be. Did she really need so desperately to be away from him? And how far was Luke Cavendish responsible for her restless depletion of spirit? How did she really feel about him now? If he asked her that, what would she tell him? Would that be the truth? He could see Luke now, placed directly in his line of vision. He was talking to Helen as easily and intimately as though he and she had never parted. Alain could not understand this. He was unable to imagine ever achieving such post-marital amity with Chloe – the prospect of losing her was, as it always had been, unbearable, unacceptable, not to be considered.

His solicitude became angry. 'Chloe, you are not making sense. Of what use can it be, either to your work or your 'ealth, to wear yourself out like this?'

'I'll be more careful,' she promised.

'No.' He shook his head. '*Chérie* – come home. We will look for a nurse for Moriarty, a nice starched nanny in a uniform, full of discipline and principles.'

'They are far too expensive,' Chloe protested. 'Besides, Miranda would hate it.'

'Well, I hate this,' he said fiercely.

'Please don't. I feel selfish and guilty enough as it is. And I miss you all so much.'

'Then come home with me.'

'Don't ask me again, Alain. You're taking an unfair advantage of that guilt. I need this time, you know I do.'

Alain threw up his hands in the wholehearted way that proclaimed his nationality. 'It is the only advantage I 'ave,' he said sadly.

'No it isn't. You have them all, if only you knew.' She touched his cheek. Was *that* the truth? Alain wondered. If it was, why didn't it *feel* like it?

'Chloe? You look a bit down. Is something wrong?'

'Hello, Dinah. In a way. Alain seems to have changed his mind about my being here. It makes me wonder if I'm doing the right thing.'

'He's probably just reacting to the occasion. He didn't expect to have to rub shoulders, let alone noses, with Luke.'

'He managed it at Christmas.'

'It was easier then. We were all wearing our shiny new haloes and going round being unnaturally nice to each other.'

'Just as we are today.'

'Yes, but Chloe, you've moved out of your house. That does make things a lot harder for both of you.'

'No harder than it probably still is for you.'

Dinah surprised her. 'It has been, but it's getting better. Honestly.' She smiled.

'Well, that's – it's good to hear that.' Chloe floundered among imagined possibilities. Luke had mentioned none of them.

'Come on, Chloe.' Dinah was suddenly impatient. 'We don't have to talk like this any more. Just carry straight on, that's what we said we would do. So let's get on with it, shall we?'

'I'm sorry.' Chloe was going to cry.

'Don't you dare,' Dinah threatened. She turned neatly to intercept Paul, who was circulating with glasses of chablis. 'Here – pick yourself up with this. In fact,' she grinned, 'why don't you get elegantly sloshed? It's definitely my turn to act as the drinking woman's friend.'

'Maybe I will.' She found that she wanted a drink very much. 'So – here's looking at you, friend.'

'You and Mum were looking pleased with each other.'

'Oliver!' Chloe hugged him and kissed his cheek. His thin body tensed and relaxed as he returned her embrace. 'I suppose we are, yes.'

'I am really happy. You were always good together.'

'We were, weren't we? And you, Olly? Are you pleased with yourself?' He smiled, filling his eyes with her lovely face. 'I was,' he said. He had fallen in love with her at almost the same hour as his father had done, and with that incandescent first-time confidence had attempted to persuade her to love him in return. He had known nothing of his unconquerable opposition. He had supposed that all marriages, however happy, must turn a little stale, so that hers, twenty years old, must have reached that state. He had been full of hope.

'I thought I was beginning to get over you,' he said. 'Until now.'

'Then I expect you are,' she said gently. 'Now is just a trick of the light.'

'I don't think so.' He shook his head gravely. 'But I do *hope* so. That in itself is some sort of progress, don't you think?' His green eyes teased her.

Chloe touched his hand, its bones as fine as lace; he weighed so lightly on the world. 'I think it must be.'

He closed his eyes, allowing the light caress to continue in imagination. 'I'm not sure now. I can feel myself backsliding. Fast.' He hesitated. 'Does that ever happen to you?'

'You mean do I still think about your father?' she said unflinchingly. 'Of course I do. We almost overturned all our lives, Olly. It wasn't something you can leave easily behind.'

'No, I didn't suppose so,' he said soberly. 'But I was just thinking – I mean, what's the use of anything if it takes a lifetime to get over loving someone?'

'I don't think you get over it; I think you slowly, very slowly, assimilate it – the wound closes around it until it is part of you. And you can live that way. Eventually.' She would not tell him how distant she was from that desirable way of living. 'Of course, the kindest thing that can happen is that you should meet someone else. In your case, that is.'

'Ah. You've been listening to village gossip.'

'Well, Tilda did say you have been seen about with Lisa Latham.'

'Lisa's a nice girl. Grown up. Unusual.'

'And unusually sensitive – which you would also know how to appreciate.' She hoped their relationship would develop. Olly would be so good for Lisa. Like Dinah, he liked to make other people happy, and like his father, he was blessedly unaware of the mainsprings of his attraction.

Oliver lifted a finger and stroked it down the bridge of her nose, the gesture of an adult to a child. 'Lisa and I are just friends,' he said. 'We are learning how to tend our wounds, but as you say, it takes time.'

Rufus looked about the humming room and tried to identify the nudge-nudge of discomfort he was feeling. Everyone was happy. Mum was here; Miranda was like she was on Ecstasy; Moriarty was as cute as a kitten. They were all gathered together, just like they used to be. Helen had even promised him a spin in the Porsche. So what was wrong? He had another surreptitious glass of wine, his third, while he thought about it. After this, he inconspicuously left the room. Taking the spare key from the drawer in the kitchen, he went downstairs to Chloe's studio. He let himself in and sat down at her desk in front of the phone. He looked at the instrument for a bit, tapping his fingers on it a few times, then picked it up and dialled a familiar number. Of course, there was no point, really. He wouldn't be there. He never was.

'Yeah?' pronounced a lazy voice, using two syllables.

Rufus leaped nervously. 'Oh shit.' He pulled himself together.

After all, he was doing the right thing.

'Hi, Joel. It's me. Rufus.'

'So it is. How are you, Rufe? Missed you. Bad business, back there.'

'Yes. Look, I'm sorry I got you into grief with the police. It all got kind of out of control.'

'No sweat. I shouldn't have put so much pressure on you, I guess. Let's forget it, huh? So what's up, Rufe?'

Rufus let go a long breath. 'Thanks, Joel. And I'm really pleased you weren't nicked. What's *up* is – well, I'm actually calling to tell you that you're a father.'

Silence.

'Joel?'

'Yeah.'

'OK. Well, she's a girl and Miranda's called her Moriarty. She's—'

'I suppose she looks like a rat?'

Rufus grinned. 'Sure. She looks a lot like you. Quite OK, really. Not wrinkly or anything, not now. She's got loads of hair and she looks quite intelligent sometimes. Makes a hell of a row, though.'

'Yeah. Well. Thanks. Yes, thanks a lot, Rufus. It was friendly of you to let me know.'

'That's all right. I reckon you *ought* to know. I mean, you are her real father, after all.'

'That is true.'

'Are you going to come and see her, Joel? Everyone else has. They're all here, now. Both families.'

'Cosy.' There was the impression of a raised, laconic brow. 'They're getting on together, then, are they?'

'Yes. Why not?'

'No reason.' Joel was basically rather fond of Rufus and saw no reason to distress him by telling tales on Chloe at this late stage. 'But I think they might regard me as the Bad Fairy if I were to turn up now. Thanks again for letting me know, Rufe. I won't forget it. Hang loose. Be seeing you.'

'Great. Bye, Joel.'

Rufus put down the phone with a sense of achievement.

Luke had developed eyes in the back of his head as soon as he had come into the room. He always knew exactly where Chloe was and who was talking to her. He waited until Helen had coralled Alain Olivier in the kitchen – as usual, the pair of them appeared to be sharing a private joke – before moving in on her conversation with Rufus.

'I suppose it's all right, if you've absolutely *got* to stay here,' he heard the boy say. 'It's just that I miss you more than I thought I would.'

Chloe laughed. 'I'm not entirely sure how I ought to take that, darling.'

'It was meant to be nice.'

Luke was suddenly there, echoing her laughter.

'If I were you,' he told Rufus, 'I would withdraw gracefully before you get in any deeper.'

'I think you're probably right, sir.' Rufus recognised a magisterial command, however sociably disguised. He decided to go and tease Tilda about Paul Hughes. She seemed to be seeing even more of him recently. Rufus himself only saw her at mealtimes, and not always then. You wouldn't believe they were supposed to be twins.

'Chloe, why didn't you tell me where you were going?'

The feared and beloved voice was deviously polite. She ignored the churning beneath her ribs. 'Obviously, because I didn't want you to know.'

'Did it not occur to you that I might worry about you?'

'No.'

'Then I think you have been very selfish.'

'It isn't selfishness, Luke. It's self-preservation.'

'That's unfair.'

'No. You push me too hard. You always have. I had to get away – to breathe.'

He was incredulous. 'Surely you're not claiming it was I who drove you away?'

'Not entirely; but you were part of it.'

'What was the rest? Have you left Alain? *Tell* me.'

'No, I haven't. Now, either we talk about something else or we don't talk at all.'

'Dear Chloe, always laying down rules for my good behaviour.' His smile, a sudden sun, forgave her. 'You hurt me, my love; that's all.'

'I'm sorry. I thought you were angry.'

'That too.'

'I don't want us to be angry with one another. It takes too much energy, and I haven't any to spare.'

'Then let's not be,' he said caressingly.

Luke had energy. He had more than any human being had any right to have, and now he was taking Chloe's as well, or what Alain had left of it; his body urgently demanding things of hers, his emotions building up a force-field around them.

'I am so horribly tired,' she said quietly. 'If only we could settle into a nice, dull, middle-aged friendship and let the rest all fall away.'

'All passion spent; I see. Are you mad, woman? Can't you see how much precious time we are wasting? Come back to me, Chloe. Now. Today.'

Over Luke's shoulder, Oliver caught Chloe's appalled and despairing look. He excused himself from Cosmo's eulogy for the occult and extreme in cinema, and moved determinedly to her rescue.

'Hi, Dad. Paul Hughes wants to talk to you. Something about using the stage next weekend. To check sound values, he said.'

'How kind of you to concern yourself,' Luke replied nicely.

'Just letting you know. Actually, there's something I want to ask Chloe about.'

Amused and irritated in equal parts, Luke bent close to Chloe's ear and whispered softly, 'I know where you live!' before leaving them both in relative peace.

'It is almost impossible to have secrets in a room thirty feet by fifteen, plus a kitchen fifteen by eight,' Helen Cavendish complained to Alain Olivier. 'One could, of course, remove to the bedroom – but then there would no longer be a secret.'

Alain regarded her appreciatively. Her voice was like clotted cream. 'Do you have a secret, Hélène?'

'I'm not sure, just at the moment. It might not be quite convenient to have one. What is *your* opinion?'

— 93 —

He smiled. 'I think that, *comme toujours*, your judgement and taste are impeccable.'

'I see,' she murmured. 'What a pity. Then I think I need a cigarette, if Miranda still permits one to smoke.'

'She has said nothing to me.' Alain produced the beloved Gauloises without which he could not function.

'Thank you. I'll stay faithful to my Black Russian.'

'Hélène – do you still have my lighter?'

'I do.'

'I should like to 'ave it back, if you please.'

'I told you in December that it was in my flat in Paris. You did not retrieve it. You are still invited.'

'I know. I am grateful.'

'Then come. For the lighter, for a delicious dinner, to walk beside the Seine in the moonlight. Do come. For the sake of friendship, or a little more than that.'

'I'd love to, Hélène. You know 'ow much I enjoy being with you. You are the only woman, apart from Chloe, who—. But with things as they are . . . Chloe – she seems to be riding some private nightmare. I can't reach her. But I must be there if she needs me.'

'I understand, and I'm sorry for her. But I am more concerned about you. You are all strung up and detached again. It isn't good for you, and it won't do any good to Chloe to see you like that.'

He shrugged irritably. ''Ow would you 'ave me be? Naturally, I am anxious. I think I may be going to lose her after all. If you will look be'ind you, you will see what I mean.'

'I don't need to look. But you're probably quite wrong, you know. You can hardly expect them not to speak to each other, especially on an occasion like this. I mean, it's part of the great game of Heal the Rift, isn't it? Don't allow jealousy to get to you now.'

He sighed. 'You are right. I know it. But I cannot 'elp it. I won't be able to find forgiveness in myself again. I fear that.'

'You won't have to. I'm sure of it. Look, I want to talk to Luke about Adam. Now seems a useful time. I'll see what vibrations I can pick up. But you are to stop worrying, do you hear me?'

'I shall try. It's good to see you, Hélène. I'm sorry to be so—' He held out empty palms.

'Don't be. And don't forget the lighter.'

He would not do that. Chloe had given it to him. He kissed Helen's elegant hand in the exaggerated manner that made her laugh.

'*A la prochaine, belle Hélène.*'

'For godsake, Luke, haven't you the sense to leave her alone for just two minutes? You can see she's stretched to breaking point, even when she's laughing for Rufus or Olly.'

'Oh Hades, the voice that lynched a thousand shits! Don't belabour me, Helen. I'm feeling rather fragile myself.'

'Serves you right, you idiot. You're going to wreck everything again if you can't begin to think before you run breakneck after your emotions.'

'How sweet of you not to say my prick. I know,' he added disarmingly. 'I just don't know what else to do.'

'How about nothing, for a change? Just look after the school and cherish your family and enjoy being a proxy grandparent.'

'Is that what we are?' He rallied and smiled at her affectionately. 'It's an odd feeling, isn't it?'

'Yes. It must be a lot odder for Adam, poor darling. I never saw him as playing St Joseph – all the responsibility and none of the usual fun.'

Luke grimaced. 'That would mean Joel Ranger is God the Father.'

A gleam came into Helen's famously clear amber eyes. 'According to Belle, he bears more resemblance to a very sexy Lucifer.'

'Ergo – Lucifer equals God the Father. Makes some sense, when you consider the permanent Armageddon we have made of the world.'

'Which reminds me,' she said sweetly. 'How is your home life these days? Dinah is looking uncommonly perky.'

'Come to think of it, she is, isn't she? I suppose we are getting on pretty well at the moment.'

'All the more reason to keep away from Chloe, especially in public.'

'Don't meddle, Helen. You are no longer my wife.' He grinned shamelessly. 'And, given nearly a year of non-observance, you are no longer even my intermittent mistress. You have forfeited your right to interfere.'

'Rats!' Once, less than a year ago, she would have been cut to the quick by his second clause.

'Very well. But it works both ways.' He took on a look of engaging innocence. 'Tell me about you and Alain Olivier.'

'Nothing to tell.'

'Liar.'

'Ask him.'

Luke laughed. '*Touché*. But I've seen how you look at him.'

'Nothing wrong with good, honest lust. Alain, alas, is a one-woman man. But it would suit you so well, wouldn't it, if it were true – you think it would give you *carte blanche* to pursue Chloe?'

Luke looked hurt. 'I was simply taking a kindly interest in your life.'

Helen smiled. 'Just as I do in yours.'

'Dad!' Belle's imperious voice demanded Luke's attention.

'What is it?'

She was standing near the window with Alain Olivier. Luke joined them. He would have to speak to Alain sooner or later and the chemistry between them would be less unreliable if one of the children acted as a catalyst.

'It's a bit embarrassing,' Belle said, 'Although it's very nice for me. Monsieur Alain wants to pay for the party because he's the Father of the Mother. I told him you had already offered.' She flirted her eyelashes at Alain, who had always treated her as an attractive young woman rather than the permanent adolescent her own family seemed to require.

'Why don't you hold an inverted auction?' Luke suggested frivolously. 'We could outbid each other until you felt you had made a worthwhile profit.'

'Don't be silly,' Belle said severely. 'The food and wine cost a hundred and twenty-six pounds. There's tons left – people talk too much. I paid for it out of my building society account. I'd be grateful for any contributions, but I'm not greedy about it.'

'Then let's leave it with me, shall we?' Luke said courteously, looking at Alain. 'Dinah and I may be only proxy grandparents, as Helen calls it, but we'd like to be treated as the real thing.'

'*D'accord.* In that case, we shall go 'alves,' Alain said, smiling at Belle.

'Done!' cried Belle. 'That will be sixty-three pounds each. Cheques preferred.'

'Thank you for doing all this for us, Belle,' Alain said warmly. 'It was a charming idea.'

'Oh, I just happened to be the first to think of it.' She looked quickly round the room. 'Have you seen Cosmo lately? Sorry, I've got to track him down. Catch you both later. There's going to be music.'

Alain was turning away as Luke spoke his name.

'Yes?'

Luke refused the parcel of negative emotions offered by the syllable. 'I've wanted to ask you,' he said easily, 'if you might be kind enough to repeat the lecture you gave us. It was very popular. Indeed, you have already made a conversion; one of the sixth-form girls is applying to Imperial College to do an engineering degree.'

'I am glad to 'ear it,' Alain said politely.

'Then will you talk to us again, to the Lower Sixth? There are one or two students whom I would particularly like to listen to you.'

'I regret,' Alain said firmly, 'but I 'ave no time at present.'

'Then, perhaps in a few weeks?' Luke had no clear idea why he was being so insistent. It seemed that he wanted to make some sort of a connection between them; apart, of course, from the one that already existed. He did not know if it was something to do with guilt, or it was simply that he liked the man and, in different circumstances, would have been his friend.

Alain, disturbingly, looked him straight in the eyes. It became instantly plain to him that no such connection could be made.

'I am sorry,' Alain said with finality.

'So am I.'

There was nothing further to be said between them.

Belle discovered Cosmo in Adam's studio, lying on top of the pile of coats on Adam's bed, a half empty wine bottle in his hand.

'What the hell do you think you're playing at?' she protested furiously. 'You're supposed to be doing a job. And that's Adam's bed.'

'So? I'm taking a break.' He patted the coats. 'Come here.'

'No. You get back out there and serve the desserts.'

Cosmo put down the bottle, grabbed Belle by the wrist and pulled her down on top of him. Clamping her head between his fingers he rammed her mouth into his and muzzled her into a painful kiss. Belle wriggled and kicked and beat him with her fists, emitting a strangled gurgling noise as if she were gagged. Cosmo wrapped his legs around hers and hung on grimly with every muscle while he wrestled her beneath him and on to her back. Still kissing her, he forced her head into the pillow while he dragged her forearms behind her and cuffed them together with one long, sensitive and apparently cast-iron hand. Next, kneeling over her, he ripped open her shirt and began to do astonishing things to her left breast.

'What's *happened* to you?' she raged, realising her mouth was no longer occupied.

'Shut up,' muttered Cosmo. He gazed at her moodily, for a very short time because she was wriggling again, then swooped upon her in a recently acquired manner and fastened his lips upon the breast. Just as his healthy, well-formed and normally rather pleasant teeth opened around the tenderest piece of flesh on her body, Belle translated appalled intuition into action and frenziedly wrenched herself aside.

She sat up and knotted her shirt, glaring at him in outrage.

'You were going to *bite* me!'

'Well, you needn't gape at me with "*J'accuse*" written on both eyeballs. Biting is what we're *supposed* to do, isn't it? I haven't even tasted blood yet.'

'You stupid shit!' she yelled, getting up and kicking him savagely on the shin. 'Even I know it's *only a play*!'

Cosmo, unaccountably, seemed to find this very amusing.

During the days after the party, Chloe began to live as if a bomb had been magically placed inside her, a tiny, delicate mechanism whirring faintly beneath her breastbone, the timing of which she knew nothing. She did her best to discount it, occupying herself with Miranda and the baby and with feverish attempts to find some direction for her painting, but she knew that the whirring would continue until Luke returned to stop the clock.

He did not come for four days. On Thursday, in the early evening, she recognised his knock on her door. When she opened it he entered so quickly that she had to step back, as if he had feared she would not let him pass.

'You knew I'd come.'

'Yes.'

'Are you glad?'

'I'm not sure.'

'Well, I am.' He grinned expansively. 'I'm over all the moons of all the planets in the universe. Come here!' He picked her up and whirled her round, kissing her as her feet met the ground, a joyful exuberant kiss that knocked the breath out of her.

'Luke – don't.'

'What's the matter – I've let go, haven't I? That was just by way of a greeting. We can try some other mode, if you'd rather.' Chloe moved out of his reach.

'"They flee from me that sometime did me seek",' he observed sorrowfully. 'Don't be so defensive, my darling.'

'You make it impossible to be any other way. Why did you have to come here?'

'Because it's important that we talk to each other sensibly and truthfully, without you constantly trying to cut me off or freeze me out. And without the beady-eyed family watchdogs.'

'But we've said all the important things, months ago. We agreed on what we were going to do and we put ourselves and everyone else through hell getting to that point. And now you behave as if that decision had never been taken.' Her voice rose in protest.

'It isn't the decision that's important; it's how we really feel. I want the truth between us, and you keep pushing it away.'

'No, I'm pushing *you* away. It's different.'

'Why?' He shrugged away her determination. 'You don't want to.'

'But I do. How can I make you believe me?'

'You can't. This isn't a one-sided thing. You're forgetting that I *know* you – that I can't *not* know how you feel.'

What she felt was panic. 'Not any more. I have changed.'

'No. You think you want to, but you can't.'

He was so close to her; she had not meant to let him get so close again. He made an impatient sound and pulled her against him. Since she could not move she allowed herself to be kissed, standing in his arms like a woman in a coma while her lips grew sensitised and swollen and sent insidious couriers to eager and treacherous parts of her body.

'You can drop the zombie act,' Luke said pleasantly, 'or I promise you I will rape you. I think I might enjoy it, just at this moment.'

She said contemptuously, 'I suppose you think it would do me good?'

'It might conceivably bring you to your senses.'

'God, you are so bloody arrogant! Do you really think force could ever be any persuasion?'

Luke put his head on one side and smiled engagingly. Now that he had got her good and angry, perhaps she would really begin to talk to him. 'No, probably not,' he decided. 'I won't bother with rape. Just listen to me, will you, please? Chloe. These are words to hang in your ears. Look in your mirror and you will see how they shine. You love me. You always will. Just kiss me once, the way you want to. That's all.' His smile held all the innocent sweetness which had been an early revelation to her when they had first met. It flowed into her and she wondered if it would hurt her so very much, after all, to kiss him just once more and feed the hungry animal that screeched and yowled inside her; then she knew that of course it would; it would hurt both of them, very much.

'Sit down, please,' she ordered him quietly. 'I hear you, but I need you to listen to *me* for a while. If you will.'

Always responsive to her changes, he obeyed.

'I don't know how to tell you this. I don't want to. It is such a terrible thing – no, hush – but I think I must, because part of it belongs to you. And also because it will show you, as nothing else has been able to do, that we are farther apart than you could know.'

He said gently, 'It will be easier if you don't cry.'

'I'm sorry.' She bit her tongue to stop the tears. 'I don't want to go on.'

'I rather think you must.' He attended gravely.

'Yes. Then – you remember the day I met you at the Lightning Oak?'

'Of course.'

'I know I must have seemed like a madwoman then. In a way, I was.' She waited for an extra propulsion, which did not come. 'The day before – the day before we met, I had a pregnancy terminated. It was your child. Ours.' She watched his face become blank and then catch up with her words. Shock did that to you. The words were like thorns in his eyes.

'Oh, my dear. Why?'

She shook her head. She was trembling. She felt filthy, inside and out. Her soul was dirty. It was one of those little creatures in the white nightgowns with great black stains upon them, falling down canyons of mortal sin towards the jaws of a welcoming hell. The despairing image had hung on the wall of her convent classroom when she was five years old. She had hated to get dirty ever since.

'Why?' Luke repeated. 'Why didn't you tell me you had conceived? What possessed you to go to such hideous lengths, without even talking to me? It was my child too. I can't bear to think of what you have done. Can you explain it to me? You must, because I sure as hell do not begin to understand. I thought I knew you.'

She began to give him her reasons, as they had appeared to her, but she did not think he was really able to listen.

'Why?' he said again when she had done. 'It was the

one thing in the world that would have made it right for us to begin our life together. Nothing you say can stand up to that.'

'But it did stand up to it,' she said dully, 'or it seemed to, then.'

'And not now? Is that what you're saying?'

'I don't know,' she said wretchedly. 'How can I have you with me and say so? That's why I had to think it through by myself, and then do what I did without you. If I had told you, you would have tried to take me over completely; you would have given me no chance. I couldn't take such a risk.'

'Were you so very eager to get rid of it?' he asked brutally.

'I would have given anything possible to keep it. But there wasn't anything.'

'So you gave up my child's life, and my happiness, and your own. It doesn't appear to bring you much joy.'

His harshness was her final undoing. She sat down on her bed and wept without control. He watched her for a time. Eventually he said, 'I would have thought I could forgive you anything. But I don't think I can manage this.'

She was further destroyed by the tenderness this aroused in her.

'You shouldn't,' she said. 'So now you understand that we have come too far apart ever to turn back?'

'I don't know. I have to think about this. I'm leaving now, Chloe.' He lifted her phone and looked at its number. 'I'll call you, soon.'

'I'd rather you didn't.' She rose and walked beside him to the door. When they reached it he turned and gathered her in to him, rubbing his face in her hair, holding her as though both of them were burning or drowning. 'I'm so sorry,' he said.

This time she wanted his kiss, though she knew it was not given in absolution but out of a sad pity which it shamed her to receive from him. She thought, all the time that his mouth was so kind upon hers, that now they had surely come to a place where they could make an ending. When he had gone she sat down on the bed again and let her body shake and tremble as it needed to do. Every molecule seemed to take part in a dance of displacement and chaos. Yet, when the tremors had ceased and the dance was done, nothing at all had changed.

As Luke stood at the end of the hallway, debating numbly between lift and stairs, the lift arrived and Miranda stepped out of it. She took one look at his bleak face and knew that he had been with Chloe.

'What are you doing here?' she asked cheerfully.

He recalled the ostensible reason for his presence. 'I have a carload of stuff that Dinah sent over for Moriarty.'

'That's lovely. But I live on the next floor.'

'I had something to say to your mother.'

She had never seen him look like this. His huge energy was lost and what was left without it seemed to have nothing to do with him.

'I was going to see her myself,' she said, 'but I can catch her later. Come back with me and visit Moriarty. Adam will be home soon; he'll help you bring the things up.'

He went with her like a compliant sleepwalker, but he was unable to rouse himself sufficiently to admire Moriarty's superior talents for sleeping, yelling, eating, defecating or bringing up wind. Miranda noted the tension in his hand as he clutched his glass of Belle's leftover Chablis.

She said diffidently. 'Something is wrong. I suppose you don't want to tell me about it?'

Luke answered softly, as if for himself, 'I have of late lost all my joy.'

Fear, more than curiosity, prompted her. 'I thought it was all settled – between you and Chloe.'

'Did you?'

'You seemed OK together at the party. I mean – normal. You know.'

'Normal is not how I feel at this moment, Miranda. But that does not mean I am about to unload my sorrows upon your attractive bosom.'

'You're angry. I'm sorry.'

'Not with you.'

'With Mum?'

'With myself, mostly, I believe. Now, stop fishing, will you?'

'All right.' She shrugged. 'I just don't like to see you so sad.'

'No. It doesn't suit me, does it?' he said ruefully. 'Look, you mustn't concern yourself. I don't want you and Adam to start worrying about me, or about Chloe, again. There is no reason for it.'

'Oh, that's all right,' Miranda said instinctively, 'I won't tell Adam you were with her.'

'Why not?'

'Well, I suppose, just because he *might* worry – though not as much as me. Or maybe it's more that, if I don't tell Adam, then I can't talk to him about it – and that way I won't think about it so much either.'

Luke laughed. 'Dear Miranda – I can see why Adam thinks you are the sun and the moon. But even he might think it exaggerating matters to predicate a universal catastrophe upon a little romantic regret.'

He smiled again and she allowed herself, temporarily, to be convinced.

Chapter 6

MORIARTY HAD TURNED INTO A SCREAMER. Whether she had snatched trouble from the air or whether she was, as the insouciant insist, simply exercising her lungs, she was unable to say. But she was very well able to howl and she did it with variety and bravura. Her best performances enlivened the dead of night, but she also gave matinées and the occasional Coffee Cantata, after Bach. Miranda was incredulous and horrified. She had expected her daughter to continue to be the reasonable being to whom she had been explaining the world for all those months of shared blood and simple pleasures. This horrendous din which stole their sleep and quickened their heartbeats piled insult upon ungrateful injury. She expressed herself forcefully upon the subject to Moriarty but achieved not a semiquaver of difference.

'Let's take it in turns,' Adam offered. 'You sleep with her one night, and I'll take the next. That way we both get some rest, even if it's not enough. Unless she could sleep by herself?'

'No, she can't. Or rather, I can't let her. I have to be with her, I don't know why. You go back to your own room. There's no point in both of us being permanently exhausted.'

'Well, maybe. But not every night. Let's see how it goes.' Adam hoped he concealed his relief.

Miranda, despite the fact that his release had been her idea, was immediately resentful of his freedom to accept it. The next time Moriarty yelled, she made a face at her and left her to get on with it.

'Do you think it's because I'm giving her formula food?' she asked Chloe. She had produced very little milk herself and, anyway, they had already agreed that bottle-feeding fitted more practically into everyone's lives. This did not prevent Miranda feeling guilty, and Chloe recognised this.

'I don't think there *is* any reason,' she told her soothingly. 'Some babies just seem to do this. Tilda did – though Rufus, astonishingly, was almost silent until he began to talk—' She stopped abruptly.

'How long did Tilda go on doing it?'

'I can't remember exactly. Two months or so, I think.'

'Two months! That's a life sentence.'

Later that week, Chloe awoke to a loud hammering on her door. *Luke*, she thought, still half asleep.

'Mum?' Miranda called urgently. 'Please come. I think Moriarty is really ill.'

'I'm coming.' Chloe struggled with the arms of her dressing-gown.

'What's wrong with her?' she asked as she opened the door.

Miranda was ragged with worry. 'She's terribly hot and she won't stop crying.'

They ran up the stairs. 'I think it's some sort of fever,' she gasped. 'Adam's still next door. I tried to rouse him but he just wouldn't wake up.' They raced into the studio, Chloe ahead.

'For godsake!' she protested, entering Miranda's bedroom. The modest space was a tropic of sultry heat. Puce with rage and discomfort, Moriarty lay in her cot, swaddled in bedclothes, screaming her lungs out and beating the air with her fists. 'What are you trying to do, kill her? It must be nearly thirty degrees in here.' Chloe turned back the thermostat, then picked up the roaring bundle and cast off some of its wrappings. 'There, darling, we'll soon make you more comfortable,' she crooned. 'Mummy has mistaken you for an exotic plant.' She laid the still complaining child on a small plastic-topped table and snapped her fingers. 'Nappies. Clean pants. Any more cream?'

'Oh hell, I didn't even think to see if she was wet. I was panicking.' Miranda rummaged in a drawer. 'Will moisturiser do?'

'It will have to.' Chloe's movements were deft and gentle. It was surprising how quickly it all came back. She dashed away a sudden tear and tickled the baby's tightly packed little stomach. 'If I were you I should get properly organised. It makes life a lot easier.'

Miranda heaved a deep sigh as she watched her daughter regain her status as a member of the human species. 'You do it all so quickly,' she despaired.

'So will you, very soon, believe me.'

'God – the little swine is actually smiling.'

'Yes, well, it *is* nice when it stops,' Chloe said drily.

'What?'

'Torture. Here, you take her now. You can wrap her in her shawl and hold her for a while. But take it off when you put her back in the cot. You have double-glazing, a heavy blind and those thick curtains – you need to lower the temperature at night, and keep the window open, just on the catch. There's nothing wrong with Moriarty except that you were parboiling her.'

'I didn't know.' Miranda was subdued. 'The book said she has to be kept warm all the time.'

'It just means you have to maintain an even, sensible temperature.' Chloe sighed. 'I'm going back to bed now. And in future, make sure there's a real emergency before you drag me out of it.'

'I'm sorry, honestly,' Miranda said pathetically. 'But how do I tell when it *is* a real emergency? This looked like one to me.'

'This,' said Chloe with measured callousness, 'was Lesson One.'

Back in her own room, she asked herself what had been the cause of her irritation. It was not Miranda's foolishness; she had made a common mistake. No, it had been her own emotions that had been so disturbing. She would never have admitted to Miranda the paralysing sense of foreboding she had experienced when she had heard her terrified cry at the door. The child had been dead and buried long before Chloe had reached her. It had been as if that were what she ought to expect; that what happened to Moriarty might be a punishment for her own misdeeds, as though nature had not done with her but must somehow, no matter how unfairly, get even.

'No!' She cried aloud in self disgust. It was all nonsense, and dangerous nonsense. This was how to drive herself beyond reason. She could see that plainly enough. But her enemy was not what she understood; it was what she felt to be just. 'Catherine,' she prayed helplessly. 'What am I to do? How can I stop loving this child so much? Why can't I simply accept that there is a space that is not to be filled? Help me, Catherine, help me to find the blessed grace of detachment.'

She knew what Catherine would have said. She would have told her once more to look for that grace, and also to take some solace from her work. She knew she must try to do that. Trying, in itself, must eventually succeed, if only in concentrating her mind.

The problem, or one of them, was what to take as her subject. Joshua Reinhart, who sold a lot of her pictures, had asked her to produce some more of the sensual landscapes she had done last summer. She had told him it was unlikely that she would be able to repeat that particular mood.

Joshua, who was a sensitive man, had asked no questions but said simply, 'Then you had just better see what wants to come next.'

The answer, so far, had been: nothing – or perhaps a single small square of canvas to be painted black; black, over and over until it had become the absolute essence of black.

'Black, black, black—' An old lyric returned to mock her. 'I want my baby back.' And after she had dealt with that there was 'Black is the colour of my true love's hair,' the anguished elegy for love which she had so often sung as a girl, long before she had put herself in the way of meeting Luke.

She began to make charcoal studies of Miranda and Moriarty, rough, hasty sketches, crackling with movement or heavy with repose. She drew Adam too, seated at his desk, communing with his computer as if with a familiar dinner companion, smiling, cajoling and waving his hands in emphasis. Often, his head a little inclined, he would fix his gaze on an unseen source, seeming both to listen and to hear. The sketches were not her best work but they forced her to live in the moment by challenging her to catch it as it flew. Miranda, who had to work long and hard to achieve such seeming carelessness, despaired of ever matching her.

'I'd like you to do them every day, for the rest of my life,' she said, 'and publish them in a huge book, and a video too, just before I die.'

'Sorry. I won't be able to oblige,' said Chloe. 'I was rather relying on you to bury me.'

'Mum! Don't be ghoulish.'

'You were the one to mention death.'

'Yes – but I can't *imagine* it.'

Chloe gave her a hug. 'Don't ever try.'

Chloe, who had been the cause of it, could imagine death

only too well. A new irrationality took her over. She began to draw not only Moriarty as she grew and altered, day by day, but her own child as well, the child who might have been. Sometimes she drew a boy with the foreshadowing of Luke's dark, intense features; sometimes a girl, an elfin, contented little creature whom she surrounded with sunlight. They had become two or three years old before she was made to realise just what it was she was doing.

She was drawing the boy when Luke phoned. She had not expected to hear from him, although that, too, was irrational.

'Chloe?'

'Yes.'

'Will you talk to me?'

'Yes.'

'Your voice is fragile. How are you? What are you doing?'

She told him she was drawing the boy, his child, that she could not help thinking of him as a living child. 'I know he isn't, of course. I do know what I've done; that I've reduced him to raw, ripped-out flesh, unwanted, without respect – as if he were a tumour.'

'I'm coming over. Now,' Luke said urgently. 'Just be still. Don't think.'

'No. You must not. I don't want to see you again. How can we, with this between us? Before, we only dealt in lies, deceit, betrayal. Now we have moved on – oh, an order of magnitude. Why should you want to be with me? You can't forgive me. I can't forgive myself.'

'Please, listen.' Luke was desperate to trap her attention, to stop the somnambulist's voice that could speak only of death and remorse.

'I've thought about it all the time since I saw you. It was a shock. I was hurt. It distressed me that you hadn't told me about the baby. I said things I regret. But I think I can understand why you thought you had to do it. It's all right. It makes no difference. I love you. I can't change that, whatever you do.'

'That isn't the point. It hasn't been for a long time.'

'Sweetheart, you are feeling like this – and doing these sketches – because you need to mourn. You need to weep and to put flowers on a grave. You can't do that. Instead, you are looking after a living, healthy child who belongs to your daughter. Of course it is too much for you. It is making everything worse. Chloe, you must come home.'

'You *don't* understand. I need to be here. I have to work through it in my own way. I know I sometimes don't make sense. Please – leave me for a while, Luke. I *will* talk to you. When I can.'

She thought over what he had said about mourning. It was true; she could accept that she needed to mourn. But what was she to do with her guilt? Luke wanted to discount it, to lift its dead weight from her with the countervailance of his love and his forgiveness. He could not comprehend that such a release was not in his gift.

She could see no way forward. Her mind turned and tumbled a mass of disconnected debris in its wheel; half thoughts, unfinished images, jagged lumps of emotion; nothing of reason – all anxiety, all loss. She was inside the glass globe of the snowstorm which had been her favourite plaything as a child. It had housed a perfect Victorian village in miniature, complete with a tiny, various population with names, occupations and eccentricities, whose complex lives she had chronicled in a weekly journal. She had shaken the snowstorm rarely and with great gentleness, aware that to do it roughly would be to loose an avalanche of fear and change upon her helpless dependants. Now she stood in the path of the avalanche, as helpless as they, and like them, pent apart from the others outside the glass.

Recently, more often than not, Luke spent Saturday afternoons alone. Today Dinah was up in the Cessna with

Philip again. He had watched them from the garden as they banked slowly around the church spire, imagining her squeaks of fear and delight. Flying had become her new obsession. It was the latest in a long line of off-centre pursuits into which she had thrown herself with the whole-hearted abandon that was her most lovable and occasionally most maddening proclivity. Luke liked it a lot better than last year's exhaustive investigation of what non-historians were arrogant enough to call the New Age. Dinah had undergone hypnosis for the avoidance of anxiety and chocolate, reflexology to cure an aching foot, had enjoyed colour therapy and aromatherapy and consulted pendulums which answered queries yes or no. She had opened up her third eye and improved the health of her chakras with the Mahatma, learned to make Tibetan mouth music, play temple bells and make a horrible noise on a didgeridoo. She had read Tarot cards, Navaho animal cards, and cast reeds for the I Ching. She had been rebirthed and realigned, and had interviewed a Renaissance alchemist and a Tang dynasty Mandarin through the medium of a comfortable dowager in Hackney. Her crowning achievement had been the uncovering of a previous incarnation in which she had saved her sister's life at the expense of her own. The sister, it was revealed, had been Chloe, who happened to be with her during the consultation. Both women had been pleased with the discovery.

The New Age had been abandoned together with the sisterhood when Dinah had lost heart for her enthusiasms in losing Luke to Chloe. Now, here she was again, restored, invigorated and concentrated upon the single, ancient desire of wingless humans to turn themselves into birds or angels, or failing that, to inhabit mechanical imitations. Luke could identify with that; he would have enjoyed the experience himself if he had been less fully committed to the school.

When Dinah had left in Philip's safe and solid company,

Belle asked Luke if he would drive her to Guildford station.

'I wouldn't ask,' she told him in the car, 'Only I don't quite know how I feel about this audition and I need moral support.'

'I thought Helen was going with you?'

'She can't. She's coming to Adam's this evening.'

'I see. Does that mean you'll be staying over again?'

'Yes. If that's OK?' Belle was deferential.

'I suppose it is. You seem to spend a lot of your time over there.'

'I'm helping Miranda with her college work, and a bit with Moriarty. Dad?'

'Mmm?'

'If I do get this part, will it be OK if I stay with Adam while they do the filming? It would be much easier, and cheaper, than travelling every day.'

'I expect so.' He smiled at her. 'If you do. I have the impression that you are not quite sure whether or not you really *want* it.'

'Yeah. Funny, isn't it? It would be a mega-huge chance. It's just – it has come a bit early. Before my A levels. Even before drama school. What do *you* think, Dad?'

'I think you should give it all you've got, and see how you feel if you do get it. Just for the experience.'

Luke drew up outside the station and she leaned over to kiss him.

'Good. That's what Helen said. You know – I'm really glad you married her before Mum.'

'You think she made you into an actress?'

'No, but she is certainly helping. And I think I'm more like her than Adam is. And more like her than I am like Mum.'

'God's boots! I hope not,' Luke said piously.

'Why? Oh, yes. You got divorced. Well, I'm *never* going to divorce Aunt Helen.'

* * *

When Luke re-entered the house he found Oliver, back from a shift at the vet's, preparing to take Holmes and Watson for a walk. The dogs thumped their tails against his legs and did their best not to leap with unseemly joy until they got outside.

'Mind if I come along?' Luke asked. He did not feel like working and had a sudden unusual sense that if he were to stay in alone he would actually feel lonely. Also, if he went out with Olly, he could not be tempted to phone Chloe. 'This sun's too good to miss.'

'Good idea,' Oliver said. It was six months since they had walked together. The request seemed to him a further indication that things were getting back to normal. 'I'd planned to go up through the woods to the top of the downs. There's a superior selection of sticks up there – you know how fussy Holmes can be.' Ever a perfectionist, Holmes would consent to chase only after impeccably smooth sticks of a certain length and thickness. He was also rigorous as to the style of the throw, which must be of a good distance and offer the opportunity for him to catch the stick in his mouth. Watson, lazily content to be outclassed, would run in the opposite direction and sit down to admire the catch.

The game continued all the way up the steep, green path through the woods, the dogs dashing wildly about, snuffing and searching, purblind among the leaves, then speared by a sudden shaft of sunlight. When they came out into the full sun at the top of the ridge, they were met by a tangible body of heat and scent that seemed to present a different element, so forceful was the shock on entering it. The dogs stopped to pant for a moment, then raced away together. They knew all the paths and rabbit runs and would come back when they were whistled.

Luke and Oliver wandered along the ridge until they found a wide slope of grass, studded with blue and yellow flowers, stretched across the hillside like a woman's dress laid out to dry. They flung themselves down on their backs and sighed with mutual contentment as the sun hit their faces.

'I love this countryside,' Olly said fervently. 'I'm so glad we came to live out here.'

'So am I,' Luke agreed, thinking as he must of Chloe, who had walked with him and lain down beside him in other such enchanted places, when for the last few weeks of a single summer their private world had seemed inviolable.

They lay without speaking, listening to the bright scissoring of birdsong and the distant, ocean sound of traffic.

'Don't let me go to sleep,' Olly murmured. 'I have to meet Lisa at four.'

'I won't,' Luke promised. 'I'm glad you've taken to Lisa. I was hoping you might become friends.'

'Is that why you went out and left me to talk to her that day?'

'I don't know that it was a conscious thing, Olly—'

But he had been happy to avoid Lisa. He was doing his best to help her during regular private conversations in school hours, and preferred to keep the relationship on that basis.

Oliver sat up and ran his fingers through his hair. It was almost shoulder length now, surrounding his thin face in a streaky brown and gold halo like his mother's. He was a good-looking boy, Luke thought, and he had Dinah's generous spirit. He hoped the silly girl would have the sense to turn in his direction.

'Dad?' the paragon pronounced hesitantly. 'How much do you actually know about Lisa's suicide attempt? I probably shouldn't ask – but I know she doesn't want to talk about it, and it would help if I knew.'

'Knew what, exactly?'

'Well, I suppose – who it was that she thought was worth *dying* for. I mean, I look round at school some-times and I just can't get my head round it. There really

— 116 —

isn't anyone with that kind of pulling power or charisma about them.'

'Not for you, perhaps. Obviously, Lisa felt differently.'

'Right. So – *do* you know?'

'No, I don't,' Luke said. The lie was both necessary and compassionate. If Olly was at last beginning to forgive him for falling in love with Chloe, who had been his first true passion, he was hardly likely to welcome the news that Lisa, to whom he was tentatively transferring his affections, had also been in thrall to his father, and to such an extreme degree. Luke did not believe that Lisa would ever tell Oliver herself; her instincts were better than that. Nevertheless, it might be a good idea to make sure of it. He would talk to her. He did not want the two of them to lose each other's friendship before it had been given a chance to grow deeper. He had enough on his conscience already.

'I think you are right to feel you ought not to discuss it with her,' he said truthfully. 'The best thing for Lisa is to allow this business to fall slowly into the background of her life. What you *can* do is to help to make the present and the future more interesting to her than the blighted romance of the past.' Here, his sense of irony mocked him with his own situation.

'Wow! You don't ask for much, do you? But you're right. Maybe I'm just curious. I promised her I wouldn't be. But aren't you?'

'A little – as to why it became such a desperate thing for Lisa.' This too was true. Luke had never understood why the girl had not worked her way through her schoolgirl crush like the rest of them. There had been rather a lot of them, over the years; he saw this as a hazard of the work itself rather than anything to do with his own questionable charms. Chloe had not agreed, but then she was – had been – partisan.

'I don't know.' Olly sighed and scratched his head, dislodging a small beetle from his hair. 'I'll never understand this love business. It seems absolutely crazy to me. No one ever wants the right person – or if they do, and they get them, either they can't stick to them or they lose them to someone else.'

'That about sums it up,' Luke agreed. 'Welcome to the idiotic world of the adult. Or would you rather change species?'

'I've thought about that. I should like to be one of the larger cats; something fast. A puma or a cheetah.'

Luke wanted to grab him and hug him to pieces, but he was not sure if he would like it, not yet. It occurred to him, as a corollary to all this, that another secret that must never be told was that he himself was aware of Oliver's passion for Chloe. Dinah had sworn never to let him know, but Luke had simply guessed. It had not been difficult; there had been the apocalyptic scene following his confession of adultery. Overwhelmed by his first experience of male humiliation and enraged beyond all possibility of emotional control, Oliver could not help betraying his feelings. His need to tear his father apart with bare hands had obviously been less on Dinah's behalf than to exorcise his own hideously graphic vision of Luke and Chloe making love.

'Don't worry,' he said now. 'I shall tread on eggshells all round.'

'So shall I,' Luke said soberly.

'What?'

'Well – with Lisa.'

'Oh. Yeah.'

Walking and talking with Olly were all very well. So was getting on with Dinah as if they were a companionable brother and sister whose relationship consisted of eating together and exchanging news about the other people in their lives, but contained nothing that was deeply personal. It was easy and pleasant and empty of meaning, as were their occasional bouts of sex. Yet it appeared to be enough for Dinah and equally sufficient to restore Oliver to domestic security. What was comfortable for them, however, was a veritable briar-patch for Luke. While each of them supposed his mind and heart to be properly engaged in the renaissance of his marriage, they were in fact given over almost entirely to Chloe. In spirit, he was still deceiving his family as fully as he had been last year – even Belle, bless her, who had no idea she had ever been deceived in the first place. It was an impossible situation, he could see that; but to everyone else it looked not only possible but hopeful and positive. Unless he did something to alter it radically, it could go on like this for a very long time.

Chloe, Chloe, short-sighted, pigheaded light of my days and nights, why won't you turn around and look at things as they are?

Belle did not yet know if she had the part. There was to be a second audition, which Helen had assured her was normal practice. She came home and sank her teeth into that evening's rehearsal of *Dracula*, thirsting after blood. She remained grimly disappointed by the second act. The problem, as always, was Cosmo.

'It's no use – we can't get any further until you get it into your great bovine skull that *you are not here to enjoy yourself*,' she began. Paul and Tilda rolled their eyes at each other and settled in for a period of discomfort.

'The whole thing depends on you. Do you realise that?'

Cosmo opened his mouth and shut it again.

'And what it mainly depends on is your having a sense of tragedy – of real mental suffering and sorrow that will go on and on until the last whatsit of recorded time.'

'Syllable,' Cosmo snapped.

'You haven't just got to understand it – you have to *internalise* it – draw it all inside yourself, so that, for the audience and even for the other actors, it all flows out of *you*. You have to radiate suffering, like – like Christ on the cross. Have you any idea what I'm talking about?'

'Of course I have,' said Cosmo savagely.

'Well, I've seen no sign of it. You play the Count as if he were Robin Hood, and your vampire companions were his merry bloody men. OK, so what do *you* think is the essential tragedy here?'

'Do you have to be such a pain in the arse?'

'Go on, answer me.'

'What's the point? You're obviously giving a lecture so why don't we take the short cut?'

'You have no idea, have you?' she said contemptuously. 'All you care about is looking good and moving like some stupid action hero.'

'Either get to the point or I'm out of here,' Cosmo said icily.

Belle fractionally lowered her tone. 'The point is this: what we have here are two entirely separate, mutually exclusive societies – vampires and mortals, who might as well be on different planets. The vampires wish the humans no harm, but they need their blood to exist, like we need animals and plants. But human beings are not like animals or plants; they are like the vampires themselves, who are divorced from them only by that one, tragic need and by their immortality. So – if a vampire and a mortal fall in love, what you have is a classical tragic situation, something unacceptable to society and to the gods. Yes?'

'Like incest,' suggested Tilda thoughtfully.

Belle gave her a startled look. 'Not really,' she said.

'All right,' Cosmo said tightly. 'But there's something you've forgotten. Dracula is also a very, very angry man, and with justification. No man's punishment should last for ever. Maybe you ought to bear that in mind.'

Suddenly he grinned and let the tension trickle away. 'Don't *worry* so, Belle. I'll be all right on the night. I promise you I'll purge their hearts of pity and terror.' He gave her his good-natured smile.

— 120 —

'Yes. Leave it out for a bit, why don't you?' Paul said pleasantly. 'Cosmo really is shaping up pretty well.'

'*Is* he?' Belle was surprised. 'What do you think, Tilda?'

'Same as Paul. You worry too much. It's all coming together, slowly. I think you ought to relax a bit. Why don't we take a break and we'll play you what we've thought of for Act Three? We're using a modern interpretation of Hildegarde of Bingen. It's really fantastic.'

Sighing, Belle looked at her watch. 'Oh, all right. It's nearly time to eat, anyway. You're all staying? Only Mum wants to know how many.'

Tilda shook her head. 'I'm going home. Dad and Rufus are on their own. You stay, Paul, if you like. You can do the music without me.'

'No. I'll come with you, if that's OK?' Paul said. He knew that was what she really wanted. It was at mealtimes that Chloe was most missed. Without her presiding spirit, the charmed circle of the family rite became merely three people sitting round a table. Another face would make this a little more bearable.

Belle, too, had thought along these lines. 'Look, why don't you all come over here for Sunday lunch,' she suggested to Tilda. 'I know Mum would love to have you. I'll ask her, shall I? Adam's coming, and the M&Ms.'

Tilda brightened. 'That'd be nice. It will be sort of like another party.' But only 'sort of', without her mother.

'Of course I'll ask Alain Olivier,' Dinah said cheerfully. 'I think there's a turkey in the freezer and I could knock up something involving loads of cream and alcohol for pudding. I need *notice* for anything more elaborate.'

'Sorry. Thanks, Mum. Would you ring Alain *now*?'

'All *right*! Really, Belle, I don't know why you don't become an army officer instead of an actress.'

As Dinah had expected, Alain Olivier was surprised by her invitation. She knew perfectly well how he felt about Luke and had observed his increasing difficulty in concealing it.

'It is very kind of you, Dinah,' he said, his English lightly starched, 'But I 'ave 'ardly seen the children this week and I want to try to make Sunday lunch a little special for them, 'ere at 'ome. I'm sorry to be so ungrateful, but I 'ope you will understand.'

'Completely,' Dinah replied warmly. 'It was Belle's idea, so I had to ask. I'm sure *you* understand that, too?' She heard Alain's throaty chuckle.

''Ow understanding we all 'ave to be, do we not? For the sake of the children, as you say. And for how long, I wonder?'

'If only I knew,' said Dinah feelingly.

'I wish so much that things were otherwise,' he said gently.

'So do I. You're a lovely man, Alain. I wish you – oh, lots of good things.' She visualised his fine, asymmetrical brows as they shot for his hairline. His '*Merci, Madame*,' was wryly amused.

Tilda had worked out her own understanding of Alain's refusal. Sunday had always been an Olivier family day, and Dad was doing his slightly desperate best to keep it that way. She wished he wouldn't bother, really, as it meant they were all trying a bit too hard to be normal.

Lunch, however, was delicious. Each of them chose a favourite course. They began with the crunchy fried whitebait Rufus loved, which was nicely balanced by Alain's medallions of pork in white wine and cream sauce. There was a salad featuring three kinds of olives. The pudding Tilda had requested was the one that used to provoke the loudest squeals of delight when they were little; it was a *château flottant*, a snow palace of soft meringue carved in the shape of a castle, its turrets glistening with caramelised sugar, set in a moat of toffee sauce. It was sheer bliss.

'That was the best meal for ages, Dad. Thanks,' Rufus said, chasing the last of the sauce round his plate. 'I wish I'd invited Dwayne.'

Alain gravely acknowledged the accolade. 'Invite him tomorrow,' he suggested.

'Can we ring Mum now?' Tilda asked. 'She might be feeling lonely, with Miranda and Adam gone to the Cavendishes'.'

Alain hesitated. 'You 'ave already called today,' he said. 'I think it's beginning to make her feel guilty – you tell her so often how much you are missing her.'

'Good.' Tilda set her jaw. 'Then perhaps she'll come back sooner than she planned.'

Alain sighed. 'She'll come back when she's ready – and when she thinks Miranda can manage without her.'

'Why can't she manage now? She's got Adam. Especially at weekends – why can't Mum come home then, like she said she would?'

Alain expelled another hard-driven breath. He was running out of excuses. 'Chloe is 'aving a lot of difficulty with her painting. It's a new thing for her. She feels the new environment might 'elp. Tilda, everyone needs some – what you call "space" – now and then. Just let 'er 'ave it – and don't question 'er *every* day. Can you do that for 'er, do you think?'

Tilda frowned and tutted. 'I suppose so, if it's that important.' Then she asked quietly 'She *is* coming back, isn't she?'

Rufus instantly tuned in to her doubt. 'Yes. She is, Dad? Before the summer holidays begin?'

'I believe so,' Alain equivocated.

'*Ask* her.' Tilda insisted.

They were back where they had started. 'I will,' he promised. 'And now, if you please, we should discuss the coming week. I shall be in Paris on Wednesday and Thursday nights. There will be plenty of food in the fridge. Clean up after yourselves and don't leave any mess for Mrs

Cubitt. Now – who is feeding the animals, and who is walking Baskerville?'

'Can I carry on with Baskerville?' Rufus begged. It meant that Dwayne could accompany him, giving them extra time together. They had a lot to talk about; the pirate game was turning out to be far more boring and rather less lucrative than they had hoped.

'I'm happy with that,' Tilda agreed. 'I have so much other stuff to do; I haven't really time for walking. Sorry boy!' Baskerville came to her and allowed her to scruff up the fur on his neck.

'Huh! Not unless you're off to the woods with Paul,' Rufus mocked.

'Shut up, you horrible child.' She hoped she was not blushing.

'Cheek! Considering we were both born the same morning.'

'No one would ever guess,' Tilda sniffed.

Looking at her, Alain thought how right she was. She was growing up fast. Tall, graceful and increasingly at ease with herself, she was developing a physical confidence to match her remarkable musical talent and the new acting ability that Belle had drawn out of her. Winged with plans for the future, she was leaving her brother behind, caught in amber, an eternal schoolboy on the lookout for mischief. It was a fact that girls developed more quickly than boys, but with twins it could take you by surprise.

'Don't you think,' he enquired mildly, 'that it is time to stop insulting each other as a matter of course? It 'as become very boring for the listener.'

'But it isn't *for* the listener,' Rufus explained earnestly. 'It's just for us.'

In the interests of justice Tilda agreed. 'He's right. It sounds daft. It *is* daft. But it's the way we are.'

'It doesn't really *mean* anything,' Rufus expanded solicitously. 'It's just a habit – but we sort of stick to it, like you do to old toys.'

Alain was impressed by his power of analysis. Evidently, surprises could arrive from both directions.

He smiled at his son. 'Then I look forward to a future visit to Oxfam.'

Alone a little later, Alain fought an almost irresistible desire to pick up the phone and implore Chloe to come home. Or, if she would not do that, at least to set a date for her return. The children's instincts were also true for him – it was not missing her, in itself, that made him wretched; it was not knowing when she would come back; and that, sometimes, when he thought of the way Luke Cavendish still looked at her, he wondered if she would ever come back at all. Forget the phone – he wanted to jump into the car, race breakneck to London and carry her off by force, if necessary.

It wouldn't work, of course. The attempt would only distress her. In fact, to protect herself against such impulses, she had vetoed any unexpected visits. He wondered if his patience could possibly stretch far enough to satisfy her need. He began to see, with a clarity he had not previously possessed, just how much his characteristic equilibrium had come to depend on the certainty of her loving presence. Without her, he was no longer himself. What could he do? A cold nausea moving in his stomach told him he could do nothing but wait. The feeling of powerlessness terrified him. He was able to imagine a complete personal disintegration.

He was still sitting at the kitchen table, his hands balled into fists. He realised this was to stop them shaking. He was a truly pathetic object, was he not? 'Mon dieu, mon dieu, mon dieu,' he whispered. He poured himself a glass of the white wine left over from lunch. It steadied him a little and he reached for the further comfort of his packet of Gauloises. Putting his hand in his top pocket for his lighter, he brought out the Asterix disposable Miranda had given him. As he used it, he thought of Helen who had taken his gold one hostage until he should reclaim it in person. Helen would also be in Paris this week. He thought it would probably do him good to talk to her. Helen had the ability, unusual in a woman, and particularly in a woman with whom one had enjoyed a sexual relationship, to distance emotional problems and examine them in a manner that was both detached and sympathetic. She was a good friend. Alain felt now that, rather than look any further over the precipice on his own, he would be very grateful for the company of such a friend.

As he picked up the phone to call Paris, he remembered that he ought to speak first to Mrs Cubitt.

'My mother isn't at home,' Dwayne told him in the smooth school accent he used for adults. 'She has a mobile now; I'll give you the number.'

'Madame Cubitt? It's Alain Olivier.'

'Oh, 'allo Mr Olivier, luv. 'Ow are you?'

Her friendly voice washed back and forth as if he held a seashell to his ear. Almost expecting whalesong, he smiled at the sound of birds.

'I am well, thank you. I wanted to confirm that I shall be away for two nights, as I expected.'

'Wednesday and Thursday, ain't it?' A masculine voice murmured protestingly on the waves. 'That's aw 'right, Mr Olivier, luv. I'll stay over, as usual.' The male voice became more voluble. It must surely be the man she had described to Chloe as her 'gentleman friend'. Did every woman have one?

'Thank you, Mrs C. I'm sorry to 'ave interrupted your Sunday.'

'Don't you worry. I'll see to it that everything is ship-shape. 'Ow's Mrs Chloe? Aw' right?'

'Yes, thank you. *Au revoir*, Mrs C.'

Chapter 7

'MORIARTY – IF YOU DON'T STOP SHRIEKING this second, I promise I'll find out where the Reichenbach Falls are and drop you over them!' Miranda yelled, her face redder than the baby's.

'That tone of voice won't stop her,' Adam protested. 'You're scaring her half to death.'

'No such luck. And exactly what are *you* doing to help? Or did you consider that to have been constructive criticism? Here!' She held the raging bundle out towards him.

Adam backed away. 'Look, stop this, will you? I've got to go. I'll be late.'

'Will you really? I wonder why. God knows you slept well enough. What do you do, plug up your ears? She was howling nearly *all night*.'

'It was my turn to sleep.'

'Maybe. But *I* wouldn't have left *you* on your own all those hours. You could at least feed her now and give me a breathing space.' She laid Moriarty over her shoulder and rubbed her heaving back.

'I can't, honestly. I have a one-to-one tutorial with John Bowles at nine-thirty. He's giving me a comprehensive assessment and a lot of advice. It's important.'

'Off you go, then. We wouldn't want you to miss hearing you're going to be the next Martin Amis.'

'You know, you can be a royal pain when you try.'

'And you don't have to try,' she said wearily, putting the baby's face down on her lap and massaging her feverishly against the rhythm of her crying. 'Just – get out and leave me alone!'

Adam shrugged and made for the door. He opened it, then turned back, his face penitent. 'Look – I know you're dog tired and your hormones are shot to hell. And you don't eat properly. I know none of this is as much fun as we thought it would be; but things *will* get better. Everyone says so. Meanwhile, why don't you try just to be good to yourself today, and when I get back I'll take over completely until tomorrow. OK?'

Miranda did not feel either grateful or gracious so she said nothing.

'Miranda?'

'Yes. Fine. Whatever you like.'

He looked disappointed. 'Right. I'll see you, then.'

She turned her head away.

When the door had closed, temporarily at least, on the possibility of further quarrelling, Moriarty obligingly diminished her cries to a kittenish mewling. Miranda laid her down on the sofa and buried her face in the warm, fat little stomach. She shed a few tears, induced by bone-tiredness and the panic demon, arbiter of her unfinished work, that slept under her pillow and thrust its wicked, chittering face into hers first thing every morning.

'I do love you, you know I do,' she said passionately, 'but I can't understand why you have to go on like this when the doctor says there's absolutely nothing wrong with you.'

Moriarty waved her fists and looked evasive. Bubbling noises were heard and the look turned to satisfaction. Miranda sighed, averted her nose and prepared to change her yet again. It was one of life's less exciting mysteries that so much more seemed to come out of babies than ever went in. She supposed the colour was interesting, once you got past the smell. It would go well with copper, magenta and

— 128 —

a strong, clear blue, somewhere between cobalt and teal. She might use such a combination for the fantasy part of her project; the clothes she would make for pure pleasure, to be looked at, not worn – an exuberant exhibition of wit, imagination and exotic materials – more art than fashion, and more theatre than either of those. That was if she could ever get back to being *capable* of exuberance or imagination or wit, or to any damn state where she was not deprived of sleep and forcibly subject to unending hideous noise, like some mad captive who could no longer tell you her name.

Changed and full of her four-hourly feed, Moriarty held a brief consultation with her hands and feet, patted Miranda sweetly on the cheek and fell into an instant deep sleep. This was a thing she did only in the daytime, apparently as a matter of principle. Miranda sighed with relief and awarded herself a few precious minutes to drink two cups of strong coffee and eat a small slice of brown toast with orange and ginger marmalade; she loved anything tasting of ginger. She carried them to the window seat and made them last, looking out with damp and shaky gratitude at her own private version of Carpaccio's Venice – the eastern river prospect of the mauled and miscellaneous city of London.

'Earth hath not anything to show more fair'? Well, dear old William's much-loved wordsworth was still true for her. But you could no longer rely upon unassisted eyesight; nowadays you had to look at London with a forgiving heart to find it fair. On the surface it was just another of the world's great overcrowded cities where tall, thin, angular buildings swaggered brutally towards a river in the various gangsters' hats that enabled you to tell them apart, shouldering out or gunning down the small, exquisite members of older, finer cultures. There was still a lot of sky in the picture, of course. That, happily, remained the same, give or take a few greenhouse effects. Miranda, who gazed at her part of the scene religiously, every morning and evening, treating it as a mantra to protect her sanity, had come to see it as a series of upright, archaeological stage sets, layered one over the other like the painted gauze flats in a classical ballet, leading deeper and deeper into history. Lift away today and you had Victorian London and the hellish hulks riding the river with the tea clippers and the Queen's Navee. Peel back further, and the sedate Georgian mansion – now belonging to a wine-merchant and half hidden by his warehouse – was the only building on this side of the river, its green gardens stepping formally down to its quay. Back further still, and you could worm through a hectic jigsaw of brick and beam and plaster to watch the skimming water boatmen of Tudor times; heraldic barges roaring down to Greenwich, busy lighters running out to the gaudy, flaunting galleons, facing seaward, straining at anchor on the changeable wave. Did the water, then, stand up in slabs of grey and flint – or did it catch the flash of oars in a mirror of living crystal? Had it, perhaps, even been blue?

'I love my magic window,' Miranda told the sleeping child. 'I don't want to leave it, ever; not permanently. It draws me. And I draw it. That's a pun, my darling. Not a very clever one. Grandfather Alain likes them, and so did Shakespeare. Do you know, I was born in this room, though I can't remember it because we moved soon after that. Chloe didn't make the hospital either; I was in a tearing hurry to get at the world, just like you.'

Moriarty made a non-committal snuffling sound. Miranda hung over her in a haze of redoubled love. 'I'm going to do some work, now,' she said. Before she did, she sang to her, very quietly, the first verse of You Are My Sunshine, just in case she might, earlier, have given her the wrong idea. Most of their mornings began much like this.

That evening, after three more feeds, a lot of sleep and an enchanting episode when she stared waveringly into

Miranda's eyes for a full two minutes, Moriarty was ready to exercise her lungs again. Miranda, who had worked hard and had not bothered with lunch, realised simultaneously that she was starving and that it was nearly nine and Adam had not come home. Furious, as Moriarty reached her higher register, she swept the finished garments off the sewing table and threw them across the room. There was no satisfaction whatever in this as they weighed only about half a kilo between them. Picking them up, she heard a soft knock at the outer door. Adam. Bloody man! Not only was he more than two hours late and *anything* could have happened to him – he had forgotten his imbecile key as well. Flinging the clothes back on the table, she stamped to the door and shouted at it.

'Why can't you put it with your other keys like a normal person? What the hell do you mean by turning up at this time?' She thought she heard him laugh. Bastard.

'Well, I did mean to come in and be sociable – but if you feel like *that* about it—'

'Oh lord.' She opened the door and looked sheepishly at Luke.

'I'm so sorry. I thought—'

'Miranda,' he beamed, kissing her cheek. 'It's lovely to see you again.

'Yes, it's – oh, I'm so glad – Adam should be here at any minute.'

'Don't worry about him,' he said, escorting her back into the room as though it were his rather than hers. 'He has never been much good at time-keeping. He goes off on a trail and forgets everything but the scent.'

'I know. But things are different now. Or ought to be.'

'How is she?' Luke went over to the cot, shedding his jacket on a chair.

'As you hear.'

'May I?' He took Moriarty out of her blankets and cradled her in his arms. She stopped crying and opened her eyes very wide. He offered her his thumb and she closed a starfish hand around it, grunting with concentration, her mouth pursing and pouting like a peony opening and closing on fast-forward film.

'I'll hang on to her for a while, shall I?' He made the two of them comfortable in an armchair. 'It's wonderful, how hard they can grip,' he said tenderly. 'She really is a beauty, Miranda. Where do the blue eyes come from?'

'Chloe's mother, like Rufus 'n' Tilda's. She has Joel's skull, though. His hair, too, if it stays as dark as that.' Odd, how easy it was to mention Joel. There was nothing judgemental about Luke.

Would his child have had such eyes? he wondered, stricken. His own were a similar dark-ringed, noticeable blue. He felt sick with sorrow.

'And she has your skin, like a pale magnolia. It's a striking combination!'

Keep on talking, Miranda thought. It had been centuries since she had received anything resembling a male compliment. 'If only she'd give up the Wagner, she'd be absolutely perfect,' she said.

'When Adam used to scream,' he remembered, 'Helen would put him next to the stereo and turn up the volume until she couldn't hear him; symphonies, piano concertos, jazz, anything. It seemed cruel to me, but eventually he stopped competing.'

'How could she tell?' They both laughed. 'I wonder – does he love music so much because of that treatment, or in spite of it? I might even be driven to try it myself. I'm going out of my mind.'

'Can't have that. Look in my jacket pocket; you'll find a temporary cure.'

She extracted a bottle of Shiraz. He had intended to drink it with Chloe who liked its blackberry richness. He had found her already entertaining the fellow who sold her paintings. She had introduced Luke briefly, but had made it quite clear that she did not want him to stay. Out in the hallway she told him angrily that he was never to call on her again without her permission. It had depressed him. For once, he knew what it was like to be on the wrong side of a thorough dressing-down. Poor Chloe. What a state she was in; and why on earth wouldn't she let him help her?

Miranda brought him the wine in one of the enormous glasses he and Dinah had given them when Adam had moved in next door. He sipped it, then set it down, careful not to disturb the baby. Miranda treated hers like a very small espresso and gave herself a refill, looking vaguely surprised to find Luke's glass still full. She was halfway down again when she remembered that she still had not eaten anything.

'I'm ravenous,' she announced. 'I'm not waiting for Adam. How about some pasta with prawns and things?'

'Not for me. You go ahead.'

'Shall I?' Her body sagged. 'No. Maybe I'll wait, after all.'

'My dear child, you're simply tired to death,' Luke realised. He stood up and carried Moriarty to the cot, easing her down as though she were dynamite. Motionless, deeply asleep, she snored benignly. Luke went into the kitchen and made swift preparations for prawns and asparagus with five-minute linguini. He found some lemongrass and remembered to put in plenty of ginger.

'I didn't know you could cook,' Miranda called.

'As long as it's quick. I did quite a lot of it when Dinah went on strike.' In ten minutes he was back with two aromatic bowls.

'Mmm, this is marvellous,' Miranda said, by no means between mouthfuls.

'Good. There's more. It won't keep.' She was looking too thin.

When they had finished his eye wandered to the walls; there was always something new to look at. 'I see you've finished the pastel series.' He went over to examine them properly.

The last sketch in Miranda's personal advent calendar faced him squarely between the straddled knees of a straining, sweating naked woman whose face was unrecognisable in the rictus of the extreme effort of labour.

'So that is what it is like,' Luke said respectfully. 'I don't think I've ever been so near to feeling it from the inside. Foolish as it sounds.'

'Thanks. On balance, I think it's worse after they're born.'

He looked at her sharply. 'Do you always feel like that?'

'You mean is it postnatal depression?' She smiled sourly. 'No, no such excuse – just – oh, let's not think about it!' She topped up their glasses and glared accusingly at the empty bottle before asking him casually, 'Did you see Mum before you came here?'

Luke knew it was not a careless question. He must tread very lightly. 'She has a visitor. The gallery owner.'

'Josh Reinhart. She's been out with him all day. He's supposed to be trying to "talk her down" – kind of ground her in her painting again. As if she were a cat up a tree.'

'Will it work?'

'No. She has to come down by herself, when she finds her confidence.'

'I think you're right.'

The light had gone out of his face. He looked sad. She could not help feeling sorry for him. 'Luke, do you still feel the same about her?'

'That is not a fair question,' he said quietly.

'Isn't it? I think it is. It does affect me, you must know that.'

'All right.' He sat beside her, offering a courteous, wary attentiveness. 'Tell me how.'

Unnerved by this simplicity, she let words tumble about her like alphabet bricks. 'I suppose it's – I haven't got over finding you like that. I'm sorry, I think I must be a bit drunk or I wouldn't be saying this.'

'It doesn't matter.' He waited.

'You see, when I found you and Chloe on that bed, in that very private place, a great deal of what I felt must have been pure jealousy. You looked so complete, so absolutely right together; that was the most upsetting part of it.' She did not want to go on. 'Because, by that time, I knew that was something that couldn't be said about Joel and me.'

'I'm sorry. Sorry that we did that to you.'

'It doesn't matter now, because of Adam. I don't even know why I needed to tell you – perhaps because I couldn't tell Mum. I'm sorry too.'

'No reason to be. It helps to understand yourself.'

'I don't.' She gasped and caught her breath. 'I'm all over the place, just now. I don't feel like me at all.'

Luke put both both arms around her and held her securely, as he did with Belle during her rare bouts of unhappiness. 'Sweetheart, things are not as bad as they seem. But it is obvious that you need a long period of rest. I'll talk to Adam, shall I, and Chloe?'

She shook her head forcefully. 'Please don't. It was just an extra bad day. Usually, Mum takes Moriarty for the afternoon. And Adam – where *is* Adam, anyway? He's got to be back by now, or he would have phoned.' Her voice was ragged. 'I'll just bet he's at Chloe's. Josh Reinhart will have left by now.' She rejected tears. 'It's what he does. He slopes off there for what he calls "a bit of peace and some lucid conversation".'

'I'm sure you're wrong.' Out of his depth, Luke patted her back.

'Am I?' she asked grimly. 'We'll see.' She shot up and was out of the room before he could catch her intention.

Chloe, exhausted by the pressures of imitating her normal public self for the well-intentioned Josh, had gone to bed early and was floating near the shore of sleep. She was not pleased to be dragged on to the shoal by the panic assault on her door that had become quite frequent, despite her protests.

'What is it?' she called from her bed.

'Is Adam there?'

'No, why should he be? For heaven's sake, Miranda!'

'Are you sure?'

'Are you mad?'

'Well, he's not home.'

'Go away. I will not have this. I'll speak to you in the morning.'

'He's not there,' Miranda reported despondently. 'He could be anywhere, couldn't he? Anywhere he bloody well pleases. He has all the freedom in the world.'

'Which you no longer have?' Luke said gently.

'You're not kidding. I may as well be in jail.' She wandered into the kitchen and came back with the bottle of ginger wine Adam had bought her.

'Have some? Can't find anything else.'

'No, thanks. But I'd like some coffee.'

'You mean you think I've had enough.'

'Yes. But I really would like coffee.'

'Oh Luke—' She suddenly seemed to melt all over him. 'It's all going wrong,' she moaned into his chest. He rubbed her back. He wondered if Chloe had any idea how run down she was. It was unlike her to be so careless of one of her children's welfare. She had, after all, put her life on hold for them. And his. Not that she would ever see it that way.

'Miranda, listen to me.' He employed the voice that could persuade streetwise schoolchildren to believe in exams, themselves and a future that could be more pleasant than not. 'I think you are getting things all mixed up in your mind. Moriarty and the problems specific to her are one thing – what happens between you and Adam is quite another.'

'No. It's all the same,' she said wetly. 'It has to be, unless we are both consecrated saints. Adam doesn't do nearly enough for Moriarty and I can't help resenting that. It gets in the way. And sex has taken to the road with its red-spotted hanky, so what's the point of it all?'

'Love?'

'Dunno. Doesn't feel like it any more. I know I look godawful, so you can't blame him if he's given up on it.'

Luke tucked a finger under her chin and surveyed her tear-streaked face. 'You look like an unusually lovely girl who is angry because she can no longer control her life. Anger wears you out, Miranda. Even more than howling infants. We never have complete control; I think you ought to accept that.'

'Luke – you are so—' Without any conscious intention she kissed him. Astonished by the softness of his skin, no different from Adam's, she sailed away on a merry little wave of sexual desire, the first she had felt since the birth.

Luke waited until she realised that he was not taking part in her excursion, then patted her shoulder and moved apart from her.

'That was as nice and as daft as you are,' he said mildly.

'Oh lord. I'm sorry. I shouldn't have.'

'No.'

'You smell just like Adam. Oh, what the hell! I won't pretend I didn't enjoy it. It was an impulse of pure gratitude, because you are being so nice to me. The pleasure was an extra.' She grinned wickedly.

'Thank you. I enjoyed it too. But we are not going to repeat it.'

'No, of course not.' She looked suitably chastened and bowed her head. Raising it, she caught his eye and they both laughed, relieved to find that, by the alchemy of common sense, the episode had made them better friends.

'Why don't I make that coffee?' Luke suggested. Passing the phone, he asked if he might call Dinah. Although they kept separate hours, they were always courteous about it. Instead of using the instrument he passed it to Miranda.

'What? Oh no! I didn't. O god – I remember now. I switched it off when Moriarty first went to sleep. I could have sworn I put it on again. Poor Adam; he could have been trying all night.'

It was after midnight when he tried again. Luke had left an hour ago.

'For Christ's sake, Miranda. I thought something serious had happened.'

'I'm so terribly sorry. I can't seem to remember things any more.'

'Never mind. I couldn't get back. The press agency got a leak that Leo and Pansy were getting married tonight – ten o'clock at the drummer's place in Surrey. It was a terrific scoop; I had to go.'

'Of course you did,' she said humbly.

'Look, I'm pretty near Sheringham now, so I may as well sleep at home.'

'Fine. I'll see you tomorrow,' she said. She did not say, I thought this was supposed to be home.

Dinah had read of surveys claiming that men thought about sex every two minutes. If this were true, it went a long way towards explaining the unbalanced and lurching progress of the planet. On the other hand, you had the example of Philip, who could fly a plane with only a few hundred thousand brain cells on the controls.

Since knowing Philip, carnally and otherwise, Dinah was coming to believe that the real nature of things was that the more sex you had, the more of everything else you became capable of doing. Men had simply kept this hidden from women for as long as they could. Naturally, many women had worked it out for themselves, a bold sequence of sexually intelligent housewives flaunting their pheromones along with Sappho, Messalina and Catherine the Great;

women with enough power to their elbows, bosoms and brains to allow them to choose how often, with whom and in which position they employed them. And now Dinah had joined this happy band of sisters under the sheets. In giving herself to Philip, she had also discovered new needs and appetites of her own, not all of them sexual. This gave her a confidence in life that she had not felt since she first stood up and walked. Her days were fast and dazzling and her humour was permanently mischievous and good. Never a selfish woman, even in this pleasant extremity, she was anxiously conscious that Luke had no part in any of it. Surely, that was something she could change?

'I'm going for a swim,' she told him one night, bringing black coffee to him in his study. She bent to read a title on the pile of folders beside him on the desk. 'War Novels from *War and Peace* to *Birdsong*.' She turned and firmly sat down on them. 'Great books. Come with me?'

'It's nearly midnight.'

'Exactly.' Her lopsided grin invited him. 'We'll have the whole place to ourselves.' She dangled the keys to the pool in front of him.

'Oh, why not?' He threw up his hands. It was little enough to do to please her, and the thought of the water was balm to a mind bemused by Cosmo Leigh's preference for describing the film rather than the novel. His disquisition ran from Abel Gance to Francis Ford Coppola, with a friendly nod to ITV's Napoleonic saga, *Sharpe*. As it happened, Luke himself was addicted to *Sharpe*, identifying enthusiastically with the gallant, proletarian officer who used his sword and his wits with electric effectiveness by day and unbuckled lustily at night to a succession of bodices ready-ripped by their wearers. Richard Sharpe was played by the lean, soft-spoken actor Sean Bean, whose nervous system reverberated like a well-turned guitar. Belle, at twelve, had written to him, asking for an assignation and sensibly enclosing a photograph of Miranda. She had received a courteous reply, explaining that Mr Bean was happily married. Belle had gone about big-eyed for a while, and had then sent a copy of her invitation to Ralph Fiennes, who was not. His memory thus leaking pleasantly, Luke gave Dinah his hand and they went out into an airless summery night that closed around them like a premonition of the pool, heavy with the pungency of earth and leaves after rain.

They walked through the quiet grounds, cutting across lawns that glistened in swathes of light from sleepless windows and turned black as they were extinguished. The swimming pool was set back among trees near one of the five small lakes on the Sheringham estate. Its humped bulk stood strangely against the moon, but the sense of it hit you as soon as you entered; for you found yourself under the vast, upturned hull of a boat, designed by its local architect, Mike Barnes, to resemble a church he had seen on the island of Orkney. When asked how a swimming-pool related to a church, he replied with limpid simplicity that he liked the shape and that water had as much to do with boats as fishermen had to do with Christ. However eclectic his inspiration, he had produced a building that was dearly loved and in use for twelve hours of every day.

Dinah had brought candles. She set a dozen of them, short, fat and long-lasting, along the edge of the shallow end. She and Luke shed their clothes and slipped naked into the water, tensed for the first sensation of cold. They swam a quick, uncompetitive length to warm up, then floated together in the flickering glow.

'We used to come here so often in the early days,' Dinah said. 'In the old pool. Remember?'

'I do. It smelled of chlorine. This one hardly ever does. Clever.' This was not what she wanted him to remember. She swam up beside him and slid her hands between his legs. 'Remember?' she repeated.

He shuddered as her fingers played an old familiar tune. 'I do now.' After the fingers she used her mouth. She used it remarkably well.

'I don't remember this,' he said. 'I thought you disliked it.'

'Tastes change.' She smiled.

He laughed softly. 'Not that one, I think.'

'Well, it's all mixed up with the water.' She towed him towards the rail. 'Hold on,' she directed.

He obeyed and was subject to another, more invasive ministration; for a moment only, then she was gone, her laughter echoing back to him.

'You little bitch,' he cried, lashing the water. 'Wait till I catch you.' Dinah, a fast and stylish swimmer, had nearly completed a length when he drew level. He captured her in a life-guard's hold and brought her back to where they could stand. 'Where do you want it?' he enquired silkily. 'Up against the wall?'

They found the right depth and she stretched her arms along the rail; she had a mental flash of Philip, tying her hands. Then she could see nothing, think of nothing; only feel, only Luke. There *was* only Luke, wasn't there? He had been her life for so many years. That must still be true. Smiling, she opened her legs, convinced she was opening her heart.

Luke, pumping hydraulically and hugely enjoying it, was visited by the stray thought that a water scene would fit well with the more ebullient side of Sharpe. It wasn't that his mind was not on what he was doing; it was that it wasn't required to be.

When they had finished they floated again, resting and recovering; the end of the episode had been explosive. In *Sharpe* they would have accompanied it with all twenty-one guns of the *1812 Overture*.

'Luke! Why are you howling like a mad hyena?'

'Pure relief,' he claimed. It might almost be true, since they had barely slept together for months.

They swam lazily for a while before pulling themselves heavily out of the pool.

'O Lord – towels,' Luke said.

'It's all right. There's an emergency supply.'

'We *could* just skin-flit across the grass.'

'Not in my lifetime.'

The lightness that had buoyed them up with the water departed from both of them as they dried and dressed. They did not speak after they had left the building, but walked home occupied with their thoughts, keeping a little apart as they navigated through the dark.

Water; he wished it had not been water. Luke thought of Chloe and the recurring dream she had. She had told him it had prefigured his coming into her life. It had been about him, or about her need for him, before they had even met. She had never been able to recall his face when she awoke, but she knew they had made love fathoms beneath the sea, beneath consciousness, resting in green weed, open to wonder. It had been a union in which they had reached a perfect knowledge of each other. The sex had been a metaphor for the knowledge.

He felt leaden and troubled as he re-entered the house. It surprised him; it was a long time since he had suffered from post-coital *tristesse*. Behind him, Dinah lingered in the garden, afflicted by a similar mood of unexpected seriousness. She had meant to do something that would bring Luke closer to her. She knew that she had not got it quite right; there had been something too hectic, even almost false, about her abandoned gaiety. And what she was feeling now seemed very much like guilt. It was very odd. *Could* one feel guilty for making love to one's husband? She would like to ask Philip what he thought about that. Perhaps she would, if she could find the right way to pose the question.

'Come up to Jebb's Field for a bit?' Oliver asked Lisa. It was lunch-time. They had already eaten in the school dining-hall and had another forty-five minutes before their afternoon classes. Jebb's Field was an area of grass and trees up behind the school buildings, at the foot of the downs. Its main attraction was that it was out of bounds to all students bar the sixth form. It was especially popular on a summery day like today.

'I can't. I have to see your father. You go. I'll come up later if there's time.'

'Why didn't you say? I wondered why you were so quiet at lunch. I thought I must have said something to upset you.'

'Sorry. I didn't know I was. I'm fine, honestly. He just wants a progress report. He's kind of, keeping an eye on me. Look, I'd better go now, or I'll be late. See you after school if it takes too long.'

'OK – and listen, try to think of him as a human being, will you? And the rest of my family.'

Lisa nodded and hurried away. She knew why Olly had said that. It was because although they saw each other nearly every day and he visited her at home or the restaurant as a matter of course, she had so far avoided the Cavendish house. She knew she would have to conquer her reluctance if their friendship were to follow its natural course, but she and Olly were not exactly going out together, not yet, so she could allow herself some leeway. She instinctively drew back from the opportunity for suffering that was implicit in the prospect of watching Luke in the bosom of his famously happy family. Her greatest fear was that she would be newly overwhelmed by the horrible, inescapable lust and humiliation that had been her foremost experience of being in love. It was bad enough to feel that way in front of Luke, as she was forced to do by the time-table, but she could not bear to go through the loss of self and dignity in front of Oliver, even if he were unaware of it. And then there was Mrs Cavendish, who was kind and concerned and had wanted to help her, whose sunny good nature was a constant reprimand for the facts that Lisa could not explain to her in her role as the school's psychological counsellor. No, she simply could not handle any of that. The next half-hour might be bad, but it was better than having to pretend. At least she would see Luke alone, and would be able to gauge the strength of her feelings without distractions. What she was trying to do was to feel a little less for him at each meeting. She knew this was ridiculous, but she also knew that she *wanted* to stop loving him, and considered this to be a healthy and positive desire. She was not sure, with the monolith of Luke still set before her, whether or not she had begun to want to love Oliver.

When she entered his room, Luke was shying the last and worst critique of the war novel from his desk to an unkempt pile on the sofa he kept for interviewees of a nervous disposition. Lisa let it sail past her, then sat down beside it, as signalled, and began automatically to tidy the pile.

'Don't bother. I shall probably chuck them at the lot of you. Not yours.' He smiled at her. 'It was one of the three passable ones.'

'Three out of fifteen. Not good,' she said. His standards were very high.

'Not good *enough*, anyway. Now stop fiddling with them and tell me how things are with you.'

She studied her hands. 'Well, I suppose they are getting better.' This was self-evident. She no longer immured herself in a darkened room, or wept until she was too tired to weep any more.

'Why is that, do you think?' he asked gently.

'I don't know, exactly.' She looked at him. He burned less brightly today. Nothing she could pin down, just a diminution of his psychic, even his sexual energy. She hoped nothing was wrong. She said 'I expect it happens naturally – a kind of biological cycle. After everything has been as bad as it can be—' she shrugged.

'The only way is up?'

'I suppose it must be.'

'You know, you sound as though you almost regret that.'

'Perhaps I do, in a way.'

'You prefer to remain unhappy?'

She wished his voice were not so kind, that his conversation did not always seem much more *intimate* than anyone else's. It was an unfair trick; but, of course, it was not a trick – he couldn't help it, any more than she could help wanting him so much. She had said it was getting better, and it was true up to a point, but she had also said it because it was what he wanted to hear. Men did not like women to weigh on their consciences. She knew he felt badly about her because he was responsible for her, even if he was not responsible for her inconvenient passion.

'I don't want to be unhappy. But I think it was better than feeling – well, in a sort of limbo. I mean – I know I have to get over you. I can't have you. It wouldn't be right that I should. I can see that now. I couldn't at first. I think that's why I – did what I did. I think I was trying to blackmail you in some way. I don't know what I thought it would make you do. I was too mad to know. Mad equals insane, in love; not mad equals angry.'

'You seem remarkably sane now,' Luke said. 'I think, if you can view it all with such clarity, you are probably very nearly cured.'

'Cured?'

'Of the demon love.'

'Do *you* think of it as a demon?'

'It can be. If one is made to suffer, and has to do so alone. You told me when you came out of hospital that the worst thing about it was the feeling of loneliness. Do you still feel like that?'

'Sometimes. Not so much.'

'You sound surprised.'

'Well – I'm back at school. There's a lot of work. I have good friends.'

'Including Oliver,' he said, as though it were anyone's son.

'Yes.' Her cheeks flamed.

'I'm glad he's becoming more sociable,' he said without pressure. 'He has been a bit of a loner himself. The animals and all that.'

'I know. But it was his choice. Everyone likes Olly.'

It was obvious to Luke that she did not wish to discuss what she felt about Oliver. It was therefore out of the question to ask her not to tell the boy about her feelings for his father. In fact, he thought it very unlikely that she would; she must be the first to understand how cruel it would be.

'There is one thing I want you to know,' Lisa said, her expression unreadable. 'What I have felt, and learned, because of you, have been the best things that have happened to me, as well as the worst. Does that make sense?'

'Perfectly,' Luke said.

'So, it's not altogether a bad demon?'

'I probably should not have introduced the demon. Too much of a romantic notion. I'm often told that teaching literature is like spreading a disease; so much of it is essentially a history of the idea of romance. The more we analyse it, the closer we come to it, the more we become subject to it. All that drawn-out desire, all that exquisite pain. How can we possibly immerse ourselves so deeply and fail to be affected? I was in love with Emma Bovary when I was fifteen. I have watched dozens of girls fall in love with Heathcliff or Julien Sorel, and legions with Lord Byron.'

'At least Byron was real,' Lisa said shortly. 'I don't know if your contagion theory is true. One has to learn about loving somehow, and it's quicker by literature than by life. Anyway, it says as much about you as it does about me. You *chose* literature, were drawn towards it. You might have chosen physics. And I might still have felt the same. We can't know. But you are real to me; not some romantic anti-hero.'

In the end, he let her win because she seemed so much more cheerful, and because he hoped she was right, that she did have the sense to tell the difference between the fiction we write and the fictions we live. There probably *was* no difference; by now, he would be the last person to see it if there were. It was simply a useful idea to offer to girls – rarely boys – in Lisa's situation.

'I'm going now,' she said. 'I have to meet someone. When shall I come back?'

'Whenever you like,' he said. 'Next time, we'll talk about Oxford.' She was pleased with that. She was no longer to be given close appointments, like a patient of doubtful stability. It seemed her progress was speedier than she thought. It occurred to her that, if she could soon provide sufficient evidence of having got over him, she might manage to keep him as a friend. That would be a great deal better than nothing. 'Love is a wound within the body that has no outward sign.' She had sent him those words he had taught her, by the poet Marie de France, just before she had decided to die. They had been – and were still – a perfect mirror for her emotions; but she was beginning to feel that the wound might one day bleed a little less.

Chapter 8

'IT'S OPEN!' MIRANDA SHOUTED FROM THE BEDROOM, referring to the outer door. It was ten o'clock on a Wednesday morning, and the health visitor had said she might call. She checked the rhythmically heaving mound that was Moriarty in the cot, and went through to the studio.

Joel was standing in front of the pastels.

Her heart constricted. She felt cold. 'What the hell are you doing here?'

'These are very good. You have really found your confidence. I came to see how you are.' His smile attacked her, sensual, insolent and very white.

'I'm fine. Now you can get out.'

What shocked her more than his presence was the instant familiarity of him; the shape he made in space, the sweep of his hair, his lightness, the way he seemed to weigh on the air rather than his feet. Always an elegy in black, he had changed his Harley leathers for well-cut linen; everything else was the same.

'Ah now, don't be unpleasant. You spoil yourself.' He touched her morning kaftan. 'That's nice. Regal. Statu-esque. You printed it yourself?'

'Christ, Joel! Will you just go?'

'I don't think so. I was rather hoping to see my daughter before I leave.'

'You *what*?'

'Motherhood doesn't make you deaf. I just got to thinking about you both, and I wondered how you were doing.'

'It is absolutely not your business.'

'Oh, but it is.' He came close and there was a great lurch inside her like a ship going aground. 'After all,' he said, laying a long-fingered hand upon her stomach, 'I put her in there. What's her name, again?'

She hit his hand away. 'Moriarty,' she answered automatically. 'It wasn't supposed to stick, but it did.' She realised she ought to have said almost anything else, preferably something so explosive as to have blown him backwards, blaspheming, through the wall, exorcised, dismissed. She had not thought of anything because he was standing so near to her and his hand was full of heat and life.

He laughed. 'I'd heard that.'

'Who from?'

'It's not important. I'd like to see her, please. And after that, I'd really like us to fuck. I want to be inside there again, Miranda. I've missed you.' His voice was honey on his tongue, alchemically transmitted to hers. She scrabbled for a hold on reality.

She gasped, 'You must be out of your mind to come here like this. You asked me to have an abortion; why should you want to see the baby you didn't want to live? You haven't even spoken to me for months. You had no idea whether or not both of us had died during the birth. And now you cruise in from whatever mad planet you live on – and expect me to make love with you?'

'Why not? You always enjoyed it.'

She raged. 'You are unbelievable!'

'Yes, but don't you want me, just a little, just a lot?'

'No!'

'Liar,' he said amicably.

'I'm with Adam now.'

He ignored this. He pulled delicately at her kaftan. 'Won't you take this off? I would love to see how you look, now that you've had my child.'

That brought her fully to her senses. 'She's *my* child, Joel,' she said fiercely, pulling away from him. 'She is nothing to do with you.'

'I know that,' he said mildly, 'but I would like to see her. Just once.'

'Why?'

He shrugged. 'Curiosity, I guess. I'd like to know how our two sets of genes worked out together.'

'Well, your curiosity will just have to kill you.'

He frowned. 'Well, put it this way. I am not leaving until I have seen her. If you want me around when Adam gets back, that's OK with me.'

'I see,' she said contemptuously. 'Blackmail was always your pastime.'

The stubborn look left his face. 'Ah no,' he said quickly. 'I don't mean that. I'm sorry. I just – I – really want to see the baby, Miranda. I don't, not honestly, even know why.'

He was looking at her as if she would know. She hesitated. Joel had never displayed such a normal, human vulnerability to her. Certainly, he must have come here for the sake of Moriarty. He had hardly come for her own, when he had been content to let her go and to cause so much pain to her family. His sexual overtures were to tease her, to take her off her guard. They were a form of amusement.

'I don't know what I will feel, when I see her,' he said. 'But I want you to give me the chance to find out. I know I have no right,' he finished humbly. He held out his hand to her; as if he were blind, she thought. This was a Joel she did not recognise.

'I don't know.'

'It's probably the most natural thing I've ever wanted to do.'

'That's true.' Except for the loving, the sex as he insisted on calling it. She hovered. Her instincts, trashily lacking in reason, taste or common loyalty, trooped off, deserting to Joel. The truth revealed itself in obvious colours; she actually *wanted* him to see Moriarty. She frowned.

'Stay here.' No way was she letting him into the bedroom.

She came back with Moriarty and dumped her into his arms. 'There. Now ask her how she had the temerity to be born.'

Joel said nothing. He adjusted his hold until the baby's head rested comfortably against his arm, rocking lightly on his heels as she showed signs of waking. He watched the minute, effortful changes in her face, the tiny muscles relaxing and contracting; he smiled when she put her index finger in her mouth, opening and closing her lips around it in her imitation of a sea anemone.

'I thought it was always their thumb they sucked,' he whispered.

'She's an individualist. You don't have to whisper. She won't wake now. She was roaring half the night.'

He was still smiling, his eyes on the busy little face. 'You sound as if you think that could be my fault.'

'Heredity has a lot to account for,' she said gloomily.

'Well, I think it can be proud of itself,' he declared. 'She's a beautiful little creature, Miranda. I can't quite believe she's real.' He was not joking; she could hear that.

'So you don't want to take her to the nearest abbatoir?' she asked nastily.

'Be quiet. That can serve no possible purpose now. It's too mean and small to qualify as any kind of revenge.'

'It certainly is,' she said bitterly.

'Is that what you want, revenge?' He spoke almost vaguely. His gaze was fast on the sleeping child, his face wiped clear of irony or mischief or the blank withdrawal of self that were the things in him you would try to paint.

Moriarty stirred, making small, cheery noises. Her hands curled into fists like ferns and belaboured space until they found Joel's chest. He laughed and she opened her eyes. 'Hello,' he breathed, looking back at her with his own identically shaped pair, black into black-rimmed blue. Oh my God, Miranda thought.

Moriarty squealed and grabbed the end of his nose. He took her hand and guided the fingers over his face. He closed his lips on two of them. The child was now fully awake and completely happy. A mere spectator, Miranda wanted to lay her head down upon the table and beat it against the wood until she was senseless. She was observing something neither she nor, she imagined, anyone else had ever seen; she was watching Joel fall in love. Just for the moment, the very painful moment, she found it unbearable.

'Excuse me,' she said. She left them together.

In the bedroom she took in great gulps of air and tried to slow the racing of pulses and juices, to turn herself into a stone woman and a good mother; someone who could not undignify herself by tearing back into that room and howling, 'You never looked at me like that.'

She left them alone for nearly half an hour before he came looking for her. By this time she had laid the shredded pieces of her pride together and applied tacking stitches.

'Are you OK?' he asked. Moriarty was asleep again in the crook of his arm.

'Perfectly.'

'Right. I'm going now, but I'd like to come back. Quite soon.'

'I'm not sure that's such a good idea,' she temporised. 'There is Adam to consider.'

'She isn't Adam's; she's mine,' he said determinedly.

She looked at the two of them together and the sheer unlikelihood of it undermined her will to argue. She could not blame him. He had seen something he had got to have. She had felt like that when she had first seen him.

'You don't have to tell him I was here,' Joel said.

'But I do,' she returned.

In the event, however, she did not tell him. She had intended to; she had even rehearsed the words she would use. But when she attempted to speak them, she could not get them out. He would be angry, he would be hurt, and she did not want to deal with that now.

Adam was pleasantly surprised to find her in an unusually soft and solicitous mood. Recently accustomed to coming home to a termagant, he whole-heartedly blessed the change and hoped, with fingers crossed, that her hormones might have stopped behaving like enemy aliens.

On Friday morning, Miranda tidied the flat, put clean clothes on herself and Moriarty, took a list of art supplies and Italian foods to Chloe, who was going up to Soho, and settled down to the Botticelli-based fabric designs she was considering for her fantasy costumes. She worked with deep concentration, veiling faces behind translucent flowers and insubstantial gauzes, washing shade on shade in *Primavera* colours. At eleven she took a coffee break and gave Moriarty an affectionate rendering of 'My Girl', telling herself that the grunts and squeals that greeted it were a precocious attempt at song. Back at the sketchboard, she worked up the best of her designs and carried out a mental review of the shapes that might flatter them. She kept her mind on a very short leash, as she had done for the past two days, determined not to let it roam off on its own.

When Joel reappeared at half past eleven, she felt trapped and helpless, then swiftly relieved. He had said he would come. This time she would make it absolutely clear that there must be no more such visits. It would be over and she would never have to think about him again.

He lounged in the doorway, smiling as if he were scanning a fax of these thoughts as they came. He held a bunch of blue and white flowers in one hand and a realistic toy panther under his arm.

'She's too young for that,' she said foolishly, nodding curt acceptance of iris and gypsophila.

'Not for long. What ought I to bring?'

'Nothing. There's no need.'

'I want to!'

She waved a dismissive hand. 'I have to talk to you.'

'Me too. Will you fetch her? I can hold her while we talk.'

She knew she should refuse but it seemed too pettily ungracious. 'Try not to wake her. She needs to sleep for another hour or so.'

'Right.' He settled the baby next to him in a corner of the sofa. Miranda went to the window and stood looking out, though she had no confidence that its magic could help her now.

'She seems to be so – finished,' Joel marvelled. 'She's right there already, in every detail. I guess I expected her to be – well, more like a lump of plasticine.' He paused. 'Do you think she looks like me?'

Damn you, Miranda thought. She scraped her nail down the protesting pane.

'A bit,' she said. It was far more than that; there was the black hair that was going to remain; there was the shape of her skull and her eyes, and now, more noticeably, the meaningless co-ordination of facial muscles that was suddenly recognisable as Joel's. She thought of Adam's short story and the hopeful act of love he had intended it to be. She wished passionately that things might have been different.

Joel said, 'Yeah, I reckon she's mine all right.' He had been completely unprepared for the pang of love and the primitive desire to protect that had overwhelmed him at first sight of the tiny animal he had unwittingly caused to exist. Such emotions – indeed, all emotions – were difficult to assimilate as any part of himself. Miranda had been right to visualise him as simply seeing something that belonged to him and being determined to keep it against the odds; it was the way he preferred to see himself. It was a simple and positive attitude that avoided the murky complexity of the psychological swamp in which others, especially women, chose to live.

'I've thought about her a lot,' he said. 'You too.'

'Don't bother.'

His eyes were on her hair, which he liked to look at and to touch.

'No bother,' he said. Very gently he took Moriarty's finger out of her mouth and gave her his own. 'I don't want to go over the past,' he told Miranda. 'Things are different now. I've decided to help. Both of you. Financially, and in whatever other ways we can work out. For as long as she needs it.'

'Joel, I don't want anything from you.'

'It's for Moriarty.'

'No.'

'You're being unreasonable.' He got up and stretched. 'Look, why don't we take her out for some fresh air, and see if we can get a little of it into our heads?'

'I am *not* going to play mamas and papas with you.'

'Don't be so bloody tight-arsed,' he retorted. 'What's the matter, haven't you had any good sex since she was born?'

'Do you have to be so pathetic?'

'I thought not,' he said delightedly. His voice dropped to a caress. 'Come here. Now, don't start crying. The moon's in June and everything is going to be the way you want it.' He folded himself round her with the sexual tenderness that always felt like something more, and for a second or two she allowed herself to rest in it. A second further and she realised she ought to have known better.

She broke away. 'Stop that. I don't want it. I don't

want you. And Moriarty doesn't want your beastly drug money.'

'I don't do drugs,' he said sharply. 'Ask the police. I sold a couple of paintings to Yamamoto, and I'm going to make and install a water-garden, with sculptures – for his penthouse roof. He's paying me three thousand.'

'Really?' she said. 'But that's wonderful.' Pleasure routed anger. 'I'm happy for you, Joel. You deserve it.'

'Thanks. My exhibition is fixed for the end of July. I hope you will come to the opening?'

She recognised a need to retrench. 'I don't know.'

'Oh, come on. You can't be *that* tight-arsed.'

'Shit, Joel!'

'OK, OK.' He held up his hands, innocent of mischief. 'I'll be serious. I won't tease you. I won't even harass you sexually if you absolutely insist – if – *if* – you will let me visit my daughter occasionally.'

'What do you expect me to say? It was all finished. You didn't want her.'

'I know how you feel. I'm as surprised as you are. But it's simple enough; I'm her father and I want a part in her life.'

She sighed. 'It *sounds* simple, but it isn't.'

'It will be. Just try to relax about it.' He took her casually by the shoulders as if to give her a quick, social kiss. If she was honest, she more than half expected the thorough physical trouncing she got instead. Joel had always known how to rouse her to fever-pitch. It was like unravelling time to have him here like this, behaving in such fascinating opposition to everything she knew of him except the part of him that made her flare and glow like a tree of candles.

She gave in to weakness and let him kiss her and touch her and reduce her to tears. Then, having lost all confidence in her emotional integrity, she clutched at a straw and told him Chloe would be back at any moment and that he must leave.

'Tell her I don't bear her any grudges,' he grinned,

unforgivably. 'And I want you to talk to Adam. Make sure he knows I intend to help. He knows I have the right.'

'I can't believe you would do this,' Adam said furiously. 'Don't you possess a memory any more? What the hell were you thinking about?'

'I wasn't. He was just – *there*! I suppose I couldn't think quickly enough.'

'Just there? Why was that? A bit sudden, wasn't it? Did you ask him to come here, is that it?'

'Don't be ridiculous.'

'Well, you seem to have been pretty pleased to see him.'

'That's not fair, and you know it. How can I help it if he takes it into his head to see Moriarty? Maybe I shouldn't have – well, talked to him for so long; but it was such a shock, seeing him again. I was in no condition to think things out.'

'I seem to recall that was always the effect he had on you. Your reactions to Joel are strictly between your legs. So tell me – did you sleep with him?'

'No, I didn't!' Miranda shouted, her face scarlet. 'How can you say that?'

'Because, if you ever do, you know what to expect.'

'Oh, stop. Stop. You're behaving like some outraged Victorian husband. I've done nothing wrong. I talked to him, that's all. It's Moriarty he's interested in, not me.'

'You can hardly expect me to believe that. It was the existence of Moriarty that exposed him for the vicious little psychopath he is.'

This was getting them nowhere. Miranda carefully lowered her voice. 'I *do* have a memory, you know I do,' she said steadily. 'But Joel doesn't want to remember. He just puts a clean slate in front of him, erases what he doesn't like or can't bear. Like his mother's cowardice and his stepfather's belt. His childhood was completely without love. And now, he really does want some sort of relationship with Moriarty – but I don't know what to think about that.' She was appealing to him.

'Well, you damned well ought to. Is she going to thank you for giving her a father who deals in drugs and psychological blackmail? Someone you yourself consider to be emotionally damaged?'

'That isn't all he is,' she defended, angry again. 'There is his work.'

'His work! Give me a break. Surely you aren't going to tell me his great genius excuses him for becoming such a poisonous human being? Even Picasso's women didn't pull that one.'

'Don't be so childish. You have no need to be jealous, if that's what this is.'

'Is it? I don't know,' he said more calmly. 'Some of it, perhaps. But mostly, it's pure, reasonable anger and resentment. And just the smallest measure of fear that you really are as stupid as you seem, right now.' He paused, holding up a hand to stave off interruption as he struggled to make his conviction power his words.

'I do not want Joel Ranger anywhere near Moriarty. Do you understand?'

'Neither do I,' Miranda replied wearily. 'But he is her father. We can't change that.'

'Does that mean you won't prevent him from seeing her?'

She looked at him in desperation. 'I don't *know* what to do. I thought you would help – but all you can do is blame me.'

'Really? I wonder why.'

'Oh God, why can't you be sensible?'

'You mean why can't I change my opinions?'

'No. I don't. Only – you didn't see Joel with Moriarty. You don't know how different he is with her.'

'Regeneration by the power of love, is that it now? When will you learn?'

'You can't judge properly unless you see for yourself.

Why are you being so stubborn about this? I've never seen you this way. You are just as unlike yourself as Joel is.'

'Oh great! There's nothing to choose between us.' He threw her a look of disgust and swung towards the door. 'I can't see any point in going on with this. You obviously need time to sort out your priorities. It's important you do that now, before it's too late. And after this, I could do with some space, myself. I'm going to Sheringham for the weekend. Now. I'll see you on Monday night. I'll phone.'

'But Adam, can't we—'

'I'm sure it's the best thing.'

'Oh, then – go to hell!'

'Why this is hell, nor are we out of it,' he said savagely. Mephistopheles's gleeful, ironic revelation to Faust, a world view Miranda considered better suited to Joel's saturnine disposition than to Adam's, which until now had been characterised by kindness, calm and lack of complexity.

Belle was overjoyed to find Adam at home on Friday evening, and intrigued by the absence of Miranda. She could not believe her luck when Luke departed for a formal dinner and Dinah announced that she was going over to work on Philip Dacre's computer and would probably stay late. Olly, as usual, had simply melted away without anyone noticing. Belle turned herself into a listening ear and dispensed coffee and sympathy in an aura of '*In XS pour Elle*'.

Adam had not intended to discuss his problems with anyone, least of all Belle, but she said reasonably that he might as well tell her as go about radiating doom and despondency, in case he thought he wasn't. It took her some time to establish that there had been a serious quarrel, and longer to elicit its cause. As she displayed her genuine revulsion at the undiminished gall of Joel Ranger, she was simultaneously working out an emergency plan of campaign. Adam might never be driven farther apart from Miranda than he was at this juncture. Therefore, she had two nights and two days in which to seduce him. Tonight, she decided, would be best employed in the production of a deeply caring sister act. She would continue to draw him out, listen attentively and speak ever soft, gentle and low. They would talk only about him, and she would be diplomatic about Miranda. There must be no suggestion of sexuality between them. Not an eyelid would she bat.

'I can't tell you how sorry I am,' she said when she had coaxed out most of his anger and frustration. 'But I'm sure that once Miranda has thought it all out, she'll realise she can't allow Joel to have any place in your lives. You did the right thing to leave her alone.'

'I hope so, Belle. But suppose Joel comes back? Tonight, even?'

'Don't be so lurid. That's insecurity talking. Joel doesn't *know* you're away.'

'Miranda might call him.'

'If she did,' was the uncompromising reply, 'it would be the end between you, anyway. But I know she won't,' she asseverated with more honesty than was useful to her. 'She loves you far too much. You ought to know that by now. And besides, she wouldn't be such a fool.'

Adam grimaced. 'We'll see.'

On Saturday night, Luke and Dinah were going out to dinner with Mike Barnes, the swimming-pool architect, and his wife Maggie, who were old friends. Adam was invited, but refused on the grounds that he was going to watch Belle's afternoon rehearsal and was uncertain when it might end. This had been his own idea. Belle had shown him a depth of understanding last night and he felt grateful and closer to her.

The rehearsal was a considerable eye-opener. He had expected Belle to be good; he had seen her hold her own against his redoubtable mother in *The Importance of Being*

Earnest. But he had not expected a production entitled *The Soul of Dracula* to be so many-layered, and for all its Gothic and romantic excess, ultimately so serious. Like many a dramatist, Belle had sought to expose some of the cruelties and stupidities of moral and civilised society by pitting the free will of a human soul against a barbarous authority figure, in this case the wickedly unforgiving Old Testament God. Dracula had committed a single mortal sin, for which it was impossible he could do penance. He had shed, drop by drop, until his victim died, the blood of the man who had desired and murdered his wife. God's punishment for his honest lack of contrition was to condemn him to prey on the blood of others for eternity. The prose of the piece, most of it Belle's, was beautifully measured and sometimes lyrically poetic. Her sense of hubris and catastrophe was solidly Aristotelian, while her instinctive understanding of character and motivation owed nothing whatsoever to Bram Stoker and a very good dinner to Shakespeare, and of course Kinski. What stood out, for Adam, was the highly wrought interior world shared by Belle and the striking boy who played the harsh, barely sympathetic Count. Yet, according to the other players, they had never performed so well together before today. It had disturbed him, that tension.

'Just good luck,' said Belle when he kissed her in congratulation, 'that we happened to hit it at last while you were here.'

'It was wonderful. *You* were wonderful. Let's go out and celebrate. Or had you all planned something already?'

The rehearsal had been the second act of her seduction campaign. Act One – soften him up with sisterly sympathy and allay fear of sexual advances. Act Two – demonstrate just what it could be like if there *were* to be such advances. Act Three – all in good time.

'I'm sorry!' she said to Cosmo in the dressing-room, very loudly because it was not the first time.

'But you said you would! We did something really sensational today. And I booked a table, and everything.'

'Next week. I promise. If I can.'

'I don't know why I bother,' Cosmo said in disgust.

'Adam's my brother and he's got problems. Can't you be a bit unselfish, for a change?'

Guildford on a Saturday night in summer presented itself as one gargantuan street feast. Pubs, bistros and smart bars spilled their customers into cobbled streets and alleyways, where they sat at small tables, waving hands and glasses, or promenaded about, meeting and talking with friends in an atmosphere in close community with the Greek or Italian *passeggiata*. Music sprang out of doorways, mugged them and joined forces with the mugger next door. Dress was optional, but this year most people still opted for black, the women in tiny Lycra dresses lit by brilliant scarves or hairslides like tropical birds, men in jeans and T-shirts or linen suits with the jacket slung over a shoulder or the back of a chair. There was the quick, extra-fashionable flash of Day-glo orange, lime or lemon, wisely eschewed by anyone over twenty-five. Belle, whose only influence was her personal whim, was got up like Carmen in a black lace mantilla and a red dress like a coat of Chinese lacquer which ought to have been a flag of warning to Adam. It failed because, being male, he had forgotten when he had last seen it. The dress was velvet and rather warm where it clung, but it had low shoulders and was very flattering, and Belle enjoyed a private sense of the continuity of things.

They walked languidly up and down for a while, greeting acquaintances and examining window displays, then chose the smartest of the bars in which to drink one expensive cocktail, harried by unendurable music. As they pottered back up the High Street, admiring the descent of the sun at the top of its steep climb, Adam suddenly whisked them up a brick passage only a little broader than his shoulders. It led to a small restaurant where, it transpired, the staff were not only young and attractive but knowledgeable and dedicated, especially the chef. They brought dry, golden wine and seafood dishes like delicious paintings, mainly by Klee and Dufy, though Belle consumed, in happy isolation, a pudding designed for greedy gods by Georgia O'Keefe. Replete, she signalled a waitress. 'Do you have a single red rose I could beg?'

'Whatever for?' Adam asked innocently as the red flag dropped at last. Belle raised her eyes and crossed them, an accomplishment much envied at her primary school. 'Breathes there the man with soul so dead?'

'Why do Cavendishes always borrow other people's words when they want to exaggerate?' he complained. He regretted the lines from *Faust*; they were far too good for Joel Ranger and too unkind to Miranda.

'We were brought up that way. Almost my first memory is of Dad holding me up and saying he thought I was very like a camel.'

'He was right. Come on; we'd better find a desert for you to carry your enormous dinner across.'

'We camels carry only water. Anyway, it will be only a cultural desert. Hang on, here comes my rose.' She leaned over and placed it in his buttonhole. 'So, have you decided yet? Are you Don José or Escamillo?'

'From camel to Carmen is a stretch too far for my imagination.'

'You are playing for time.'

'All right, Belle. I remember the dress.'

'And what else?'

'The restaurant. La Grenouille.'

'Coward.'

He smiled and rose from the table. 'Let's go. We need a change of scene. And subject.'

'You must remember this,' Belle trilled sweetly as they went down the lane.

'A kiss *is* just a kiss,' he returned drily. Normally, she scared him when she played this game, but tonight it all seemed harmless, somehow. It was relaxing to be with Belle after the non-stop pressures of his problematic life with Miranda and the baby.

They walked down to the river which flowed through the centre of the town, and meandered along its bank. Belle stared soulfully at pairs of lovers entwined beneath the rows of ancient willows on either side of the slow-moving water. Adam discovered that he was holding her hand. They admired the moonlight and the swans asleep in the reeds, talking very little. She agreed biddably when he said it was time to go home.

'That was lovely. I really enjoyed myself,' she said when they had settled in front of the TV. 'Now I've got something nice for you, just to say thank you.'

Adam suffered as his reprehensible depths reprised the magenta underwear.

'It's a bottle of Tokay,' she said. 'I know how much you like it.' She had bought it with some money Rufus Olivier had given her for recording half a dozen late-night movies, plus some of her weekly allowance. If she could get Adam to drink enough – just enough, not too much – then there would be a good chance of moving on to Act Three.

She fetched the bottle from the fridge and liberated some French chocolates screaming 'Eat me!' from the top shelf. She found Adam taking up a whole sofa, pushed back his legs and wriggled herself comfortable against them.

'Don't worry,' she advised. 'I'm too tired to attack you. I'd rather rape these chocs.'

He laughed and ruffled her hair, which still smelled of 'In XS'. 'You certainly are a cure for the blues,' he said, 'whatever comes with it.'

'Thanks. Here – there's only one *baba-au-rhum*, but you can have it.' She made no more overtures except to fill his glass one and a half times and feed him chocolates with her fingers. They talked about the play and the difficulties that would arise if she got the TV role, and about Adam's failure to come up with a new idea for a short story. They looked at, but did not watch, a good bad movie starring Al Pacino and Andy Garcia. Belle was the first to say she was going to bed.

Just before the turn of the night, when dreams run too deep beneath the surface of consciousness to be recalled, Adam moved over in his sleep and was caught in a soft wrapping of arms and legs. Small hands began to drift over him, touching and stroking so lightly that he knew he did not have to wake. He gave a moan of pleasure and Belle lay breathless beside him, her body barely grazing his. She did not want him to waken until she had completed her private act of worship. She had waited for this since she was eleven years old. She would not hurry the experience, or allow it to be anything less than perfect. When he was sleeping deeply again she began her inventory of all that would shortly be hers forever. She sat on her knees beside the pillow and applied butterfly contact to his hair and his eyes. She kissed his mouth with her breath, her longing, her intention, but not quite with her lips. She pulled down the duvet so that she could look at him in the first light that penetrated the white curtains. She laid her head against his chest and breathed him in, his skin as smooth as hers beneath her cheek, its brown-egg colouring matt and uniform. She stroked his nipples and smiled to see them stiffen. She removed the duvet completely and gazed at his penis, curled like a snail without a shell. They should have shells, she thought, or something. They are too vulnerable. She watched it, thinking of what it meant to her, what it could do, wondering if she could lift it merely with her eyes. Apparently she could not. It was time for Adam to take part in the ceremony. 'With my body I thee worship,' she whispered. She kissed his mouth and then the penis, and placed herself astride his thighs. She began to stroke him awake. She wanted him to wake inside her – or as nearly as turned out to be physically possible – so that he would recognise that they belonged to each other, and that there could be no doubt of that from this moment on.

Until that moment, for Adam, it had been a dream of a dream, the kind you wouldn't wake from in a hundred years if you could help it. He knew what was happening, but not that it was *happening*; not that dreams could, on very rare and carefully prepared occasions, come true. He rose and fell with the pliant body that was covering him. It was familiar and unfamiliar, narrow and long-boned, fitting his own because it was like his own. He was kissed by a mouth whose taste he seemed to know, and he kissed ecstatically in return. Scented hair fell on his face. He opened his eyes.

'I hope,' said Belle severely, 'that you are not going to pretend that you didn't know.'

'I could. Almost,' he said. 'But I won't.'

'Then it's all right.'

She subsided on him again and he turned her slowly, kissing her and murmuring to her, on to her back. This time, there was no possible doubt that he knew what he was doing. There was nothing in the world or out of it that could have stopped him.

Afterwards, it would be different. He would be Adam after the Fall. However illicit-delicious the apple had been, he was going to suffer for it. She had thought it all out, what she would say, several months ago.

'You must not look at it from a moral viewpoint that doesn't belong to you. Why do you think I wanted you to see the play? You know there is nothing intrinsically wicked about what we've done. How could there be, when it was done because we love each other? You as much as I. You know that now, don't you?'

He would not deny it. She was too strong, and too innocent.

'We have hurt no one, and we never will. It will be a lightness in our life, a blessing; our secret sanctuary against the world.'

'I don't know if I have the courage. Especially when I *really* wake up.'

'You will, you'll see. Nothing is going to change very much, after all. Except that we'll have this – knowledge – between us which no one else will ever discover.'

'No, and they must never know. Not anyone.'

'Don't worry so. We've got it now, all of it. We can't marry. And I don't think we should try to live together. I do have the sense to know that wouldn't work. We can go on with our lives just as we used to – but we will always have this to keep us safe.'

'What about Miranda?' He was not even sure what he meant.

'I don't want anything that belongs to Miranda. Only what's always been mine.' She sat up so that she could read his expression. 'It has been, hasn't it?' she asked. 'I want you to be honest. It's important.'

'Yes, it has,' he admitted. He felt a combined sense of relief and terror. He had been honest, or he thought so. He endured the cheerful anarchy of a family Sunday morning with a benign goodwill that concealed numb disbelief with undercurrents of wild excitement. He looked at Luke, who had so obviously fathered both him and Belle, and tried instead to think how very different – opposite in every way – Helen was from Dinah. Not that incest was anything special these days; they committed it three days a week on television. Nevertheless this was a staggering experience, his and Belle's, and he feared he was condemned to swoop from fear to dark, delirious joy and back again, like poor unhappy Quasimodo on the end of his predestined bellrope. The Hunchback, the Vampire Count, the incestuous lover. He had made himself a place among the great outsiders of society; precisely where he ought to be, Belle would tell him, if he had any true ambition as a writer. He thought that perhaps he was becoming a little hysterical.

'I'm going back to the flat, now,' he said to her gently,

at the end of the morning. 'I need to think about all this, without you around to distract me.'

'I *told* you,' Belle said clearly and kindly, 'You mustn't *think* about it. Just – let it be.'

Miranda saw at once that Adam was still very much disturbed. Even her greeting appeared to interrupt some grim interior debate.

'I'm glad you came home early,' she said, hoping he might attempt a positive response. She gave him Moriarty to hold, as a comfort blanket, should he need one. He held her stiffly, his fingers tense.

'I came because there's some work I have to finish,' he said. His manner was oddly polite, as if they had only recently met. He had not kissed her, but she had not expected he would. She did not know what to say. Neither of them believed in holding on to quarrels, but this had been their first serious one.

'Do you want to talk first?' she asked hesitantly.

Adam looked blank. 'What about?'

'Don't be like that. It doesn't help.'

'I don't know what you mean,' he said distantly. He felt he was in shock.

'Please, Adam. I need to know what you think we ought to do.'

He wrenched himself into time, place and issue. 'You know already,' he said. 'My feelings haven't changed. Have yours?'

'I'm not sure. I would like to talk to Joel again, and I think you should, too. That seems a sensible step.'

'Then you must take it on your own,' he said deliberately, 'and see where it leads you.'

'Why can't you be *with* me on this?' she pleaded. 'Everything would work out if you were.'

He sighed. 'You know how I feel. Won't you, please, just leave it for now? I really do have a lot to get through.'

He was closed to her. She gave in. 'In that case,' she said, 'you won't mind if I go out. It's the last of the Graduate Student Fashion Shows this afternoon. I've only managed to see one, so far.'

'Fine. I don't mind.'

'I do *need* to see the clothes. Loads of people are getting pictures for me, but it's not like seeing them on the catwalk.'

'I've said it's fine with me. In fact I would like, very much, to be alone. Oh, hell. Come here.' He hugged her tightly in sudden aching contrition. 'I'm sorry. I can't help it right now.'

She hugged him back but still did not attempt to kiss him. 'I know. Neither can I,' she said. 'Oh, Adam – I don't want it all to slip away from us. It used to be so good.'

'It's a difficult time,' he said stupidly.

'I feel as if a bulldozer had been let loose in our lives while we were somewhere round the corner,' she wailed. 'Nothing is right any more.'

Chapter 9

LUKE PHONED CHLOE TO REMIND HER THAT SHE had said they might talk. Polite as as a well-mannered child, he asked if he could come to see her.

'When?' she asked, thinking she would make some excuse.

'Now.'

Panic fluttered. 'Surely – you're teaching?'

'It's Wednesday.'

'Oh. Yes.' It had been a Wednesday afternoon when he had first appeared in the summer field where she was sketching Arden Court. They had continued to meet on that day until Nemesis had caught up with them in the form of Joel Ranger.

'I'm in London,' Luke confessed. 'Well, actually I'm upstairs, at Adam's.'

She sighed. 'You'd better come down.'

'You are too thin,' he said tenderly, briefly keeping the hand she had tried to avoid giving him. 'What are you doing about it?'

She shrugged. 'I take vitamins. When I remember.'

'Are you still – have you recovered from the – the baby?'

'The termination.' The bleak correction seemed a blow to punish them both.

'I wish I could look after you,' he said passionately. 'You shouldn't be living here on your own like this.'

She said very distinctly, 'I don't need looking after. I am not on my own.' She was determined, he saw, to separate herself from him; he understood that she wished to protect herself. He moved away from her, to the window. Confronted by the close-packed centuries of brick and stone, glass and steel, he thought of the numberless women, within the boundary of his vision, who had mourned or died or felt relief, or had too little time to feel at all, about the wilful termination of a life within.

'Termination,' he said savagely. 'A horrible word. An official's word. Without any human attachment, like that other Roman sentence of death – "decimation". And "abortion" is even worse. Did you know,' he demanded roughly, still looking out of the window, 'there are three thousand of them, every week, in Britain? The latest annual figure is a hundred and seventy-six thousand.'

Chloe fought nausea. 'How do you know?'

'I called a couple of organisations – one pro-life and one not – their figures were identical.' He gestured nervily in the air like a smoker who has forgotten his cigarettes. 'I don't suppose it makes you feel any better – how could it? – but at least you know you're not alone.'

'It's immaterial. I'm responsible for my own actions. Why did you call them?'

He said humbly, 'I thought they might tell me how I could help you.'

She was shaken. 'That was – kind.'

'They weren't much use. You see, you took all of the responsibility on yourself. I wish you could have given me a part of it. Talk to me, Chloe. I need to understand what you are feeling.'

Still, she held it all back from him, her grief and her

softness as a woman, just as she had held back her hand when he arrived.

'What do you want?' she asked levelly. 'A share in my guilt?'

'God, no. I loathe this unnatural nurture of guilt. It's a legacy from those damnable nuns of yours.'

'No. We have had this argument before. The nuns would say I am forgiven.'

'Then why not forgive yourself? If you must adhere to an archaic system of guilt and absolution imposed from outside, then you might at least go all the way. For myself, the only thing I couldn't forgive was that you excluded me from something that affected an essential part of both of us.'

'I know. I was a coward. I didn't dare take the chance that you might influence my decision.' She shook her head. 'Oh, Luke I'm sorry. I know you mean nothing but kindness now – but you can't change anything.'

'Neither of us can change what has happened. But one day you will have to let it go. You must begin to believe that you can move on and make things new. You are in a trap you have made for yourself. You don't have to submit to the torture. You can release the spring and go free. Only, let me help you,' he begged.

'I'm sorry. I can't.' The phrases fell heavily between them, grey, unshiftable boulders of negativity. She had removed to some cold star and looked down without interest on past, present, future.

Luke took hold of her and shook her until tears flew out of her eyes. 'That's better,' he said. 'You should know by now that the frozen goddess doesn't cut any ice with me. What are you trying to achieve?'

She said, 'I don't know,' because it was easy and meant nothing.

'Then you had better find out, because you're not the only one who is responsible for your present state of mind. I am. I am. It has all been happening to both of us; all of it, since the day we met. I won't go away. I won't leave you alone. Not ever. You have got to try to think it out. For instance, you have left your husband. Why?'

'I haven't.'

'Well, it looks that way to me, and I imagine it feels that way to Alain. So, ask yourself exactly why you are here?'

'I know why,' she cried. 'But you want different answers. Well, you cannot have them.'

He made his voice very gentle. 'Not yet, maybe. But it *will* be different. You will set yourself free. It's the way the world works.' He sounded so certain and looked so determined that she was brushed by a flicker of his energy. But it was only a flicker; her struggle to prevent him reaching her had worn her out.

Luke knew this instinctively. 'I'll let you rest now,' he said. He led her to her bed and made her lie down. She went unprotesting, and lay staring into space. She thought how she longed to feel his energy and certainty run through her as it had done in the past.

'Chloe?'

'Yes?'

He stroked back the hair from her face. 'You don't have to be so alone.'

She put up her arms and he held her in a long, unsensual embrace. Both of them knew it could not remain that way for long. Just before it became unbearable he let her go.

'You'll let me come back?' he said.

'All right,' she said, because of how much she wanted him to stay. What she felt as he left was not love, it was more like the tug of entwined entrails. She recognised this as a moment of extreme weakness for which the reckoning might be considerable.

Next weekend, without any family pressure, Chloe went home; 'scuttled' would have been her chosen verb. She was aware that her reasons did not bear examination and, rather than subject them to it, settled for being unreasonably angry with Luke.

Arriving early on Friday evening to see Alain's car already in the drive, she knew she would find him in the kitchen performing the culinary abracadabra with which he banished the gremlins of the power industry. The back door was open and she moved through a scent barrier of mint and honeysuckle to reach him.

'*Mon dieu, mon dieu, mon dieu.*' The mantra represented the zenith of his delight, as it did the nadir of his sorrow and much in between. 'Why did you not tell me you would come?'

'I told Tilda, yesterday.'

'*Ah, bien.* She has kept you a surprise. *C'est parfait. Embrasse-moi.*' In his arms she was filled slowly and effervescently with relief, like a human glass of champagne. She had not realised, until then, that she had been afraid she might have stopped loving him. It was an idiotic fear, but so much of her was idiotic and fearful at the moment. She held Alain very tightly, nuzzling into the open neck of his shirt to renew her acquaintance with the warm skin at the base of his throat where a pulse throbbed familiarly with the scent of herbs. He kissed her with a slow tenderness that restored her, as he intended, to her position as serene ruler of all that was his and hers; for the weekend, for ever, whatever she wished. There would be no strings, no entreaties, no mention of her abdication.

The children, despite Alain's careful programming, demonstrated no such subtlety, but their demands for her permanent return were equally reassuring.

'It just feels odd not to have a mother,' Tilda told her briskly. 'I don't know what to say when people ask.'

'Tell them I'll soon be back. Anyway, what people?'

'You know, just people.' Tilda managed to sound both vague and socially justified. 'Everyone, really.'

Rufus surprised himself by supporting her. 'It's like, the house feels sort of empty – as if we'd all gone on holiday. Especially coming home after school.' He had not actually meant to say this, as having Chloe out of the way was convenient, possibly even necessary, to the smooth execution of Walk the Plank Enterprises.

'And the animals really miss you,' Tilda added triumphantly. 'I mean, just look at Baskerville.'

Chloe sighed. The big dog's head lay in her lap and his eyes were glazed with worship. 'I'm here now,' she pleaded.

Tilda pressed on. 'Arnie is too thin, Grace sulks all the time, and Spothilde hardly ever comes out of the blue casserole. They *need* company in the daytime. It's what they're *used* to.'

'Spothilde?' asked Chloe.

Rufus said grandly, 'We are learning to compromise.'

'Congratulations. Is there a short version?'

'Spotty,' said Rufus, grinning.

'Hildy,' said Tilda. 'She answers to either. Or not.'

Chloe's laughter made them both feel they must have got it right at last. The evening that followed was so enjoyable that she began to think that, perhaps, she could simply stay on, that everything would be as it had been before; before Luke, before the termination, before Moriarty, before the glass had turned and the avalanche come down. It was a comfortable frame of mind and she allowed herself to fit into it for as long as it might last. She enjoyed Tilda's music, Rufus's demonstration of the wonders of the Internet and Alain's gentle teasing about the too thin body she was walking about in, which clearly belonged to some other woman. She apologised to each of the animals for her absence and attempted to purchase forgiveness. Arnie, the muscle-bound ginger tom, snapped up the skin of her salmon before stalking off on his Queen Anne legs to broadcast his genes. Grace, his svelte black companion and mother of the diminutive Spothilde, leaped into her lap and solicited for cheese, sitting delicately side-saddle on Baskerville's black leather nose. The kitten, fed until she bulged, located the cream jug, then retired to curl up in a yellow duster in the blue casserole.

It was all so everyday, so normal, so much how they had always been. Why should she not come back, come home, and let it continue?

During the night she turned over and awoke suddenly, surprised to find Alain beside her. He too was awake.

'How nice,' she said, putting her arms around him. 'I was expecting a blank wall.'

He rearranged her slightly. 'And I was not expecting a second chance until morning.'

Morning brought an unexpected breakfast guest. It was Dwayne Cubitt, who looked unusually hollow-eyed and anxious.

'I'm sorry, Mrs Olivier,' he said nervously, 'but I had to get out of our house and I couldn't think where else to go.'

Chloe swooped him into the hall. 'This is the place,' she assured him. 'Breakfast? Rufus is having a bacon and egg burger. How about you?'

'Yes, please.' Dwayne subsided gratefully in Tilda's vacated chair.

'Would you like to tell us what is the trouble?' Alain enquired kindly, flipping the eggs over, 'Or do you prefer to speak only to Rufus?'

The boy shrugged miserably. 'It'll be all over the village by now. Surprised you didn't hear it from here. It's my mum. Dad's just found out she was having an affair with this bloke, Ben Simmons from Abingley Common. He's chucked her out.'

'Wow!' offered Rufus by way of solidarity.

'Literally. More than once. But Mum's stronger than him and she kept getting back in again. They've been at it all night. They made the most incredible noise. Really embarrassing. So, then I got Elvis and he joined in, and then Clint came and *he* joined in. I've had as much as I can take, for now,' he finished wearily. 'Can I stay here for a while?'

'As long as you like,' said Chloe gently. 'I'm so sorry, Dwayne.'

'Don't worry, old Shitface,' Rufus said affectionately. 'They're bound to make it up.'

'No, they won't. Mum's packing. She's going to live with Ben Simmons. She wants me to go with her. I'm supposed to think about it.'

'Abingley Common. That's seven miles away,' said Rufus doubtfully. 'Do you want to?'

'I don't know. I just want it not to have happened,' Dwayne said sadly. 'I don't think I've really taken it in yet. I mean – Mum, of all people. Whatever was she thinking about?'

Chloe looked nervously at Alain. 'Try not to worry yet,' she said. 'You don't know what they'll decide to do in the end.'

'I do,' Dwayne said quietly. 'So would you if you'd seen Mum's face. It was like something had happened that she'd been waiting for all her life.'

'Romance,' said Tilda sombrely. 'I expect that's it. What's he like, this Ben Simmons?'

'I've never spoken to him. He's a woodsman and caretaker. He works on that big estate near Friday Street – Arden Court.'

Chloe thought the world might stop. She looked at Alain, but his expression remained one of compassionate interest. Perhaps the name of the house had never entered his consciousness. That would have been understandable in the circumstances. If Miranda had been here, or Adam, memory would have flared across the room like sheet lightning.

Not only the house but the man. Ben Simmons was Trespassers W. Adele Cubitt had fallen in love with Trespassers W. That was the name Chloe had given the unseen caretaker of Arden House, a figure whose Pinteresque absence had continually threatened his presence. It was not he, but she and Luke who had trespassed. Trespasses will not be forgiven.

'I remember,' Rufus discovered now. 'Wasn't that the place where you used to paint, Mum? The Gothicky one with all the towers?'

'Yes, it was.'

'I liked those pictures,' Rufus said. 'They looked as if they were on fire.' She smiled at him. She knew that the little time of peace was over. All she could do was to meet Alain's eyes and see him discover that too.

'Did you know Mrs Cubitt was going to do this?' he asked when they were alone. He spoke with the colourless courtesy of a man in a suit behind glass.

'No. She thought she would always put her family first.'

'She 'as changed 'er mind. Why? Because 'er 'usband 'as found out? Crises can precipitate truth.'

'I don't know, Alain.'

'Is she consumed with a longing for romance, as Tilda believes? Adultery is, of course, romantic; marriage not.'

'She may be.'

'And you?' he asked. 'Will you also change your mind?'

She turned on him. 'No! Why should I? Please, don't talk like this, Alain. This is nothing to do with us.'

''Ave you been seeing 'im?' The sudden harshness jolted her. ''As 'ee come to you in London?'

'No,' she said firmly. A lie would do more good than the truth, if there was any good to be done.

'I don't know if I can believe you.' He thrust his fingers through his hair, indicating a true dilemma.

'But you would have, only yesterday. What difference does Adele make to us?'

He thought about that. 'I suppose Mrs Cubitt 'as shown us 'ow fragile is our own situation. It is this – I want to trust you, but I must always remember that 'ee seduced you once and wishes to do so again.'

'What you are saying is that you don't trust Luke,' Chloe said in desperation. 'Does that have to mean you won't trust me?'

'I am not certain,' Alain said gravely.

In the afternoon, what appeared to be a compact floral marquee was seen to move into the Oliviers' drive. This was Adele Cubitt, dressed to stun the tongues of all detractors, her fit, stumpy body erect beneath its stately pile of orange hair. She had come to ask if Dwayne could remain where he was for a few days while she settled her affairs. Chloe hugged her and said that, of course, they would be glad to have him.

'But you are sure?' she asked, anxiously searching the bravely made-up face. 'This really is what you want?'

'I know I once said diff'rent. But I love Ben, Mrs Chloe, and he loves me. It's too late in my life to let anything get in the way of that little miracle.'

'I probably shouldn't ask – but did that miracle never happen with your husband? You have been together so long.'

''Im!' Adele snorted fiercely. 'I married 'im because I fell pregnant with Elvis, didn't I? 'Ee's never been a proper 'usband, nor a proper father. I've brought them boys up single-'anded, and we'd all've been better off without 'im. 'Ee's never done a day's work in 'is life if 'ee could 'elp it. I don't know why the good Lord wastes oxygen on 'im.'

'The boys have turned out well, though – each with his own business.' Chloe felt the need to be positive.

'They're all right. They're good boys. Dwayne's the only one I worry about. 'Ee's different, bein' so clever an' all. I want 'im to make up 'is own mind who 'ee's goin' to live with. D'you reckon that's all right? At fifteen?'

'I think it depends what his regime would be. It's

important he keeps up his work. I believe he wants to go to Cambridge.'

'Regime! Chaos, that's 'is father's regime. But Dwayne doesn't let that stop 'im. 'Ee 'as 'is own room an' 'is own world.'

'Well, leave him with us until he can see clearly what he needs.' She took Adele's large, hard-working hand. 'I wish you great happiness, you know that. And I admire your courage.'

'It doesn't need courage. But thank you. 'Ere – wot you cryin' for?'

'I'm not sure. Probably for the same reason one does it at weddings, whatever that is.'

'Get away with you! I'll see you next Wednesday, same as usual, aw'rite?' She looked keenly at the two large windows framing the upland sweep of the downs. 'Those look as if they could do with some knuckle.'

On Sunday evening, Rufus and Dwayne were going to St Mark's to ring the two treble bells before Evensong. They had been caught experimenting with them, with cacaphonous consequence, and the rector had decided they might as well learn to do it properly. They found they enjoyed it; it also gave them valuable extra time together, as well as what Dwayne punningly described as 'vicarious virtue'.

Chloe, who wanted to talk to Catherine Chandler, walked with them through the village, thinking that a mother figure might be some comfort to Dwayne, even if it were not his own. She was correct only in so far as Dwayne, who thought she was the most gorgeous woman he knew, was well-pleased to be seen with her in public. It did not seem to him possible that she belonged to the same generation as his mother, who, although he loved her dearly, was undeniably built like a grand piano and had a voice like something happening in a breaker's yard.

When they had rung the changes, the virtuous pair

tugged surplices over their sweatshirts and joined the church choir for Evensong. Singing was another thing they greatly enjoyed. Rufus had sung every kind of music with Tilda for as long as he could remember, while Dwayne had harmonised alongside his father, whose reputation as the lead guitar and singer with his own pub and club band was higher than his wife would give him credit for. Church music, Dwayne had discovered, was something else, something unexpectedly beautiful and satisfying, like so much that had come to him since he had won the Sheringham scholarship and made new friends with minds that stretched as far as his own. His voice, now a sure, dark-ish tenor, married well with Rufus's lighter one, which was still apt to crack, if not break completely, at inconvenient moments; he could still *do* a treble, but it was only to be trusted in private. They looked forward to being Don Giovanni and Leporello.

Chloe let the service, one of her favourite non-Catholic ones, wash in and out of her, becoming part of the music, or it of her. They were using Gregorian chant and its rigour was just what she needed in her present state, which she knew to be a lack of grace. She did not know whether God existed or not, but if he did – and if he bore any resemblance to the patriarchal figure who had both kept artists going (some of them) and held them back for too many centuries – he would certainly deplore her present muddled condition. When the church had cleared after the last 'Amen', she plumped up the little grey squirrel on her kneeler and rubbed its nose as though it were Baskerville. Anthropomorphism again, she accused herself; what a batty old lady she was preparing to be. Quite soon, at this rate. She got up and made her way to the quatrefoil opening in the wall that was her hotline through the cold stone to the wisdom and strength of the long-dead Anchoress of Sheringham. She sat down on the bench beside it and rubbed her hands over the rough surface as she had rubbed the squirrel's nose, touching it as if it were animal, not mineral. Catherine was there, as always, at the end of her senses and her imagination.

'I have made no progress, none at all,' she confessed at once. 'My attempt to make sense of my life has succeeded only in making it unintelligible to either Luke or Alain. Both of them agree that I should do the only thing I don't want to do; I ought to come home for good. What do you think?'

What do *you* think? Think.

Oh, Luke wants me home because he thinks I'm losing my wits and my health in London. And possibly he wants me near him, though that's debatable; Alain is right to think the studio is more convenient for purposes of seduction. Theoretically. And of course, Alain just wants me home; he never wanted me to leave. He gave me a sort of ultimatum last night, tried to *make* me come back. But I can't, not for the wrong reasons. Not to be watched and guarded and live in the prison of his jealousy. Why now? Why does he suddenly have to be like this now?

Perhaps he has seen that nothing has changed.

He has no need to worry. I will keep faith with him. I will. I just need time to work everything out. It is getting more confused now. I am sad for Alain because he's angry and jealous and unhappy. But it also alienates me. I don't want that. And God knows how I feel about Luke. The same as ever, probably, if I can be completely honest. I never *have* felt differently; that was always the trouble. Shall I simply go on like this, in love with Luke, loving Alain, until one of them dies – or I do? I wish I could be like Adele Cubitt, with her single, tidy little miracle.

You are a self-regarding, inward-looking, spoiled product of the end of your century, and it is not easy to feel sympathy for you. Have you done any work since you came here last?

A little. It is all about the child who is gone.

— 182 —

That is good. Do not stop. Go where it takes you. Slowly. Allow yourself peace in which to work, no matter what confusion surrounds that.

Thank you. Don't despair of me, Catherine. I need your strictures. There is no one else.

There are too many. *Pax vobiscum.*

Et cum spirito tuo.

Outside, arrested between the crooked rows of grave-stones, excused their worn uniforms of lichen to bathe in the summer sun, she spoke the thought that had emerged from her trance. 'Must I define myself as a pendulum swinging helplessly between two poles? Is that any kind of description of a human being? Let alone an artist?'

'Look at it this way,' Rufus said, as he walked with Dwayne along the upper path, past the Lightning Oak. 'If you go with your mother, you'll be seven miles away from school and us and everything. *And*, you'll have the unknown Mr Simmons to contend with. If you stay with your father and brothers, you might miss a bit of female TLC, but think of the glorious freedom! Let's face it, your dad doesn't give a pink shit what you get up to.'

'Yeah? You should have seen him when the police came round. He went off-the-planet ballistic.'

'Yes, but that was a one-off occasion. I hope.'

'Me too.' Dwayne shuddered as he recalled his parents' inarticulate but painful reaction.

'So. What d'you reckon?'

'I'll stay at home for a while, see how it goes. It's easier for me, and it's better for Mum and Ben Simmons not to have anyone else around, just at first.'

'Great!' Rufus did a quick somersault. 'Now we'll really be able to get on with business.'

But here he was sadly mistaken.

When they got home, Alain invited his son to drink coffee

with him in his study. Such formality always made Rufus nervous.

'Anything wrong?' he enquired cheerfully, securing a couple of chocolate biscuits before whatever doom it was should fall.

'Do *you* think there is?'

Immediately Rufus felt himself look guilty, which was totally out of order as he really couldn't think of a thing. 'No,' he said boldly.

'*Ah, bon*. Then Madame 'Ollings 'as made a mistake.'

'What – April?' This was mystifying.

''Er mother.'

'Oh?'

'She 'as telephoned a few minutes ago. She was in some distress. Can you imagine why that should be?'

'No.' Rufus could not.

Alain smiled; quite pleasantly, but that was no guarantee.

'Not even if I were to mention video-tapes?'

'Oh – well, yes. Sort of. You know.'

'Tell me.'

'Well, I just copied something for April.' His tone was generous.

'Remind me of its title.'

'Some romantic shi— nanigans. *Romeo and Juliet*, I think. She fancies Leonardo di Caprio.'

'*Oui*?' Alain looked surprised. '*Tu es sûr*?'

'Absolutely.'

His father consulted the pad next to his phone. 'Not, then – *Tracy and Samantha Get It On with the Big Boys*?'

'Never heard of it.' It was patently true.

'I see.' Alain smiled again. 'And 'ow about—' He consulted the pad again. '*Ah oui, The Teletubbies, the Pirate Version*. One of your sixth form called about that one. He seemed rather annoyed.'

'You what?' Rufus howled. 'What is going on here, Dad?'

— 184 —

Alain sighed. 'You really don't know, do you?'

'No, I bloody don't! Oh – sorry.'

'You have obviously got your tapes and your customers a little confused.'

'Oh damn it,' Rufus groaned tragically. He had no idea what had gone wrong, but it was obviously going to land him in more trouble.

'My advice is to wind up your business as soon as possible,' Alain said frigidly. 'It is, as I am sure you know very well, illegal.'

'It's only for people from school. I don't think that's illegal. Is it?'

'*Je t'assure. Ecoute-moi, mon fils.* I understand that you are restless and that you like to have some little extra dimension to life, but can't you find something more intelligent than this?'

Stung, Rufus said sadly, 'I don't see how it could have happened. I put the lists of tapes and customers on the computer; I don't recognise either of those titles.'

'I thought your computer was down? Though, even so, I doubt if it can be the guilty party here.' He was now plainly amused again.

'It was. I mended it. Look – I think these are tapes that never got recorded on. I got a job lot from Clint Cubitt; he must have given me ones that were already used. Just wait till I get hold of him!'

Alain ignored this. 'My dear short-sighted boy,' he said, looking remarkably pleased, considering, Rufus thought. 'Do you tell me you are capable of mending a computer?'

'Yes. I do it for everyone. I like doing it. What has that got to do with it?'

'You like doing it. Yet, to make a pitiful amount of money, you prefer the repetition and ennui of this video rubbish? Oh Rufus – go away and think about it!'

'Is that all?' Rufus was dazed.

'*Allez, allez, allez!*'

*   *   *

Chloe had left on Sunday evening, explaining that Miranda had an early lecture next morning, so she must be there to take care of Moriarty. She and Alain had not made love again on Saturday night, nor had they found it possible to talk to each other to any useful purpose. Each one was bemused by the weekend's experiences, uncertain what, exactly, had hit them, but painfully feeling the blow.

Quite late on Sunday night, Alain reached for the phone and dialled Helen Cavendish's number. She was presently occupying her flat in Eccleston Square during the filming of her three-part TV thriller.

'Hélène. *C'est toi?*'

'Alain. *C'est toujours moi. Et tu proposes?*'

'*Tu es directe.* You don't beat about the tree.'

'Bush. Why waste time? Are you coming over?'

'Not tonight. I can't leave the children. But I can arrange something. When would you like that to be?'

'Tuesday. I shall be free from five-thirty. Come early.'

'Until then. Thank you, Hélène.'

'*Ce n'est rien.* Though I hope it *will* be quite something.'

She heard him laugh and thought that he had sounded as if he needed to.

On Monday morning Tilda woke up suddenly and early, feeling anxious and exhausted. She had dreamed the Joel dream again. This time he had pulled her up behind him on the Harley and they had left the ground and flown up into the night sky like masters of sword and sorcery. Reaching out, she had let tiny constellations flow through her fingers, and his hair had licked her face as he turned to shout at her in exultation. She had even managed somehow to have *A Night on the Bare Mountain* playing around them in the starry dark. Joel had discovered a new self, someone light and unthreatening, pure enjoyment informing every inch of his body, accepting this glorious newness like a marvelling child. She had held on to him with perfect confidence as they zoomed and dived about the purple heavens for what seemed many hours, cloudscapes unrolling about them in multicoloured banks and scrolls. At last, they had quite literally come down to earth. Tilda got off the bike and stood waiting for his smile, for the continued sense of shared loveliness. But when he turned to her it was the old Joel she was looking at, his eyes tired with the same old irony, his pleasure or pain on lease to no one. He saw her unguarded happiness and only stayed to watch it fade before he shrugged and walked away.

She had felt sad and foolish and cheated, and had awoken with those feelings clinging to her like a ragged, dirty web. Her instinct was to carry them, without the personal details, to Chloe, who would touch them with the wand of her maternal love and make them fall away. But Chloe had gone back to Miranda and that beastly studio. And anyway, the wand was not so immediately available as it once had been. If only her mother would *talk* to her, tell her what was going on in her mind. Tilda was sure there was a lot of it, whatever it was, and that things were nowhere near as fine and dandy as either parent made out. It was so frustrating to be treated like a child when one was quite clearly no such thing.

At school that day, she was quieter than usual and kept as close as she could to Paul.

'Something wrong?' he asked her as they shared an apple and a coffee-to-go beside the tennis courts.

'Not really. Just – things seem sort of bitty and unre-solved.'

'What sort of things?'

Everything, she thought. You, Mum and Dad, the future – looming like an iceberg with its exams and choices and slippery banana skins. And sex. 'It all needs sorting out in my mind. I'd rather not try to do that now.'

'Very sensible. Especially as it's the wrong time of the month.'

'Don't be so smug and – blokeish.' Tilda huffed and upturned her cup of coffee on the grass. She wanted to throw something – anything – away. Sometimes boys who thought they understood were worse than those who simply didn't. She looked at Paul's intelligent, worried face and did not know what she wanted from him. Only yesterday, everything had seemed more simple, her life moving forward with a gentle, pleasant momentum. Today, she seemed to be standing on the edge of a chasm she could not leap.

At four, Luke Cavendish sent for Tilda. He was in his study, entertaining a small, lightly built girl with a sharp, bright-eyed face, her dark hair shaved close to her skull.

'This is Antonia Valder. She comes from Prague and has recently lived in Paris and Amsterdam. She speaks French as well as English, and as she is joining your year, I thought you would be the ideal person to introduce her to everyone and generally look after her.'

'I'd be glad to,' Tilda said. She liked the look of Antonia and had had more than enough introspective gloom for one day.

'I'll leave her to tell you all about herself,' Luke smiled, 'but one thing I do know is that she is another musician.'

'My father has played the violin with most of the European symphony orchestras,' the girl explained as they walked down the corridor. 'This time it's the London Symphonia. So everyone expects me to be a musical prodigy.'

Her accent was interesting, Tilda thought; it ran up and down the scale like Alain's, but there was a handful of gravel thrown in and no missing aitches.

'I do play the violin, in a tortured sort of way, but my father is usually the first to beg me to stop. I'm not bad on a honky-tonk piano,' she added cheerfully, 'but best of all, I like to play my computer.'

'You'd better meet my brother, Rufus. He's an advanced computer freak. By the way, can you sing, Antonia?'

'Ant, please. I loathe the name Antonia. I quite like singing. Why?'

'I have to make up a chorus of vampires for our *Dracula* production. It's a lot of fun and you'd meet most of the good people in our year.'

Tilda suggested to Rufus that Luke Cavendish would be grateful if he too were to take some part in the tending of Ant. He might, for instance, like to take her to the Sheringham school and village disco next Saturday.

'A girl,' Rufus swore. 'No way. I'm going with Dwayne.'

'I thought you could both look after her a little, that's all. We'll all be going together, really, but Ant won't have got to know many boys by Saturday. Go on, it won't hurt.'

'But I don't like dancing.'

'I've never even seen you try.'

'Blood and sand! It's the first time Dwayne and I have been let off the leash since the deadly curfew.'

'Don't be mean. She's new around here, and a foreigner; and she needs to feel wanted.'

'You make her feel it, then. I don't want her.' Then he had an appealing idea. 'Tell you what, though. I'll hang out with her a bit if you'll record four more videos for me. For the last time, I promise. On your grave.'

Tilda groaned. 'Don't ever give anything away, will you? OK, done.' There was a percussion of hands that would not have disgraced Spike Lee. Tilda was quite pleased with herself. It was high time Rufus was exposed to the civilising influence of a little female company. And she did have rather a lot to do herself, apart from befriending Ant.

As a reward for future virtue, Rufus decided to give Joel a call. Just in case. You never knew. He contacted the fizz and buzz of a mobile.

'Joel? It's Rufus. Stinking reception.'

'I'm on the roof of the Yamamoto house, fixing up this sculpture garden. That's water you hear, not interference.'

'Didn't know artists did stuff like that.'

'They do anything, Rufus, anything anyone wants or can be persuaded to want. There are no borders any more.'

'Eh? Where?'

Joel chuckled. 'Between life and art, my man.'

'Oh, right. I guess not. Listen, the reason I called—'

'I can guess. The answer's no.'

'Oh.' Rufus was crestfallen. 'Why?'

'We have already had this conversation.' The reply came back with edged, diminished patience. 'I don't do any of that. Don't ask me again. Not me, not anyone else. Forget that trade. It can only do you harm. I mean it.'

'I see.' It actually sounded like the truth – not that you could possibly tell. 'OK. Thanks, anyway. Hey, did you get to see Moriarty yet?'

'I've seen her. But it's not something your family would like to know about. I want to thank you for telling me when you did.'

'No sweat. So, what did you think?'

'I thought she was a good mix.'

'Yeah. She's cute, for a baby.'

'She is. Well, I have to go. Be seeing you, Rufe.'

Rufus wished this were true. He missed Joel; he had added a lot of zing to life. So had the beloved Harley. Shame about the drugs, too. Art must be paying well, these days, without its borders. Maybe he and Dwayne ought to go in for it. They could be the – who was it? – Gilbert and George, of Sheringham; stand around in their underpants at posh people's parties, moving from time to time to spit in their faces or piss on the smoked salmon canapés. They could call themselves No Borders and be famous in fifteen minutes – or was it *for* fifteen minutes?

Sheringham Village Hall had been mercilessly stripped of the posters of lovable and neglected felines illustrating the need to support the afternoon bazaar in aid of the Cats' Protection League. This evening's event, perhaps the most luminous in the calendar, rated the full fig of Maggie Barnes's Chinese lanterns (saved from the profligate 1982 production of *Chu Chin Chow*) and Butcher Sweeney's Christmas lights. The walls had been covered in red paper, the electric lights dimmed, and the general effect was that of a luxurious bunker during some undatable war.

As well as the disco, run as usual by Clint Cubitt, live music would be provided by Bedrock, the popular band led by his father, Charlie. When their large, loose group of relatives and friends began to congregate at the back of the hall, towards the end of the third set, neither Rufus nor Dwayne was displeased to find Antonia Valder among them. At school they had found her friendly, easy to talk to and determinedly independent. Tonight, they noted with approval that she was sensibly dressed in jeans and a shirt. She had a nice face and cool hair, and the sense not to paint her lips like a Marilyn Monroe sofa or turn herself into an undead panda with gross hollows of black eye-shadow. They agreed that they could put up with her, now and again.

'Your father plays very well,' she told Dwayne as the fast set ended with a stomping *Brown Sugar*, aimed at the funkier over-forties who had to be allowed to do their air-punching, elbow-pumping thing at some stage. After that it was back to the present with the lad bands and Skunk Anansie, while Charlie went to down a pint of lager and chat up April Hollings, who was behind the bar in the committee room next door. April was in the sixth form, sixteen and technically touchable, though not within the public eye. For the moment, Charlie contented himself with making her giggle. He began to contemplate all sorts of new freedoms, now that Adele had gone. After all, he was entitled.

'So, ask her.' Dwayne nudged Rufus impatiently. He thought he might ask April Hollings himself. He had danced with her since they were in nursery school. They moved well together and she didn't waste time flirting with him like she did with everyone else.

'I will. In my own time,' muttered Rufus.

'Just do it.'

'Oh, shut up.'

Goaded, he stalked up to the group of girls in their scary Saturday night outfits, each sheathed from clavicle to crotch in a tiny stretch of blazing colour, like living, wriggling tubes of Chloe's Winsor & Newton. In the middle of the pack, Antonia was coming to the end of some story that had made them laugh. He waited till they had finished spluttering and nickering and caught her eye.

'Hi, Rufus. How're you doing?'

'Fine. Want to dance?' It was easy, after all.

'Yes. Thanks.'

She left the group and they walked away towards the music. Halfway, she stopped and asked, 'Do you really, badly want to dance?'

'Not specially,' Rufus admitted.

'Then, d'you know what I'd rather do?' She bent her head, alert and birdlike, close to his ear. 'I'd like to go outside and do some puff. You do smoke, don't you?'

'I certainly do,' Rufus said happily. Rich were the rewards of virtue. He steered her out of the reverberating building into a mellow evening with a hazy, yellow sun pinned in one corner and a white paper moon in the other. They could walk up across the football and cricket pitches and into the woody anonymity that was Sheringham's permanent backdrop.

'I've got this excellent stuff I brought from Amsterdam,' Ant said.

'You mean you smuggled it? Wow!'

'I've done it several times. We've always moved around so much, with my father. It's easy; I seal it and put it in a bag of herbs in my shoulder bag. Then I put my glasses on and carry my violin case, and I look so prissy that customs never stop me. And usually my parents are both fussing so much about their instruments, in at least three languages, that the poor guys don't have a chance. It's a good life,' she finished, grinning. 'Here – d'you want to do the roll-up?'

'You are quite a surprise,' he told her, his fingers working busily. 'I'm glad you came to Sheringham.'

'Mmm. I think it could be fun. Now – tell me what your computer can do.'

'Haven't seen you all night,' Dwayne said when he and Rufus met up at last. 'Have a good time?'

'The best. You?'

'Not bad. Dad and I did our Everly Brothers spot, which seemed to go down pretty well. And I had a good workout with April Hollings.'

'What kind of workout?' Rufus asked suspiciously.

'Ah. That's for me to know,' Dwayne teased. 'How did you get on with little Ant?'

'Ace.' He explained. 'I think she's going to be a godsend. She has this thing set up on the Internet with a guy in Amsterdam. The correspondence *looks* like it's all about music – but it's all about moving drugs. Just dope and speed, like we want. There are couriers coming over all the time.'

'I don't know,' Dwayne said seriously. 'It could be too big for us. Too complicated. It's better to fish in your own backyard if you can. We don't want to be pulled in with a whole lot of city street kings.'

'It's not like that. It's quiet and private. Honestly. Ant will give us a good start. We can use the video money, what there is of it.'

Dwayne still looked doubtful. 'I'm not sure I like the feel of it,' he said. 'And we still have the problem of the curfew.'

'There's always a way,' Rufus said expansively. 'You just have to know what you want and go for it.'

'Exactly,' said Dwayne. The trouble was, they might not always want the same things.

Chapter 10

BELLE AND TILDA, UNABLE TO PERSUADE COSMO to drive them to the South Bank unless he was invited to remain in their company, opted to travel by train. Belle had not seen Adam since the life-changing events of his last visit home, and Tilda simply felt that she needed to see her mother again. The train was sluggish and unconvinced of its business, and Belle was abnormally impatient, even for her.

'I wish you would calm down and sit still,' Tilda told her as she changed her seat for the second time.

'I don't *feel* calm. I feel like a hurricane waiting to happen.'

'You're like this more than half the time, now. There's nothing wrong, is there, Belle? You would tell me, if there was?'

'No. Everything's all right. There's just too much of it.'

'I know what you mean. I feel much that way myself. You know – we used to talk about things. Everything, once. It helped.'

Belle sighed. 'I know,' she said. 'But they were different things.'

She sank her chin in her hand and stared out of the grimy window through the wastes of Clapham Junction. Tilda, who knew better than to feel hurt, sat back and worried about her friend.

In the lofts, Chloe, Adam and Miranda were each spending Sunday in their separate studios, a secret, too well tended, thriving behind each hothouse door.

'How lovely. Come on up.' Miranda's voice on the entryphone held the gladness of promised relief.

'The thing is,' said Belle as they stepped into the lift, 'I'd really like some time alone with Adam. He always helps me to get my head in gear. So, if that doesn't happen naturally, can I rely on you to give me an artificial hand?'

'Naturally,' Tilda smiled, worrying more than ever. She wished she knew the exact nature of this thing that Belle had about Adam. It used to seem like a game designed to tease him; now she was not so sure.

'Hi everyone!' cried a completely different Belle on Miranda's threshold, a fizzing indoor firework thrown into the peaceful afternoon.

'I'm afraid it's only Moriarty and me,' Miranda apologised, 'but I expect we can drum up the others for you.' She kissed them both and placed her daughter in Tilda's open arms.

'Hello, beautiful,' Tilda crooned, lowering her nose into the warm smells of soap and milk and baby skin. 'I wouldn't mind a word with you, first,' she said. 'About Mum.'

'Why don't I leave you two to talk,' said Belle helpfully, 'while I go and annoy Adam for a while.'

'So what's on your mind, my love?' Miranda asked.

'I want you to tell me, honestly, if you think there's anything wrong with Mum. Or with Mum and Dad. They behaved so strangely last weekend – it was lovely at first, but then everything went quiet and sad.'

'Well, I know they were both very upset about Mrs Cubitt.'

'I think it was more than that. They were sad for themselves, not her.'

'No. Now, you are simply imagining things,' said Miranda robustly. 'Look, I'll get Mum up here and you can see for yourself. She's perfectly OK. In fact, she has even started sketching in watercolour again.'

'You're *sure*?' Tilda pleaded. 'You're not just saying that to make me stop worrying?'

'Absolutely certain,' Miranda wondered irritably if it would not be more sensible simply to tell Belle and the twins about Luke and Chloe's troublesome affair, and thus avoid all this undignified subterfuge. She supposed it would be cruel, but the whole thing was becoming ridiculous.

'Well, if you say so.' Tilda drew back and moved in from another angle. 'You know, I still can't see why you need her here any more. You seem to do most of your work at home. You have Adam. Why do you have to have Mum as well?' She tried not to sound resentful, but it was not easy. When Miranda had lived at home she had monopolised Alain's interest, charming him almost as though he were one of her legion of admirers. Now, just as Tilda was beginning to triumph over that painful cause for jealousy, her sister had taken it within her extensive rights to monopolise Chloe. Well, it was not on.

'I'm not getting into that,' said Miranda wisely. 'Talk to Mum about it, not me. She chose to come here. It was her idea, if you remember.' This was true in essence, if not in precise detail.

'Maybe. But something has changed since then, I know it has. I just don't know what it is.'

She looked so uncertain that Miranda recovered her sympathy. She stood behind Tilda's chair and began to massage her shoulders.

'Poor love, you're all knotted up. Relax. There really isn't any need to worry so much. Look, I'll get Mum up here, and we'll have a nice afternoon tea, with cucumber sandwiches. And you talk to her and just – play it by ear.'

By now, Tilda had begun to think that Miranda was kind and reasonable and that her curmudgeonly thoughts had been unfair.

Belle stood outside Adam's door. She felt sick and her heart was jumping about in her chest as if it wanted to crack her open and burst out like the disgusting thing in *Alien*. If this was love, you could keep it. Or perhaps it was fear? What would he say? How would he be? Would he want to back off and go into a rigid denial?

Oh God, there was only one way to find out.

She tried to still herself and empty her mind, as she did before going on stage. She could not tell whether or not it worked. 'Get a grip!' she muttered to herself. 'If you can make it happen again now, he will be yours for life.'

She let herself into the studio with the key she had providently kept after Moriarty's welcome party. Adam was sitting at his desk, lost to the world, his fingers moving in a pensive *andante* over his keyboard. She came up softly behind him and covered his eyes with her hands.

Adam froze. His eyelids fluttered in her palms. Then he sighed and placed his own hands on top of hers. There was a long silence.

'Well, Delilah,' Adam said, barely breathing. 'You have rendered me eyeless. What next?'

'The mill and the slaves? There must be a better idea. How did you know it was me?'

'Don't be foolish.'

She nodded, satisfied. How could he not know? She bent to rub her cheek against his hair. 'Are you glad I'm here?'

'It's more complicated than that. But yes, gladness comes into it.'

She set free his eyes and took his hand, pulling him out of his seat. 'Please – I need to go to bed with you. Or I won't be able to believe it.'

He made a sound as if in sudden pain. 'Belle – we need to think about this,' he began.

She slapped him hard across the face. 'No,' she spat. She kissed him with a savagery Cosmo would have found intoxicating, grinding her teeth into his lips, drawing blood and licking it into her.

He broke away. 'Come on,' he said despairingly and pushed her into the bedroom.

On the bed they behaved like two ships grappled together in a high wind, the furious seas roiling around them, whipped into a vortex by their own turbulence. They were exultant, flaming, overwrought, carried away on the waves of her determination and his willingness to accommodate fate.

'How exclusive we are,' she said afterwards. 'A free élite, outside the rules. Reflected only in each other.'

'Pure narcissism,' Adam said. 'That's *why* it's not in the rules. It's too inward-looking, a closed circuit. That's not good for society!'

'We don't have to worry about that. You've got Miranda and a baby; that should keep society happy.' She was a true fantasist, he thought. The whole of *The Thousand and One Nights* was playing inside the theatre of unreality that was her mind. But nothing was stronger than the imagination of a fantasist. If you wanted proof of that, look where she had got him.

'How can you tell whether you are in love or not?' Tilda demanded of the room in general. She and Miranda had produced the promised afternoon tea and, one by one, the others had joined them for the ritual. Adam, who had gone out, saying he needed some air, returned with one of Parvati Neerim's Raj-Type Chocolate Cakes, a moist and midnight creation whose hollow centre was crammed with mango and fresh cream.

'There's no way you could ask the question,' Belle said definitively, 'if you were. It's something that just *is*. You don't make it happen. It comes from outside, like a – a state of grace. Isn't that right, Mrs Olivier?' She appealed to Chloe to deflect interest from what she realised was too great a certainty.

'If you are very lucky,' Chloe said, a mite drily.

'And if you're not?' Miranda asked.

'A state of *dis*grace, I suppose,' Adam said lightly, feeling feverish. He smiled at Tilda. 'Why do you ask?'

'Oh, we were just talking, some of us at school.' She looked around the circle of faces. 'Only Belle seems to know, so far,' she challenged.

'I based it on something my father once said.' Belle shook her head as if it did not matter very much, after all. 'He's a throwback to the all-time great romantics, my father. Isn't he, Adam?'

'Yes, he is.' Adam gave her a brotherly smile.

'Do you take after him?' she continued wickedly.

'You'd better ask Miranda,' he said to punish her.

But he succeeded only in punishing Miranda, who was sorrowfully conscious that he had shown no romantic inclination whatever towards her since their last argument about Joel. 'I think,' she told Tilda, 'that everyone is different. One can only speak for oneself. There are no rules to life – you are sure to be disappointed if you think there are.'

'Having lived twice as long as you, my darling,' Chloe said softly, 'I believe I am coming to the same conclusion.'

'I've had enough of this,' said Belle sturdily, leaping up and dropping crumbs on the floor. 'Let's play Monopoly.'

There was a universal groan.

'On one condition,' Adam said. 'That all sharp and blunt instruments are first put under lock and key.'

'You can play the boot,' Belle told him sweetly.

She bewildered him. Half an hour ago it had been the *Arabian Nights*; for the next hour and a half it was going to be the Family Soap.

Belle lay across two seats and stared at nothing while the

train juddered and shook them homeward. Now and then she sighed.

'Are you going to tell me what's on your mind?' asked Tilda, who had been patient as far as Carshalton Beeches.

Another sigh. 'I'd like to. But I think I'd better not.'

'It must be something pretty stupendous, anyway,' Tilda decided. 'I can tell by the way you look – kind of happy and glorious.'

'Well, I *did* win at Monopoly. And I got the TV part.'

'Belle! Why didn't you tell everyone?'

'Because I don't think I'm going to take it.'

'But it's your chance to start being famous.'

'Yes, but once you start, you have to go on, or you lose it. I think I would rather start later on, when I've finished drama school. Otherwise, there would be just too many plates in the air.' It was a pity she would not need to stay with Adam for the filming, but she could always find another excuse when she needed one.

'You're being excruciatingly sensible,' Tilda said admiringly. 'But you always are when it's about acting.'

'I hope so,' Belle said. 'Happy and glorious, eh?' She chuckled.

'You know what I mean,' said Tilda in her school-marm voice.

Happy and glorious, Tilda decided, was what she too would like to be. If sex – even unattainable sex – could make Belle look so exalted, whatever must the real thing be like? (She closed her mind, for the moment, to the peculiar morality of Belle's case.) Anyway, she told herself with daylight bravura, she was sick of being tormented by outrageous dreams about unspeakable Joel Ranger when Paul was the one she wanted. It was an unwanted intrusion in her life, as if one of Rufus's computer viruses had invaded her system – it had got to stop.

There being no time like the present, especially if one was just a little shaky about one's enterprise, she made an appointment to see her GP on the way home from school and arranged with Paul that he would come round that evening to work with her.

Dr Amanda Graham gave her a brief examination and prescribed the Pill without any personal questions, adding that Tilda ought not to rely on it solely for the first couple of months. 'It takes some time for the body to get used to it.'

'I expect it does,' Tilda agreed, thinking more about the sex than the contraceptive. She wondered if she would become an addict. Obviously most people did, or how else could you explain the way they behaved?

'Did you make any progress with your mother?' Paul asked when they took a break. They were adding some muted piano and flute to the eerie, atmospheric sounds recorded by the orchestra to haunt Act Three of *Dracula*.

Tilda shrugged. 'You tell me. She said it wasn't natural for me to worry about her so much – that I was at the age when I should be rebellious and critical and embarrassed by every word she uttered. But why should I be, when we've always got on so well? It seems to me that *she's* the one who is rebelling, running off to London and living like a student again.'

Paul laughed. 'I guess it can happen at any age. But does it matter? And is it really any of your business?'

Tilda was surprised. 'I *thought* it was,' she said, frowning. 'She is so hard to understand at the moment; I can't *help* worrying.'

'You worry too much.' He put his arm around her. 'It's time you began just letting things happen.'

'What do you mean?'

'You should let life surprise you sometimes, instead of always needing to be one or two safe steps ahead.'

'I see.' She thought guiltily of her little wallet of pills.

'Don't be offended.'

'I'm not.'

'Really not?'

She moved closer and kissed him gently. 'Really.' After a time they altered the tempo and the kisses became less gentle. Still holding Paul's hand, Tilda got up. 'Come on,' she said. 'We'll tape the rest in my room.' It was not an unusual invitation; the room was furnished for study and entertainment as well as sleeping. But this time he sensed it was different.

'Are you sure?' he asked.

'Don't worry,' she teased him.

When they entered her room she threw the tape on the bed and kissed him again, pressing against the length of him, rubbing her body over him until she got the inevitable result.

'Tilda, this isn't fair,' he protested.

'It is. I promise.' She stood back, smiling invitingly, and began to unbutton her dress. She felt detached about it, as if she were acting rather than just being, but she knew she wanted what would happen next even though she felt numb all over just at this moment. Her dress was denim and the buttons difficult to undo. Her smile became fixed.

Instead of touching her, Paul sat down on the bed and watched her fumbling. 'What are you doing, exactly?' he asked. 'What is this supposed to be?'

Her chest tightened and she stopped unbuttoning. 'What do you mean?'

'I mean I want you to consider precisely what it is you are trying to do. Is this an attempt to seduce me? Do you want to make love with me? Do you want me so badly you can't bear not to do it?'

'Well, I – oh God, I've blown it, haven't I?' Her body gave way and deposited her glumly at the other end of the bed. She began to cry. Paul got up and sat beside her. 'There's no need for that,' he said kindly. He started to fasten her buttons. She tried to help and their fingers tangled. He kept hold of her hand.

'I'm sorry,' she said miserably.

'It doesn't matter,' he assured her, 'but why did you suddenly feel you *had* to sleep with me – as opposed to simply wanting to?'

'I didn't. I don't,' she said painfully. 'I mean, I *do* want to. I'm just so nervous about it. I can't seem to behave naturally.'

'But I thought we decided,' he said patiently. 'You can take all the time you need.'

'But then it's sort of – hanging over me. I'd rather we got it over – the first time, that is – and went on from there.'

Paul shook his head vehemently. 'That's crazy. Making love isn't just something you want to get over. Or, if it is, it means the whole thing is over. I learned all about that with Fiona Thompson.'

'Does that mean you want us to finish?' Tilda asked tragically.

He clapped his hands loudly in front of her face. 'Don't women ever listen? Tilda, I think I love you. I think you probably love me. That seems to be more than enough to be going on with. Isn't it?'

Her veins filled with relief. 'Of course it is,' she said shyly.

'Then, no more sexual harassment, please,' he begged. 'Making me have an erection and then unbuttoning your dress. You're not a slag or a cock-tease, so why behave that way?'

'I'm so sorry,' Tilda said wistfully. 'I just wanted to do something that would make everything feel right.'

Paul smiled. 'That's a lot to ask of that particular act; though I admit it tends to make you feel that way, at the time.'

'Mum says it's the most astonishing feeling you can have. She wouldn't try to describe it for me because it's such a special, individual thing. Oh, I miss her so, Paul. I wish she would come home.'

Adam had barely spoken to Miranda since she had told him

she was going to allow Joel to see Moriarty occasionally. He had kept to his own apartment and they had neither slept nor eaten together. Miranda did not know whether she was more miserable than furious, or vice versa. His behaviour was so alien to his nature that she had no idea how to deal with it. He had never left her alone before and she was badly hurt by it.

When Joel arrived one morning, his satirical anti-hero's face shining with pleasure at the sight of Moriarty sleeping peacefully, he had only to put out his hand towards Miranda and she was shot full with arrows of desire. She stood, stuck and bleeding like a female Saint Sebastian, and helplessly watched his smile of absolute understanding grow and grow. The hand he had politely extended homed to her breast, which stood up and shouted for joy.

'I take it I may come in?' he said mildly.

'Yes,' she said. Oh, yes please. Was this her uncontrollable hormones at work again? Or was it that seductive section of olive-skinned throat and chest between the open edges of his shirt – white, for once, and laundered to a choirboy dazzle – which implored her to touch?

She did touch, brushing and stroking with the tips of her fingers, imitating his as they found their way inside her kaftan, then pulled open the ribbons that fastened it.

'Lie down,' he said. He kicked the door shut behind him and began undoing his belt.

'On the floor?' she murmured faintly, already there, warmly transmuting to a pool of liquefied lust.

With inspiration like this, Joel was at his mad, bad, Byronic best. He treated Miranda as a map of Europe and set off on a lordly progress encompassing the entire Grand Tour. He drove his coach and horses with breathtaking speed and control, accompanied by his grooms, his manservants, his tame doctor and his domesticated bear, each of whom had a different pair of hands (or paws) and individual ideas of how to use them. It must have been the bear, surely, who turned her over and rogered her on her knees? And later, in balance or recompense, it was certainly the poet, the artist, the most realistic of all romantics, who took her sweetly in the missionary position, then wrapped them both in the folds of his soft, lawn shirt and raised his head to gaze into her eyes, repeating, 'Miranda, Miranda, Miranda – if I were ever to say "I love you" to any woman in the world, that woman would have to be you.'

There was nothing, nothing at all, she could trust herself to say in return.

Sore and satisfied, still sitting upon the floor, they ate cheese on toast and played with Moriarty who, Joel claimed, had recognised him at once because she laughed at him and made a grab at his nose. Miranda forebore to mention that she did this to Adam every evening, or that this playtime visit was now the only remaining communication between the two studios.

'I didn't need that delicious experience to remind me how good it used to be, but maybe you did?' Joel suggested in tones for which many silkworms had laid down their small lives. 'I came here to tell you that my offer still stands. I want to help provide for Moriarty. And I want you and me to go on doing this.'

'You make it sound easy.'

'It is easy.'

'As usual, you are pretending Adam doesn't exist.'

'Does he?' Joel's white smile appeared, now rather more pristine than his shirt, which was all he was wearing. 'Do you know, I never did like the idea of your sleeping with him? I'm afraid you will have to make one of those loaded choices women are always inviting into their lives.'

'I've already made it once,' she reminded him.

'Yeah, well. It isn't everyone gets a second chance.' The smile gleamed again, advertising fluoride, sex and mildly malicious intent.

'Jesus, why does life have to be so bloody difficult?'

Miranda banged her fist on the floor, bruising her knuckles.

'To make it more interesting?' Joel reached for his jeans and neatly pulled them on without getting up. 'Look, I'm out of here. I have to finish setting up the show. You'll come to the opening, won't you? Tomorrow evening, around seven. Dress to kill, and don't dare come without Moriarty.'

This, at least, was something to which she had decided to agree. She had watched, encouraged and criticised Joel's work since they had met as first-year students and he willingly admitted her part in it. He was about to gain the triumph he deserved and she wanted to be there to see it.

When she kissed him goodbye she felt important soft parts being wrung from her body by an Aztec fist. After he had gone she remembered she had felt like that every time he had left her.

This was a hopeless fantasy she had indulged in. A fairy tale. A shirt as white as innocence did not turn its wearer into a prince.

The exhibition was in the Yamamoto Gallery on the first floor of the Docklands cathedral of commerce which housed the London offices of the Yamamoto electronics industry and Takashi Yamamoto's rooftop paradise. Two other artists were also featured, but Joel had been awarded the best space, in four interconnecting rooms with pale walls and quiet whitewood floors, which he had converted to his needs with the aid of five young Japanese who formed the in-house team of exhibition makers. Tonight, dressed in dark robes printed with the four-leaf logo, they circulated trays of wine and sake with the serene detachment of Shinto priests.

The first thing Miranda saw, as she entered the sky-high atrium at the heart of the building, was a gigantic photograph of Joel with his name flying on a banner beneath it. It testified to the fact that his was one of the most beautiful faces in the western world. She tore her eyes away and crouched to talk to Moriarty, who was reclining at a comfortable angle in the minimalist silver pram that had come in a small flat box from her grandmother in Paris. She was wide awake and her eyes were swivelling busily. She had slept all through the night and most of the afternoon and was ready to be entertained. Miranda had dressed her in a scarlet Pierrot suit, with silver pom-poms, her soft black hair providing the perfect little skull cap. She herself wore a high-cut slink of a dress, patterned in black and silver diamonds, with a scarlet imaginary flower pinned near one bare shoulder and another arguing with the magenta streaks in her hair. She paused to get her bearings at the entrance to the gallery and Joel was beside her before she could blink.

'You look sensational,' he said, kissing the sensitive spot beneath her ear. She shivered.

'So do you, Funny Face.' He bent to let Moriarty make her customary lunge for his nose. 'Why don't I carry you?' he suggested. 'You can't see what's going on down there.' He released her harness. 'We can leave the pram in the cloakroom,' he told Miranda.

When they walked together into the gallery, she thought she had never seen him look so openly happy.

'Now, focus straight ahead and upward.' He pointed. 'There!'

In a startling presentation that made the best of the height and sweep of the room, an outsize, camp and carnival homage to the motor-cycle burst through the upper wall in a shuddering vroom of pure energy that fooled the eye to make the body freeze.

Miranda gasped. 'I guess that's you, up front?' she said breathlessly, relishing the slant-eyed icon in black leathers, with the give-away white smile. 'No helmet?' She raised her brows.

'That's how it is, in art and dreams – living life without

a helmet.' He hurried her past half recognised, enticing sights, all but obscured by the crowd of friends and students, art-money moguls and potential hypers and buyers. As they passed into the next room, he spun her to the left.

'You see?'

It was the other half of the Harley. Miranda was riding pillion, her arms round his waist as it disappeared through the wall, her hair and her red skirt flying above her well-formed, naked buttocks, her long legs tensed on the pedals in liquorice-strap sandals with six-inch heels.

'You bastard!' she cried.

'Yeah, well, sorry about the knickers.'

He grinned and she suddenly got the point. 'One of your centrefold, sexist-pig dreams?' She said icily.

'You got it, moons of my delight.'

'I would like,' she declared, 'to wear a mask for the rest of the evening.'

'That would be a shame. You *could* hitch up your skirt and show them how maligned you were, instead.'

'Not, as it happens,' she admitted, laughing at last. 'With this dress, they would spoil the line. Come on, get me a drink and show me all your other tasteless secrets.'

'Beauty cannot be tasteless.'

'That sounds right, but it's probably immoral.'

'I don't care about moral.'

'I know.'

'Morality is just a viewpoint. Islamic fundamentalists consider it moral to stone a woman to death for adultery.'

She sighed. 'I'm opting out of this discussion. I want to look, not talk. Shall I take Moriarty now? Won't she spoil your ice-cool image?'

'Stuff my image. Come on, darling,' he cajoled his daughter. 'Grab the world by the nose. Later, Daddy will teach you to grab it by the balls.' Moriarty produced the gummy grimace that, by now, could probably be counted as a genuine smile.

In the first room, there were the Harley paintings, surreal intimations of machinery tearing into air, the shapes recognisable but not figurative. In one, a three-dimensional topography of disaster was built up in what appeared to be real mud: dried, caked and rusty blood; and broken, murderous shards of steel. They shared their space with the war pictures which Miranda had watched him working on: vast, confident canvases, teeming with inhuman acts of execution and revenge. Their colours were unacceptably gorgeous, as if they depicted a Renaissance feast. They were good, extraordinary, but she had always hated them. She had told him, once, there was no compassion in them, that he should look to Goya for his master.

'I know,' he said, reading her face, 'but everything else is new. You may be surprised.'

In the second gallery, small and painted a pale terracotta, everything suddenly became miniature. Decorative pewter or velvet frames occupied the walls, their contents intricate and obscure until closer examination. People burst into bright flurries of surprise as they sustained the change. Joel led Miranda first towards two glass tanks, standing on tables in the middle of the room. Each was a yard long, two feet wide, eighteen inches high, and two-thirds full of bluish water. Suspended in one, floating below the surface, was a modest enlargement of a castrated penis. It was made of some distressingly realistic plastic material and coloured in squeamish shades of indigo, worm-pink and grey. Set in the end of the glans, a single glaucous eye gazed reproachfully at the tiny figure of a woman swimming away from it, using its stolen testes for water-wings. She swam naked, and her long-legged body and the cinnabar hair streaming behind her on the internal current were plainly Miranda's.

'I thought this might be here,' she said. She liked it. It made her laugh. 'There is a companion.'

In the other tank a small male figure sat in splendid solitude upon a rock protruding from the water. His legs were wide apart and the same high-coloured penis rose between them, flanked not by testes but by the severed heads of two women, one of them Miranda's, with her flowing hair, the other, blond and pouting, recognisable as Cally Baker's. The little headless bodies floated with their limbs pathetically dangling, Miranda face down and Cally on her back.

Miranda weighed the pros and cons of punching Joel in the face and decided against it, but only because it would be bad for Moriarty.

'I suppose this one is entitled *Why Should Girls Have All the Fun?*' she said demeaningly.

'Could be. Or perhaps *The Right-on Man's Reply to Feminism – Fuck 'em and Top 'em*'.

'You're sick, d'you know that?'

'Nonsense. Where's your sense of humour? Come over here. Let's see if there's anything else you recognise.' He sounded mischievous. With misgiving, she followed him over to the wall.

At first, she thought the intricate constructions of velvet, leather, metal and semiprecious stones were nothing more than the exquisite decorations appropriate to the covers of extravagantly produced books. Looking closer, she realised that the intricacy was of the unfolding and revealing of hidden flesh. That thing which resembled the clasp of a medieval book of hours, shaped like a winged lizard with jewelled, extended claws – that rosy velvet pouch upon its back was an open vagina, the glisten of quartz between its lips. Nearby, in an ebony frame, a brooch for one of Beardsley's perverse fetishists – a leather flower petalled with pricks and arses, stamened with steel whips and tiny, inventive instruments of sexual torture. Next, there was a series of brothel windows, luridly lit to focus on the little leather and lace-clad creatures with their naked breasts and buttocks, their labia turned back with jewelled pins. In the first scene, the whore was having natural congress, standing, with her client. From then on, the level of the relationships sank to ever lower depths of perversion. There were triads, there was a group of three masked men on one woman, there was a dog, (a rather fine model of a Dobermann) and eventually, there was murder and last of all, intercourse with a female corpse. Everything was finely and minutely wrought, the technical perfection overwhelming. Miranda understood that it had been a journey towards the heart of darkness in all of us, testing our will towards excess, our need and ability to realise our fantasies. And then, with Joel's typical delight in defying expectation, the last few frames turned out to hold only wonderfully ingenious jewellery, a sighing release from the previous stress, stunningly coloured, witty and sweet.

Joel knew better than to talk to her about any of it, just yet, though he did mutter 'Beauty? Morality?' close to her ear as they moved to Room Three. Other people were talking, they could not keep quiet; words calmed their fears and clothed their prejudices, expressed their outrage or approval. They were like an aviary disturbed by cats.

Room Three was in semi-darkness and contained only three pieces of work.

A Victorian couple, dressed in stiff layers of formal clothing, performed the sexual act while the man sat on a chair with the woman, facing him, on his lap. They looked into each other's faces, pleasured and intent. They were proper, domestic, even virtuous.

A second couple sat in precisely the same position, performing the same common act. This time they were naked and their conjunction was explicit, everything seen and understood. Their faces replicated those of the first pair.

The third couple did not reveal their pleasure so clearly in their faces; this was because their faces were, in fact, perfectly clear. Like the rest of their bodies they were moulded in transparent plastic. Beneath this the workings of the major organs – heart, lungs, liver, kidneys, upper and lower intestines and the full arterial system – could be viewed in clinical and liquid detail, blood and water supplied by a hidden pump. All was in the open, all safe and sane. There was nothing more to know about the body. What you really had to worry about was the mind, the pump of passion and perversion, frustration, obsession, fetish and true-blue love. Joel provided no answers but, like all good artists, he asked the right questions.

In the last room, Miranda wept and threw herself into his arms. Moriarty crowed and held out her arms in ecstasy. It was a very little space, like a summer-house inside-out. It was dim and scented and there seemed to be trees. The air was filled with fireflies, their pointillist lamps flashing urgent sexual signals from the willing female to the male seeking in the dark. It seemed a projection of the part of Joel that Miranda would never be able to stop loving; she thought of it as the innocence lost by the abused and lonely child he had been, something he could only touch once in an unknown, magical number of days or years. And now he had made a gift of it to all who passed through this enchanting room.

When Adam entered the gallery, everyone had crowded back into the first room, overflowing into the atrium. A party atmosphere prevailed; there were shrieks of laughter and the occasional tinkling crash of glass above the energetic, argumentative buzz. Normally, if, for instance, he been covering the show for the paper, it might have been the kind of thing he enjoyed; but he had come tonight because Miranda was here and he needed to know exactly why. She had left a note to tell him where she had gone, nothing more. She had not suggested that he follow her. Though she might have known he would.

He scanned the room for her and did not like what he found. She and Moriarty were standing with Joel in front of one of his bloody great anthems to death and destruction, being photographed by Hugo Sladen, whom Adam knew because he had taken many pictures of Helen. Miranda was glowing, positively phosphorescent with pleasure.

A brick descended in his stomach. He held back, his anger building, until he saw her hand Moriarty to Joel, who held her up against his shoulder and draped his other arm around Miranda. Adam pushed through the neighing crowd in seconds, planted his back to Hugo's lens and snarled at her, 'What the hell do you think you are doing?'

'What does it look like? For godsake, Adam!'

'It looks,' he replied bitterly, 'as if you have lost your mind.'

'It's just a photograph,' she said helplessly, wishing she could be angry but already overtaken by growing fear. Instinctively, she took Moriarty from Joel.

'What's your problem?' Joel enquired neutrally. 'It'll be a great picture – the family that plays together—'

Adam hit him and was dazzled by Hugo's flash.

'You didn't have to do that,' Miranda said furiously. 'Joel only wanted some souvenirs. This evening has been important to him.'

'He can have one,' Adam said in disgust. 'He can have you. He's welcome to you.' He turned to Joel who was rubbing his tender jaw. 'Just don't ever expect her to know what she wants.'

He walked away without another glance at her.

'He's right,' Miranda said, suddenly pale. 'What am I doing?'

Joel groaned.

Justly proud of his photographs, all of which captured the verve of the moment, Hugo sent round the morning papers. MUSE'S PARTNER NOT AMUSED, sniggered the *Telegraph*; YES, SIR, THAT'S MY BABY! proclaimed the *Sun*; the *Guardian* emphasised the cultural aspect of the evening with an operatic VISSI D'ARTE, VISSI D'AMORE. Miranda wanted to die.

She had not seen Adam since he had helped to originate the headlines. Unable to concentrate on any work, she waited miserably for him to return in the evening, filling in the immense longeurs by confessing to Chloe every detail of her dealings with Joel – without, of course, the sex. Chloe was no more amused than Adam had been. She told Miranda roundly how irresponsible she was, how disappointed she was in her, and how well she deserved Adam's contempt. After this, she took the sodden lump she had created into her arms and comforted her, telling her what a good mother she was turning into, how well she thought of her almost completed collection; even that she could understand (had it been any other man) the instinct that awarded Joel the right to love and support his child. Having forgone breakfast and midday snack because there was an iron bar in her belly, Miranda recovered enough to eat a small meal at tea-time. At six, she heard Adam go into his studio. Feeling it would be inappropriate to use her key, she knocked penitently on his door.

He did not answer, so she knocked again. Nothing. She called his name, then repeated it in a stronger tone. Still no reply. Adam simply did not want to know.

She returned to her own territory and dialled his mobile number.

He had switched off his phone. She could not think what else to do.

'Will you talk to him?' she begged Chloe, who by this time was very sorry for her.

'If you like, but I think it would be better to wait until he has stopped feeling quite so hurt and angry.'

'That's the very worst thing, how much I must have hurt him. I hate myself for it.' There were definitive slamming noises from Adam's flat. They could be identified as three or four drawers followed, after a short interval, by the outer door. Miranda gave a little gasp.

'He has stopped loving me, I know he has,' she said, her voice high and taut. 'It started a while ago – I don't know just when – but this is the last straw, the excuse he needed to leave me.'

'I'm sure that's not true,' Chloe said reassuringly. 'You are just frightening yourself. I would have noticed something.'

'You wouldn't. You hardly notice anything round here except Moriarty. It's all right for you,' she added with a surprising dash of Tabasco. 'Not every man is as forgiving as Dad. You don't know how lucky you are.'

'Really?' Chloe looked at her searchingly. 'I wonder what, exactly, is the comparison you are making?'

But Miranda had finished talking. She did not want to admit that she too had committed an act of sexual betrayal. When Chloe had slept with Luke it had seemed to her an outrage; her mother had turned her safe and comfortable world upside-down. And now she had done the same. The extent of it was only just beginning to come home to her.

It closed her throat with the fear of irretrievable loss.

Just before midnight she used her key to enter Adam's flat. She was not sure what she wanted there. She moved about, from studio to bedroom, kitchen to bathroom, touching surfaces, opening cupboards and drawers as if she might find in one of them a clue to her next step, as in a Treasure Trail. But the place was empty. Adam had gone.

'I've just been talking to Miranda,' Luke said, wandering into Chloe's room at nine at night as if they were halfway through a conversation. 'Adam refuses to call her, so thought I would let her know that he's with us, for the present. And, well – express solidarity. Poor girl, she seems badly shaken.'

'She is. The scandal sheets haven't helped. God, how I loathe Joel. Adam and Miranda are in real trouble, while for him it's all a glorious explosion of cheap publicity. How is Adam, anyway?'

'He has closed up, cut himself off. Neither Dinah nor I can get to him.'

'They were so close. It's such a waste,' Chloe said fiercely.

He looked at her sideways. 'Isn't it, just?' he remarked ambiguously.

'Not another word,' she warned. 'I've had enough emotion for one week.'

'Whatever you say,' he said biddably. Then his face lit. 'I've brought you some music. I heard it and it was all about you. Or me. The composer is contemporary – Gavin Bryars – but it has some spirit in common with the medieval things you like.' He took a CD from his pocket.

Chloe dropped on to the bed and made herself comfortable. Though grateful for the release of strain promised by this change of direction, she remained wary. Music had always been part of the private language between them.

'It's called *The Green Ray*,' he said. 'There's a story attached to it – an entire novel if you like – by Jules Verne.' His voice fell into its story-telling mode, becoming richer and furred with persuasion.

'It seems that on certain coastlines – this one happened to be on Orkney – and under certain atmospheric conditions, a green ray shines out of the setting sun at the precise moment when it first appears to rest on the horizon. The legend is that if a pair of lovers share this moment, the bond between them is mystically sealed forever. In the book, a young man tries time after time to contrive this shared moment, but his efforts are continually frustrated, by events, by the weather, by a ship that passes at precisely the wrong time.' Luke smiled at her. 'You will love the music. And perhaps you recognise the story, as far as it goes?' His metaphor did not elude her, but she shook her head and waited to hear.

The music filled the room with a quality of celestial purity that made her imagine the thin blue air surrounding the ice-cliffs of an arctic landscape. A saxophone sounded in long melodic phrases the swansong of glaciers under the sun. There were chill, tingling strings, each as distinct as a frozen, separate hair, and small bells like icicles ringing. They were among the most ecstatic sounds she had ever heard, and as with all that we love instantly, it was impossible not to feel that they expressed a most significant part of herself.

When the piece was over she returned to a body as relaxed as though she had stepped out of it and left it lying on the floor. She smiled at Luke, acknowledging both his gift and his understanding of her. There seemed to be no pressing need for speech.

Following the changes in her face, he had seen her consoled and renewed before his eyes. He did not expect a lasting transformation; even music such as this could not perform miracles. But to see her like that had refuelled his hope. The need to be close to her became insistent. Her head was thrown back on a cushion, her eyes were closed, her face softened and clear. He restarted the music and sat beside her. She stirred but he did not touch her for several minutes. By then she had already waited too long. Her music-washed body was quickening, every cell coming alive to him. Alive. It was so simple and necessary to hold him, to kiss; she would not have believed how easy, this time. No prison gates clanged behind her; no fires leaped in punishment; she saw no vision of garments spotted with sin.

'In one second, you're going to tell me we must not go any further,' Luke said sadly.

'No. I'm not.' There was a wonderful release in saying it. She laughed. She had never seen him so astonished.

'I don't know what has happened to you,' he breathed, 'but for godsake let's make love before you change your mind.'

'I won't. I just have.'

They both laughed, breathless, shining-eyed, as unable to believe their good fortune as if it had come from outside, dispensed by some *outré* fairy-godmother.

They undressed hastily, thirsting for skin against skin. Naked, they surveyed the mind-mapped territory of each other's bodies and rejoiced to find the country still familiar.

'It's been so long,' Chloe said, beginning to tremble.

Around them, the music built its ice-castles on the air, its calm, transcendent ecstasies a paradoxical backdrop for the hot surge of sexual energy that powered them. There was no possibility of foreplay, of pacing, of artistry; such hunger has no patience, no finesse. Chloe felt her body bloom like a Celtic fertility figure, billowing with wanting flesh, splayed by outsize organs waiting to be filled. Luke felt the blood race to his prick, each molecule clamouring to be first. She held herself open for him as he slid into her, sharing his soft, triumphant cry. Even in their extremity of need they reached, by means of this vulnerable conjunction of melded flesh and minds space-travelling beyond thought, for the cosmic magic by which each made the other the the gift of their essential selves. The climax was extraordinary, a rush to the head as much as the loins. It left them gasping and shuddering with the suddenness.

When he had slipped out of her, Luke leaned on his elbow and searched Chloe's face, as he always had, for the lineaments of her pleasure.

'I love you,' he told her. 'I've missed you. I've missed seeing you blush all over your body – and the incredibly voluptuous sight of all that bronze-age hair on the pillow.'

'I have missed you, too. I've only just let myself know how much.'

'What made you change your mind?'

'Well, you could say that my grip on things has been stretched so far that letting go was my only option. Or simply that I did it because I wanted to. Or even that it was an impulse that came out of the music – that I thought of that young lover striving to influence fate towards happiness, while all I could do was to push away the thing I longed for. All are equally true, or untrue. It's just – I suddenly saw that this could happen, that we could love each other, here, tonight, without hurting anyone.'

'Tonight.'

'Yes.'

There was his pirate smile, demanding ransom. 'And after?'

'I will not regret this,' she said steadily, 'but it changes nothing.'

'Don't worry,' he said sweetly. 'I know you better than to believe it could.' This was untrue. Given one unbelievable event, one must at least allow the possibility of another.

'Then you won't mind,' he continued, in what she thought of as his Connery voice, 'if I take a personal inventory while I'm here – just for the memory bank?'

He began at her feet, kissing the toenails, vestigially coloured like ripe sloes, touching knowledgeable fingertips to the pressure points on the soles. Chloe gasped at an unexpected sensation. 'How can touching me *there* make me feel it *here*?' Her hand was pressed to her groin.

'It's a Chinese trick. I've been reading a manual on oriental medicine.'

'Dinah's?'

'She doesn't do any of that now; she's wholly dedicated to flying.'

'With Philip Dacre?'

'Yes. Well, I *think* that's all they do, though I may begin to wonder soon.'

Chloe gave no opinion. Dinah had told her long ago that Philip had invited her to become his mistress. Admittedly he had been drunk, at a party, and Dinah had been as much amused as flattered; but one never knew. Certainly it would be a mistake to put such information in Luke's mischievous hands. Her only reply, therefore, was to direct those same hands to the area of her vulva that was fluttering like a singed moth. At that precise moment, timely as the ship that passed unwelcome on the Orkney coast, Miranda's voice was raised at the door.

'You've shot the bolt,' she called. 'I can't get in.'

Chloe sighed luxuriously. 'She'll think I'm asleep,' she whispered to Luke. 'She'll go away.' And, of course, she did.

But their happiness was a living thing in the room with them.

Miranda decided to go in to college. She had to take her pastels in for their final assessment, and it might as well be today. It was something to do. It would stop her listening for Adam to come home, even though she knew he would not do that. She hefted Moriarty on her hip and took her down to Chloe's.

Her mother was sitting in the sun near the window, drinking the strong French coffee she liked to wake up with. She wore the gold-shot robe Miranda had made for her and her hair was loose and tangled.

'Hello, my lambkins,' she greeted them. 'Another lovely day! I just saw the most beautiful sailing ship go down the river.'

'You bolted your door last night,' Miranda said, sounding both waif-like and accusing. She planted Moriarty in the armchair. 'I wanted you and I couldn't get in.'

Chloe's grey eyes were vague. 'I was very tired – the heat, I expect. I slept very deeply. Coffee? Anything to eat?'

The subconscious knows when there is something in the air that concerns it; it sniffs and stores the scent.

'No, thanks. I must go. I'll be back around two. I'll phone if not.'

'Are you sure you feel like going in?'

'I may as well face the music. They'll have read the papers.'

'They are your friends. And at least you came out of it with your dignity more or less intact. It won't be bad.'

'You think?'

'I do.' Chloe smiled at her. It was her old open, generous smile, the one people remembered her by. 'Don't *worry*.'

'OK. See you later.' She kissed Moriarty and tickled her tummy, inciting squeals. 'Be good, honeybucket!'

She was halfway through her salad in the college café, her mind pleasantly empty, when the thought wandered into it that there had been something different about her mother this morning. Not just different, but as though she were actually another person, someone with a completely different aura. Of what? Rest? Peace? And something further. What was it? Her face had seemed fuller, too; more itself. Come to think of it, she had appeared to have regained weight overnight. The nub of it was – she had *relaxed* – something she had been unable to do for nearly a year, though she had counterfeited it often enough. But why now?

The subconscious rooted, sniffed – and snapped. Miranda knew right away what the answer was. An icy chill seeped into her with the knowledge.

'Was Luke Cavendish here last night?' she asked casually when she collected Moriarty.

'He did call in, yes,' said Chloe. And she blushed.

Her mother actually blushed. Miranda controlled a murderous desire to do her physical damage. How dare she start the whole horrible thing all over again? None of them had finished dealing, yet, with what she and that lying, damned Luke had done before. Had she gone stark, staring mad? Had he? Well, they were not going to get away with it, not this time.

'Did he stay long?' she asked, her head bent over her daughter.

'Not long. I was tired, as I said. I needed to sleep, not talk. I've told you,' she added, checking Miranda's face, which was doing a dance for Moriarty's benefit, 'you don't have to concern yourself any more on that score.'

'Fine,' Miranda said. 'Who's a clever girl, then?'

She went home and put Moriarty in her cot for her afternoon sleep. She found she was OK as long as she had something to do. She drummed up some small jobs in the kitchen and bathroom, washed some baby clothes, tidied the living-room. All the time her fear and resentment were building layer on layer of blue, incoherent funk. Her own life was already in chaos. It looked as though she had lost Adam – worse, she had thrown him away – and she had got herself into a situation with Joel which she doubted her ability to control. She ought not to have slept with him, she knew that really; but at least she had a perfect right to do so if she wanted – not like her mother, who was responsible not only for her own morals but also the happiness and security of her family. It was not the same, nothing like the same. It was not as if she and Adam were married. He was the one who had left. And anyway, he didn't even know she had slept with Joel. She sensed that her reasoning was a bit woolly here, but what was the difference? It didn't alter the facts. What was OK for her was absolutely not OK for Chloe, and that was that.

Her subconscious, which had been flaring and snuffing avidly throughout this unintelligent thought process, seized and snapped again with dogged accuracy.

She made sure that Moriarty was fast asleep, then took Adam's key from the drawer and let herself into his flat. He had taken his laptop, (not necessarily a terrible sign; he used it constantly) but his old word-processor was on his desk.

'YOU OUGHT TO KNOW,' she tapped. She was not sure why she was using capitals. They always did, didn't they? 'YOUR WIFE IS SEEING LUKE CAVENDISH AGAIN. TAKE HER HOME OR YOU WILL LOSE HER.'

She put the sheet in a brown envelope and addressed it to her father. After an anguished glance about the room that no longer seemed to have anything to do with Adam, she returned to her studio, woke Moriarty and fastened her into the silver pram. 'We're going for a ride,' she told her, 'on a big red bus.'

With some notion of further anonymity, she travelled as far as Waterloo Station, where, after a very short search of her soul, she sent her communication on its journey. Suddenly exhausted, she bought an Italian lemon cake in the Costa Brothers' coffee shop to restore her depleted energy. Then she went home to have tea with Chloe, who had at last begun on a new painting and did not notice the smell of burning boats.

That evening, Alain Olivier found that he was missing his wife quite unendurably. Something had gone wrong between them last weekend and, by now, he thought it had probably been his fault. It was foolish of him to have dizzied down into a vortex of hopelessness at the news of Mrs Cubitt's defection. He had not realised how volatile his emotions had become. No wonder Chloe had been so upset. He must make matters right with her as soon as possible; she could not be allowed to feel that he did not trust her. He picked up the phone, praying that she would be there.

'*Chérie*?'

'Alain! Darling, how are you?'

'*Je suis tout seul, et triste*. I need to see you. Will you 'ave dinner with me?'

'You mean tonight?'

'*Bien sûr*.'

She could not. Not tonight, not while her skin still smelled of Luke, while part of him was still with her, inside her; his music playing in and around her, even at this moment. She needed time to let him go again. It was not that she had thought it would be easy – now, later – when she had capitulated so crazily to whatever force had moved her; there had been no thought involved at all.

'I'd rather not, tonight,' she said. 'I didn't sleep at all

last night, thinking about Miranda. I'm so tired. Could we make it tomorrow instead?'

There was a pause. 'I want to be with you, *chérie*.'

'I know, love, I know. Tomorrow, I promise.'

He sighed. 'Very well. As it 'appens, I shall be working not far from you.'

'Good. So, come here as soon as you've finished.'

'I will. Until then. *Je t'aime. Je t'embrasse*.'

'Me too. I'm sorry to be selfish. I'll be human tomorrow. Sleep well, Alain.'

To punish herself, she switched off *The Green Ray*.

Rejected, once more Alain dived into depression. He had work to do, as always, but he did not want to work; he wanted company, friendly noise to scare away the flocks of negative thoughts. Bereft of Chloe, he sought out his children.

Rufus and Dwayne were busy on the computer. They explained that they were getting their history holiday project out of the way, early. They were producing a lengthy thesis on the cultural aspects of the reigns of the Tudors. When Alain showed interest in the Dutch letter on the screen, Rufus told him it was 'just basic, factual stuff – some contract between a Dutch composer and the Master of the Queen's Music.'

'*Bon*,' said Alain. 'Most of us think only of the great Dutch painters; we forget that there was also music.' Pleased with his son's progress, he went to see what Tilda was doing.

But Tilda was out. It seemed that, lately, she was always out, either with Paul or with Belle Cavendish, or both. All of them seemed to live for *The Soul of Dracula*, and indeed, he admired their dedication, for they would spend most of their summer holiday working on the play. Nevertheless, he missed Tilda, who was beginning to talk to him as a friend as well as her father. And now, when he would have liked to talk with her, and she was out, and Chloe was gone, he also missed the essential presence of a woman in the house. The negative thoughts began to circle, dark wings threatening. Already, he knew what he would do. He was not sure if it was out of weakness or a justifiable need. He would give in to the promptings of loneliness and a slightly angry desire, and spend the night with Helen Cavendish, who he happened to know would be free.

Alain and Helen had known each other, socially and carnally, since about the same time as Luke had known Chloe. They had always been careful to enjoy the sophisticated kind of sex that prides itself on the avoidance of too much emotion. At least, that is what its practitioners aim for. What usually happens is that this works for one and not the other – and that, nearly, is what was happening here. Helen, whose numerous liaisons were well publicised, had failed to find among them a successor to Luke, whom she had truly loved; though tragically, she had not discovered this until after her fear of domestic bliss had driven her into the affair that had caused their divorce. Now she was trying not to feel that she might have found the right man in Alain Olivier, whose heart and soul would always belong to Chloe, no matter how often (and it was very rarely) his body might stray. This permitted him to be Helen's friend and to enjoy making love to her, but not, *bien entendu*, to fall in love with her. She was beginning to think that this was a pity, even that the situation might, just conceivably, change.

'The first time,' Helen said thoughtfully, as they lay back among the mellow silk pillows in her moghul-size bed, smoking, very carefully, a Gauloise and a Balkan Sobranie, 'you were just fucking, getting rid of a whole lot of frustration. The second time, it was all for me.' She shuddered pleasurably. 'But why all that dark, desperate business?'

   '*Mon dieu, mon dieu, mon dieu!*'

She smiled. 'That is scarcely an explanation.'

'Ah, Hélène, I don't know what is 'appening to me. More and more, I am angry. It is not 'ow I am and I don't like it. My whole life feels strange to me. My skin does not fit me any more.'

'Then, *mon ami*, you must do something positive about it.'

'What can I do? Chloe is the one who must make a move – and she does not. I can't get it out of my 'ead that she may be seeing Luke again. She says she is not, but I don't know; I can't *read* her as I used to do. I feel so – powerless. Useless. *Bête!*'

Helen hugged him.

'What is that for?'

'Because you are a pearl among men, and such a delicious lover that I don't know how Chloe can let you out of her sight.'

'She seems to prefer it that way. Hélène – you are in a position to make comparisons – what is it about Luke that would let him take her away from me again?'

'It's not a matter of comparison,' she said gently. 'You know that, really.'

'I'm sorry.' He scraped despairing fingers through his hair. 'I am being absurd. It's just that I am a creature of order. I don't know how to lead my life any other way.'

She could not resist asking, 'Am I part of the order – or the opposite?'

'Of both, I think. You are my lifeline – and I am very grateful.'

He kissed her earlobe, a tiny diamond rasping his tongue. 'It's bizarre, isn't it? I took such care, once, that you should not come to rely on me. And now, I 'ave come to rely on you.'

It was not the ultimate accolade, Helen thought, but it was an advance. If Luke and Chloe finally could not keep away from each other, she would be conveniently placed to pick up the pieces. She would not wish for this to happen, however. She was too fond of Alain for that.

The rest of the night was calm and sensual, like making love in a Spanish cloister. When he left her, just after dawn, so that he would be home before his children awoke, she felt that they had become closer during this unimpassioned interlude, drifting in and out of sleep and treating each other's bodies with a care that spoke directly to the hurt spirit, closer than they ever were in their previous dance of sexual wit and excellence.

When Alain came home the house was heavy with sleep. He sat at the kitchen table, drinking coffee until after eight, when Tilda came down in her dressing-gown, rubbing her eyes.

'*Bonjour, ma fille*. You are up early.'

'I wanted to see you before you went to work. Here – the post came – they're both for you. Shall I make you some breakfast?'

Alain looked without interest at the two brown envelopes and shoved them into his pocket. 'No, thank you. There's coffee, if you would like it?'

'I'll have juice. And you'll have some toast, at least. I promised Mum I'd look after you. Did you say you were seeing her tonight?'

'Yes.'

'Well, will you try to get her to come back before the holidays are over, even if it's only for a week?'

He looked at her sympathetically. 'Tilda. We 'ave 'ad this conversation too many times.'

Tilda made a face. 'I know. I'm sorry. Just give her our love. And Dad – have a nice time, won't you?' Her voice curled up at the end as if in a question.

'Joel! I didn't expect you.'

'Yes, you did.'

Miranda stared blankly. He had phoned, but she couldn't

remember what they had said. He had not been in her mind since she had posted the letter.

'Am I coming in, or do I stand here like a dodo, holding all this stuff?'

She stood back and watched him deposit several animal-papered parcels and more flowers, horribly expensive oriental lilies. He held out a small gilded box with her name on it.

'What is it?' She didn't want it, or any of these things. They laid claims on her and on Moriarty.

'It's for coming to the exhibition. You made all the difference, in more ways than I was counting on.' He grinned. 'Was that fantastic publicity or what? Open it.'

'What. Definitely,' she said, muted. She could not be bothered trying to explain the damage done. It would please him too much. She opened the box. It contained a small, finically crafted pendant that was a microcosm of his gallery of miniatures, its intricate shapes ambiguously floral or sexual.

'It's Welsh gold. Rare now. These are moonstones – for your skin, and those are garnets – for your hair. Never tell me I am not a romantic.' He kissed her, an exuberant kiss that was not the dangerous kind because it needed no response.

'It's very beautiful,' she said quietly. 'Thank you.' He put it around her neck. It had no weight but she felt that it did.

'I made something for Moriarty, too.' He reached into his pocket.

'I just finished it.' It was a frog brooch, laquered red and green and gold, an exotic frog that only Joel had ever seen.

Miranda had to smile. 'She'll love it. I'll get her up in a minute. You're good at frogs.' They were an old, quirky obsession of his.

'I'm good at lots of things. Mainly because I know how to concentrate. Now – question time, right?' He was crackling with a bushy-tailed energy that seemed to siphon her own away. 'It's the same old question. Do you want – one: me in your bed and in your head, no strings, lots of laughs; two: tons of money for Moriarty, as long as I'm making any? I'll be as faithful as I can, and you say goodbye to the guy with the fast uppercut.' He rubbed his chin and smiled as if he enjoyed the memory. 'He's not around now, is he?'

'No.'

'Good, let's keep it that way. You might want to move out of here.'

'Why?'

'Because he might not. You could be nearer my place.'

'I won't leave here, ever!' she cried with sudden passion. 'I love this place.' She went over to the window and stood with her back to it, hands stretched as if to protect her beloved view. 'I was born here.'

'OK, OK, don't fuzz your fur at me. What's wrong? You seem like you're somewhere else. Wake up. We're talking futures, shiny new plans.'

She took a deep breath. 'Look, Joel – I've done something stupid, something I regret – and I don't know what to do about it. I just can't think about anything else, just now. I can't see any way out.'

'Honey – what is it?' Joel flipped into tenderness in his disconcerting way and wrapped his arms around her so that she cried for several reasons. She told him what she had done, and that Alain must have read the letter by now.

He looked at her in perfect astonishment. 'Jesus, girl! Are you ever a bonehead! What do you want to hit the poor man like that for?'

'Because I won't let my family break up. It's Moriarty's family too. I won't stand by and watch everything go wrong again.'

Remembering the first time, Joel stepped back and gave her a hard look. 'I'll say just one thing, Miranda: it's time you forgot about being Daddy's girl and began to grow up.

You're someone's mother now, you have to stand on your own two feet. I'll help you when I can, but you'll have to do most of it yourself. You can begin by giving me a straight answer, and maybe give yourself some, too.'

She glared at him. Why did the truth so often wear hooligan boots and carry a nasty sting?

'All right,' she said. 'But give me some time on my own. An hour.'

'You've had loads of time. This is where it runs out. I told you that after the exhibition.'

'One hour won't hurt you. Please, Joel. You could take Moriarty out to the park. You know how she loves to watch the bigger kids playing.'

Joel considered this for what seemed to Miranda an unnecessarily long time.

'Why not?' he agreed at last. 'I should probably get some practice pushing that glitzy babymobile.' He clapped his hands and marched towards the bedroom. 'OK, Professor, let's go!'

Miranda followed him. 'She'll need changing first.'

'I can do that. I've been learning about babies. You'd be surprised how much I know.'

'Learning how?'

'Oh, you know – manuals, talking to owners. An awful lot of people drive them these days.' He looked at her with sudden seriousness.

'I love the hell out of her,' he said. 'I want you to remember that.' No ifs for Moriarty, just the raw, unqualified emotion.

She was not likely to forget.

Joel's absence, though badly needed, did not help as much as Miranda had hoped. Her mind was a lump of unleavened dough, leaded with questions like small hard currants. What did she want? What was best for Moriarty? Would Adam ever come back? Did he despise her? Did he still love her? And if he did not come back, ought she to take

— 230 —

what Joel offered, because Moriarty was his daughter, and because he was fun and unpredictable and would always have the fatal ability to turn her bones to jelly? And to hurt her and humiliate her and make her fall in love with him all over again, and one day leave her flat, and Moriarty too? With Joel, excitement and fear of loss went hand in glove. He would not change, and she could not survive in the intemperate climate that was necessary to him. Nor, her intuition assured her, could her very respectable artistic talents survive against the enormity and certainty of his. Joel would be a star, and he deserved to be. But Miranda did not want to be the mistress of a star. Although, if it were Adam, and he became a successful writer, it would be different. With Adam, she could still hold on to herself, her work, her supreme place in Moriarty's life; but Joel couldn't help himself – he would take her over, dominate her, subsume her into himself. She would not be able to grow.

Oh Adam, please come home and make everything fall into place. The wish made her laugh at herself. Even now, when Adam had so explicitly left her, she just could not begin to see him as someone who would do that.

Her wits were still churning like an aged washing-machine when Chloe came in, offering to take Moriarty out for some air. There being no point in subterfuge, Miranda explained the situation.

Correctly assessing her mental state, her mother spoke soothingly. 'I wish you would try to talk to Adam before you make any decisions.'

'How can I, when he won't let me?'

'He might if you were to pursue him a little.'

'It's no good, Mum. Just leave it for now.' Her voice rose. 'I *have* to know what to say to Joel – he'll be back any minute.' She looked at her watch and yelped in surprise. 'Oh no! He should have been back twenty minutes ago.'

Chloe frowned. 'Is that what you'd expect?'

'I don't know. He might be giving me extra time. Oh hell, what'll I say?'

'Well, why don't you simply tell the truth? Say that you hope Adam will come back, and that therefore you can't take any money from him at present, but that you're happy for him to visit Moriarty at regular, pre-arranged intervals.'

'I could try,' Miranda said doubtfully, 'but I don't think it would work.'

Chloe understood that she was purposely vague. 'What is he, Svengali?' she demanded. 'This is *your* choice, not his. Listen, Miranda, I sympathise with your difficulties. No one better,' she added delicately. 'But isn't Adam more likely to come back to you if he knows you've broken with Joel?'

'There'd still be a catch-22. Adam won't accept Joel's rights as Moriarty's father.'

'He might, if he loves you as much as I believe he does – and if you can make him see that he doesn't have to be jealous of Joel.' Psychiatrist, heal thyself, she told herself grimly.

'Perhaps,' said Miranda non-committally, having no confidence in such an unlikely prospect. 'Come on, Joel, you mean bastard. Where *are* you?' She looked at her watch again. 'You don't think – well, he wouldn't have taken her home with him, or anything? To sort of, under-line his rights?'

'Do *you* think so?' Chloe asked sharply. 'Because, if you do, then I think we should give him another ten minutes before we call the police.'

'No – surely he wouldn't? He just hasn't noticed the time. He gets so involved, playing with Moriarty. He really – he's very fond of her.'

'Even so, this is hardly a recommendation. If he *is* going to see her regularly, there will have to be strict ground rules.'

'I'll call him at home, just in case. Oh God, Mum!' She

stopped halfway to the phone. 'Suppose there's been an accident?' Her face was ashen.

'Right. Now it *is* time to call the police,' Chloe determined. 'Sit down. I'll do it.'

'What did they say?' Miranda was rigid with misery.

'There have been no accidents in the area. They've sent out a call to all cars to look out for the two of them, and will ring back as soon as they hear anything. Don't start to worry yet, sweetheart. Why don't you make us some coffee, just for something to do?'

'All right. Oh Mum, I can't believe this.'

'Oh God, why are they taking so long?'

'It seems a lot longer than it is.'

'It's twenty minutes. He's been gone nearly two hours.' Miranda was spiralling towards hysteria. Chloe took her in her arms and rocked her.

'I'll do anything he wants, if only he'll bring her back. I'll – I don't even know why he would do this. *If* he's doing it.'

'If he is, he is engaged on another exercise of power.'

'But he'd be crazy to go this far—'

The phone rang. Miranda flung herself at it.

'It's for you,' she said dazedly. 'I'm not sure—'

'Hello?' said Chloe.

'Mrs Chloe Olivier?'

'Yes. Please tell us—'

'This is the East Cheap police station, Mrs Olivier. I'm afraid we have some rather bad news for you.'

'But they couldn't have gone—'

'I'm sorry to say that your husband, Mr Alain Olivier, has had an accident at the local power station. A fall. We don't yet know the extent of his injuries. He has been taken to the Queen Victoria Hospital. We can arrange for a car to pick you up and take you there at once.'

'Thank you.' Miranda was tearing at her arm. 'That won't be necessary.'

'Where is she? What's happened? *Tell me*!'

Chloe choked on hot tears. 'It's not Moriarty – it's Alain,' she gasped. 'He's hurt. An accident in the power station. He's in hospital. I must go there.'

Miranda was shaking. 'Oh God, don't let this be happening.'

'I'm sorry.' Chloe sat down and grappled with the need for oxygen, and then for clarity and common sense.

'I have to go right away, sweetheart. And you must sit tight and wait for the police to call you. And why don't you call Adam? He would want to be with you. There ought to be someone. Will you do that?'

'Yes. Maybe. But what's happened to Dad? What kind of accident was it? How badly is he hurt? Mum?'

Chloe shook her head. 'I'll let you know the second I find out myself. Try to calm down, Miranda. I know it's hard, but we must both try to get through this without breaking down. You understand?'

'Yes, you're right. OK. I'll be calm, I promise. I'll be fine, Mum. But are you sure you're in a fit state to drive yourself?'

'I wouldn't trust anyone else.'

Chloe accomplished the journey without incident within a private bubble in which she had caused time and thought to stop. There seemed nothing real about the hospital, which was like every other hospital; one hurried down corridors, stood breathless in lifts, encountered busy white coats and blue dresses. She might have been watching herself in an episode of *Casualty*.

The first tremor of reality came when the nurse pulled back a curtain and showed her a man stretched on a bed. His body seemed almost without content. Only the face was visible between the navy blanket and the white bandage covering the head. At first she thought it must be someone else. There was nothing in this still absence that she could relate to Alain, whose face could not be still, whose intelligence was never absent from it, even when he was asleep. But this was not sleep.

'He's not – he isn't—?' She knew what it meant, now, when they said that the blood could run cold.

'Oh! No, no.' The young nurse was embarrassed; she ought to have told her what to expect. She was tired; she usually did better than this.

'I'll get the doctor,' she said. 'He wanted to know when you arrived.'

'Alain,' Chloe whispered, bending over the bloodless face, '*vraiment, c'est toi, mon amour*?' The stillness was absolute. She tried to find hìm. The bones were right, but the flesh was not flesh. What, then? Marble, no. Grass, as they claimed in the funeral service? But that was much later. It took time for flesh and bone and blood to become grass. Years. Her thoughts had become slippery and uncontrollable. She grasped at them.

'Oh my dearest love, where are you? Please come back.'

'Mrs Olivier?' The soft voice was at her shoulder. 'I'm Doctor Shaw. I'm afraid he won't be able to talk to you today. He had to be heavily sedated for the journey in the ambulance.' The doctor was about her own age, his hair and face and coat uniformly crumpled. He offered her a chair which she refused.

'What can you tell me? I only know he fell.'

'I'll be able to give you more information when we have the X-rays; but there is an obvious longitudinal compression of the spine, as one would expect. He fell from quite a height – I believe he was investigating some pipework – at about twenty-five to thirty feet.'

Automatically her mind's eye went with him on the climb, saw his absorption in the work in hand, the care for self relaxed, the never-before slip of control, the helpless chute through terror to oblivion. The sound the body makes as it lands.

'What were you saying?' she asked in someone else's voice, 'about X-rays?'

'Well, the vertebrae will have been crushed and almost certainly dislocated by the fall. What the X-rays will establish is whether there is any damage to the nerve tracts in the spinal cord.'

'What would that mean? Paralysis?'

'Yes. And it would make a full recovery unlikely.'

'I see.' She marvelled at her cold composure. 'And otherwise?'

'There's really no point in my saying anything further until I've actually seen the X-rays,' he said gently. 'We'll make him comfortable on the ward, make sure he has a good night's sleep. And I would like you to go home and take a sleeping pill, and I'll see you in the morning. About ten o'clock?'

'Very well,' she said. 'There is obviously nothing I can do here, and I still have to talk to our younger children.'

'Tell me about them,' he said, sounding as though he cared. She responded to his effort and they walked down the corridor together, discussing the twins and Doctor Shaw's two student sons. She found it amazing, how matter of fact she could be; she even laughed at something he said.

In the foyer, she called Miranda, giving her the bare essentials. 'Is there any news of Moriarty?'

'Nothing.' Miranda's voice was shaky. 'The police haven't found them. And Joel isn't at his studio. I don't know what to do.'

'Hold on, sweetheart. I won't be long. Did you reach Adam?'

'No. His mobile isn't on. But I called Dinah. She'll tell him – and she wants you to call her, as soon as you can.'

'I'll do that now. See you in half an hour.'

'Chloe! Oh my dear, how is he? And you?' Dinah's affection came at her so fiercely that, for the first time, tears burned Chloe's eyes as she gave her brief explanation.

'I am so very sorry,' Dinah said. 'Nothing prepares us for such a shock. And as for the damnable Joel – what a hideous coincidence! Not even he would have wanted this to happen.'

'No. I'm worried about Miranda. I don't think she can take much more. Have you spoken to Adam yet?'

'Not yet. I will. I promise. Chloe, what about the others? Tilda is here now, with Belle. Why don't I pick up Rufus and bring him over, and then tell them everything? It will be easier for them than hearing from you by phone. They can both stay here, Dwayne too, if Rufus wants him, until you know just how things are going to be.'

'Bless you, Dinah. I'll feel so much better if they're with you. I'll talk to them later, of course, in the evening.'

'I'll tell them. We'll keep in close touch. Chloe? Listen – Luke wants a word. If that's all right?'

'I don't – well, I suppose so.' This was not the time.

'Chloe?' His voice shocked her with its harsh intimacy. 'I don't know how you're feeling; quite unreal, I imagine.'

'Yes.'

'I want so much to be able to help you.'

'You will, with Rufus and Tilda.'

'I feel there should be more. Hold fast, my love. Alain is a strong spirit.'

'I know.' She could not bear this conjunction.

'And don't worry too much about Moriarty. Joel will surely bring her back.'

'We can't assume that he *can*! Luke, I have to go.'

'I'm with you. Goodbye.'

It was clear to Dinah, who was listening as Luke spoke to Chloe, that he was still head over heels in love with her. She was surprised and interested to find how little this distressed her. She felt jealousy, naturally – she would have been inhuman otherwise – but it was no longer the white-hot-with-pincers jealousy that had tortured her into raging idiocy last year. Anyhow, jealousy did not seem an appropriate emotion in the present circumstances; it was mean and small and beside every possible point. She put it away in the back drawer of her mind, to take out and examine when these sorrowful times were past.

Next, she spoke with Adam's editor, a sensible man who knew both where he was and how to get hold of him. Ten minutes later Adam phoned. He was chastened and horrified by Dinah's news, and she had the satisfaction of hearing him get into his car and race away to Miranda while they were still talking.

Miranda was hunched on the window seat, staring over the airy carnival of summer London, seeing monstrosities. It was the Queen Mother's birthday and the weather was *en fête*, together with thousands of loyal citizens. Something about the naïvely hopeful combination of pale lapis skies and small clouds sailing like dandelion clocks was causing a fine web of hairline cracks to run, swift as breaking ice, across her heart. She was clutching the little blue jumpsuit, scattered with yellow stars, that Adam had given Moriarty, holding it against her breast. 'You are my sunshine,' she had sung, trying to knit together the favoured song and the jovial day into a talisman to keep her child from harm. She followed it with the equally potent 'I'm Into Something Good'. She was still singing, her voice a single candle in increasing darkness, when Adam let himself in with the key he had not been able to give up. He was halfway across the room before she noticed him. They said nothing at first, though both of them wept.

'I'm sorry. I'm so very sorry,' Miranda said feverishly. 'You were right. I should have listened to you. Adam – I am so scared that I'll never see her again!'

'Don't, sweetheart. Of course you will. You know Joel is only playing one of his cruel games. And I do believe he loves her.'

She shook her head, tears flying into her hair. 'It isn't that – I deserve to lose her. Because of what I did—' The words rose on a wave of pain. 'I don't know how I can even tell you. You see, what happened to my father – it was my fault.'

He held her, hushing and stroking, attempting to contain and diminish the extraordinary flood of grief. 'How can that possibly be? He fell. Miles away. It was nothing to do with you.'

'It was. It was. Please, just listen,' she begged. She told him, gasping with fear. 'You see? That's why it happened. It must have been. He has climbed like that for years; he never put a foot wrong. You know how careful he is, always. What else could have broken his concentration to that extent? He was thinking about Mum and your father, I know he was. Perhaps – oh Adam, I can't bear to think this – but he may even have jumped.' She finished on a note of hysterical horror that made him wonder if he should slap her face. But he could not do it and he held her more tightly instead, murmuring as if to a frightened animal.

'How you must despise me,' she mourned.

Pity turned him inside out. 'No, no,' he said. 'I understand you well enough to know why you did it. It was my fault as much as yours. If I had not walked out in that stupid way, you would never have written the letter.'

'I can't be sure.'

'I think you can. You had two huge reasons for insecurity dumped on you at once. You snapped. I'm not surprised; it's a mirror image of what happened last year. Then, it was Chloe and Joel who let you down; now it's Chloe and me. I'm sorry, Miranda. I love you. I always will. I've handled things badly because I saw the problem as mine – when in fact, it was yours. Forgive me?'

'I love you too, and I won't let you take on my guilt.'

'You aren't guilty, just unhappy. Alain would understand. Now listen to me a moment. There's no point in torturing yourself before you even know what happened. Whatever may have been on Alain's mind, he most certainly did not jump. You *know* that, because you know him.'

'Yes.' She looked at him gratefully. 'I suppose I do. He always tries to put things right, not run away from them.'

'As I did,' said Adam ruefully. 'Though I would have run back, very soon. I couldn't have stayed away from you.' There was an interval for therapeutic kissing.

'The other thing you have to accept,' Adam resumed seriously, 'is that you must never tell anyone you wrote that letter, however confessional you may feel. Not Chloe, and absolutely not your father.'

'Joel knows,' she remembered, stricken.

'Shit.'

'He could use it in some horrible way.'

'We'll face that if and when it happens. Meanwhile, why don't we try to find out if any of Joel's aquaintances have any idea where he might have gone? Cally Baker, say, and some of the other students.'

'I should have thought of that myself,' Miranda said. 'I just haven't been *thinking*. Only panicking.'

'Well, I'm here to stop you doing that,' Adam said lovingly. 'And I won't go away again. Ever.'

Chapter 11

ELIZABETH'S COTTAGE HAD BELONGED TO HER father, who had been a gamekeeper. In the middle of a forest in Hertfordshire, it stood on the edge of a green grass bowl which the early evening had filled with a lemony light. The house had white walls and blue paintwork and was half smothered in honeysuckle and wild roses. When Joel had first come here, while he and Elizabeth were lovers, its fairytale quality had provoked caustic denial in him; this time, he saw only what an idyllic place it was for a child. The fact that the child was not yet four months old did not impinge on his fantasy of future weeks and weekends, stretching forth in sunshine and in snow, as he and Moriarty grew into a closeness of blood and respect such as he had never experienced and had only begun to imagine. Joel could barely remember his father. His recollections of his step-father, on the other hand, were deeply graven. The strong sun which would bless his present enterprise during the next few days would not be powerful enough to erase the pale repeated logo of the belt buckle from his brown back. They were scars he disliked to catch sight of because they also contained the memory of his mother's tears. She had been unable, or not willing enough, to help him, and now he did not like to see women cry because, if he felt pity for them, he also felt anger. He preferred not to consider how Miranda might be weeping now; if she was, it was in a good cause. She was going to learn something important from this experience.

It had been very easy, kidnapping his daughter. The plan had jumped into his head when Miranda had started to waver again, driving him mad with her drawn-out indecision. When he fetched Moriarty from the bedroom he had collected some extra clothing for her and tucked it under her in the pushchair. On leaving the building, he had not turned right towards the park, but had taken her to the supermarket to buy supplies. Afterwards he had wheeled her round to the private carpark at the back of the lofts. There had been no one about to see him put the pram and the bags in the boot and the baby in the back of his dusty black Renault 5. It really had been predestinately simple. He had driven all the way here without even one hold-up, a single young man in an unassuming car. You don't *see* a small child asleep on a passing back seat, especially if she is camouflaged with an old tarpaulin used for transporting works of art, not even if you are the police and are supposed to be looking for her. And another thing that doesn't help – you have absolutely piss-all idea where to look.

Moriarty was the first person with whom Joel had shared the cottage since Elizabeth had left, a year ago, to work in a New York gallery. She had given him the key in exchange for some basic housework and tending of the garden, in which mainly wild things grew. He had told no one about his retreat, not even Miranda. He had always needed a secret place in which to be himself without human company. Here, his companions were animals; half-tame squirrels, rabbits and the occasional roe deer who came to drink from the pond where the frogs leaped and swam and stared at him while he sketched them into characters for the book he was planning for Moriarty. He would use it to teach her to read and to see in detail. In the car, he had described to her where they were going, and had told her the story of Snow White, explaining that she would have to make do with one rather large dwarf rather than the usual seven. Miranda would have found it interesting that he made no claim to be the Prince. It was all the same to Moriarty, who enjoyed the caressing sound of his voice and treated the tale as a lullaby, sleeping fast until they had arrived. She had cried briefly on waking, missing Miranda, but she liked Joel's smell and the comfortable way he held her, and the lack of fuss when he fed and changed her. She had soon produced her more entertaining repertoire.

Now they sat out on the little terrace outside the front door and waited for the sunset, listening to the conversational claims of birds and watching the shallow, fluttering wing-beats of a nursery of Dawbenton's bats, as they learned to skim the surface of the pond for insects.

'Do you know, Professor,' Joel said peacefully, luring the busy black eyes back to his face, 'if I were to live here with you – and hardly ever see anyone else – I would probably turn into quite a nice person.'

Moriarty made the small, agreeable noises that she had found to cover most subjects. 'And then again,' he said regretfully, with his beautiful smile, 'you have to go out and sell your work, you have to have at least a couple of friends – and you really do have to have a good fuck. Excuse me—' he added with formal courtesy. 'I expect, like your mother, you would prefer it if I said "make love".'

They had put Alain in a pleasant room of his own at the end of the Spinal Injuries ward. Its predominating colour was an optimistic yellow, and the presence of a small table and a couple of rush-bottomed chairs allowed him to imagine himself in Vincent van Gogh's sunstruck little bedroom in Arles. He would ask Chloe to bring him some *tournesols* to complete the mood. They would be in flower now, in the fierce hot fields of Provence where he had spent his holidays as a child, where he and Chloe had spent the last two weeks of their honeymoon, their skin saturated with that yellow sun.

Dr Shaw had just left him. He liked the man; he was clear and efficient and possessed a welcome ability to put himself in his patients' place, though Alain conceded that in his own case this would soon be difficult. He was not sure just where that place was going to be; in Paris, perhaps, in the family mausoleum near Versailles, or at home in Sheringham among Chloe's dissolute soldiers in St Mark's churchyard, or possibly they could scatter him illicitly in the Renaissance room in the National Gallery where he and she had first met and recognised their future. The twins might enjoy doing that.

Alors, mon homme, ça y est! La fin. C'est tout. It was very hard to believe in one's own death. Especially when one had been given no precise sentence. No term had been set; indeed he might continue to exist for a very long time, if he wished. He would not be able to feel or move anything below a line halfway down his ribs, and he had been advised to move very little above that line for an unpredictable number of weeks. On one level, he had accepted what he had been told; on another, he assumed he was trapped in a particularly horrible nightmare and would soon leap free of it.

And then Chloe came in, and he saw her face and believed what he had heard.

'Am I allowed to kiss you?'

Her lip trembled. He stilled it with his finger. 'Yes.' He smiled. 'You can do anything you like with my 'ead – it is apparently exceptionally 'ard, by the way – and there is nothing wrong with my 'ands and arms, or my chest; which is useful because it contains my 'eart. But I fade out somewhere below that, rather like your famous Cheshire Cat. One day, I may become nothing but a smile.' A tear fell on his nose. He wrinkled it. 'Ah, don't look like that, *chérie*, I don't have any idea of my limitations yet. Why don't you try touching me in several places, and I'll tell you what I can feel?'

She bent her head to kiss him and was relieved to feel his arms go round her. The kiss was long and left them both breathless. ''Ow is it? The same?'

'Just the same.' She managed a smile. 'It's a good start.'

He sighed. 'But, alas, we may not go further. Not ever. You understand?'

'I've spoken to Dr Shaw.'

'*Bon*.' Dr Shaw would have told her the truth, as he had asked.

He stroked her wet cheek and pushed back her hair, cherishing its buoyant red and gold. 'This cannot be a life – such as we 'ave 'ad together.'

'But it's still a *life*!' she cried. 'And you can't *know* – there are so many amazing recoveries – that girl who was in a coma for seven years.'

'Chloe, the nerves are smashed. They cannot be repaired. It would be a life without movement. I would be little better than a talking head, watching you come and go, wanting you – I am still able to do that, even if the desire is all in the mind – where it has always been, as well as all the rest.' He paused. 'I am not sure it appeals to me.'

Chloe leaned all her concentration upon each word he spoke, not daring to wander beyond the protective syllables. It was necessary that she should be for him as she had always been. She would not allow the shrieking metamorphosis to reveal itself; the winged and scaled creature she must become, the woman-into-serpent, a soulless Melusine who could no longer suffer, had no further concern with the beauty and aspirations of human love or the pain and degradation of the body and spirit; a creature of myth that could put on a woman's face when it wanted to, and wear her body skilfully to clothe her cool amphibian heart.

'Alain, you are not going to die,' she said angrily. 'I am not going to let you.'

'You are dramatically determined, *ma mie*.' He sounded

amused. 'But, from what the doctor has told me, it seems we have little choice.'

This was not true. He did have a choice. He might live on, as he was now, possibly with some minor improvement, for a number of months or years – even, God help him, decades – the duration of which, again, was unpredictable. Or he could live for a short, civilised length of time, within which Chloe and the family might begin to accept that he must leave them. They could also revisit past happiness; there had been so much of that. He could talk to his children. Wrapped in Chloe, or in his work, he feared he had done too little of that. Most of all, he needed to talk to Miranda. He thought it very likely that she was the one who had written that unsigned, pathetic letter; who else would have advised him to TAKE HER HOME OR YOU WILL LOSE HER? Like him, she was reduced to a condition of panic-fear by the least idea of family dissolution. He knew precisely how wretched she must be feeling now and he knew that he must say something that would help her, as soon as he could. He could not mention the letter, of course; nor could he tell her that he had been thinking about the writer of that letter, coming to his conclusion with faultless emotional logic when he had fallen from the steel height to this altered state. It had been a slight, such a very slight shift in his concentration that had made him fail to see the oil on the walkway he was treading so slowly and lightly, balanced like an acrobat, his body attuned to the pressure of air. It was no one's fault. And anyway, what did it matter now?

If only he could somehow make Miranda understand that her fears had been groundless; he himself had known that from the moment Chloe had entered this room, with both their lives so clearly written in her face. Whatever Luke Cavendish had meant to her, and he did not under-value that, it was unimportant now. What counted between them was the immeasureable richness they had shared, not the small amount she had given away. But perhaps, after all, there was nothing he needed to do; Miranda would surely see this for herself during the days before them.

'Kiss me again, *chérie*,' he said to Chloe. 'I am going to demand a lot of kissing. It will be rather like being very young again.'

'We've always done a lot of it,' Chloe reminded him. 'We never grew out of it.'

'I know, but now we are going to do it even more. *En effect*, one 'as to do what one can.' He said this lightly, but he felt the tremor go through her. 'You must not do my agonizing for me,' he admonished her. 'I promise I will be serious sometimes. But not yet. So – no more tears.'

'I'm sorry,' she said. 'I won't do this after today. I hope. I shall treat you as if you had simply broken your leg.'

'*Mon dieu, mon dieu, mon dieu*,' he said, delighted. 'And now, tell me – I know the children are 'ere, but did Miranda bring Moriarty? I should so much like to see 'er.'

'Not today.' Chloe measured a reasonable amount of brightness. 'She has a cold. Nothing much, she'll soon be better.'

'*La pauvre petite*,' Alain deplored. 'Such a tiny 'ead, to 'ave a runny nose.'

When the children did come in, they did not come separately, but tightly knit together in a cable stitch of supportive arms. Alain welcomed them lovingly but, in the end, he would not allow them to stay long because they were too woeful, the twins quite incapable of controlling their tears, and Miranda frozen into a horror which he feared might suddenly speak its name.

'Don't worry,' he said cheerfully as they departed, commanded to go and drink coffee in the cafeteria, 'I am not going to die just yet.'

'I hope you understand,' Chloe said triumphantly after they had gone, 'that you can't say that to them and then just turn your face to the wall.'

'No, I can't, can I?' he agreed thoughtfully. This

was going to take more time and more careful stage-management than he had realised. Meanwhile, he gave her some little commissions for them. Miranda was to discover and bring him a paperback copy of *The Golden Bowl* by Henry James, his favourite writer in the English language. Tilda was to bring in his CD of Barenboim conducting Brahms's Fourth, at a concert which he had heard with Chloe in Paris. Rufus was to lend him the best back copies of *VIZ*, the bizarre humour of which he was determined to comprehend before he died. Or decided to die. Or perhaps, to live a little longer? How extraordinary it was, and wonderful in a way, to be given such a choice.

If you had been standing that evening in the small garden opposite the lofts, looking up at the windows, your attention might have been caught by an uneven flow of human figures moving back and forth across one of the broad panes, or standing before it, unnaturally still, as if seeking something far out in the ether. One after another they came, in a restless, asymmetrical dance.

'He *can't* die,' Tilda kept saying. 'He's too strong. I can't remember him ever even being ill. He can't *die*.'

'Shut up, shut up!' Rufus said convulsively. 'Of course he won't die. Why do you have to keep on *saying* it?'

Tilda exploded into tears and ran out of the room. She would go next door to Adam's place, where she would repeat her agonised litany to Paul, who was sitting by his phone, at home in Sheringham.

'He's not *really* going to die?' It was Rufus's turn to entreat Chloe. 'Tilda's just being hysterical, isn't she? The doctor only said he *could* die, not *would*.'

'I don't think anyone can tell, yet,' Chloe said. 'We just have to wait.' She would not snatch away hope, not while they were, all of them, still so deep in shock. They would surely become calmer in time, if only because they would wear themselves out; but she would not speculate on how soon they might be able to come to terms with the probable future.

For herself, she felt both the unfairness and the rather shameful relief of being the one who had to keep the world on its axis. There was no room for the ballooning enormity of her own grief while these raw new emotions had her children by the throat, fury and determined disbelief tearing at them in the unacknowledged shadow of a prefiguring fear.

Miranda had said almost nothing since they had come home. She sat close to Adam, whose frequent, loving touch only reminded her how little she deserved his comfort. Inwardly, she gabbled a form of prayer to an entity in which she did not think she believed. Please – I'll give up anything if I can have my baby back. Please, let it be Joel, only Joel and not some terrible accident, or – you hear such appalling things; people do things to babies nowadays that one never knew about – even children do. Don't let it be anything like that. Oh Joel, let it just be you; you would keep her safe, wouldn't you? Everyone says you would. Oh God – don't let me have to lose Moriarty so that my father doesn't die. Can it really work like that? It can't, of course, that's a crazy idea. Superstition. If only I *knew* if it was the letter that made him fall. Adam says not but how can he know? If I could just tell Dad I wrote it, then at least I could ask him. I could explain that I did it because I was in such a muddle over Adam and Joel and I didn't really know what I was doing. That's almost true; more than. But oh, what would you say to me, *mon père*? *Que je t'aime*. And oh Christ, why doesn't the phone ring? I think I shall start screaming if it doesn't— What was that, Mum? Did you say something?'

'I'm going to make us some supper. Would you like to help?'

'I will, but I don't want anything myself.'

'Nor do I,' said both twins.

'I'll make it anyway,' Chloe said.

Miranda followed her into the kitchen, while Tilda flew for Adam's phone again.

Alone with Adam, Rufus glanced several times at his abstracted face. Eventually, he succeeded in framing a question that was on his mind.

'Do you think,' he said apprehensively, 'that it could have been my fault that Joel kidnapped Moriarty? You see, it was me who told him when she was born – he might never've given her a thought if I hadn't.'

Adam smiled. 'No, Rufus, I don't think so. Someone else would have told him, probably even Miranda herself. The kidnap has nothing to do with you, honestly.'

'You're a hundred per cent sure?'

'Yes, I am. It's a struggle between Joel and Miranda, and in the end, Joel knows he can't win. I think that's why he has done this.'

'Because he's angry about not winning?'

'I think, on balance, he's probably more sad than angry.'

'It doesn't sound much like Joel.' Rufus frowned.

'No, it doesn't, does it?'

'I don't really understand. But that's OK. As long as it wasn't my fault. Thanks, Adam. You've been ace.'

A little later he said, more soberly, 'Do *you* think my Dad might die?'

'I don't know. None of us does,' Adam said gently. 'We don't have enough medical facts yet. If I were you, I should try, if you can, to stop asking yourself the question. It's a bit like nagging at a wound – it just makes it worse.'

'I suppose so,' Rufus sighed, 'but I can't help thinking about it; there isn't anything else to do.'

It occurred to Adam that here was a method of relieving some of the pressure they were all engaged in building up. 'All right – why don't we go back to Sheringham and pick up those copies of *VIZ*?'

'Right now? Wow, thanks. Tilda can come too, and get the CD.'

Tilda, when invited, was dubious. 'But what if there's any news—?'

'That's what mobiles are for,' said Adam.

'You won't forget to switch it on?' Miranda asked anxiously.

Adam kissed her goodbye. 'Not any more,' he promised.

'I'd forgotten how young they are, still,' Chloe said across the sombre area of peace that was left behind them. 'Their defences are barely formed. They have nothing at all to arm them against this.'

'None of us have,' Miranda said. 'I don't know what to think, or say, or do. I feel red and raw and bleeding inside, and my brain won't work to help me.'

Chloe nodded. 'I just keep hearing echoes of Tilda – he *can't* die, can he? Alain has always given so much strength to this family; how can he suddenly be so powerless? How can he fall, when he has a dancer's balance?'

'I don't know. How can he? How can Moriarty be gone? How could any of this nightmare have happened in the space of a couple of hours? Our whole life turned upside down.'

Like her snowstorm, Chloe thought, as she had before; shaken without any care for its minute inhabitants. How intimately she used to imagine their terror, and how perfectly she experienced it now.

When the others came back, the two women were still sitting there, close together in the darkness, in front of the window.

Rufus went quietly into the kitchen and made some coffee, while Tilda, with a gesture that canvassed assent, put on the Brahms symphony that Alain had asked for. The music was a part of him that they could have there in the room with them and, for Tilda especially, it was a place in which to lay her pain.

— 251 —

They continued their vigil, silent for the most part, touching each other occasionally, until dawn.

Well after nine, Chloe came to with a jolt to find herself still on the sofa with her arm around Miranda. Her head was full of cotton wool and her bones were cramped and aching. She shook out her stiff limbs and went downstairs to her own studio to call the hospital.

'I won't keep you a moment, Mrs Olivier,' the ward nurse said. 'Dr Shaw would like a word with you.' She was a cheerful girl, but she did not sound cheerful. Chloe suspended life and breath.

'Good morning, Chloe.' The doctor's voice was tired. 'I'm afraid Alain didn't have a very good night. There has been a complication.' He paused, and she understood him to be giving her time to prepare herself.

'Go on,' she begged.

'He insists on telling you himself.'

'When can I see him?'

'This morning – but he's going to need a lot of rest and sleep in the next few days, so I don't think you should bring the family. I'll see you at about eleven.'

'Very well. Thank you.'

Her legs stopped supporting her as she dropped the phone. She collapsed on to the floor and blacked out for a swimming second. Reeling and nauseous, she breathed deeply and hung on to consciousness. When she felt a little better she put her head down on her knees and rocked herself backward and forward until she could bear to allow the thinking process to begin again.

A little later, she got up slowly and went over to the south-east corner of the room, where she pulled the covering sheet off a small canvas standing on the easel. It was a self-portrait, just the head and shoulders, the pose taken from Leonardo's *Narcissus*, in which the young man is seen in profile against a gloom of lowering crags. He is not aware of them because he sees only his own reflection in the water below, but they crowd him and enclose him, just as his dreaming self-love crowds and encloses the spirit of humanity in him. Cut off, abstracted from the world, he is a lost soul, himself his wilderness.

Chloe studied what she had done. She thought, now, that even the work of painting, of consciously following this subject, was a new act of self-involvement, a dwelling in her own pain. It was irrelevant now. Everything had changed. She took the half-finished picture off the struts and stood it against the skirting-board with its unseeking face to the wall.

Adam and Miranda were using two phones, trying to track down anyone who might conceivably have any idea where Joel might have gone.

'I can't get hold of any of them,' Miranda complained, nerves fretted with frustration. 'If they're at home, they're out; if they're in college, they're unavailable. And Joel's such a loner – no one ever knows where he is.'

'Wouldn't it be better,' Chloe suggested, 'if you both went into college and talked to everyone you can find?'

'Sure – but aren't we going to see Dad?'

There was no point in adding to her anxiety until there was something to tell. 'Not this morning, the doctor thinks. He's very tired. Delayed reaction. He needs to sleep.'

'But you're going.'

'Yes, but he may not be awake. Go, Miranda – it's better to be doing something. I'll find out when you can see him again.'

Alain was awake when Chloe arrived, though Dr Shaw said he had been sliding in and out of consciousness for several hours.

'Can you talk?' she asked when she had kissed him, breathing in his skin.

'Enough. *Je t'aime.*'

'*Moi aussi*.' She held his hand tightly. 'Tell me what happened.'

His shoulders approximated his characteristic shrug. 'I am afraid it was the Gauloises.'

'Alain! You can't have been smoking.'

'I asked a visitor – she was passing the door. She took them from my jacket, in the cupboard.' He coughed, with evident pain, following this with the look of a guilty adolescent that made her heart ache.

'You are such a fool,' she said softly.

'Ah, but the cough – it is useful, you see. Because it 'urts a little, they 'ave discovered that my lung is collapsed.'

'No! My darling, I'm so sorry. What does it mean? Can they put it right?' She cursed the ignorance with which we guard ourselves, while still wishing to be guarded. 'What did the doctor say?'

Alain sighed. 'They will 'ave to scan to see if I 'ave an embolism. If I do, and it is a big one, they might want to operate.' He repeated his sketch of a shrug.

'How can they operate, when your spine is so badly damaged?'

'I don't know. Maybe they should not try? Already, they want to operate to stabilise the bones of the back. I think this is too much, no? Oh, *mon dieu, mon dieu*!'

'You missed one,' Chloe said miserably. 'You never do that.'

'*Mon dieu*,' he obliged. 'Don't worry, my Chloe – let us just wait and see. And now, let's talk about more pleasant things.'

For his sake, she tried. They held hands, and kissed like newly-weds, and she let him take her bravely back to the days and places where they had been most happy together. But all the time her coward imagination betrayed her with her worst fears, and with the cold, scaled creature who must become strong enough to conquer them.

When Alain became tired, she kept his hand in hers while he drifted into sleep. As she watched him, seeing and fearing the extra thinness of his face, he woke again to smile at her with the sweetness of a sudden memory. 'Will you bring me that photograph of you, *chérie*? The one in the blue dress. For when you are not here?'

The letter was behind the door when Miranda came home. She shrieked and picked it up, tearing it open as Adam followed her in.

'It's Joel's writing – read it – my stupid hands are shaking.' She collapsed on the nearest chair as he took out the single sheet. 'Adam! What does he *say*?'

Miranda – please believe that I am sorry to have had to put you through this. I know how much you love Moriarty, and how distressed you must have been. Well, you can stop worrying; she is fine, very happy and I think she has enjoyed her time with me. The point of the exercise was to make you realise that I love her too. As much as you, perhaps, in my own way. She is my child, Miranda, and no one could be more surprised than I am at the way that makes me feel. But you know this, already. Now – the police. You must have called them; it was the right thing to do. But now I am asking you to explain to them that I only took my daughter because you would not give me a straight answer; and I had to show you that I love her and I need to be able to see her and take an active (and financial) part in her life. What's so bad about that? I'll bring her back, very soon. Don't worry.

Joel.

'She's all right!' Miranda was gasping and laughing. 'She's all right!'

'Of course she is.' Adam hugged her and laughed with her and wiped her tears with his hand, while bright blue murder bred in his stomach. This time, he was going to give Joel Ranger what he so consistently asked for; it might

— 255 —

be vengeful, pointless and morally dubious, but it would make him feel one hell of a lot better.

The phone rang. 'It could be him!' Miranda grabbed the instrument.

'It's me.' It was Belle's voice, hesitant and subdued. 'I just wondered if there was any news—'

'Yes! Joel's going to bring her back.'

'That's terrific. I'm really glad, Miranda. And how about your father? We're all so upset about him.'

Ashamed, Miranda realised she had not spared a thought for Alain since she had entered the house. 'We haven't heard any more,' she said quietly. 'We've just come in. Mum might know something. I'll let you know, shall I?'

'Please – and would you – give my love to Adam?'

'He's here – why don't you talk to him?'

'No, that's all right,' the small voice said hastily. 'I have to go.'

'Belle sends her love,' Miranda reported.

'Is she OK?' He wished that she had spoken to him.

'Sad about Alain. She likes him, doesn't she?'

'Yes. Everyone does,' he said softly. He felt bad about Belle. He had pushed her to the back of his mind for Miranda's sake, during the last few days, but he would soon have to bring her to the front of it and decide what he was going to do about her. He could not imagine how they could go on as they had been, now that he had renewed his commitment to Miranda. But how would he ever get Belle to see that? And did he actually want to? How on earth had his life managed to become so unmanageably complicated?

Later, Joel did phone.

'I'll leave you to it,' Adam said.

Miranda was grateful. 'It would be easier.'

'Hi, there.' Joel was sprightly. 'Are you still talking to me?'

'Only because I have to.' Miranda had herself on a very tight leash. 'Do you have Moriarty with you?'

'Sure. Do you want to speak to her?'

'I want you to bring her home, *now*.'

'First, there's something I want you to know.'

'But you *said*—' The leash was slipping through her fingers.

'Hold on. Just listen. I'm here to tell you that I can, and will, take Moriarty like this, any time I want to. Unless you give me the modest access I'm looking for. Think. I've done it once. Nothing could have been easier. And I'll do it again. I will never hurt or distress her in any way – but I *will* take her from you – and you'll never know when it might happen.'

'You disgust me,' she said passionately. 'Don't you ever try to get anything without blackmailing for it?'

'More often than not,' he said cheerfully. 'Blame yourself, not me. You made me wait too long. You'll admit that, if you're honest.'

'What if I did? It wasn't just about Moriarty. You made me put my whole life in the balance.'

'But you wanted to,' Joel said. She could see his white, insufferable grin.

'Well, I don't now,' she said coldly. 'You can see Moriarty, regularly. I can promise you that. The rest, we can discuss. But Joel – this is not the only thing on my mind just now. You have to stop this, finish it right here. My father has had an accident. He may be going to – to die.'

'Jesus, Miranda, I'm sorry. Tell me.'

She told him quickly, running between tears.

'It's all right,' he said when she had finished, his voice urgent with kindness. 'Don't cry, sweetheart. We're on our way.'

In fact, they were outside her door in forty minutes, Joel having driven safely but very determinedly, his set face cautioning other drivers aside.

Moriarty was sitting in her silver pushchair, wearing a

sophisticated new hat made of black lace, with a bunch of cherries on it.

'Here she is!' Joel beamed as though he had just that moment created her. Moriarty screwed her head round and gazed up at him, cooing.

'Sunshine!' Miranda cried. As she scooped the solid little body into her arms, an ache that she had never quite noticed suddenly stopped.

'How does she look?' asked Joel.

'Wonderful. Beautiful. Moriarty, I love you, I love you, I do!' Moriarty laughed and put her fingers in Miranda's mouth. Then she stretched out her hand to Joel with an encouraging squeal. She quite obviously adored him. Which was just as well.

Joel shook her hand, then kissed its fingers. 'You stay with Mummy, now. You've had your holiday.'

Miranda tickled her under her chin and the squeal was redirected at her. 'Where did you take her?' she asked, extremely curious.

Joel smiled. 'It's a magic place. It will disappear for ever if I tell you where it is.'

Touched by the notion, she found herself smiling back at him. 'That sounds like a Celtic legend.'

'Well, I am half Irish – the half I can barely remember.'

'I never knew that. But I'm not surprised,' she added severely, aware that they were having entirely the wrong kind of conversation. 'God knows I've heard enough blarney coming out of you.'

He put his hand on his heart. 'Never again. I promise on the *Book of Kells*. Now, can you and I sit down and try to straighten out the Professor's future?'

It was at this point that Adam chose to return from Chloe's, where he had gone to exchange the news of the day. His face darkened as he saw Joel.

'So you're back, bastard,' he said succinctly. 'I'm delighted. Now, if you will come down the corridor with me, there is something I've been wanting to discuss with you.'

Miranda, who had seen him look this way before, did not propose to watch any further fisticuffs. 'Not now,' she stated, very clearly. 'If you want to behave like small boys, you can do it another time. Adam, I would like you to leave, please. I have things to discuss with Joel myself. As you know.'

There was more bad weather brewing in Adam's face. He nodded grimly. 'Come into the bedroom, a moment, will you?'

She followed him, rolling her eyes at Moriarty who was busily making a stork's nest of her hair.

'Just this,' Adam said, his eyes glittering close to hers. 'I no longer care what you decide about Moriarty. I accept that the little shit is her father. But you – you've had your second chance, Miranda. I want you to remember that. There won't be a third. If you ever even dream of sleeping with him again—'

'I won't. I love *you*,' she declared, almost angry now herself. 'We've had all this. It isn't necessary, Adam.'

'Really? Sometimes I think we're going to be playing the same old scenes over and over again, like some crazy New Wave French film.'

'*Celine and Julie Go Boating*,' said Miranda automatically.

'Thank you,' Adam said drily, turning away. 'I'll see you later, then.'

'Yes.' She bit her lip. His idea disturbed her. It seemed quite a possible scenario, given the circumstances; part of her even found it rather attractive.

In the studio, Joel had made himself at home on the window-seat. He was stretched out, Adam thought wishfully as he passed, like the Lord of Misrule on his tomb.

Joel caught his look of loathing and waved an indolent hand in his direction. 'You win, Sir White Knight,' he said with maddening reasonableness, 'So why the poisoned chalice?'

'Do I?' said Adam.

Joel detested hospitals. He had not been near one since his mother had died, somewhere on the other side of the morphine, in the cancer ward of St Mary's. He did not think she had recognised him, but he had held her hand anyway, and tried to recall some small happiness they had shared, just the two of them, before he had left the house he would never think of as home. What came to him, his memory surprising him with a sudden taste of sweetness in his mouth, was the first time he had ever eaten a crêpe Suzette. She had told him how much she loved them and that he would like them too, and she had taken him, for a birthday treat on the day he was twelve, to a little French café in Camden Town, where they lived. The young waitress had looked at his black hair and his blue eyes – though he did not have the smile, not yet – and had dropped Cointreau on to his plate in a luminous flash like a tiger blinking. Then she had grown bolder and done it again, pouring it this time, reckless. And there was his smile, a rich reward for her gift, though he had not recognised the power of it then, nor for a long time after.

It had been a stolen pleasure. His step-father never went about with them, did not wish them to seem like a family, and would in any case have disdained such a foreign and frippery dish. His mother had died while he spoke of the sweetness, and their little time of freedom and ordinariness together. Afterwards he had hated himself because he had never given her any such delight. He was just seventeen and he had already known who he would be; but he had not told her. She seemed too far away to hear.

The nurse showed him into a yellow room which made him think of Vincent, who had died in such a room but had painted it as a vessel in which the simple objects of his life waited for him, together with time and light. The man in the bed, resting elegantly in a blue grotto of pillows, was also a spare-looking man, his face containing many planes and his hair cut short in the style now taken up by a younger generation.

He did not know what reception he expected, certainly not the one he received.

'Joel! But 'ow nice of you. I did not expect to see you.' Alain pointed to a chair. 'You are alone?'

'Yes. I know I'm probably the last person you want to see, but I hope you'll forgive me. There is something I would like to tell you, something I want to get off my conscience, if you like.'

'I see. But why choose me for your confessor?'

'Because it is something I have done to you.'

'To me?' The winged brows flew for his hairline like Vincent's crows. 'I am not aware of it. I am intrigued – a relatively happy occurrence at this time.'

'Wait till I've told you; you may change your mind.'

'Well, that would not matter very much,' Alain said with gentle irony.

'It's the letter,' Joel declared baldly.

'Ah.' The vowel did not commit itself.

'I wrote it.' There was no comment. 'You must have wondered who it was?'

'Naturally.'

'Did you think it might have been me?'

'No.'

'Well, it was.'

The crows swooped and collided. 'Why?'

Joel released a sharp sigh, as though the reason were unimportant. 'Why does one do such things? I was pissed off, I guess. Miranda was giving me a hard time about Moriarty, you know? I would have given her exactly what she asked for – suddenly she doesn't want it any more. It really got to me. I love my daughter. I wanted to fix up something sensible between us, for everyone's sake. And we have, now. But she messed me about and that made me angry, and I wanted to – to upset the comfortable family bandwagon again. I suppose.'

'Apple cart.'

'Huh?'

'What one upsets. A bandwagon is different. It implies profit. In this case, emotional profit. Are you telling me that you have been suffering from jealousy? Of Adam and Miranda, perhaps?'

'Perhaps.' Joel sighed. In for a penny, in for a pound of sheer shit.

'Ah. Will you pass me a cigarette? Over there. No, don't light it; I am not yet so 'elpless.'

'Sorry.'

'Thank you. Please take one yourself.' He drew in appreciatively. '*Eh bien*, *je vous dis*, Joel – I am not sure if I believe what you say. Why should you care? I thought you wished to overturn the cart, not set it right again?'

'That was before—' Joel felt to his horror that he might be reddening. 'I mean, Miranda will be OK about the baby now. What I said about your wife and Luke Cavendish – it wasn't true. I made it up. Just for the hell of it. That's what I wanted to – confess, as you put it.'

'*Vraiment.*'

Joel nodded. 'It was simple spite. I'm sorry. If I'd known—' He waved a helpless hand at fate and circumstance. 'I'm really sorry. It wasn't aimed at you. I don't know quite what I thought I was doing. I just – lost it.'

'And now? You 'ave found it again?'

'Why does this amuse you so much?'

'Do I sound amused? I apologise. I tend to find everything a little amusing just now. If I can.'

'Oh, right. I see.' Joel did not know how to take Alain. He certainly made it hard to believe in his possible death. In fact, he seemed quite likely to get out of bed and offer himself as a companion to the nearest bar. And his face was so mobile that he did not even look ill.

'I 'ave thought of a suitable penance,' he announced

suddenly, looking pleased with himself. 'I like very much your work. Your exhibition is the best thing I have seen for a long time. I would like to 'ave a small thing of yours – to put on this wall.'

Joel was astounded. '*You* have seen the exhibition?'

'Of course, why not? Your talent has never been in question.'

'Only my behaviour.'

Alain gestured this away. 'So, you will bring me something of yours, and you will tell me what you will be working on next – yes?'

'Yes, I will. Both. And, thanks—'

'Alain.'

'Alain.'

'*Bon*. Now, I am just a little bit tired. I will see you soon, Joel. *Bon chance.*'

He was glad the boy had come. It had been a courageous thing to do. He was almost certain he did not believe his story, but that was not the point. He hoped he would have time to get to know him better and to help him, if he could, to lessen the tragedy that lay between him and Miranda. For it was a tragedy, surely, and perhaps the root of future tragedy, when both parents could love their child so much and yet be inherently incabable of living together. He would talk to Miranda tomorrow; they would have everything clear between them. He would make sure she knew how well she was loved. That, after all, is what people most need to know. He sighed. He was very tired now. He thought he might be able to sleep better than he had done for several days and nights. There was no pain, scarcely even any discomfort; a few aching muscles in his upper torso. Dr Shaw had suggested that this was one of the better points of his condition. He smiled at this thought. It was to say, in effect, that to be half dead was better than to be dead.

Well, he would sleep now for a couple of hours, and when he awoke Chloe would be with him.

Alain died just after four o'clock, in the depths of that good sleep. He had not, after all, been consulted in the matter.

A little later, Chloe came into the room, carrying her photograph in its frame. She put it on the bedside table, then bent to kiss him awake. The sun filled the room, ebullient as an anthem, blaring across the bed and the pillows.

'It's so bright, I'm amazed it didn't wake you,' she murmured, her lips close to his cheek. Her kiss had no evident effect, so she repeated it. His skin was warm and, even here, it still smelled of the south of France. She stroked his hair, liking its fuzzy resistance against her palm. Her pressure was slight but Alain's head fell a little to one side. It was a movement that conferred instant knowledge, immediately repudiated.

'Alain?'

She found his hand and clasped it. It was coolly unresponsive and therefore unreal to her. 'Something is wrong,' she said aloud. She rang the bell beside the bed. The nurse would come. She would be able to explain it.

'Alain. Wake up, *chéri*, I'm here.' She shook his shoulder.

When the nurse came in, she was shouting at him. 'You can't just do this, Alain. I bloody well won't let you do it—'

Her anger charged the little room, stronger than the sunlight, but just as incapable of waking him.

Chapter 12

H ER ANGER ABIDED. IT BUOYED HER ON A
treacherous wave that lent her a false strength,
enabling her to care for everyone's grief except
her own. But when she sat at home, in Sheringham, with
her arms around her children, beset with their tears and
knowing this was the worst, the very worst that had come
to them, and that there was nothing she could do to take
it from them, the wave fell away with a fearful, tugging
suddenness, leaving her to an undertow of agonising apprehension that was the beginning of her awareness of loss.

If it seemed to Chloe that her world had extinguished
itself on a high scream of rage and disbelief, it became
apparent that this was not so for others. After a stunned
twenty-four hours of shared weeping and silence, an
unspoken consensus seemed to demand a gradually increasing amount of noise and activity. Quietly at first, they began
to talk to each other, offering their memories, conjuring
Alain's spirit into the room with them, as if they could
hold him there, unchanged, speaking and acting as he had
done last week or the day before yesterday. As a chorus,
the phone did not stop ringing, although none of them
wanted to be the one to answer it, to repeat the same
words over and over again to each concerned neighbour
and devastated friend.

It was Adam, of course, who made the least noise and got the most done, taking on himself the blunt, obligatory tasks that were twists of the knife to the bereaved. He dealt with the death certificate and the undertakers, and with the telephone calls other than those to close relatives. He visited Nick Bannister, the Rector of St Mark's, and they agreed on a time and probable length for the funeral service, the tenor of which would be humanist. Nick, who believed in drawing everyone into the warm circle of the church's friendship, was sadly content to bury Alain in the small, hidden graveyard that was the overflow for the dissolute soldiers. He would miss him, both as the only man who had consistently beaten him at chess, and the friend who had shared his own voracious curiosity about the world.

It was Adam, too, with a slow, healing determination, who had set out to discover exactly what everyone would like the service to contain. It was partly a displacement activity, so that they could take a breathing-space, a clearing in the forest of sadness. Not for the first time, Chloe thanked her non-existent God for him. She was especially grateful for his instinctive tending of Miranda; somehow, he had managed to get her to stop crying. This was a relief to them all because Moriarty, sensing her mother's affliction, had joined in with her usual uninhibited force – and when Miranda stopped, Moriarty stopped. The silence then spread throughout the afternoon; everyone relaxed as far as their temperament would allow, and a more contemplative sorrow held them together. The twins, who for the most part had been mute with shock, sitting close together, holding hands as they had not done since they were seven, were the first to behave in a relatively normal manner. Following Adam, Rufus initiated the argument that would fuel them for the rest of the day – what should be the main reading in the Order of Service?

'I think we ought to have "Do not go gentle into that good night". Dad really likes Dylan Thomas.'

'We can't,' Tilda protested. 'That was written for an *old* man. Dad isn't old.'

'He is *quite* old.'

'He was forty-five,' Miranda said, swallowing.

'So shut up,' Tilda told Rufus. 'We're not having it.'

'OK, what do *you* want?' her brother asked reasonably.

'I'm not sure yet – what about that thing about not being – dead – but just going into the next room?'

'*Everyone* has that,' Miranda said.

'How do you know?' asked Tilda.

'Well, I've been to two funerals; it was at both of them. It *is* comforting, I suppose, but it's not true, is it? He isn't in the next room.' This silenced them all until Adam asked quietly, 'What do you think, Chloe? You know best what Alain would like.'

'He would like,' Chloe said, the anger rising in her throat so that she could barely breathe, 'to be alive.'

It was unfair. She knew it. But she wasn't going to apologise now. Red tears winked and hazed in front of her as she fled the room.

In her studio, where they would not follow her, she leaned against the door and waited for the ache of unshed tears to go away. It didn't, so she let them fall. At least it might ease the odd sensation that the nerve that covered her humerus had somehow established itself behind her eyes. 'You will have to help me with this,' she said to Alain. 'I can't do it on my own.'

'*Oui, c'est bien emmerdant, ça,*' she heard him reply. 'But of course you can, *chérie. Evidemment* – you must.'

'Oh God, where are you? I don't believe you have simply left me; just got up and gone away from the world. It doesn't make sense.' For this, there would have been a shrug.

'Damn it, Alain, why did you have to fall? What possessed you to do such an incredibly stupid thing? Why didn't you take care, like you always do? I'll never forgive you, you hear me? Never.'

And then, at last, the floodgates opened and there was some bitter sort of relief behind her aching eyes.

Anger, she discovered, had been easy. It had been stronger than she was; it had held her up. Grief was a stripping away of strength, a quiet, efficient destruction like a butcher or a fishmonger filleting out the bones and the soft, unwanted parts. Gutted, that was what Dwayne had said he was, his shocked voice trembling back to childhood when he had heard the news. What a simple, perfect metaphor. That was exactly how it was. How she was. She had been gutted. There was nothing inside her any more.

'I am no more alive than Alain is. No more alive. He is no more alive.'

On the eve of the funeral she had held his pillow against her body all night because she could not bear to have her arms empty. In the morning, she got up early and fled the bedroom for the kitchen where no one would disturb her for another hour. She was greeted by an interrogative mew from the blue casserole and could not help smiling as the little spotted cat stretched her back and wobbled out, ready for breakfast. Scuffling noises beneath the table produced Baskerville and Grace, who shared his basket. There was undeniable physical comfort in the rubbing of furry faces against her legs. She fed them all, with an extra helping for Arnie, who with feline telepathy erupted through the cat-flap as she finished scraping the tin. She had a vision of herself, doing this each morning, waiting for Rufus and Tilda to come down – *only* Rufus and Tilda. It did not seem anything like enough people to make a household. Or a family.

She brewed some coffee and took it with her to the table. She had made it the way Alain preferred it, a little too strong for herself. She would probably always do it that way now; the idea of further change, however small, made her afraid.

She drank her coffee, too fast, and poured another. She took it slowly this time and searched for something small to concentrate upon. What, for instance, would Alain like her to wear for the funeral? He would want them all to look elegant, or fashionable and fun. The blue dress, the one in the photograph? He loved that, and Miranda had made it. And then there were their parents to think about, both his and hers, who would be here shortly. Dinah had offered them the school's guest-house, conveniently empty for the long vacation. It would certainly be easier than having them all to stay. Each of them, though charming, was also a forceful personality, and the thought of all those strong opinions under one roof was presently overwhelming.

An appreciative chuckle followed this decision. It did not come from Chloe. She stiffened, not daring to look around. It had been Alain's laughter, there was no way she could mistake it. He was here, behind her, a little to her left. If she did look round – then what? Would she see him? Or would there simply be more emptiness? He was not a ghost, she did not feel that. Nor, in any possible sense, could he be what, up to now, she had regarded as 'real'.

Yet, there was no doubt, she felt it still; it was his presence, there beside her, amused, relaxed, standing in his normal morning place before the grill, turning croissants to his precisely ordered shade of golden brown.

She would not look round. She would keep him while she could. And if he was a figment of her grieving imagination, then she was grateful for it.

'The blue dress?' she asked. 'For the service?'

Her sense of his company did not falter until, with Rufus beside her, she led the small family procession through the lych-gate of St Mark's. She looked towards the porch, where Nick Bannister stood waiting, and the path shrank into a tightrope, leading to the inevitable. She walked on with empty air above her head and beneath her feet, and it was then that she lost him, somewhere among the leaning soldiery. She reached the porch, but because the open oak door had small flowers, blue, white and gold, woven round the horseshoe of its handle, as if for a wedding, she suddenly balked and could go no further.

Rufus, feeling the break in her rhythm, stopped when she did, and waited. She could not and would not.

She thought of Catherine Chandler waiting in the wall.

Oh Catherine, I never thought to come here for this.

No one does, my dear friend. But since you are here, come in; and if you cannot praise God, you may at least assist in an act of love and beauty. Come, I will bring you through the door.

In this way, Chloe was enabled to face the flowers and the friends, and to sustain, without falling into darkness, the appalling, the insanely unexpected shock, before the altar, of the coffin.

What most people would remember about the funeral, justly, was the music. The readings, however, were also very fine. They had chosen them easily once their jangled nerves had settled to the task, for as Rufus said, by selecting pieces that Alain had loved and read aloud to them, they would create a kind of verbal hologram of him.

The service opened with a welcome and a personal memorial from Nick Bannister. Affectionate, regretful, a man talking among friends, he gathered them in to this shared loss.

The first reading, given by Tilda, set in the balance the joyous assurances to the living composed by Dame Julian of Norwich, finishing on the jubilant 'All shall be well, and all shall be well, and all manner of things shall be well.' Listening, Chloe tried not to repudiate this on her own behalf, but only to be proud of her daughter's courage and knowledge of her father's spirit.

Miranda, after searching through Alain's books, trawling

her childhood with her net of memories, had brought up the prize of Paul Valéry's wry, erotic poem, 'The Graveyard by the Sea', which she recited in faultless French. People agreed that it must have been the unBritish liveliness of her facial muscles that had made her resemble her father as she spoke.

The last offering, made by Rufus, held the surprise of mischief. He had opted to read from Russell Hoban's blackly comic fable, *Kleinzeit*, in which Death figures as a shambling, simian, unwanted pet, the kind that smells and fawns and wants horribly to be loved. The family had made Alain read it to them, over and over until he had it by heart – and now, by heart, they gave it back to him.

All of these would resonate in the memory; but the image that would remain was that of Tilda, straight-backed in a long yellow dress, seated at a grand piano in front of the Lady Chapel. Ambered in a shaft of sunlight, she seemed the virtual embodiment of a Vermeer. She played the music that she felt Alain might have asked for, and her performance was only for him. She began with one of his favourite nocturnes, elegiac, haunting, written when Chopin was already condemned by tuberculosis. Later, she explored the tender, impressionist reveries of Elgar's *Dream Children*, which Alain had once described to her as nostalgia for a more perfect childhood than anyone has ever known. With the notes flowing beneath her fingers, Tilda called up countless pictures that could prove him wrong.

At the end of the service, she left the piano and came to stand with Rufus, Miranda, Dwayne and Paul in a protective arc behind the coffin. Their parting gift was to make the whole church their instrument, the praying arches, the walls, the rampant tracery, the great sounding blocks of the pillars, as they joined their voices, clear, poised and meditative, in the marriage of words and music, body and spirit, in which Hildegarde of Bingen envisioned the love between man and God. It would never have occurred to Hildegarde, nor would it to Catherine Chandler, who probably knew her music, to doubt the existence of God, whereas many did who were there today. No one, however, would leave the church in any doubt as to the continuing existence of love.

At the graveside, Nick Bannister spoke the old biblical words of committal which everyone wanted to hear, for their bleak beauty, and for the ancient, inbred assurance of something well and decently done. Nick's delivery was warm and slightly bracing; he found that this could inhibit too great an extremity of tears. He noted, however, that the one person who could not control this extremity was Helen Cavendish, and also that her ex-husband remedied this by clamping her arm in a bruising hold that widened her remarkable eyes in pain. Chloe, who knew that Luke was present, but did not look at him, was aware of her tears and somewhat puzzled by them.

Shamed by Chloe's own composure, which she guessed to be a matter of emotional exhaustion rather than iron control, Helen thought how different she had looked the last time she had seen her.

When Luke had told her about Alain's accident, Helen had gone at once to the hospital. Afraid of what she would find, she had walked down the ward with her hand in her pocket, turning his lighter between her fingers. He had meant to take it when he came to Paris, but had forgotten at the last minute. Helen had failed to remind him, conceiving a superstitious fancy that he would continue to come back to her as long as it was in her possession.

A nurse directed her to his room, saying she would shortly be there herself. The door was open, but she stopped short on the threshold, cramming the back of her hand against her mouth to prevent herself making a sound.

On Alain's bed, Chloe lay curved around her husband

like a maternal animal; her arm cradled his head, her body cleaving to his as though to keep him warm. She held his hand in a fierce grip that must surely bring him back from any brink and make him fast to her. It was a little time before Helen realised he was dead. She waited a while longer, and when she could trust herself to walk, went silently away. She loves him, she thought humbly; she always has. I never had a chance.

After the service, about thirty people were invited back to the house, the majority arriving on the heels of the family. Tilda, waiting on the steps to welcome the stragglers, was horrified to see Joel come through the gate.

'What are you doing here?'

'I should like to speak to Miranda, just for a moment. Will you tell her I'm here?'

'I suppose you do know what's happening today?'

'Of course. I was at the service. You played beautifully.' Tilda stared at him.

'You've changed,' he said. He was looking at her as he had during the night rides they had shared. 'I like the difference.'

'You haven't,' she said. 'You're still unspeakable.'

'Nevertheless, I should like Miranda to speak to me.'

'She won't want to.'

'Out here will do.'

'Please – can't you leave it till another day?'

'I'd rather not.' He stepped forward. 'Would you prefer me to come in and look for her?'

'No,' she said quickly. 'Stay there. I'll fetch her.' His smile distressed her. It appeared to be compassionate.

'I didn't expect to see you today,' Miranda said neutrally.

'I wanted to pay my respects to your father.'

'I see. Thank you.'

'Don't look so wary. You know I liked him; he was one of the good guys. And a good father. But what I wanted

— 273 —

to tell you was – I went to see him, the day he died. In the hospital.'

She stiffened. 'Why?'

'He was Moriarty's grandfather. I wanted to make the connection, tell him how I feel about her. And then – we had a chat about the letter.'

Miranda froze. 'What did you tell him?'

'I said I had written it.'

'Are you serious?' Her voice spiralled in disbelief. 'Why would you do such a thing?'

'Oh, just a charitable impulse. Don't knock it.'

'I'll never understand you. So – what did Dad say? Did he believe you?'

'Of course he did. Why wouldn't he? It fits. It's the kind of thing I do. Isn't it?'

She shook her head. 'Joel, I don't know how I feel about this.'

'Look at it this way – knowing how he thought about you, would you rather he believed it was you – or someone who didn't matter a damn to him?'

'But *I* know it was me.'

'We're thinking about Alain, not you. You can go on feeling like shit if you like, but at least you'll know that *he* didn't have to.'

'Yes. I understand that. It's just—'

'What else can I say?'

'No, I do see. I suppose I ought to thank you.'

'Not if you don't want to. Don't go away and start worrying about it.' He took her hand and squeezed it. 'I'll see you soon. I'll call you. *Ciao*.'

'He didn't do it for Alain, or for you,' Adam said when she told him. 'He did it for himself, to store up points with you for the future.'

Miranda had thought about this. 'That's possible,' she admitted. 'But either way, the result is the same. I'm glad Dad didn't die wondering which of us wrote that horrible letter. I'm going to regret sending it for the rest of my life. Whatever you may think of him, Joel has made it that little bit easier for me to live with that.'

'OK, but just don't start feeling beholden.'

But she did. Only a little bit.

After applying professional restoration to her make-up and her equilibrium, Helen left her starry public persona in the dressing-room and circulated the gathering with a sympathetic ear for everyone. Among the first to claim her was Belle, the epitome of funeral chic in one of her less startling Dracula costumes.

'I hope you weren't offended, Aunt Helen – but now I'm really glad I didn't take that part. I'll be able to spend more time with poor Tilda. It must be the most terrible thing to lose your father.' She glanced towards the window, where Luke was talking to John and Claudie Latham. 'I couldn't bear it if anything happened to Dad.'

Helen shuddered. 'Neither could I.'

'You're still very fond of him, aren't you?'

'Yes, I am. Probably more than I have any right to be.'

'Oh, *rights*! Can I ask you something very personal?'

'You can ask. I might not reply,' Helen smiled.

'It's – well, did you and he ever – sleep together after the divorce?'

'What a forthright creature you are!' This was not something Belle should know.

'It's just that – Adam and I used to wonder about it. It would have been an exciting relationship. Forbidden fruit, but so close. Almost incestuous.'

'What an interesting idea. Belle, this is a very odd conversation, considering why we are here.'

'I suppose it is. But Alain wouldn't mind.' What Belle was seeking was reassurance; she was proud to be an individualist in love, as well as in every other part of her life, but she would feel less lonely on her pinnacle above the crowd if she could believe that Helen was up there too.

'He would laugh,' Helen said. 'You always amused him. But he also thought you were developing into "*une vraie femme fatale*".'

Belle accepted the change of topic. 'Oh, I do hope I will,' she beamed. She looked so pleased that Helen hugged her for her innocence. Not for the first time, Belle regretted that Helen was Adam's mother. She badly wanted to tell her about them. What would Helen think if she did? That would be a real test of individuality. All the same, she was wise enough not to offer it.

'Are you all right, Belle?' asked Adam, coming up behind her as someone swept Helen away.

'I was just thinking about you.'

'I've been wanting to know how you were. I seem to have been kind of overwhelmed since this happened.'

'I'm well. I miss you. Being close to you. You know.'

He caught his breath. 'Yes, I know.'

'We'll catch up later. You're doing a good job. Everyone says so. Look – I think Miranda wants you.'

'I wish I could get her to move around and talk to people. She just sits miserably in the corner, clutching Moriarty as if anyone who comes near intends to snatch her. It's weird; she seemed fine in the church.'

'Yes, but she'd psyched herself up for that. It was a performance. She just needs to collapse for a while. I'll go and talk to her, shall I? You go and find yourself a drink and a breathing space.'

'Thanks. I'd like that.'

'*Nada*. I love you.'

Adam looked round hastily to see if anyone had heard.

'Now *that*,' she said severely, 'deserves a kiss.'

She gave him one, very chaste and sisterly, on his cheek.

Claudie Latham's habitually eager attentions to Luke were only slightly diminished by the occasion, despite his attempt to discuss her daughter's problems rather than her own. He could well (and thankfully) imagine why Lisa had never confided in her mother.

It was Helen who read his beleagured body-language and came to the rescue. It occurred to her that she might ask him for a modest reward.

'I have a small moral problem,' she told him. 'Perhaps you can help. Why don't we go outside in the sun and I'll tell you about it.'

'I take it that means you need a cigarette? Moral, eh? Intriguing.'

They found a bench under a plum tree. Baskerville, who had found it first, retired beneath it to consider some stolen slices of ham. Helen lit her Black Russian, drew on it with deep relief, and handed Luke the gold lighter. He examined it. 'Haven't I seen this before?'

'Probably. It's Alain's. He left it in my flat in Paris.'

'I see.' He looked at her tenderly.

'You don't seem surprised.'

'No. I was with you at the grave. Until then, I hadn't realised how much he meant to you.'

'I hadn't long realised it myself. He was a beautiful man.' She struggled with tears. 'Oh, Luke – I so hate to have to use the past tense about him. It's like a knife in the wound.'

'I know, love. It's a bugger, death. It's the last thing you expect to interfere with your plans.'

She laughed, a small, watery implosion. 'The very last. But it isn't only death that is bloody and unexpected; love can be like that too. Well, you know that yourself.'

Luke held up his hand. 'Don't. I can't think about that today. Tell me what it is I can do for you.'

'It's the lighter. I want to keep it. I've had it so long and it feels like part of Alain. But Chloe gave it to him and he wanted it back. I can't steal emotions that don't belong to me.'

'Haven't you anything else, something he gave to you?'

'He only gave me flowers or crazy, delicious food. No jewellery, nothing lasting. He was honest enough not to treat me as his mistress. I must give the lighter back – but I can hardly present it to Chloe myself. I don't want her to have even the whisper of a suspicion. So – would you do it for me, Luke?'

'It will be difficult,' he said doubtfully. 'Understandably, she's trying to pretend I don't exist, just at the moment. She has even avoided shaking my hand, let alone looking at me or talking to me.' He sighed. 'Never mind,' he said bracingly. 'Give me the lighter, anyway. I'm bound to think of something.'

'Thank you, my darling. It would be a relief. Otherwise I should keep it under my pillow and in my pocket like a besotted *ingénue*.'

'I know the script,' he said, smiling. 'I once stole one of Chloe's favourite camel brushes, one she used when she painted Arden House. And then there's all the music I can break my heart to. Helen, beautiful Helen – why didn't we just stick together and save all the heartache?'

'Because we couldn't stop falling in love. We still can't.'

'Ah, but this is the last time for me. For you – I hope not. Truly. Oh, God's boots, now I've made you cry again.'

With mixed feelings, Luke went upstairs and hesitantly located the bedroom Alain and Chloe had shared, a place he had never wished to see. It was a pleasant room; like the rest of the house it was full of books and sunlight. He reflected that sunshine had surrounded this death, in the church, in the graveyard and now in Alain's house; it seemed a lapse of taste, making it harder to accept the loss.

He ignored the signs that Chloe lived a third of her life in this room, her robe flung across the bed, the Florentine mirror, a gouache of Provence. He opened the long wardrobe and searched for a grey cord jacket that Alain had been fond of. He slipped the lighter into the

— 278 —

inside pocket, then pointlessly clasped the empty shoulder with his palm, rocking it slightly on its hanger. He was about to close the door when Chloe's scent reached him faintly from the other end of the cupboard. He slammed Alain's door and stood back, his throat aching, willing himself to leave. Then he tore open the other door and plunged his face into her clothes.

Philip Dacre's benevolent gaze roamed the room for Dinah. He was tired of sharing condolences and of deflecting the kind of parent who thought this a fit time to quiz him on their offspring's future. He wanted to get away from here, and he wanted Dinah to go with him. He saw that she was perched on a window-seat with a glass of brandy in her hand, deep in discussion with the Cubitt boy. He made his way towards her, his progress impeded by pleasantries.

Dwayne had wanted Dinah's advice, as school counsellor, on the best way to get his mother to leave the Oliviers' whisky alone. She thought him rather puritanical, given the occasion, but nevertheless sipped her brandy in a ladylike manner and did her best.

'Why don't you ask her to go for a walk with you,' she suggested practically. 'She hasn't seen much of you lately, and you both need to catch up on things. And the fresh air will help.'

Dwayne was doubtful. 'She's drinking because I told her I want to stay with Dad, permanently. She didn't think I would and she's very upset. But I'd feel really spare with her and Ben – and I've got everything worked out the way I need it at home.'

Dinah nodded vigorously. 'I think you ought to stay where you feel most comfortable, especially with exams coming up next year. I'll have a word with your mother, if you like?'

'Would you? Thanks, Mrs Cavendish. Oh – good afternoon, Mr Dacre.' Automatically, Dwayne put his best voice forward. He didn't bother quite so much for Dinah, who had known him a long time and anyway, was easy-going and a normal human being; whereas Philip Dacre was an ambulant institution demanding of respect, with his Gielgud vowels and his posh family and his impressive size and presence. When you thought about it, it was funny how well the two of them always seemed to get on together.

'Good afternoon, Dwayne,' Philip said mildly. 'I must say, you look very well in that suit.'

'Thank you, sir.' The suit belonged to his brother Elvis, who had cast it into the outer darkness for possession of three buttons rather than the newly requisite four. Dwayne didn't mind wearing it; a suit showed you were serious. He wanted Mr Dacre to think he was serious. He had decided now: he was going all out to get into Cambridge.

'The thing about death,' Philip said quietly to Dinah, his bulk obscuring her from the rest of the room, 'is that it shocks one into realising how easily it can happen. It was like that when Catherine died – the hideous shock, and the feeling that we had both been so dreadfully cheated.'

'I'm so sorry, Philip,' Dinah said, reaching for his hand without thinking. 'This must bring it all back to you.'

'It does, yes – but more than anything else, it makes me think about the future. I don't want to waste any more time, Dinah.'

She tried to decide precisely what he meant. Did he want her to race off and make love to him, to distance the grinning spectre in the time-honoured and most natural fashion? If so, she was more than willing, once she had concocted a suitable excuse for Luke.

'Come home with me, now,' he urged her. 'Will, you, please? I need to talk to you.'

'Won't tomorrow do?' Making love was one thing; serious talk was another.

'No, it won't.'

'All right. You go ahead. I'll follow when I've sorted things out here.'

'Olly – don't you think you're drinking a bit too much to be polite?' asked Lisa anxiously.

'So what? People do get drunk at funerals. That's partly what they're for.'

'Yes, but it's not like you. Is something bothering you? Apart from M. Olivier dying, I mean?'

'Not really,' Oliver shifted restlessly. 'Look, do you mind if we leave soon? I'd like to go off somewhere up in the hills. I've had all I can take of this.'

'I'd like that too – if you want company, that is?'

'Yeah, fine. I just want to speak to Chloe before we go.' He turned away abruptly enough to prevent her coming with him. Chloe was talking to Mike and Maggie Barnes. He waited until they moved on and planted himself stiffly in front of her. She gave him a tired smile and touched his cheek.

'Hello, Olly, my dear. Thank you for coming.'

He said awkwardly, 'I didn't know if you would want me to.'

'Of course. Why ever not?'

'Well – you know.' He burned with embarrassment. 'It didn't seem quite the right thing to do.'

'Why, Olly,' she said gently. 'What are you imagining?'

'It's difficult to put it into words,' he said painfully. He wished he had never started this.

'It might help you if you were to try. I think you might be suffering from a mixture of emotions that need – well, separating.'

'OK, then, obviously, it's because of the way I've been feeling about you. It seemed like an insult to Alain to turn up at his funeral.'

She flinched, though by now she had learned to recover quickly when someone used a phrase that underlined the day's finality. 'That's nonsense, Olly. You liked Alain, didn't you?'

'Yes, I did. And I'm terribly sorry this has happened. I feel so guilty. I can't seem to work out exactly why. I suppose it's – retrospective?'

She shook her head. 'It's because you are still alive. You can go on feeling – for your family, your friends – even me. And he can't. He can't.' She turned away.

'Chloe, I didn't mean to make you feel like this. I'm so bloody selfish!'

'No, no. Most people here would probably say they felt something similar. It's all right, Olly. It's all right.'

She wrapped her arms round him and he held her with all his strength.

She patted his shoulder and waited for him to release her.

Lisa, intently watching their faces and following the choreography of their conversation, discovered the obvious with a dull drop in her stomach that she reluctantly recognised as a symptom of jealousy. In different circumstances this would probably be a good thing.

It seemed a good idea to give Oliver time to recover from what had obviously been an emotional blitz, so she decided to go and wait for him in the garden. She spoke briefly to her parents, then edged her way carefully around the small dark-clad groups clutching their plates and glasses and twittering repetitiously only a few decibels below the level of a cocktail party.

Out in the broad hall, she shut them all in behind her and blessed the relief of silence. Her eyes were drawn towards the garden, through the open front door, and she did not immediately see the figure leaning against the wall. Drawing level, she stopped in astonishment.

It was Luke. Facing the wall, his forehead pressed against his arm, his attitude was one of absolute despair.

Lisa did not know what to do. Her instinct was to put

her arms round him, but that did not seem to be an option within their present relationship. For a cowardly second, she considered slipping past without acknowledging his presence. It might even be the best thing, but she couldn't do it.

She said 'Luke' in a diminished voice.

He made a sound like a man waking up to pain, and pushed himself away from the wall.

'Is there anything I can do?' she asked anxiously.

He looked as if he were not quite sure who she was. 'Lisa,' he affirmed. 'No, thank you. I would like to be left alone, if you don't mind.'

'I'm sorry,' she gasped, and darted out of the house.

Luke pulled himself together, preparing to find Dinah and tell her he was going home. He heard the living-room door open behind him.

It was Chloe. She stood still and did not speak.

'I was just leaving,' he said.

'Oh.'

'How are you?' His hands moved, sketching nothing. 'Can you cope with – all this?'

'So it seems.'

They looked at each other defeatedly, knowing there was nothing that could be said across the uncharted space the day had set between them.

'I'll go, then,' Luke said. 'Will you tell Dinah?'

'Of course.'

Chapter 13

C HLOE HAD EATEN NOTHING ALL DAY AND HER
blood sugar was low. Instead of going up to lie on
her bed and make a bid for oblivion, which was
what she wanted to do, she went to the kitchen to give
herself a hit of caffeine and sugar. As she came through
the hall, a gust of laughter blew out of one of the rooms.
It did not distress her; laughter at funerals was a salutary
thing. It was a signal that the mourners were satisfied they
had done their duty; they had seen their old friend as far
as the banks of the Styx and now they were ready to turn
away from the Underworld and resume the lives they newly
recognised as precious.

In the kitchen, coffee was already made, its aroma
struggling in a familiar Gauloises-cloud that clutched at
her stomach. Alain's mother was sharing a corner of the
table with Joanna Carrington. They, too, were smiling, as
though tenderly amused by some pleasurable memory.

'*Assieds-toi, ma chère*,' Edwige Olivier invited Chloe in
her friendly growl. 'You look exhausted.' She emphasised
the extent of the exhaustion by circling in the air with
her cigarette; the room was hung with the wraiths of
such circles.

Chloe was heartened by the sight of her fine-boned
face, so like Alain's apart from the intelligent deep-set

eyes like black olives. The two women made room for her between them and Joanna put coffee and a sandwich in front of her. 'Eat something, darling,' her light, regal voice commanded. 'You need to keep up your strength.'

Joanna was physically a previous edition of Chloe herself, a larger one since life had added a few footnotes, but her heavy twist of hair had kept much of its red and gold and she still had the same full mouth and clear grey eyes.

'Thanks, Mum. I'll try.' Her mother had always ascribed healing power to food. Mothers do; she did it herself, especially with Rufus, for whom it was actually true, up to a point. She ate obediently, though the food tasted like cotton-wool.

'How long have you two been hiding in here?' she asked. 'You must have so much to catch up on.' They were good friends and did not see enough of each other.

'Too much,' agreed Edwige. 'I 'ad 'oped to stay longer in England, but I'm taking the chair at a conference of European medical schools next week. It should be interesting; it's about abortion law and practice.'

Chloe's pulses raced; she might have expected the subject to come up, she was well aware of that; but today she was thinking of Edwige only in the context of her family, rather than the wider one embraced by her profession as a consultant gynaecologist and well-known lecturer in her discipline.

'Joanna and I were just discussing some of the more flammable aspects of the debate,' she went on. 'It does not seem to become any more simple, despite some very good legislation in Europe.'

'Yes, it's still very controversial,' Chloe said colourlessly. She was beginning to feel sick; that horror had no place here. She had ejected it from her mind without mercy at the moment she had heard of Alain's accident. She could not admit its existence now.

Joanna was looking at her shyly. 'Actually, Chloe, what

we were chiefly talking about, in the end, were our own experiences.'

Chloe gasped. '*Your* experiences?' she repeated.

'Don't look like that, darling. An awful lot of our generation have had abortions.'

Chloe fought a sense of something suddenly and unnaturally dislocated. 'It's just – well, you never told me.'

'No. It was before I met your father. We were careless, I'm afraid, or rather, we probably didn't have the sense to care. He was my first boyfriend. We were eighteen. It was still illegal then. It was a horrible experience, degrading and terrifying. It broke my heart. I *would* have told you, of course, if you had ever had the same trouble. But you never did.'

'No, I never did.' She laid her hand on Joanna's and kissed her cheek. 'I'm so sorry, Mum. It must have been such a lonely time.'

Joanna reddened. 'Oh, heavens, it was so long ago. But attitudes take so long to change, don't they? For a Catholic, for instance, it's still a double dilemma, setting a woman at odds with her religion.'

'Ach, *quelle bêtise!*' Edwige's contempt had the hawk and spit of a plasterer's hail to morning. 'The Church is run by men who want to keep women as little children. 'Ow many men 'ave 'ad an infant?'

Joanna pushed her hair behind her ears as though clearing decks. 'I must admit that though, unlike you, I am still Catholic, I have narrowed down both doctrine and dogma to a small spectrum in which I can believe.'

On one of their argumentative days – for both loved an argument, especially with each other – this would have become a prime basis for dispute. They were two women who were accustomed to their lightest word being transcribed to tablets of stone, Edwige as a doctor and Joanna as the director of her own interior design company. They sparred every time they met; but not today.

'For me, it was simple,' Edwige said more gently. 'I did

as I pleased. I was a student. I did not want a baby. *Alors, ça y est*! Nothing to do with morality. I chose. Me.' She turned to Chloe. 'What do you think?'

She had feared the question. 'I believe that every woman must choose for herself,' she said slowly. 'But the consequences – emotional, practical, physical – will be different, and most likely unpredictable, for each one. I don't see how it can be possible to make laws to contain us all.'

The Gauloise circled. 'Ah, but we must 'ave "guidelines", or we can never reach any mutual agreement. We still need laws to ensure that every woman *does* have that choice – and that no one can make it for her – unless she is mentally incapable, and even that depends on many factors.'

'I think it is also very important,' Joanna insisted, 'to make women feel that they are no less themselves, or somehow less womanly, if they make use of abortion. There has been so much injustice in women's lives: damage to their bodies, and yes, Edwige, also to their souls. Why, Chloe – my dear girl, what is the matter?'

Chloe shook her head. She looked through sudden uncontrollable tears, envisioning her eyes as a rain-streamed windscreen through which the events of her life were clearly visible despite the flow.

'It's all so wretchedly sad,' she said, her voice shaking. 'Sometimes there seems to be no way forward.'

She spoke with no intention of ambiguity but her mother exclaimed in pity and took her into her arms. 'I know, darling,' she said, biting her lip. 'We have been dreadfully selfish, gabbling on like this. I know how much you must be missing Alain – I don't know how to help you. I wish I did. But I promise you – look at me, Chloe, because I want you to believe me – one day, however far ahead, it will get better.'

That's what Luke would say, Chloe thought; if his saying it were not so wildly inappropriate. Or my thinking of it. I suppose it's what everyone says. They have to; otherwise, how would life go on?

'I'm all right now,' she said. 'I'm glad you told me about the abortion.'

'You ought to 'ave told Chloe before,' declared Edwige severely. 'A modern young woman needs to know that 'er mother is on the same side in this.'

'Perhaps you should talk to Miranda about it,' Chloe suggested innocently. 'You may be surprised by her views.'

The black-olive eyes gleamed. 'You mean she is part of this new, young pro-life backlash we are 'earing so much about? Then I will do so.' She had the bit between her teeth, where she liked it best. Not for nothing did her family usually address her as Madame Mère; the sobriquet bestowed by Napoleon upon his notoriously combative mother, Letizia Buonaparte.

It might do Miranda good to argue, Chloe decided; she would be forced to uncurl out of the ball of misery she had become since the service. For herself, she would have to examine Joanna's revelation when she had the space to think about it properly. Why, for example, was her main reaction one not of disappointment, but something akin to relief? Whatever her mother's experience had been, surely it could not affect her attitude towards her own?

For the next few days, the grandparents provided their own individual forms of support to Chloe and her children.

David Carrington, always loathe to spend any length of time away from the architectural designs which were his work, his pleasure and his chief means of self-expression, had been doodling on a sketchpad more or less continuously since his arrival. The upshot was that he and Rufus – and Dwayne, naturally – were going to demolish and rebuild the old wooden summerhouse, which no one would use because it was damp and smelled of cats. The two boys, limp with gratitude at the possibility of doing something other than being miserable, were so enthusiastic that they flattened the place and laid the new foundations before supper on Sunday.

Grandpère Hervé Olivier, large, dark and booming, with a Victor Hugo beard, awarded himself a holiday from his own vast importance in his famous Paris hospital, and decided to get to know his younger granddaughter. Unable to stand still unless conducting an examination or an operation, he marched Tilda up and down the Surrey hills as though on a Brobdingnagian ward inspection, asking questions and dispensing wisdom as they went. Tilda, who had early moved through the stages of fear and shyness to unconditional love of this ebullient and selfless giant, discovered that there was very little she could not tell him about her life and thoughts. By the time they had covered twenty miles of the Pilgrims' Way, she began to see that if she could take a very few sensible decisions, now, she might be able to clear a path as straight and simple for herself.

Miranda, far from arguing with Madame Mère, had simply presented her with Moriarty as the living representation of her side of the debate. Edwige was conquered the moment her splendid Roman nose was seized in the tiny, increasingly capable hand. She was soon as willing as Miranda to declare that the prodigy had certainly mastered the opening notes of 'La Marseillaise', even if no one else could make it out.

These pleasant and intimate relations left Chloe and Joanna the time they needed together. It was a dangerous space, this emotional cocoon for mother and daughter, a space into which confession might effortlessly have dropped. At first Chloe was almost tempted – everyone wants to lay their head on their mother's breast and claim peace – but she soon realised that such a confession would benefit neither of them. What had happened was not Joanna's concern, nor should it be her burden. The tragedy was her own, hers and Luke's. One thing she saw more clearly in the present context, surrounded by those who knew nothing of that other loss, was that it had been mutual; that Luke had suffered, and that she had disregarded that.

A fortnight after Alain Olivier's funeral, Dinah Cavendish invited her husband to a candle-lit dinner for two in his own living-room, where she set the small table with a gypsy shawl and wild flowers. She found the dining-room rather depressing when the children were not at home. Once, she and Luke would have filled the room with sufficient life and noise on their own account, but lately it required an effort. They usually ate in the kitchen but tonight would be a memorable occasion and she wanted to make it as enjoyable as possible. If it *was* possible.

Luke followed her preparations with a questioning look.

'What's this in aid of?' he asked, as they sat down. 'Have I committed the sad, male lapse of forgetting some arcane anniversary?'

'No.' She smiled. 'But it might possibly become one.'

'You can't be pregnant?' His alarm was genuine. Dinah was unpredictable.

'You're right. I can't.'

'Fine. Then – you tell me.'

'I'd like to eat first, if that's all right?' The lamb she was cooking was very good and they might not feel like it later.

He was intrigued, but obediently helped to demolish the lamb with aubergines and the apricot tart before laying down his fork and complaining, not unkindly, 'Dinah, you are all nerves and electricity tonight. I wish you would, please, tell me what's on your mind.'

'Very well.' She took a deep breath and told him, rather too quickly.

'What did you say?'

'I said that Philip has asked me to marry him.'

'You're married to me.' This was not quite the appropriate answer, but it would serve while his brain caught up.

— 290 —

'We'll have to get a divorce.'

'A divorce?'

'That's right.'

'You want to divorce me and marry Philip Dacre?'

'Yes, I do.'

'I can't believe it.'

'I realise that. Why not?'

'Obviously, because I had no idea what was going on.'

'Didn't you, Luke, honestly? None at all?'

'Not really.'

'You've not noticed how much time I've been spending with Philip?'

'Vaguely, I suppose, but I didn't think anything of it. You work for him; and there's the flying. I may have joked about it, but I never realised there was anything serious going on between you.'

Dinah sighed. 'I'm sorry. I thought you must know.'

Luke smiled wrily. 'Well, it *is* your turn to provide the nasty surprise.'

'Is it really nasty?'

'Dinah – we've been married for twenty years. Or so.'

'Twenty-two. Do you want us to go on – being married?'

'It hadn't occurred to me to stop.'

She hesitated. 'No, but – suppose you could have married Chloe?'

'That's not fair.'

'It is. Absolutely. Think about it.'

'Chloe has nothing at all to do with this.'

'Hasn't she? I think she has; because I don't think I could ever have been unfaithful to you if you hadn't hurt me so badly by falling in love with her. It's all right,' she added, touching his hand. 'It doesn't matter now. It's embarrassing really, but I seem to have transferred my affections to Philip with the minimum of heartache and very little in the way of guilt.' She thought this was about eighty per cent true. The rest would come.

'I'm delighted for you,' Luke said, lightly sarcastic. 'At least, I may be, when I've got used to the idea.'

'Oh, I hope so, Luke,' she said eagerly. 'I don't want things to be any different between us.'

He laughed. 'Are you by any chance offering me therapeutic sex – just so I won't feel left out?'

'Don't be so daft. You know what I mean. There's no reason why we can't—'

'Be civilised about this?' He grinned broadly.

'Yes. Why not?'

'Well, hang on. You're way ahead of me. I'm still trying to get the idea on line.'

'I know, and I'm sorry,' she said, beginning to see that she had beem clumsy. 'I didn't think it would be such a shock.'

'I'm not in shock – or even shocked,' Luke discovered. 'I believe I *ought* to have realised.'

'You might have, if your mind hadn't been elsewhere.'

He had no answer to that. She offered him brandy and they drank in silence.

'Are you sure this is what you want, Dinah?' he asked eventually.

'Completely. And I hope you will have the same, one day. I think you will, but you may have to wait a while.'

He shook his head emphatically and no further reference was made to Chloe. He forced himself forwards. 'Look, I don't know yet exactly how I feel about this, but you're beginning to convince me that it really is going to happen. And I can see that, even if it does, you and I will never be less than close. What I can't see, not entirely, is how the children will react.'

'Don't. That's the part that brings out the grovelling coward in me,' Dinah admitted. 'I don't know how I'm going to face Olly.'

'What about Belle? We're the rock-solid foundation of

the whole world that she takes so winningly for granted. This is going to be far harder than we can imagine. There will be rivers of blood and lakes of tears.'

'I know. I'm beginning to think the whole thing is crazy.' She smiled shakily. 'Maybe we should just forget it?'

'You have *got* to be sure, Dinah.'

'I'm sorry. I'm scared. I am sure, honestly.'

Later she said 'Sleep with me, Luke? Just for tonight.'

'Ah – so it's *that* kind of anniversary.'

A warm sound rippled up through her throat. Her laugh had been the first thing he had noticed about her, twenty-two years ago.

In school next morning, Luke visited the headmaster's study before the weekly morning assembly.

'Make sure we're not disturbed, won't you?' he solicited the secretary in the outer office.

'I'll see to it, Mr Cavendish. You go right in.' She looked at him fondly. Philip was sitting behind his desk. He rose when Luke came in.

'Good morning,' he said cheerfully. 'You're an early bird today.'

'And I've just found a big, fat worm,' Luke replied, grinning his pirate's grin. He stepped around the desk and landed a well-trained right-hook to Philip's silken-shaved chin.

Philip staggered back against the wall, his rueful expression demonstrating his perfect awareness of justice.

'Feel better now?' he asked, discovering blood on his jaw.

'A lot better,' Luke said. 'That's going to look pretty horrible in a few minutes. I'll take assembly for you, shall I?'

'Don't be so stupid!' Oliver looked at his mother as if she were an unruly small girl in a playground. 'You can't possibly mean it – not after all that stuff last year. I mean,

I could understand it if you just wanted to get your own back on Dad – show him what it's like to be on the other end of it for a change. But surely you don't have to go as far as divorce?'

'I do, Olly,' Dinah said. 'You see, it wasn't about getting even – well, maybe a tiny bit, at first. It wasn't really about anything much, not to begin with. I just found I had a freedom I didn't have before, and, well, I used it for pleasure, for fun. I didn't expect to fall in love, but it kind of . . . sneaked up on me. Luke and I will always love each other too, but we seem to have moved in the opposite direction; it's friendship that has sneaked up on us. But we'll always be together as your parents. That isn't going to change.'

'Then what is?' Oliver demanded. He was floundering in a sea of unformulated questions and didn't know what he should say.

'Nothing, yet. Philip intends to retire early, at Christmas. Luke will take over from him.'

'And you'll go and live with Mr Dacre?'

'Yes. We are going to live in London. We think that will be easier for everybody.'

'You mean *you* don't want to have to live with all the school crap and the village bloody gossiping. Gee, thanks, Mum.'

'Gossip dies down very quickly when the subjects have left the scene. Does that really bother you, Olly?'

'What do *you* think?' His contempt sliced through her. 'No, it doesn't. Strange as it may seem, I don't like having my family break up.'

'All families move apart eventually,' she said. 'It doesn't make them any less a family.' She knew at once that this was a mistake.

'Mum – you're so full of shit. I don't think I want to hear any more of it.' He nodded at her as a physician does when confirming his own worst fears, then escaped from her company before he either hit her or burst into shaming tears.

*   *   *

'It's not fair!' Up in the hillside boudoir of flowers, Oliver punched the air above Lisa's resting head. 'We've gone through all that once. How could she be so fucking selfish?'

Lisa was curious. 'How do you mean, gone through it?'

'Oh.' Wheels raced in his mind but they seemed to be affected by leaves on the track. 'What the hell,' he said. 'My father had an affair last year. My mother found out and they stopped it and everything was patched up. Mum and Dad seemed to be getting on really well.'

'Who was it?' Lisa asked casually. 'The woman he had the affair with.'

'I'd rather not tell you. Sorry.'

'I won't tell anyone. I swear.'

'Why d'you want to know?'

'No reason. Just to complete the picture.'

'All right. It was Chloe Olivier. Damn. I ought not to have done that.'

'Don't *worry*.'

Lisa was making her own mental adjustments. She felt as though some science-fiction time-tornado had blown her backwards a full year, giving her an emotional overview of a period she had lived through in a black box of her own obsession. All the time she had been driving herself to the conclusion that, if Luke Cavendish could not, or would not, love her, then she would be better dead, Luke Cavendish had already been in love with Chloe Olivier. And so had his son. Poor Olly. What a miserable time *he* must have had. Yet he told no one, and his gentle, sympathetic behaviour had not changed. He had possessed a courage she had not been able to find in herself. For the first time, she saw her attempted suicide as a purely selfish act, done without any acknowledgement of the existence of others; not of her parents and the friends who cared for her, or, more damningly, of Luke himself.

She had never really *listened* to him, she had simply turned everything he said to her into acceptance or rejection. He says I'm pretty, he says I'm clever, ergo he must feel something for me; or, he says he can't respond, he says I'll grow out of it; he obviously wishes I would just disappear. He was right. She had used, or rather, abused him as the romantic icon he had warned them about, flattened him into an imaginary and literary hero, that unsatisfactory character: dark, charismatic, cloaked in unavailability, who demonstrated the insufferable male virtues of the nineteenth-century omniscient patriarch. She had refused to see how peripheral she was in his life, and had degraded both her intelligence and instinct in making him the unwilling centre of hers. The wave of humiliation that swept through her now was more cleansing than painful.

'Lisa?' Oliver shook her arm. 'Are you in there some-where?'

'Yes, I am,' she said. 'Shall I tell you what I think? I know you're upset – anyone would be. But it seems to me that if even one partner in a relationship needs someone else to make them happy, then the whole thing is over. If *both* of them feel that way, then—' She shrugged.

'What a cool girl you are,' Oliver smiled. 'In the old sense, I mean.' The good thing was, she made him feel he might become cooler himself. 'I'll try to get my head round the idea,' he said. 'Not much choice, anyway.' He moved closer and kissed her very quickly on her lips, which relaxed with a little flutter. 'Bee-stung,' he said affectionately.

They lay back and stared up at the sky. They did not talk much because they each had a lot to think about.

'I hate you!' Belle roared at her parents. 'Both of you! Don't talk to me any more.' She flung out of the kitchen, stormed upstairs for her coat and bag, and reappeared, still puce with fury.

'I need some money,' she raged. 'I'm going to Adam and Miranda's.'

Luke handed over two twenty-pound notes.

'Let us know when you're coming back,' he said.

'I'm not – if I can help it.'

Dinah pleaded, 'But how will you get to your rehearsals?'

'I'll manage,' Belle snapped, and made her exit in a percussion of righteous anger and steel-capped boots.

'Oh Christ, Luke!' Dinah subsided on to the nearest chair. 'We shouldn't have let her go like that.'

'No, I think she needs to get away and sort her feelings out. She's had a hell of a shock; there was no way we could have prepared her for this.'

'I know. My poor baby,' Dinah mourned. 'I feel like a criminal.'

'Yes. It's bad, but we knew it would be. You'll be able to talk to her in a couple of days. Adam will calm her down, you'll see. I'll give him a call.'

Luke had already spoken to Adam. He had found him disconcertingly unsurprised by the news that his father and stepmother were to divorce, but astonished – and regrettably, amused – when he learned which of them was the initiator.

'Well, there's a turn-up,' he said philosophically. 'I wouldn't have believed it. Dinah and Philip Dacre; there can't *be* a less likely couple. But what about you, Dad? How do you feel about it?'

'Oh, I'm working my way round to it. After all, I don't exactly have room to complain, do I?'

'I suppose not. Well, I'm sorry, anyway. You've been the best parents anyone could have, and I'm going to hang on tight to both of you.'

'Thanks, Adam. Dinah will be glad to hear that. You can imagine how she's feeling about you all.'

'Yeah. Three huge sacks of guilt on her back.'

'And Miranda.'

'Oh God, Miranda! She'll go mad, Dad. You know

she thinks families ought to be permanently joined at the fingers and toes, like those rows of paper dolls she cuts out for Moriarty. I wish you could have waited a bit longer. She's still very flaky these days.'

'I'm sorry, Adam. I'll come over, soon, and talk to her about it.'

'That would be good. And listen – good luck, Dad. I hope this works out, for both of you.'

Dinah's burden of guilt appeared to have expanded overnight. Already weighted by the three sacks on the children's account, plus a smaller, more elegant container on Miranda's, she woke after a near sleepless night, convinced that she must go and apologise to Chloe.

She had no precise idea what she wanted to say to her, but she jumped into her aged Morris Oxford and racketed round to the Oliviers' before this detail could shake her conviction.

Out of habit, she slewed the car to a halt with its blunt nose in Chloe's lavender, climbed out and bent to inhale the wide-awake scent. As she ran up the front steps, the door opened and Baskerville flurried out, looking very clean, with Tilda behind him on the lead.

'Hi – we're just off to see Belle,' the girl said cheerfully. 'Any news or messages?'

What could Dinah say that Belle would want to hear? She took the paw Baskerville was offering her. 'Good boy,' she said distractedly.

Tilda understood perfectly; she had already heard Belle's excoriation. 'Shall I just give her your love? That can't hurt,' she suggested.

'Would you? And Tilda – there's probably no point, not yet – but try to persuade her to come home?'

'I will,' Tilda promised. 'I have a vested interest. Paul and Cosmo are riding shotgun. I'd better go. Mum's in the studio, by the way. The French windows are open; why don't you go round?'

*　　*　　*

Dinah heard Chloe's voice as she came round the corner of the house. There must be an earlier visitor. She caught a phrase in French – she could not get the sense of it – and then Chloe's low-throated laugh, a sound she had not heard for a very long time. She was curious to see who had provoked it. She stepped on to the patio in front of the open glass doors. Chloe was standing at her easel, her head on one side as she considered the next brushstroke. There was nobody with her.

'Chloe?'

She spun round. 'Dinah! Come in. How nice.'

Had there been a momentary look of disappointment? 'I thought there was someone with you.'

With regret, Chloe relinquished Alain's lately recovered presence. He had come back one evening while she had been crying over the photograph album, and had taken up inconstant residence in the kitchen and the studio. She did not see him, but when she spoke to him his side of the conversation was quite clear in her mind. The sense of his being with her was very strong.

'No. I seem to have started talking to myself,' she told Dinah. 'Trying to fill the space, I suppose.'

'I do it too,' Dinah said softly. 'It relieves the pressures of family life – which are pretty spectacular at present. My God, Chloe!'

Her attention was caught by the easel, which, to her surprise, seemed to hold up a mirror to the August brilliance of the garden outside. 'Oh, I'm so glad. I didn't know you were painting like this again. Those colours – they look as if they'd blister your fingers.'

'Yes, it does seem to be coming back,' Chloe said thankfully. 'I think it's because I've begun to understand that grieving, and the anger that seems to go with it, can have no accomplished end; one wraps oneself round in it until one has as much motive power as an Egyptian mummy.

So I decided I'd try to put some of that trammelled-up energy into a re-exploration of what I have, rather than what I've lost.'

This was the result of one of her 'conversations' with Alain; it was certainly what he would have counselled.

They studied her painting, in which she and Alain, young and lyrically happy, were picnicking on a beach. That is, it *was* a beach, but it was also Alain's grave on the hillside, up on the edge of the village. Behind them, the cliffs with their starry plant-life and the sand like melting fudge belonged to Provence, but the glowing patch of grass, the roses and the climbers that overgreened the headstone where Alain leaned to pour the wine, were the essence of an English summer. The hugely blue sky, the checked tablecloth and the lion-bright sun were shared; we are Europeans now.

'It's an afternoon that will go on for ever,' Dinah said, her eyes full.

'I ought to call it "Homage to Stan Spencer",' observed Chloe, standing her brushes in the water jar. 'I'm going up there in a while, to the grave. Would you like to come with me?'

It was an offer to remove any barriers that might remain between them, and Dinah took it as such.

'Yes, I would. Thank you. But first, there's something I need to get out of the way. I'm not even sure how to put it—' She began to make a corkscrew of her hair.

Chloe recognised the sign of perplexity. She smiled. 'Is it something that matters?'

'Yes. Because I feel I might have hurt you – or at least been clumsy. It's that Philip and I made our decision so soon after Alain— He was so insistent. It was as if the hounds of hell would get him if we didn't settle everything right away. It was bizarre. I agreed because I knew it was his way of letting Catherine go at last, as much as taking me on.'

'If so, it is because you have enabled him to let go,' Chloe said. 'As for me – I didn't really notice the timing; I've been too preoccupied with things here.'

'There's more to it than that,' Dinah worried. 'But I'm buggered if I can put my finger on it.'

Chloe laughed. 'You're priceless. Don't think about it. I'm happy for you and Philip. A little surprised – but we've been out of touch.'

'Not angry – or kind of indignant?'

'No. Why?'

'That's very generous of you, considering— Hey, *this* is it: a year ago I would willingly have murdered you because of Luke – and now, after all the tears and strife, here I am, about to divorce him for Philip.'

Chloe sometimes wished Dinah's approach to delicate subjects was less bull-at-a-gate, but she liked her for her strenuous honesty. Besides, they couldn't avoid Luke's name for ever. As an exercise in confronting it, she considered how she might banish Dinah's guilt feelings in one illuminating flash by telling her that she had slept with Luke only two days before Alain's fall. This was something she had pushed aside, grabbing at logic through the thick fog of emotions, because it was not relevant to what happened after it. It was in the same mode, for Alain's sake, that she had also pushed aside the loss of her child.

'Dinah, I don't have any problems about this. Honestly. I think you ought to forget the past and concentrate on getting where you want to be, with as little agony as possible for all of you.'

Dinah gave her one of her exuberant hugs. 'Chloe, I love you. Thank God you are still my friend.'

'Vice versa,' Chloe said.

'*Why* can't I?' Belle demanded for the umpteenth time. 'It would be perfect. I'd always be here when you wanted me. We'd make it a number-one priority that Miranda doesn't find out. We'd soon get used to that; secrecy would become a way of life. Like spies.'

'No.'

'Oh, Adam, don't be a coward. OK, I know we ought not to be using this bed, but when I saw you all curled up asleep, I just had to get in. I *promise* we'll only do it in your place from now on.'

'Mmm. I forgive you. But the answer is still no.'

'But just think – we could be together like this so much more often.' She rolled across the bed, stretching her delectable little body to show him what he would be missing.

'It wouldn't work. We'd be bound to slip up. And even if we didn't, how do you think I would feel, living with two women I'm making love to?'

'Like an oriental potentate.'

'They are probably less potent than you expect. I certainly would be. Anyway, I'm already going far enough in cheating on Miranda. I draw the line at having you permanently in the house. I do love her, you know.'

'As much as you love me?'

'It's not the same. This is – something separate. And more than half crazy. You know very well how it is.'

'Yes, I do. But everything feels weird and different now.' She looked forlorn. 'I *need* you. I don't *want* to go home, not if Mum's seeing horrible Mr Dacre. What a slithy bastard!'

'You've got to stop thinking of it that way, for your own sake, sweetheart. Dinah didn't do this to hurt you, though she probably feels every bit as bad about your attitude as you'd like her to. But you ought to try to be kinder to her. She deserves some happiness. Things haven't been as easy for her as you might suppose.'

'Why haven't they?'

'That's her story. Ask her to tell you sometime. It might help you not to be so judgemental.'

'I'm not,' wailed Belle. 'I just want everything to stay the same.'

'That's what children want,' Adam said, not unkindly.

'But you're old enough, now, to know that it never does. That is the single reliable fact about life.'

'But *we* won't change,' she said, frightened and determined, weaving her limbs back into his. 'We'll always be together.'

'It looks that way,' he said. If only he could feel it as simply and weightlessly as she did. Her innocence made a double burden for him.

'Then I can stay, just for a while?' she cried. 'Please, Adam?'

He sighed. 'For another week. No more.'

'God, why are you being such a remarkable pig?'

'Because I want you to do the grown-up thing with Dad and Dinah. And because we've taken a lot of chances, Belle. We're taking one now. If you stay, we'll do something stupid sooner or later – oh bloody hell, what was that?'

'The door. It's OK, I locked it. Get up! Jeans, shirt. Here.'

'Jesus, Miranda.'

'And Joseph!' Belle giggled. 'It's your fault. Saying makes it so. Hurry *up*. Shoes!' She thanked her stars for the swiftness of leggings and T-shirt and was on her way to the door.

'Don't make the bed,' she hissed. 'You never do.'

'What's this, Belle, expecting burglars?' asked Miranda, carrying Moriarty through the door. Behind her came Cosmo with the push-chair and Tilda and Paul with a sociably panting Baskerville.

'Sorry, didn't know I'd locked it. What are you lot doing here?'

'I found them outside,' Miranda said, unloading Moriarty into Adam's arms. 'Come on, let's see if we can find them anything to eat.'

'You won't come to rehearsal, so we've brought it to you,' Tilda said to Belle. 'You don't look very pleased about it.'

'Did Mum send you?'

'No, why would she?' She decided to withhold Dinah's love for the present. This didn't appear to please Belle either. 'I've only missed two rehearsals,' she said. 'I was coming to this one.'

'Yeah? On what train?' demanded Cosmo. 'There's a strike on, or didn't you know?'

'Obviously not.' Belle recovered her hauteur.

'And since we don't know how long it will last, the best thing is for you to come home with us in the van. OK?'

'No, it's *not* OK. Who asked *you* to start ordering me around?'

Cosmo looked world-weary as only he, and of course Kinski, knew how. 'Someone has to,' he growled. 'I don't know if you realise it, but we're back to school in a couple of weeks – and then the first night is going to seem like tomorrow. This is your thing, Belle – but it looks as though you just don't care any more.'

She glared at him. 'You are such a prick. God, if you all can't manage without me, just for a couple of days! I've got stuff on my mind. You know that.'

'So, you'll come back with us?' Paul asked gently before Cosmo could needle her again.

Belle surveyed her options. They were not good.

'I won't go home,' she declared. 'That's definite.' She looked at Tilda. 'I know it's not the best time,' she said, 'but do you think I could stay with you?' The Oliviers' was the only other place where she felt at home.

'I'll call Mum and ask her,' Tilda said. 'I think it will be all right. She says she wants us to carry on as we always have.'

Chloe was agreeable as predicted.

'I can come back at weekends?' Belle entreated Miranda a bit later as she was leaving. She did not include Adam in the request.

'Whenever you like,' Miranda said. 'Think of us as your second home.' As they closed the door she said, 'Poor kid. I've never seen her like this before. She really is in pieces.'

*　　*　　*

In the back of the van, propped on Cosmo's heap of red velvet cushions, Tilda said, 'Sorry if we hustled you. But we do need you – and having a job to do really can be helpful when you're upset. If Mum can keep going, so can I, and so can you.'

Belle was ashamed. 'I know you're only trying to help.'

'Well, it's not *just* you,' Tilda said honestly. 'Don't you think Miranda needs Adam to herself for a while? And whether you like it or not, sometime soon you'll have to talk to your parents.'

'All *right*!' Belle huffed. 'I'm here, aren't I?'

'Yes, and I'm glad.' Tilda nudged her affectionately. 'I've missed you.'

'You've got Paul.'

'Yes, but I need you too.'

Belle began to relax. There was much to be said for a relationship that was heavy on affection but light on intensity. 'That's good to know,' she said. She recollected that, while Tilda had actually lost her father, Luke was still alive and still the same, as far as she was concerned. It was she who had decided to put him on hold and run away. She wriggled closer to her friend and leaned against her, shoulder to shoulder.

'So how are you coping with Act Three?' she enquired.

Chapter 14

RUFUS AND ANT HAD ENCOUNTERED A SETBACK. The Dutch courier in whom they had placed their confidence had been arrested at Heathrow and the drugnet had been erased from the Internet. The encoded e-mail containing this information had declared itself their last such communication. There would be no repercussions. No names, addresses or faces had been exchanged. Ant had never even told Rufus exactly how their supplies had come into her hands.

'This is a good thing, if you ask me,' Dwayne told her. 'Suppose it had been *you* they caught?'

'Not possible. The system doesn't work that way.'

'Either way, I'm just not interested any more. I've had the drugs thing. It's time to move on.'

Rufus, who was looking depressed, said nothing.

'You could be right.' Antonia surprised them. 'This was a no-risk business, and we trod on no one's toes. But if we tried to start up locally, we might well land ourselves in trouble – especially with your record.'

'But we've got to do *something*.' There was near panic in Rufus's voice.

Ant shrugged. 'We don't *have* to sell. Personally, all I really want is a little high-class dope now and then.'

'Me too,' Dwayne agreed. 'Come on Rufe, take it as fate.

You have better things to think about. Like your mum needs all the help she can get; you're the man around the house now.' He sighed. 'And when you consider what an infantile arsehole my dad can be, it looks like I have to be the same. You know he actually asked April for a date? At his age!'

'Well, she is pretty advanced for hers,' Rufus said snippily. He was not comfortable with April. 'Do you mean to be so depressing, or have you been born again, or something?'

'Don't blame me; blame life,' advised Dwayne.

'I do. It sucks,' Rufus said unhappily. 'It has since Dad died.'

'It takes a long time to get used to something like that,' Ant said sympathetically. 'You have to be kind to yourself for a while.'

'Yeah? Like how?'

'Well, you do things you enjoy and you promise yourself not to have any negative thoughts while you're doing them.'

'I can't think of anything.'

'Try harder. Something to get rid of all the angst.'

'I'm British,' Rufus said. 'I don't have angst.' He thought a bit. 'I've never really got drunk,' he said.

'So, do it tonight. We'll look after you, won't we Dwayne?'

'You may regret this,' Dwayne told her. 'OK. I'll call April.'

Rufus groaned.

'What's up?'

'April. She's so . . . blond! And curly, and – her tits are so big!'

'Exactly,' Dwayne grinned. '*And* she's hot-shit at physics.'

Antonia looked thoughtfully at Rufus. Dwayne was right about him; he had some speedy growing-up to do.

*   *   *

'The trouble is,' Rufus complained as they entered the first pub at the top of the High Street, 'I don't know what I like best. So I'm going to start at this end and hope I've found out by the time we get to the bottom.'

'How many pubs are there?' asked Ant.

'Millions,' April said.

This intelligent beginning led Rufus, with ever fuzzier logic, from bar to bar and drink to drink, from fizzy lager to dizzying wine, to whisky, to brandy, to buzzy blue cocktails, and thence to a general expansive feeling that he would like to do something outrageous. But what?

'I know!' he said to the wavering faces above the three glasses of Highland Spring water opposite. 'Valways wanted t'shtarta barroombrawl!' He didn't hear the replies, but it took him less than five minutes to accomplish his ambition, with the willing accommodation of a beefy group of seniors from the local grammar school, in the oak-lined snug of the Ram's Head. The argument, such as it was, was whether Blur or Oasis was the bigger load of crap. It was impossible to say whether or not Rufus had won the point for the latter, because the landlord and three barmen, with the balletic expertise of long experience, laid rough hands upon the participants and gave them a two-second start before they called the police. 'Now *they* were a decent group,' Rufus said elegiacally. As the pub stood near the bottom of the High Street, it came naturally to run in a downward direction, and he did so, followed closely by Dwayne and the grammar-school boys, and less enthusiastically by Ant and April, whose platform shoes did not agree with the cobbles.

Across the bottom of the street, the river ran peaceably beneath its fine old bridge, lit up by starlight and wrought-iron coach-lamps. The banks were peopled by lovers, drunks and good citizens enjoying the weeping-willows and the water-fowl. The stars and the lamps danced exuberantly as Rufus ran full-tilt on to the bridge, pursued by a bear-like prop-forward, who stertorously overtook him and cut off his exit. There being only one way out, he took it, turning sideways and making a running jump for the parapet. For a moment the water blinked below him; then a hearty shove and he was below the water. Cold and shock sent him to the bottom and fed him a mouthful of icy slime. Spluttering, he tried to rise – the river was not deep – but the mud clung to his clothes and shoes, and the surface seemed farther away than he expected. Then his foot was netted in a skein of weed and he panicked, kicking deeper into the weed and silt, his lungs bursting as he tried not to swallow. As he opened his mouth something took him from behind and propelled him to the surface, breaking through in an exploded chandelier of heavy, brilliant drops. 'Keep still, you idiot,' Dwayne's voice commanded, and he went limp with relief as they carried out, with the instinct of frequent partners, the life-saving routine for which they both held certificates of proficiency.

'Thanks, mate,' he gurgled as they were assisted out of the water and on to the bank. Here, his gratitude was over-taken by his digestive organs, as the sixth-formers laid him face-down on the grass, covered him with a flack-jacket, and sat down to observe the ritual reappearance of mud, weed, water, Blue Dynamite, brandy, single and double malt whisky, red and white wine and three nationalities of lager.

'Sorry, really,' said the awed prop-forward. 'If I'd known he'd had such a skinful, I wouldn't have been up for the fight.'

'Not your fault,' said Dwayne, shivering under April's cardigan. 'He wanted it and he got it. I believe it's called a rite of passage.'

'Then let's hope he made it to wherever,' the prop-forward said reverently. 'As passages go, you wouldn't want to buy a ticket.'

'Where's the best place to take him?' Antonia wondered

when the sixth-formers had left, with warm good wishes for a swift recovery. 'We can't let his mother see him like this.'

'My place,' said Dwayne. 'I'll ring her and say we're staying over. My dad's playing in Aldershot; he probably won't be home till morning. Rufus can sleep in Clint's old bed – it's still in my room – so I can keep an eye on him.'

'You don't think he needs a doctor?' worried April.

'What could he do? He's seriously pissed, that's all. The river water isn't toxic – not that there can be much of it left. I'll look after him.'

'Is he conscious?' Ant asked doubtfully.

Dwayne examined the body. 'Semi, I'd say. The sooner we get him warm and dry, the better. April, you go and deploy your charms on a taxi-driver. Tell them it's for Elvis Cubitt's brother, right?'

Rufus awoke three times in the night to purge himself with self-pity and terror that he might never get to the end of it. 'If this is drinking,' he gasped pathetically to Dwayne, who was holding his hair out of his face above the lavatory bowl, 'I don't think it's my scene, after all.'

'This was not drinking; it was drinking to unfeasible excess,' Dwayne said. 'It's supposed to be about quality, not quantity. You can try again, in a couple of weeks.'

Rufus shuddered and was sick again.

After he had taken the sorry object back to bed, Dwayne went to the kitchen to give their jeans and shirts another spin in the dryer. They had smelled like a sewer. Even cleaned up, Rufus was going to look pretty rough; Chloe was bound to want to know why. They had better say he thought he was coming down with a flu bug; that should cover the green face, the hollow eyes, the probable shakes and the certain uncertain stomach. He only hoped she would not reinstitute the curfew when she saw how he looked. It seemed to have been forgotten in the aftermath of the funeral. He didn't like to deceive her, not even as minutely as this. She was the nicest woman he knew, as well as the most gorgeous, and he didn't want to add even a sliver to her current distress.

Anxious about Helen after seeing how profoundly Alain's death had affected her, Luke had asked her to spend an evening with him. To surprise her, he had hired a small cabin craft, and they had puttered up the Thames, enjoying the eccentric British mixture of riverside houses and trees. The air slid past their faces like a silk scarf, and Luke stretched out on the deck, half asleep, while Helen smoked and watched the wake follow them with its nagging intimations of time spent and non-returnable.

At Kew, he produced a picnic: there was lobster salad and sparkling wine, and the fresh figs that were Helen's favourite fruit.

'This is perfect,' she said gratefully, curling against the bulkhead to see a rosy sun going down. 'I don't know when I last felt so relaxed. I seem to have lost the knack of it lately.'

'I know the feeling. Life in Sheringham has become a permanent dance among hot coals.'

'It must be difficult having to sort out the future of the school as well as the family.'

'The family is the hard part. Both Belle and Olly seem to think I ought to be able to keep my erring wife in order, like some grim Victorian paterfamilias. Belle was rivetingly withering – I was utterly crushed until I realised she was quoting, free form, one of Strindberg's nastiest speeches from *The Father*.'

Helen chuckled. 'That child is me as I would like to be. I adore her. But what about the school?'

'Everything's fine, though it was a *little* sticky, telling the governors that I'm taking over Philip's job and he is taking over my wife.' He grinned. 'I suppose it was mischievous, but he and I opted for strength in unity and did it together, like Tweedle Dum and Tweedle Dee. The Board boggled. You could hear the clatter of eminent jaws dropping.'

'And they actually agreed to back you?' Helen was incredulous.

'What else could they do? Half of *them* are divorced, and they had already selected me for the job. The really good thing is that now they're all so sorry for me that I can have just about anything I want, next year. I've begun with two more scholarship places.'

'You know, your eyes still light up when you talk about Sheringham; you love it as much as ever, don't you?'

'It's part of me. The best part, probably.'

'I used to think like that about the theatre. But now I wonder if it has been a kind of – substitute, for a different person, one I might have been.'

'No one would agree with you,' he said, troubled by this new mood.

'More and more, I have a sense of it's all being quite pointless; dressing up and leading a life of pretence while somewhere along the road, overwhelmed by the fiction and the glitz, real life has quietly crept away.'

'That isn't true,' he protested softly. 'You have always had both; you had Adam – and me, and all the people who love you. Not to mention the Great British Public. You only feel this way, now, because "real life" has just hit you rather too hard.'

'It wasn't *my* life,' she said miserably. 'It was just time-out in Alain's.'

'Nonsense. He liked you far too much to think of you in those terms – apart from the other attraction.'

'Perhaps. Maybe all of them did. But what does it amount to, in the end? I'm tired, Luke – of the directors and co-stars and rising young playwrights; of being seen in the right places and the right clothes; of wondering how long I can get away with parts that are too young for me. I want to stop. Soon. And look after a man and a garden – even a child, if that seems possible. But I can't have them;

it's too late. And anyway – I wanted *him*.' She hid her face in her hands and he moved to put his arm around her.

'I hate to see you so wretched, but I know you. You could never stop acting; it's your life-blood. As for the garden, you'd soon get bored and turn it over to a likely young plantsman. And do you remember, when you had Adam, you swore you'd never repeat the experience? And you were in your early twenties then.' He smiled, a little anxiously.

She responded reluctantly. 'Tread on my dreams, why don't you?'

'No, no; I don't want to do that,' he said quietly. 'They are too much like my own.'

'Luke – darling, I'm sorry. I'm being selfish. You must be feeling grim.'

'Not really. But I seem to have become a spectator in my own life.'

'What will you do,' she asked cautiously, 'about Chloe?'

His face closed. 'There nothing I *can* do,' he said painfully. 'She has made it quite clear that she doesn't want to see me.'

'That's now; but you must give her time, a great deal of it. She has so much to work out. And I can't believe that everything she felt for you has been dragged out and killed as a sop to her conscience.'

He shook his head. 'No, I think I've lost her this time,' he said. 'She will never leave Alain, now that he is dead.'

Helen scanned the darkening surface of the river as if a hand in white samite might extrude some weapon useful to her argument. 'There is one thing you could do,' she said. 'Why don't you write to her?'

Chloe opened the envelope without looking at the hand-writing. When she held the letter in her hand, her reaction was indistinguishable, she thought, from fear. Whatever she was about to read, she was not ready for it.

This is my third attempt at a letter, Luke wrote. *Last time I saw you, I could speak no sensible words, and even now, when I am faced only by the idea of you, the difficulty persists. I can see you quite clearly; you have a little frown of apprehension between your brows. It isn't necessary. I shall write nothing to move or distress you. I'm not even sure I can reach you at all. I am so much aware of the gulf between the tragedy of your situation and the irony of mine. For the present, it seems unbridgeable, and perhaps this is how it ought to be.*

Nevertheless, our lives and our children will inevitably bring us together from time to time, as they always have. I hope we can find a way to be easy with each other. I promise nothing but agape; no sign of eros, not even the breath of a feather.

Chloe, I want to thank you for being kind to Belle, who has an instinct for what she most needs when she is in trouble. I know, as I think she does, that you and Tilda will help her to find her way back to us. It is characteristic of you to care for another's pain, no matter how great your own.

I won't write again, but if you should need to make use of me, please call me.

Yours,
Luke.

Nothing to fear, nothing to provoke her to tears or guilt. No pressure of any kind. She ought to have known. He had even made her smile with his teasing assurance of agape. Virtuous friendship. That was exactly what, in a tidy world, ought to exist between them. Perhaps it could. The letter lifted a weight from her spirit, and its warmth remained with her.

Adam and Miranda had gone out for the day. They were quietly celebrating the news that Miranda's work had received the highest commendations from her assessors, and the fact that Adam had been offered a permanent place on the paper. Their relief, on both grounds, was enormous.

Tilda was baby-sitting. They had thought it unwise to ask Belle, in her present state of mind. It was the last week before the Winter Term, and Tilda was glad to have a day, with no distractions other than Moriarty, in which to fine tune her role in the play. Belle had been censorious about her missing rehearsal but was forced to admit that it was her turn to look after her small niece.

She had whizzed, wordperfect, through the first and second acts, and was relaxing on the window-seat with a hot chocolate, when a visitor arrived.

She had expected anyone but Joel.

'What on earth—?' she said.

'Hello, Tilda. I've come to see my daughter. Didn't Miranda tell you?'

'No – she must have forgotten. I suppose you'd better come in.'

They measured each other up and down.

'I'm not dangerous,' he said.

'I know.'

It felt odd, different, meeting him here, on neutral ground. There was nothing here to say that he could not or ought not to be the same Joel who transported her across the skies in dreams.

'Is she awake?' he asked.

'I don't think so.'

He went into the bedroom and came back without Moriarty. 'She's zonked. Mind if I make myself some coffee?'

'Go ahead.'

She returned to the window seat, observing that people down in the street were already wearing jackets and cardigans. At the same time she was thinking about the discussion she had had with Grandpère Hervé, on the Pilgrims' Way, upon the nature and purpose of dreaming.

Dreams, they had decided, came in two main categories: either they were silly pieces of string, tied to daft balloons imprinted with any old words or images that had cropped up lately, or they were weighted bell-ropes, sounding out warnings, passings, and occasional carillons, with regard to one's deepest needs and fears. The Joel-dreams were bell-ropes, sounding the changes of enchantment, arousal and shame. They had become more frequent in the past few weeks. Following her grandfather's advice, she had begun to take them out and look at them instead of shoving them under her pillow. This had been her previous instinct, she now understood, because she had found it demeaning to be forced to admit by night to a longing she could not bear to recognise by day. She had also explored the bases of this repulsion. First, Joel had belonged to Miranda, and was still attached to her as Moriarty's father. To steal him, even in dreams, was to betray her sister. Second, she had always despised Joel, for his amorality, his cock-certainty and his disposition to wound others. This, she now accepted, made no difference; lust and despite were not mutually exclusive. There was also the question of what Joel himself might think of her fly-by-night obsession, should he know of it. Every time they had met, it seemed to her that he had consciously set out to make her aware of her sexuality. (That she was aware of his own, he took lordly for granted.) At first, unawakened and barely understanding, she had thought it a cruel method of ridicule, pinning her into her role as awkward little sister. Now she was not so sure. Joel liked women, he enjoyed their sexuality. Maybe he had just tried to make her feel more like a woman. And had succeeded more thoroughly than he could know.

What occurred to her now was that none of the reasons were important; what she had to do was to exorcise the dreams. Her cinematic education had taught her how an exorcist operated. She must confront the demon she wished to banish, and the strength of her confrontation would strip it of its power. Of course, exorcists derived their strength from God; Tilda would have to make do with the burning necessity to get on with the rest of her life.

Joel came back into the room and sprawled gracefully across the sofa. Looked at objectively – or not – there was no doubt that he was a thing of beauty, an on-the-edge kind of beauty like that of his artifacts.

'So, what have you been up to?' he asked.

She told him about the play.

'Sounds good,' he said. 'I might check it out. I've thought of doing some work on vampires myself. I'd like to explore just why the whole notion is so damn sexy.'

Tilda swung her legs off the padded sill and leaned towards him; body language, was what you called it. 'There's lot to think about,' she said. 'The relationship between sex and death, the Victorians' romantic eroticism of disease, their preoccupation with blood.'

'No wonder. Think of all those highly charged con-sumptive geniuses: Chopin, Keats, the Brontës . . .'

'And the act of feeding on their victims, part kiss, part penetration. The links between pleasure, pain and power.'

'The triumph of the dark side, unlimited knowledge, nothing forbidden, knowing one can't be killed.'

'Ah – now you're identifying with the vampire.'

'Naturally. With all that time, just think what an artist I could become. Don't you?' he added. 'Identify?'

'I try to, on stage – but I'm not like Cosmo; for instance, sometimes I think he really needs them to exist. The vampires we've created, most of them, are still half human. They feel a moral horror at what they've become. Like Louis in *Interview with a Vampire*.'

'Moral horror? OK – but who appealed to you more, sexually, in that film: Louis, clutching the rags of his conscience – or L'Estat, who absolutely accepted what he was and gloried in what it enabled him to do?'

'I identified with Louis, but I'd rather go to bed with L'Estat. How about you?'

His smile, without fangs, was appreciative. 'I'm with you all the way. Not much humour in poor Louis.' He looked at her as though sifting known quantities against others unknown. 'But since L'Estat is unable to be with us on the grounds that he doesn't exist – perhaps you would like to come to bed with me?'

He had asked much sooner than she had expected, but that was all right.

'I might like it,' she said coolly, heart hammering, 'but I can't be certain because I haven't done it before.'

His brows shot up. 'My God, I wasn't expecting a virgin.'

'Do you have any objection to them? I'm on the Pill, if that's the problem.'

'No. But have you considered how your friend – Paul, isn't it? – might feel about it?'

'It's complicated. I don't intend to go into it, but it can't be with Paul, not the first time.' The truth was that it was now too much of an issue between them, Paul's repulsion of Tilda's nervous attempt to seduce him had placed them in a double bind. Tilda could make no sexual advances because, knowing her fear of the act, he would suppose she offered herself without desire. Paul, therefore, held back whenever an embrace threatened to reach the critical point, and became angry if Tilda pressed it. Though obviously frustrated, his overt attitude was that they had for ever to 'let it happen', while Tilda knew the relationship would make no progress until she had conquered her Fear of the First Time and taken him forward with her.

The solution, for both the demon dreams and the problem of Paul, had gradually transferred itself from the night skies to her daylight consciousness. Only the opportunity had seemed impossible.

'Are you absolutely sure about this?' Joel asked her. He was looking at her as if he had found some new and delightful species.

'Look – do you want to sleep with me or not?'

She watched the spread of his lazy, cat-and-cream smile. He stood up and held out his hand. 'Will you get the Professor ready to go out, while I make a phone call?'

'But why? Where are we going?'

'Not very far.'

Twenty minutes later, they were racing the silver poussette through the short-cuts of Docklands. Joel pulled up suddenly and twirled Tilda to face the road.

'Do you mind if I blindfold you?'

Her heart missed one of the hammer notes that was its latest theme.

'Why would you want to do that?'

He laughed. 'Don't worry; this isn't another kidnap. It will just make things more special. Honestly.'

His eagerness was childlike, safe. 'Oh, why not?' she shrugged. 'Who said anything had to make sense?'

He unwound the voile scarf from her neck and tied it over her eyes. 'You have a beautiful neck.' He kissed the nape. 'That – and the shape of your head – you're like Nefertiti.'

She could not respond because the kiss had sent frozen silver streamers shivering down her back. He put his hand between her shoulder blades and the current of pleasure swivelled and turned like a shoal of tiny fish.

'Hold on to the push-chair. Here. Let's go.'

He guided her across an expanse of smooth paving; then she heard an electric door slide open ahead. Moriarty chuckled and squealed. They moved into an echoing space, which accoustics told her was probably domed.

'Hello Moriarty,' said a welcoming female voice, its accent elusive. 'Are you going to stay with me for a while?' There were more squeals, followed by unmistakable xylophone music.

'She has been here before,' Joel explained. 'She likes Dong-li.'

'She sounds happy enough,' Tilda agreed.

'Then come with me.'

They took a lift and came out on to hushed softwood floors. They walked through separate spaces whose relative sizes she could guess at from the reverberation of their voices.

'Stop here, and turn to your right. Three steps.' She obeyed.

'It will be quite dark when I remove the blindfold.' His voice was intimate now, brushing her ear. Sound had become muffled, the floor soft and giving beneath her feet. They were as closely contained as though they were in a velvet box. For a hair's breadth she was panicked by images of confinement: walls meeting walls, Dracula's coffin, Juliet's tomb. Then the scarf came off. Joel held her lightly and let her look.

At first she could see nothing, only leaping points of light behind her retina. She rubbed her eyes and still they leaped.

'Fireflies!' she cried, stretching out her arms.

'Projections of fireflies,' he affirmed, observing their flight across her spellbound face.

'Where *are* we?' She moved her hands as if touch might tell her. There was only the scent of something; she could give it no name but it was distilled from a paradise garden among the rooftops of Samarkand. Her eyes began to adjust to the gloom. There seemed to be the shapes of trees: citrus perhaps, and aromatic cedar. Or were they magical projections of trees? It must be so, because they were in an outdoor place, a wood that murmured and exhaled in the dim, pin-pricked light. Joel kissed her again, on the mouth this time, and she gave herself over, transported, to the magnification of every sense.

He locked the door and lit a pair of tiny terracotta lamps. They knelt on the floor in the warm light and he began to undress her. She was shaking slightly but they paid no attention to that.

'Mother of God!' his childhood said reverently. He

gazed at her breasts and her thighs and the curve that played the viola from one to the other. He saw the fall of her hair over her white shoulders. Of all earth's visible perfections, these were the ones he most worshipped. He set his fingers to travel where his eyes had rested and Tilda could no longer control her shaking.

'Don't, love,' he whispered, stroking her with the gentleness of the very last brushstroke of all. 'There's nothing to be afraid of.'

'I'm not afraid, exactly. It's more like how I am when I'm about to play in public.'

His reply was to tickle up an arpeggio of interesting responses in the unlikely area of her navel.

'You should be a pianist,' she smiled.

He kissed her for the compliment and she became confident enough to take off his shirt and begin her own fingering exercise. Rapt, she could not believe how easy it was after all; that you could shed your clothes and prejudices and protections all at once, so that you were weightless, made of light. When they were naked she held out her arms to him as joyfully as she had to the fireflies.

She had expected the pleasure, but never the outrageous, the extreme, the out-of-orbit intensity of it. Once more, she was flying with him through the night, constellations dancing at their fingertips and champagne sensations exploding all over her body, inside and out. Joel, pitched at his elemental best, was an erotic virtuoso who knew how to make a gift of his own artistry to his pupil. By the time the little room was grounded, and the stars were fireflies again, Tilda had learned that all that he had taught her was already part of herself. There were no demons.

'Was it how you thought it would be?' Joel asked, tracing learning curves on her reconstructed flesh.

'It was far more than that.'

He nodded. 'You were made for it. You could give up music and become one of the world's great courtesans.'

— 321 —

'No, thank you.' Her smile sparked. 'But thank you, as well.'

He delighted in her. So soon, and she was as poised as a dancer accepting her bouquet. He looked possessively at her lean body, lit like a La Tour by the tawny lamplight.

'I want to draw you, paint you. Lots of times. You will let me, won't you?'

Tilda sat up and gathered her hair, tying it back with the blindfold scarf. 'I don't know,' she said. 'This is only supposed to happen once.'

'I only asked if you'd model for me,' he teased. 'But since you certainly enjoyed what we have been doing, why not repeat it?'

'Because it might become addictive,' she said honestly, 'and I don't want that.'

'Then just let me draw you. Once. Nothing more.'

'I might. Not yet, though.'

She wanted to sleep with Paul first. Not to make comparisons, nothing like that, but as an important part of establishing her world around her as she wanted it to be. Paul and music; they were her world. As long as she could be perfectly certain about that, there could be no danger in Joel.

'You see, I haven't made a present of myself to you,' she told him, making an effort to explain something she did not fully comprehend as yet. 'But I think I was getting you to make me a present to myself. Do you see, at all, what I mean?'

Joel did. He liked the sound of it. Tilda was nothing like her sister. She was not like any other girl he had met. She would hang on to her space, maintain her independence. He could relate to that. There was a strength in her that made him feel both free and, strangely, safe in her company. He looked forward to discovering where that would lead.

Alain was no longer a presence in the house. Chloe was

not sure exactly when he had left. There were a couple of days when she had gone up to London, another when she had been hectically busy at home. Next morning, when she had started to tell him about them, she had realised at once that she was talking to herself. At first she had been afraid to be without him. She had got into the car – surely the most prosaic of all haunted places – and driven anywhere; but he had not been beside her. She had roamed the house in an agony of wanting him back; not the imaginary shade, but the living man. She had wept again for a day, aching in an emptiness without boundaries. That night she had slept as she had forgotten she could sleep. Slowly, the emptiness was beginning to fill itself with the knowledge that, soon, she must come to terms with his absence, his death. In return for her acceptance, she would eventually receive peace. That was the bargain; there was no other.

'Mum?' Tilda came into the studio after school, her expression resolute. 'I wanted to ask you what you think about something.'

Chloe abandoned the large preliminary sketch on the drawing board.

'What is it?'

'It's going to sound bad, however I put it—' She speeded up to get it over. 'The thing is, I've started the Pill and I want to sleep with Paul. It's not an impulse thing; I've thought about it a lot.'

'Tilda!'

'You're horrified, aren't you?' Tilda looked smitten.

Chloe tried to recover quickly. 'It's a bit of a surprise,' she murmured.

'Well, what *do* you think?'

'Give me time, darling. I know you're growing up fast, but I hadn't realised quite *how* fast.'

'Well, do you think it's too soon after Dad? What would he have said?'

Chloe knew. 'He'd have said his three "*mon dieu*s" and

told you that if you had absolutely no doubt, if you *knew* it was right for you, then you should follow your mind and your heart.'

'That's what I thought,' said Tilda, relieved.

Chloe smiled. 'Well, it was nice of you to ask.'

'That's OK. But don't be upset, will you? Everybody gets round to it sooner or later. I'm quite a lot later, on average.'

'Really?' Chloe said politely. Then, 'Tilda, do you love Paul?'

'Yes, I do. And I think we'll stay together. I suppose we've found each other rather soon. I mean you don't expect to meet the mirror of your soul at sixteen. But there it is. I'm glad about the sex, Mum. I just wasn't sure what you'd think.'

'Give me a hug,' Chloe said. 'I love you. I hope Paul makes you happy.'

'Then why are you crying? Don't, Mum.'

'It's all right, sweetheart. It's traditional. There's some Kleenex somewhere.'

'The end of my childhood, you mean?' said Tilda perspicaciously. 'Don't worry – I'm probably still a child or I wouldn't have asked.' She had no questions, or indeed anything at all to say on the subject of Joel. Quite apart from the obvious need for secrecy, he simply had nothing to do with it.

'By the way,' she remembered, 'Belle says can we have the rest of the home rehearsals here; only she still feels weird at home, with the divorce, and having to pretend everything's normal.'

'Yes, but she has to live at home. Not too many stopovers.'

'We just don't need any extra stress. It's not that long till the first night. Oh – and Rufus is bringing Ant to supper.'

'Is he?' Chloe's maternal hackles rose. 'Is she becoming a particular friend of his?'

'I guess.' Tilda said. 'She's good news. I like her. Oh, you mean is she his girlfriend? I doubt it. You know Rufus.'

'I'm not sure I do, any more,' Chloe said thoughtfully. 'Perhaps I'd better do something about that.'

'It's all right,' Tilda said loftily. 'Sex scares him.'

'It scares everybody,' Chloe said feelingly.

Later, trying to put together her thoughts on Tilda's decision, Chloe concluded that her behaviour had signalled her instinctive reaction to her father's death. Knowing that she would now never replace Miranda in Alain's affections, she had elected to miss out that phase of her sexual development and go on to the next; in fact, to the real thing. Seen from this viewpoint, her desire to make love was positive and life-affirming, a textbook progression. Chloe recognised that this was not a very romantic reduction of the growth of first love; nevertheless she found it a reassuring one.

The Winter Term was like a runaway train; everyone had to hang on for dear life while it careered inexorably towards drama, diversification and divorce. While Philip Dacre contemplated his great good fortune in winning Dinah at a time when the ceding of Sheringham would have left him at a total loss, Luke Cavendish found his work was now twice as hard, as he prepared to take Philip's place as Headmaster of the school and Dinah's as the heart of his family. He was confident of his fitness for the former, but mothers, he knew, were irreplaceable. He had heard nothing from Chloe and this, too, saddened him, though the reports of her well-being he obtained from the twins were increasingly cheerful. Helen did her best to console him. Her own depression had lifted when she had been invited to provide a deliciously wicked Snow Queen for Christmas Day TV.

Dinah, despite her high percentage of certainty that she was doing the right thing, found her resolution undermined by the prospect of losing Olly and Belle. Although they treated Philip with horrible politeness – Olly called him Mr Dacre and Belle always addressed him as Sir – they deflected his every attempt to build a closer relationship. When Dinah begged them to make the new house in Notting Hill their second home, Oliver claimed he needed to stay close to the vet's surgery at all times, and Belle insisted she already had a second home, thank you, with Adam and Miranda. Meanwhile, would they please not bother her, because she had the cast of *The Soul of Dracula* to whip and scorn into shape.

She did this excessively, apparently without noticing that their performance was almost faultless from the fourth week of term. The cause of her distemper was that the extra rehearsals, due to the approach of the first night, left her no time to visit Adam. Cosmo tried to make her feel better about everything by subjecting her to sudden voracious embraces when she was not expecting them. Her response was to buy herself a stage flick-knife and use it. It was only plastic, but it harboured a nasty jab. There was an explosive incident when she awoke him with it as he was snatching a tranquil forty winks in his coffin.

Tilda and Paul watched, fascinated, as their friends' off-stage relations declined and their dramatic partnership, perversely, soared to new heights. They too were exceptionally busy. They were not only producing the music for *Dracula*, but also studying for their own music exams and trying, more or less, to keep up with the normal curriculum. Such hectic productivity did not provide an atmosphere conducive for Tilda to pass on what Joel had revealed to her. She decided to wait for the New Year.

Rufus was also uncharacteristically occupied, his tutors having offered him forceful persuasion to acquaint himself with several topics that had eluded him during the course of the year. Dwayne and Antonia were willing coaches; so was April, who was, as promised, shit-hot at physics. A new seriousness had overtaken the group. Even their recreations were genteel pursuits, such as dancing or listening to music, without any extra stimulation. Regretfully, Rufus read the writing on the wall. 'Your playdays are over,' it said. In the light of every recent event and future probability, he knew it to be appropriate. Dad would have wanted him to do as well as he could at school, and that was what he would try to do. He only wished he had begun while Alain was still alive. He would also have wanted him to look after his mother, to be the 'man of the house', as people kept suggesting. Well, he could do electrical stuff, and paint walls, and fix simple things around cars. That was a start. It all looked pretty grim, but perhaps something would come along to cheer things up. Come to think of it, why didn't he try mending a few computers, see if he could get a little something going there? Dad would really approve of that; after all, it had been his idea.

The runaway train came to its first shuddering halt at the first night of the play. While the players, backstage, sweated streaks into their grease-paint, green with stage-fright, Chloe, still at home, poured herself a generous measure of dutch courage and worried, as she had done all week, about the prospect of meeting Luke. It would have to happen sooner or later, but tonight was not the occasion she would have chosen.

A year ago, when the world was different, the play had been *The Importance of Being Earnest*. Belle, driven by her first immortal longings, had hijacked the production from a hapless junior master and had persuaded Helen to lend her famous face to a blasphemously young and (almost) sexy Lady Bracknell, matching her line for line with her own precocious talent. There had been a black market in tickets and extra performances by public demand.

But what Chloe remembered now was the nerve-racking subtext to the evening. It had been the first time that she and Luke had met since she had ended their relationship. Every Olivier and Cavendish had been present, and all but the blissfully ignorant young had colluded in the strenuous pretence that nothing – let alone a passion beyond the bounds of reason – had ever occurred between them. The only defaulter was Luke himself, who had blackmailed her into promising one last assignation, a promise she had not kept.

There would be nothing other than memory to distress her tonight. In theory, there was nothing to prevent their meeting in the friendly fashion projected in his letter – nothing, that is, except the closer and more disturbing recollection of the night they had heard *The Green Ray*.

She topped up her glass and concentrated fiercely on the contents of her wardrobe. Tilda wanted her to wear the grey velvet opera cloak with the gold lining. She had refused on the grounds that it was too extreme but now she changed her mind; it was just the thing for an evening with the Count. She threw it back and swirled it around her shoulders in the manner of Christopher Lee, who had stalked her own teenage fantasies. 'This is the children's night,' she reminded her reflection as she twisted and piled her hair before the Florentine mirror. 'You'll be all right if you just keep that in the forefront of your mind.'

Her reward was a resounding 'Yes!' when she appeared downstairs where Rufus was waiting in his dark suit and Alain's magenta shirt to escort her to the school.

'I can't believe it fits you already,' she murmured, touching the brilliant collar. '*Tu es beau ce soir, mon fils.*'

Rufus swelled. That was what she used to say to his father.

'Can I drive?' he begged when they reached the car.

'When it's legal.'

'It just seems more the way it ought to be,' he said wistfully. 'You know, the man does the driving.'

'I know,' she said. She kissed his cheek and scented Eau Sauvage, also Alain's. 'Thank you for the offer, my darling.'

Sheringham's splendid theatre was packed to capacity. The

audience, like Chloe, had entered into the spirit of things and had taken their sartorial inspiration from Hammer Films. There was a lot of scarlet and velvet and lace, and not a few heaving bosoms; notably that of Claudie Latham, who embarrassed her daughter by heaving hers at Luke Cavendish as they entered the foyer where he and Dinah were ritually shaking the hands of all arrivals for the last time. Lisa, in virginal white with a single blood-red love-bite, sighed and took herself off to sit with Oliver. She hoped her mother would soon begin to grow up. Perhaps the menopause would help.

Chloe, just about to enter, saw the queue ahead of her and the tug of memory was unbearable. Shaking Luke's hand was the last thing she wanted to do, especially in front of Dinah.

'It's terribly crowded,' she said to Rufus. 'Why don't we use a side door?'

Rufus was horrified. 'But Mum – *everybody* shakes hands.'

'Oh, very well, if you insist.' She was ashamed of her cowardice.

'Good evening Luke, how are you?' she said, quite normally, she thought.

'Chloe, I'm delighted to see you.' He sounded more or less normal too. Their fingers touched. That was that, then.

Except that touching his hand still produced the life-awakening, circuit-making, Sistine Chapel effect from last year. She pressed her cheek against Dinah's and moved on into the auditorium where expectation was rising like steam. She located Adam and Miranda in the middle of the third row and excused herself into her place beside them. She felt buoyant and slightly hysterical. She must have had too much wine.

'You're late,' Miranda said, examining her tenderly. 'You look lovely. I thought you might have chickened out.'

'So did I. But I decided to bat on instead.'

'That is the worst joke I have ever heard,' Adam said affectionately.

'Thanks.' Chloe preened herself.

'Hush. It's beginning,' Rufus hissed.

The performance was a manifold astonishment of sadness, beauty and ingenuity. Belle made everyone surpass and surprise themselves, and this included her audience, who were tossed like rag dolls between their beliefs and their instincts, their aesthetic and their morality, to land, invigorated and argumentative, at her feet. After seven curtain calls, they let her go and filed out, accompanied by the spare, haunting themes of Paul's score.

'Are you sure you won't come to the party?' Miranda asked Chloe as they were wiping away the evidence of pity and terror. 'Helen is here, and I saw Mike and Maggie earlier. One drink?'

'No thanks, I'll just have a quick word with Belle and Tilda and then slip away. It's what I want. I'll see you later, if I'm still awake. I've put you and Adam in your old room.'

She was not awake when they came home. She was deep dreaming, down on the seabed in a cradle of blue-green weed. Luke was with her and they loved each other without guilt, moving to slow, oceanic rhythms, known to them from long ago. She did not remember the dream when she awoke.

No sooner had *The Soul of Dracula* completed its six-night run, cold-turkeying its habituated cast into wrenching withdrawl, than the runaway train took off again, hurtling headlong towards Christmas. For the first time in the experience of both Oliviers and Cavendishes, there was the expectancy of more sorrow than pleasure in keeping the feast.

The twins told Chloe that, as far as possible, they wanted everything to be the same as it had always been. On Christmas Eve they lovingly wreathed Alain's photograph in mistletoe and set it on the mantelshelf in the sitting-room, so that he could watch them, in spirit, while they dressed the tree. They worked together methodically, as he had taught them, distributing one colour at a time, reminding each other, by sacred tradition, of the provenance of each beloved piece of painted plaster and shining glass, of the ragged robins from Woolworths, the bells and Birds of Paradise from Galléries Lafayette, Tilda's precious orchestra of gilded cherubs, Miranda's cardboard children in Victorian dress, the miraculous miniatures of great cathedrals that Grandpère Hervé had made, the endearing felt animals they had sewn themselves, the train, the plane, the sailing ships, and Chloe's spiced pomanders, whose scent filled the room. Lastly, there were the sweets and crackers, in case of visiting children, and the glittering finishing-spray of silver frost.

When they had done they brought in Chloe, whose privilege it was to set the angel on the topmost spur. They kissed her afterwards, in place of Alain, and exchanged the first Christmas greetings. They stood together, holding each other, in front of his photograph, while he looked back at them quizzically, a little bemused and just about to smile. Chloe wiped her eyes with her hand and made a declaration. 'No more tears,' she commanded. 'Tomorrow Moriarty will be here. Let's try to make her first Christmas something we will all remember.'

'Except Moriarty,' Rufus regretted.

'I hope they're going to stay with us for the whole week. That will give some of it a chance to sink in.'

Luke and Dinah had agonised long over various prospective plans for what Oliver referred to unhelpfully as 'the Feast of the Immoderate Consumption'. What would make it bearable for him and for Belle? What social arrangement, if any, would be acceptable to them, coming as it did before an event they considered to be the betrayal of a life contract, the bloody drawing and quartering of the body familiar?

'We could *ask* them,' Luke suggested, though doubt-fully.

'They may think that if we don't know instinctively what they want, it's because we don't care enough.'

He groaned. 'If they do, it's because their mother is a psychologist. So, what do you think, then?'

'There are two ways to go. Either we have Christmas together, as normal – only it won't *be* normal, how can it? – or I spend it with Philip, and you and the children begin as you will go on together.'

'So which do you prefer – Scylla or Charybdis?'

'I want to stay, of course. But what would *they* want?'

'You see? We have to ask them; it's the only possible way.'

When Belle and Oliver were consulted, they asked for time to consider. The jury was out for three days. 'Make them sweat,' Belle said vengefully. Like Rufus and Tilda, their decision was that they would like things to be as much as possible like previous years; and that everything would be a hundred percent better if Adam and Miranda, and especially Moriarty, came to stay for at least a week.

'If only we could make holograms of ourselves, and leave them with one lot while we troll over to the other,' Miranda had sighed.

'Or if Moriarty were twins. It was on the cards, after all.'

'You're not helping. What shall we do?'

Adam thought for a while. 'What time does your lot have Christmas dinner?'

'Dinner time. Sevenish.'

'Then it's solved. We have ours at one, so that we can just party afterwards. So – we have lunch chez Cavendish, and dine later chez Olivier.'

'Oh God.'

'And after that, we'll move diplomatically from one to the other. OK?'

'KO,' said Miranda ambiguously.

The plan worked as well as it could, in the circumstances, and Moriarty was so spoiled by both families that it was just as well (if indeed it was the case) that her memory was not yet developed. The present she liked best was from Joel, who had worked on it for weeks. He had made her a rocking-horse, carved and caparisoned in the style of the Tang dynasty.

New Year brought even more delicate problems to the Cavendish house, chiefly because no one had really wanted to confront it. Dinah, who had so far been unable to choose a date for leaving her family, was jolted into panic when Belle and Olly, appearing in tandem as they did on these occasions, stated that they simply could not bear the idea of the four of them singing Auld Lang Syne together, and no one was to be upset if they went round to Tilda's and Lisa's respectively. Next, to Dinah's overwhelmed surprise, they had each hugged her until it hurt and told her how horribly they were going to miss her; then they had made a tearful escape, leaving Luke to pick up the pieces.

'I think it's time to go, love,' Luke told her, utterly miserable now that the hour approached.

Dinah's chest seemed to cave in and fall so that she could not stand. This was a crazy thing she was doing. Surely, she must not go?

Luke held her and let her gasp and shake in his arms while flashes of the past lightened across his mind; their first meeting, at a dinner party they had left indecently early; their wedding on the beach in Cornwall, near his grandfather's house; the children being born, Olly sliding neatly into the light without a sound, Belle roaring, they swore, before she had left the womb. And Dinah. Laughing, so often laughing. They had been happy together. They had been a happy family, and for so long. Until he had met Chloe. And this was Dinah's answer. He could only hope it was the right one for her.

— 333 —

They stood holding each other until Dinah said sadly, 'I'll tell Philip to expect me, then?'

'Yes,' Luke said. 'I think you should.'

He let her go.

Miranda, hunched on the window seat, was searching for signs that Spring had any intention of getting out of bed and fighting its way through the wet grey web that clung to the city. She knew there were trees down there, guarding pugnacious little fists of buds, still too insecure about the weather to let them unfurl. She didn't blame them really, with the rain blustering through the streets, head-butting its way around corners and sticking its icy fingers right in your eyes.

'I think I'm turning into a squirrel,' she told Adam as he came in with Moriarty in his arms. 'I can see nothing but shades of grey.' She sighed deeply. 'I wish something nice would happen.'

'Seems a little unfair on the squirrels; I mean, their world is so constantly and closely changing colour. We could make it happen,' he added. 'Something nice.'

'Mmm. Any ideas?' She took Moriarty from him and began to play pat-a-cake.

'Yes. I have, as a matter of fact.'

Something in his voice made her look at him. 'Why are you smiling like that?'

'I was thinking it was time we got married,' he said casually. He waited. 'Well? Don't you have an opinion on that?'

Miranda clutched Moriarty tighter. Her eyes were large and startled. 'Do you really mean that? You want us to get married?'

'Of course I do,' he said patiently. He knelt beside her and took her hand and one of her daughter's. 'Will you marry me, Miranda? And we shall be a proper family, you and Moriarty and me.'

Her melon smile appeared and threatened to split her

face. 'Yes! Yes! Yes!' she shouted. 'But I can't believe it's happening.'

'You seem so astonished,' he wondered. 'Has it never occurred to you that this is the next step?'

'It used to,' she said truthfully. 'But then I stopped thinking about it. At first because we were happy enough as we were – and later – I suppose I felt I no longer deserved it.' She met his eyes, conscious of her betrayals.

'Don't say that. None of that matters. This is just you and me staking a claim on the future. If you want to, then I think this is the time.'

It was the right time to show her that he was irrevocably committed to her, and for her to show him the same commitment. He hoped that their marriage would also give Joel that message, and that it would make it more difficult for Miranda to give way to whatever remaining affections she had for him, whether as Moriarty's father or something else. By now he had assimilated the fact of Ranger's continued involvement in their lives. Although he disliked it and would always be jealous on that account, there was also a shaming relief in being able to weigh that situation in the balance with his own extraordinary relationship with Belle. For as long as it lasted. He knew it could not go on. It would probably come to a natural term, one day; though, to be honest, it did not feel that way at present. Anything but. However, they would be all right, he was certain, as long as they kept this thing between them in its safe space capsule, way off the planet, moored somewhere near Mars. Or was it Venus? With Belle it was always both. And because of her, he too had been forced to recognise an unlooked-for dichotomy in his nature.

'So, do we book the – what? Church? Registry office?'

'Do you think we could do it at St Mark's, in Sheringham? I'd really love Nick Bannister to marry us. He won't mind us not being the right kind of believer. All us kids have sung in the choir, and Mum's always going there for something or other.' Her smile was pure joy. 'Oh, Adam, I feel so –

I don't know – renewed! You've made the sun come out. I love you.'

'I love you too.' He looked out of the window. 'Where? I can't see it.'

'Not out there! In here. Quickly – come to bed. I want to hold you as close as I can, and to know you'll always be there.'

She was absurdly happy. Like Chloe, she knew herself to be a born marriage-maker, and Adam was perfectly, amazingly, exactly the right one to make it with. What was more, she would make sure it lasted. There would be no further self-indulgent sex with Joel, who was no more capable of understanding what it took to make a marriage than he was of handling even the most simple relationship with a woman; apart, it would seem, from Moriarty. That, too, would have to be carefully monitored. Looking over Adam's shoulder in a satisfactorily blissful position, Miranda felt that her mission in life was clarifying itself nicely. Joel might well be still in her blood, but such diseases could be cured when necessary. She had her careeer to think about, and Moriarty, and in the fullness of time and womb, as Adam had mentioned, the engaging possibility of another set of twins.

They stayed in for the rest that day, consciously building their nest, making love and plans and playing with Moriarty, who caught the atmosphere and carolled away to herself like a cherub learning its scales.

They would each set out with a similar handicap in the marriage stakes, and both had learned something about the checks and balances needed in dealing with the life of the emotions. For a modern partnership, it was a practical and rather hopeful beginning.

'You are my sunshine,' sang Moriarty quite clearly, from her cot at the foot of the bed. It was clear, at any rate, to Adam and Miranda. On the other hand, she was only ten months old.

*   *   *

Wary of possible extreme reactions, Adam was careful to give Belle the news when they were alone, though expecting Miranda at any moment.

'I think it's a great idea,' she said calmly. 'Congratulations.'

She could always surprise him. 'I was afraid you would hate it.'

'Why should I? You can't marry me.'

In fact, she was rather pleased. It would change nothing, as far as she could see. And Adam would remain here, where she could always reach him, even if, upon some yet unthinkable occasion, he might not want her to. Then there was the proven and useful fact that while marriage was prone to bore a man, infidelity hardly ever did. Granted, most men might be unfaithful more than once, but Adam would never need to; she would be all the women he could ever want, from Mary Magdalen to Madonna, and including that actress he liked – who was it, now?

'Adam, who was that film star you liked?'

'What?' Adam was disoriented.

'The dark one. French.'

'Juliette Binoche?'

'No. Before her.'

'Oh – Isabelle Adjani.'

'Yeah, her. Good actress. Good choice.'

'Belle, are you *sure* you don't mind about this marriage?'

'I've said so, haven't I? Look, do we have time to make love or not? Someone's picking me up at one-thirty.'

'Not. Miranda will be here in five minutes.'

'Really?' She grinned wickedly. 'Then come here.' She pulled him over against the wall. 'Here's a quick way I saw on *Blue Peter*.' Kissing and licking him into submission, she unzipped his jeans and hitched up her slick of black leather skirt. As Adam gasped and pressed against her, she hooked her leg over his hip bone as, in fact, she had seen a prostitute do in another very educational TV series. There was some swift, efficient business with fingers, then she sank her teeth into his neck, which she had got to like recently, and he was exploding inside her before he knew what had bitten him.

'I wonder if that's the derivation?' she mused in the pedantic Cavendish manner as she tidied herself.

'Of what?' Adam demanded, rather crossly, she thought.

'Hooker,' she said smugly.

As had happened before on a similar occasion, there was a knock on the outer door of the flat. 'It's Miranda,' Adam said, guiltily checking his zip. Belle looked at her watch. 'It's Cosmo. I told him to be here on the dot.' She threw open the door and Cosmo swaggered in, wearing black and frowning as always, because he knew how well they suited him. When, instead of scowling back, Belle put her arms around his neck and kissed him on the mouth, he was not surprised – he had learned, as Adam never would, not to allow her the advantage of surprise – but he was intrigued. Why, he enquired of himself, would she do this in front of her brother?

Thoughtfully and quite gently, he pushed her away. 'Are you ready?' he growled.

'I'm all yours. Bye, Adam. I'll call Miranda later, to say congratulations.'

'What was that about?' Cosmo asked as they made for the lift.

'Oh, they're getting married, poor sad old things.'

'Christ, yes.' Cosmo shuddered. 'Are you ever going to want to do any of that?' he asked, offhand. 'Marriage, kids, the whole scary bit?'

'Not me. I'd only give birth if I could have snow leopard cubs.'

'Sometimes I think you're halfway insane,' he said comfortably.

'That's OK. Madmen live nearer to the truth. Like in Dostoevsky.'

'Maybe.'

In the lift, Belle faced him intently. 'Promise me something, Cosmo. Promise you'll come to RADA with me. I need you around when I'm working. You're the only one who really knows what I'm getting at, in any deep sense. I can't be without that.'

Cosmo smiled. 'I know that. Of course I'm coming with you. I always was. I need you, too – to goad me into being as good as I can be. Not as much as before, though – I'd like you to remember that.'

'It's a deal.' They slapped hands solemnly.

'Maybe we'll be a famous partnership, like Laurence Olivier and Vivien Leigh,' she said dreamily.

'Does that mean we have sex?'

'Sometimes.'

'Today?'

'Maybe tomorrow?'

Chloe had encountered Luke twice since the first night of *Dracula*. Once, their cars had passed each other in the village and he had slowed so that she feared he meant to stop. She had waved quickly and driven on. The second occasion was more dangerous, according to those who believe in the magical powers of coincidence. She had been walking in the fields with Baskerville and had stopped to climb up the trunk of the Lightning Oak and gaze out across the greening dip of the valley scattered with sheep and lambs. Her eye was caught by a movement high up on the opposing slope before it gave way to the forest. A man and two dogs were approaching the bench, set under an ancient beech, which stood almost in line with the fallen oak. There was no mistaking Holmes and Watson, or Luke's old rust-coloured jacket. She watched him sit and look across to her side of the valley, then saw him stand and wave his arm. Safe at such a distance, she waved back. They sat and looked at each other, small as sheep, across the two miles of exuberant new life pressing up out of the earth and covering it with beauty. It was not the Green Ray, but perhaps it was a more appropriate substitute.

Early next morning, Chloe was awoken by Miranda burbling ecstatically over the phone, and she knew that closer communication with Luke was no longer to be avoided. At eleven o'clock she called him at the school.

'Chloe! Marvellous. How are you?' The warm voice exulted. 'It was so good to see you like that yesterday. Your hair was burning right across the valley. Well – Adam has given me the news and I couldn't be more delighted.'

'So am I,' she said. 'They seem so happy about it, and it's just the thing for Moriarty.' Funnily enough, it wasn't at all difficult to talk to him; she couldn't think why she had been so reluctant to do so. 'The thing is, Luke, I think you and I – I mean, there's a lot to discuss. They want the wedding to be a small, family affair, and I'd like to do the best I can for them.'

'So would I. Why not meet as soon as possible? Today, if you like.' There was the faintest hesitation. 'I'm free after lunch.'

Chloe had many reasons to recall that weekly freedom; they rose up too vividly. 'I'm afraid not,' she said, concealing her relief, 'I have to see Nick Bannister at St Mark's. He wants me to do another large canvas, for the south wall this time. I'll – I'll talk to you again, when I have more idea what the children want.'

'Very well. It's nice to hear your voice, Chloe.'

Nick Bannister was waiting for her in the church, occupying himself by playing some unliturgical music on the piano.

'Thelonius Monk.' Chloe recognised one of Alain's favourites.

'God loves a genius.' He grinned. He closed the lid and led her to the space on the south wall that was designated for the new painting. It was to be a Resurrection and she would have a whole year to work on it. It would be a companion piece to her triumphant celebration of the life of the village, and especially of Catherine Chandler, covering the north wall near the Anchoress's cell.

They looked at this now, the colours reaching out and drawing them into parallel worlds in which the living communed with the dead. There were perfect physical details of the village and the countryside, and there were multiple moods, with the light shifting transversely across the canvas from a gold-washed spring dawn to a deep blue midnight. As rich and complex as the histories it represented, it was a formidable achievement.

'Do you think you can do it again?' Nick asked her. She had been very doubtful; she had refused him twice.

'I believe I might, now. I hope so; I want to. I brought these with me.'

She showed him the rough sketches she had blocked out. 'They're just a beginning, barely that. I'll change them a hundred times.'

Here again he saw the layered realities, the worlds touching, the interweaving of the spirit and the flesh. This was the quality he loved in Chloe's work. She had a medieval awareness of these relations which the western world was in danger of losing. It was also why he loved her as a human soul. She claimed that she did not believe; it was true that she might not recognise the same image of God as he did, or the next man; but Chloe was one of the most passionate believers Nick had ever known. He knew that she had been through a period of spiritual darkness, even greater, he thought, than was warranted by the loss of Alain. She had not allowed him to help her, though he had offered himself as anything from listening ear to psychoanalyst. She had preferred to confide in Catherine Chandler, who may well have been a hundred times more use to her. He wanted her, very much, to be happy again.

She said, 'I wanted to thank you for agreeing to marry

Adam and Miranda. We are all so grateful. Perhaps they ought not to have asked you, but Miranda makes no boundaries where her heart is concerned. She loves Adam, she loves you, she loves this church – therefore, where else could it possibly happen?'

'Nowhere else. She is absolutely right. Will you put the wedding into the new picture?'

'That's a lovely idea. Yes, Nick, I will.'

She hoped that, for Miranda, the marriage would signal a resurgence off her old, true self and restore the confidence lost with Alain's death and Joel's manipulative behaviour; she realised there had been more to that than she would ever know and could only hope that time would lessen the difficulties of that relationship. For herself, she began to hope for similar changes. The fact that she was ready to begin work on the painting must surely mean that she was also prepared to experience and explore the meanings and concepts that would crowd in on her when the canvas took on a life of its own.

When Nick left her with a benedictory kiss, to go to one of his 'beastly meetings about money', she crossed the aisles to the wall of Catherine Chandler's cell and pulled up a chair beside the four-leaf opening chanelled to her otherworld ear. There was an immediate sense of welcome.

'Catherine, dear Catherine – I would like your opinion because I am in doubt. Do you think I am a fit person to paint a Resurrection?'

If you are not, God will make you so by the time you have completed it.

'You see no blasphemy in it, or hypocrisy?'

Why does your generation bring disorder to the hierarchy of sin which the Church has been so careful to categorise? Blasphemy is an indignity offered to God, a great and shameful sin. If you do not believe in God, you are unable to offer such indignity. As for hypocrisy – a small but unlovely sin – you do not feign to be anything

— 342 —

which you are not. Your work glorifies the natural creation. There is no sin, large or small, to be found in it. On the contrary, as I have often told you, your work is where you will find your salvation – and your solutions.

'You know why I ask.' Chloe's voice was low.

I know. But the part of you that asks still looks backward, and sees guilt; the part that embraces the Resurrection looks boldly to the future, and can envisage redemption.

'You think so? How am I to be redeemed?'

A sharp sigh seemed to gust through the stone. If you will not acknowledge the existence of God, you will have to fend for yourself. You have already made a beginning. Continue! Work. Allow yourself to love without boundaries. Become a whole person, instead of struggling against yourself. Live, clear and single in mind and heart.

'That would be wonderful, a release. It is what I yearn for – but it's hard to do, and I can't convince myself that I deserve it.'

A dry, light breath teased her ear. There is always the comfort of having no alternative.

Chloe smiled and put her hand through the carved leaves as if it might meet its companion. 'Catherine, you do me so much good. I *wish* you might come back to us, and we might meet.'

We do meet. We are together now.

'I just want to feel—' What *did* she want, exactly?

That I am not merely another duality you have created within yourself?

'The ghost of my Catholic childhood? I don't believe that.'

Then rest in what you have; it is all you need. Chloe, you *have* everything that you need. You have only to see it for yourself.

'I'll try. I will try.'

As she withdrew her hand from the quatrefoil, she heard the west door creak open. 'Goodbye, Catherine,' she whispered. 'Next time, I'll tell you my plans for the painting. I think you will approve of them.'

I already do. God be with you, my dear child.

'And with your spirit.' The response came automatically.

She heard the footsteps come down the aisle and turned towards the sound. She had recognised them as easily as the figure on the hillside.

'I hope you don't mind,' he said hesitantly. 'Once I knew where you would be, it became impossible not to see you.'

'I don't mind.'

'Thank you. Were you talking to Catherine Chandler?'

'Yes.'

'And does she still answer?'

'More clearly every time.' She smiled. 'Does that seem mad to you?'

'Not specially. I just wish I could persuade Shakespeare to do it – or Flaubert. And then there's Donne and Dostoevsky and Henry James—'

'Rembrandt, Vermeer, Leonardo, Sam Palmer.' She laughed. 'Perhaps they would, if we wooed them with every ounce of ourselves. But Catherine is a gift. A kind of blessing. She was simply there, in the wall, waiting for me when I most needed her. There is no explanation.'

'So much of the best of life is inexplicable.'

He still seemed hesitant with her, a state that was alien to him. She saw now how great a negative effort he was making on her behalf, not to choose words that might put her to flight, not to come too near, unless he should give in to necessity and touch her, not to reveal the unchanged wholeness of the love he had given her and had never taken back. She saw it all because she had wanted him to come here, because the effort was as great in herself.

Luke wandered across to the brass knight, asleep on his tomb with his dog at his feet, and began to trace their outline with his toe. The sun got up and shook itself behind a stained-glass window, showering them with drops of coloured light. 'Love, for example,' he said. 'As it happened to us. There's no reasonable explanation for that. For all the sense it made at the time it first started, and considering its effect upon our lives, it may as well have been a fire, a flood or some other cataclysm. But it was the real thing, Chloe. And it still is.'

The air crowded in around them, thick with shining atoms of dust, mercurial points of enquiring expectation.

'And if I say yes – yes, it is the same – what will you expect of me?'

'Nothing.'

'Nothing?'

'That's enough. The rest is up to you. And time. You must have plenty of that. But don't wait, will you my darling, until we are utterly decrepit?' He smiled and held out his hand to her.

She came and stood before him in the coloured shower and raised herself on her toes to place her hands on his shoulders. Their kiss was a simple seal. There was no passion in it, there was not even a promise. What it did was to signify that they had understood a moment of true coincidence, when the demand for nothing and the promise of nothing flew up together like doves from a magician's sleeve, in the mutual gift of freedom.

Outside the church, they walked in new-rinsed content-ment down the path leading to the lych-gate and the ever hospitable Dark Horse, where Luke had suggested they could discuss the imminent wedding over a drink.

'Just a second.' He stopped. 'I believe the lych-gate has been reserved for a private party.' His voice curled in amusement and Chloe looked more closely beneath the gingerbread thatch. 'Luke, it can't be.' She frowned. 'And anyway, shouldn't they be in school?'

'Free study period,' he explained. 'You can't claim they're not using it.'

'But they're still children,' she said, melting into tenderness. 'I never thought this would happen so soon.'

'They grow up more quickly than we did; they don't see the point in waiting when they have their sights on a good thing.'

'Evidently,' Chloe sighed.

What they were looking at was the younger image of their most recent selves. Antonia Valder, poised on one foot, the other, shoeless, bent up behind her, the toes wriggling in pleasure, had her small hands firmly fixed on Rufus Olivier's broadening shoulders, and was kissing him with enthusiasm.

'I think we'll choose the other path,' Luke said, steering Chloe towards it. 'It's a longer walk, but we'll get there soon enough.'

She went with him thoughtfully, considering the treacherous nature of time, and what it might do if you let it fly.